I0787358

COWBOY FALLIN' IN LOVE AGAIN

BRIDES OF MILLER RANCH, N.M. BOOK 6

NATALIE DEAN

Copyright © 2021, 2022, 2023 by Natalie Dean

ISBN: 978-1-964875-17-0

All rights reserved.

No part of this publication may be reproduced, distributed, or transmitted in any form or by any means, including photocopying, recording, or other electronic or mechanical methods, without the prior written permission of the publisher, except as permitted by U.S. copyright law. For permission requests, contact Natalie Dean.

The story, all names, characters, and incidents portrayed in this production are fictitious. No identification with actual persons (living or deceased), places, buildings, and products is intended or should be inferred.

DEDICATION

I'd like to dedicate this book to YOU! The readers of these wonderful Miller Family stories. Without your interest in reading these heartwarming stories of love, I wouldn't have made it this far. So thank you so much for taking the time to read any and hopefully all of my books.

And I can't leave out my wonderful mother, son, sister, and Auntie. I love you all, and thank you for helping me make this happen.

Most of all, I thank God for blessing me on this endeavor.

AND... I've got a special team of advance readers who are always so helpful in pointing out any last minute corrections that need to be made. I'm so thankful to those of you who are so helpful!

OTHER BOOKS BY NATALIE DEAN

CONTEMPORARY ROMANCE

Miller Family Saga

BROTHERS OF MILLER RANCH

Miller Family Saga Series 1

Her Second Chance Cowboy

Saving Her Cowboy

Her Rival Cowboy

Her Fake-Fiance Cowboy Protector

Taming Her Cowboy Billionaire

Brothers of Miller Ranch Complete Collection

MILLER BROTHERS OF TEXAS

Miller Family Saga Series 2

The New Cowboy at Miller Ranch Prologue

Humbling Her Cowboy

In Debt to the Cowboy

The Cowboy Falls for the Veterinarian

Almost Fired by the Cowboy

Faking a Date with Her Cowboy Boss

Miller Brothers of Texas Complete Collection

BRIDES OF MILLER RANCH, N.M.

Miller Family Saga Series 3

Cowgirl Fallin' for the Single Dad

Cowgirl Fallin' for the Ranch Hand

Cowgirl Fallin' for the Neighbor

Cowgirl Fallin' for the Miller Brother

Cowgirl Fallin' for Her Best Friend's Brother

Cowboy Fallin' in Love Again

Brides of Miller Ranch Complete Collection

Miller Family Wrap-up Story

(An update on all your favorite characters!)

Copper Creek Romances

BAKER BROTHERS OF COPPER CREEK

Copper Creek Romances Series 1

Cowboys & Protective Ways

Cowboys & Crushes

Cowboys & Christmas Kisses

Cowboys & Broken Hearts

Cowboys & Second Chances

Cowboys & Wedding Woes

Cowboys' Mom Finds Love

Baker Brothers of Copper Creek Complete Collection

CALLAHANS OF COPPER CREEK

Copper Creek Romances Series 2

Making a Cowgirl

Marrying a Cowgirl

Christmas with a Cowgirl

Trusting a Cowgirl

Dating a Cowgirl

Catching a Cowgirl

Loving a Cowgirl

Marrying a Cowboy

Callahans of Copper Creek Complete Collection

KEAGANS OF COPPER CREEK

Copper Creek Romances Series 3

Some Cowboys are Off-Limits

Some Cowgirls Love Single Dads

Some Cowboys are Infuriating

Some Cowboys Don't Like City Girls

Some Cowboys Heal Broken Hearts

Some Cowgirls are Worth Protecting

Some Cowboys are Just Friends (Coming August 2024)

Though I try to keep this list updated in each book, you may also visit my website nataliedeanauthor.com for the most up to date information on my book list.

CONTENTS

1

Papa

Cast a line, reel it in, maybe feel a bite, rinse and repeat.

Montgomery Miller, better known as Papa Miller to pretty much everyone in their entire state, let himself relax bit by bit.

Not that his life was stressful. He recognized that he led a blessed existence, but that didn't mean his family didn't have their own troubles. And the biggest trouble for the past four years or so had been Eric.

Charity's ex was a weasel of a man. It was one thing for their marriage to not work out. It was another entirely for him to cheat on her, break her heart, and then blame it all on her.

He was a terrible excuse for a human—that was for certain.

Thankfully, his brother still had a great team of lawyers on retainer despite retiring, and they'd more than handled Eric in the courts. Too bad he still constantly tried to get in touch with Charity. He was determined, that one.

Letting out another long breath, he cast again. He didn't get away from the manor often, mostly because he loved being home, but every now and then he needed to get out and fish, hunt, or gather.

He knew that his family was wealthy enough to never need to make their own food, but he felt it was a part of his heritage that was incredibly important to him. All the fortunes of his family came from the land and the animals they raised, and while Montgomery had no desire to pursue the large businesses of his two siblings, he still wanted to honor his heritage.

Besides, he found peace in the garden. Peace and memories that he never wanted to get rid of.

But then his phone rang, interrupting the quiet. Papa considered ignoring it. After all, everyone knew that he preferred to disconnect from the world on his mini getaways. But then again, since everyone knew that, it usually meant people only tried to contact him if it was important.

With that in mind, he answered it on the last ring.

"Hey there, Char—"

"Papa, Papa! You have to come back! You have to get here!"

He hadn't heard his eldest sound so panicked in years, her voice skipping and full of sobs. "Charity? What's wrong!?"

"It's Cass, Papa. There's b-been an accident. You have to come home, Papa. They can't get her out of her car."

Montgomery Miller liked to think he was a capable fellow. That he'd gone through a lot and was good at dealing with many of the troubles life threw his way. But at his daughter's words, the entire world fell out from under him.

"They what, Charity?"

"She's upside down, and there's water. There's *so* much water! I-I-I-"

"I'm leaving now, Charity. I'll be there as fast as I can."

"O-okay. I'll text you what hospital they take her to."

"You do that, sweetheart."

"I will, Papa, but please hurry."

"As fast as I can."

Without even taking the time to change, Papa left everything behind and rushed into his car. Words wouldn't come to him, but neither did much else. All he knew was that his family needed him.

And his whole world was his family.

CHARITY FLUNG herself into his arms the moment he stepped into the hospital room. He held her, held her so very tightly, and forced himself to keep his voice level.

"How's..."

He trailed off when his eyes landed on the hospital bed, his heart stalling out in his chest when he realized that it was empty. For a moment, the worst fear in the world made his stomach clench and his blood turn to ice.

"She's still in surgery," Clara said quickly, seeming to know exactly where his mind went. She was always so perceptive, that one. He didn't know if it was a quirk of hers or just a perk of being a middle child, but she was remarkable at reading her family. "She's alive, she's just..." Clara's voice hitched too, and it was Charlie who comforted her, grabbing his sister's hand in his and squeezing it. "She's alive," she repeated finally.

"Papa, I can't lose her," Charity cried into his chest, bringing his attention back to her. "She has to live! She's too young. She's too... too..." The small, upset sobs against his chest made Papa's heart ache and his eyes water. Charity was always so strong, so untouchable; it was something heady to see her falling apart.

"It's okay, sweetheart. She's not going anywhere. She's in surgery, and they already got her a room. They don't get rooms for people who aren't likely to make it out alive."

He had no idea if that was actually true, but it had enough truth in it to pull his daughter back away from the edge.

"Y-you think so?"

"Yeah, I do. And I called Cici on the way here. She's on a flight first thing tomorrow morning. We're all gonna be here when Cass wakes up, and we'll be here for her recovery."

"Because there *will* be a recovery," Clara said with determination, back ramrod straight. "There will."

"Exactly."

Although Papa kept his tone low, comforting, inside he wasn't nearly so calm. That cold, biting grip of fear was quickly moving through him, sinking its fingers into his body until there was hardly a flicker of warmth in him.

He had been through this before, confronted with something terrible that was threatening to take away someone he loved dearly, someone wonderful and loving. He'd been there when she was taken away before her time, leaving a family of mourning and broken people.

And now he was going to have to do it again.

But Cass wasn't sick. No, she was healthy as a horse and perhaps one of the most active of all his children. And yet she was in danger anyway. Held upside down in a car accident and partially submerged in water. Papa didn't have the details, but he wasn't sure he ever wanted them.

"Have any of you eaten?" he asked finally. Naturally, his children shook their heads. "I realize you're not in the mood now, but I'm going to see if I can put in a special delivery order at one of the restaurants in town. Once Cass is here, I don't imagine any of y'all will want to leave her, and I'm not having ya pass out on her."

"Thank you, Papa," Charity said miserably against his chest.

"Of course, it's what I'm here for."

CASS WAS in surgery for eight long hours. When she finally returned to the room, she was unconscious, and more metal and bandage than she was human.

The doctors said that she wasn't going to be waking up anytime soon, that they were keeping her under until her next set of operations. Because she was going to need many. Finally, Papa got the full story of what happened, and it… well, it wasn't good.

But he listened, he took notes on his phone for everything he needed to know or look up, and he stayed with his children as they talked to Cass, picked at the food he had delivered, and eventually passed out one by one.

He waited until they were all well and truly out, including Charity, then snuck out of the room.

It was a testament to how little some things changed that he knew exactly where the chapel was. Even in all the years that had passed since Mama's death, his body followed the same path like it was second nature.

It was silent when he entered, the small chapel entirely

empty, and he slid into a pew. Wordless, he sat there for a long while, until finally the tears welled up.

Then Papa cried. He cried and cried and cried, finally allowing all the fear and loss in his chest to spill out. It was a curse, really, to only be able to really let go when he was alone but then feeling ever so lonely once he was. But the truth was that he didn't know if he could survive losing another beloved family member.

Because even after so many years, Mama was still largely a gaping wound in his chest. He loved her; there wasn't a single day that he didn't miss her. And even with her, they'd had time to come to terms with her death, time to prepare. Not a lot, but at least a little. If Cass died...

His cries turned into outright sobs, broken and guttural. He couldn't outlive his child. That wasn't right! What had his family done to deserve the never-ending loss? His little Sundance had to live. She *had* to!

"God, I ain't never tried to bargain with you, 'cause I know that ain't how it goes. But I'm begging you now. Please, please don't take her. If you need a life, take mine. I've lived too long as it is, but my girls... my girls are just babies."

Sure, Charity had been married and divorced. And Cici was about to complete her BA and was going right on to her master's. But they were still his babies. All of them. So young and full of potential, their entire lives stretching out before them.

"I ain't got nothing left to do, but Cass, you made her special. She has an entire world to conquer. Don't cut that short, Lord, please. *Please.* If I've earned any of your grace, please, give me that. Give my family that."

He dissolved into choking tears by the end, his throat thick. His faith was usually such a comfort to him, a glowing lifeline that he could grab whenever he was reeling too far from center. But at the moment, with his daughter fighting for her life, it sat like a burning poker in his chest.

He knew the proverb of Job. He knew that being good or kind didn't guarantee an easy life. But Papa couldn't help but wonder if he or an ancestor had done some sort of evil to have earned such strife.

Losing Mama, his darling, his beloved, had been the most damaging, trying experience of his family's lives. She'd always believed that heaven was all around them, but watching her slowly wither, had made it seem like it was hell instead, burning and merciless around them.

He'd survived it, though. He'd trudged through for his children because they needed him, and even then, Charity had unintentionally picked up so much slack. And eventually, it had gotten to a point where he could do more than go through the motions. Where he could enjoy watching his children thrive and grow and become the wonderful people that they were.

But he didn't know if he could make it through another loss like that. His brothers had always said he was the most sensitive of all of them. After all, he was the only one that hadn't turned his inheritance into some thriving business that increased the family wealth. And maybe they were right. Montgomery Miller was a big ol' softy, and unfortunately, the fine print of that was that it made his heart that much easier to tear apart.

"I can't do this, God. I can't. Please, don't test my family like this."

Normally, Papa could feel peace after a prayer, a sort of settled wholeness. But all he could feel right now was the silence and emptiness pressing in all around him.

2

———

Papa

ass lived.

Cass lived!

Papa wasn't going to pretend that it was all roses and daisies from that night where he wept in the chapel, but the important part was the doctors said her chances of survival were greater than the alternative. So Papa lived with that, held her hand, and comforted his children while making arrangements.

The doctors had also made it clear that it would be a long time before Cass would be able to return home, and once she did, she would need a lot of extra care and mobility needs. Things that Papa had never had to think about, like a wheelchair entrance to their house and an independent way for Cass to get up the stairs. Even something as simple as the toilet and tub needed alterations.

Papa didn't like to think about money, but he was eternally grateful that he came from wealthy folks when the cost started to pile up. He had no idea how most people could afford everything, and he shuddered to think at all the people who had to make do with less than they needed.

He should do something about that. Later, once everything was set up for Cass. It helped to give him and the children something to do other than just sit in her hospital room and stare at her.

Eventually, Cass had been allowed to wake up, and the doctors said that her chances of survival were incredibly high.

Then it had been a matter of course, and their attention had turned to her rehabilitation and getting her able to go home.

Papa had thought that would be the home stretch.

He was very wrong.

He supposed he should have known better, considering how independent and proud Cass was, but she didn't take to her weakened state well. Those first few weeks where she was fully conscious were rough, with her throwing things, screaming, and randomly dissolving into sobs. Each time she acted out, it hurt Papa down to his core. His poor baby was suffering, and all he could do was watch and speak words of kindness. He wasn't even allowed to hold her.

It was awful.

But he clung to the thought that it would get better. She wasn't Estelle, who had been in a slow decline, wasting away without recourse. Every day Cass got a little stronger, and the doctors were able to wean her off some of the strongest pain killers that made her mood swings worse.

It was a long journey, yes, but eventually they did get her

home. They got her into therapy for the PTSD from it all, and they worked through every day together.

There were some days that were harder than others, especially when type A Cass pushed herself too far, and there were nights where Papa locked himself in his room and just cried. But each week was a little better than the other, until he began to see more and more flashes of his little Sundance.

He knew that she'd never be fully back to normal. One didn't go through what she went through without changing. But he hoped that she could find her center again and integrate her new world with her old.

So the days marched on, always progressing. Always exhausting. But Papa tried not to take a single one for granted. Cass's accident had reminded him of how fleeting life was and how easy it was to lose what was most precious to him.

"You know, you don't have to drive off during my appointments. Maybe if you stuck around, you could talk to the doctor a little longer than two minutes."

Papa looked up from his coffee that he was drinking at the counter, newspaper in his hands. His children always teased him about being old-fashioned and keeping his subscription to the local, brick and mortar newspaper, but he liked the feel of it, the ritual.

"What, and sit there like a bump on a log? No, thank you."

His eldest daughters were sitting at their kitchen island, eating breakfast. Cass had been allowed solid food for several months, but her appetite still wasn't what it used to be. He supposed that made sense considering that she didn't horseback ride, help Charity with construction or repair, or play any of the sports she used to. She couldn't even swim. But thinking about such things made him glum, so he quickly pushed those thoughts down and listened to the conversation.

"Aw, come on. Surely sitting around for an hour and playing on your phone is worth talking to a hottie with a body."

Papa didn't miss how Charity's cheeks flushed pink. Interesting.

"Please never call your doctor that again," Charity said.

"Pfftt, come on, sis. You've even got an in with his daughter. She loves you, from what I saw."

"That's just because she consistently beats me at speed."

"Yeah, you probably shouldn't have taught her that game. She's become too powerful."

Huh, could it be Charity was actually sweet on someone? That would certainly be lovely. Charity deserved something good. Something precious, warm and safe.

But first, Papa was going to have to check this doctor fellow out. Only the best for his children.

3

___

Jeanette

Suddenly, something was shoved into Jeanette's face, obscuring her vision of the checklist she was finishing up.

Blinking, the librarian looked up to see it was Savannah, a new student she was rather fond of.

"Can I help you?" she asked. Sure, Savannah wasn't entirely the best with social cues, but her heart was almost always in the right place.

"This is a card."

"I see that. It looks lovely."

"It's to my dad's birthday party." Savannah shifted from foot to foot, her grin dimming ever so slightly. "I'm inviting you."

Oh, how utterly sweet.

"Thank you, sweetie, but I won't be able to make it. I don't really get out much."

That was putting it mildly. Jeanette had a very set routine that didn't allow for any unnecessary social situations. Ever. It wasn't that she hated people. No, she found many people were lovely if given the chance. It was just that she took comfort in her loneliness. In the quiet. And spending too much time around too many people reminded her of a different life. One she'd given up on long ago.

"O-oh, are you sure?"

Jeanette didn't miss the split second of the crestfallen expression Savannah allowed herself before schooling her face back to neutral. For not always getting every social cue, the girl certainly had masking her emotions down pat. Jeanette couldn't help but wonder what had happened to the young girl to give her that skill.

"I..."

Since when had she become such a hermit that she couldn't even leave a little grace for a young girl who had just moved and didn't exactly have an overwhelming amount of friends?

Well, she knew the answer to that. It had been a slow, slow slide ever since her husband passed nearly twenty years ago. It had been little things at first. Staying in on the weekends to rest and recover. Then avoiding birthdays because of the looks of pity in people's eyes. Then she'd moved entirely to a small town where no one knew her or expected anything of her.

Yes, that had certainly been a lynchpin in her abdication from a social life.

But Savannah's lip was trembling slightly and the paper in her hand continued to droop lower and lower. Clearing her throat, Jeanette made up her mind.

"I'll try my best to make it."

It was like the sun came out and Savannah visibly brightened, her neutral mask slipping off her young face. "Yay! Thank you so much! It'll be a lot of fun! I promise!"

"Oh, I'm absolutely sure of that. You have a good day now, Savannah."

"You too! I'll see you at lunch!"

"You know, you should probably eat in the cafeteria with all the students your age."

"No, that's alright. I like it here with you better."

With that, the young girl was bounding off wherever her surprisingly long legs wanted to take her. She was going to be a real skyscraper, that one.

But even tucking the invitation into her purse and returning to work wasn't enough to get Jeanette's thoughts back on track, and they slipped to her one and only love.

They'd only been married for four years, just beginning to talk of starting a family. Everyone around them was always so surprised by how slow they went, but that was just what worked for them. Jeanette had met him in her senior year, and he had been just one year below her, but they waited until halfway through college before beginning to date. And then they dated until they were both graduated before he proposed. It was wonderful, comfortable, and never a rush. They always just enjoyed each other and the moment.

And then he died.

It had been sudden, with no great reason or terrible accident. One moment he was there, and the next, he was gone. Something called a pulmonary embolism.

Just like that, there went her comfort. There went her

dreams. There went everything they had spent over a decade building together.

All gone.

The sadness began to well all the way up to her eyes, combining with melancholy to make quite the potent combination. Jeanette had to stand up quickly, pushing herself away from her desk to go to the back reading area.

Thankfully, there were no children there at the moment. Not that she minded kids being there. After all, she'd created the comfy space with them in mind. But at the moment, she needed to be alone. Just long enough to catch her breath.

Busying herself with tidying the small space full of beanbag cushions and student-sized overstuffed chairs, Jeanette made herself focus on the good. With nearly twenty years of practice, it was easy to slip into her internal chant.

There was the library, of course. Her bright point. When she'd first been hired, the school's reading area was... threadbare at best. While Jeanette wasn't exactly rolling in money, she'd been able to thrift, coupon, and work out deals with other schools to slowly improve the place.

Newer bookshelves, the reading area, a slideshow informing students of new books or highlighting one of her favorites. Several new computers. A thriving comic section as well as books from all over the world. She'd even managed to pinch nearly a hundred coloring books for various ages that had been donated to an estate shop in the city.

Yes, she was alone, but not really. She had her books, she had the children, and she had all the joy she created with them.

And that was enough for her.

Or at least that was what she told herself. But as she returned to her desk and sat down, she couldn't help but feel that loneliness creep in behind her. And not the familiar loneliness that she was comfortable with. The one that recharged her. It was a different one, cold and insidious with its bite. Whispering that she was alone because she deserved it. Because she wasn't good enough.

Swallowing, Jeanette took out the invitation and looked over it once again. Was she ready for something like that? The thought was entirely overwhelming.

Well... she supposed that she could always cancel last-minute if she wanted.

4

———

Papa

*P*apa sipped carefully from his cup. Not because it contained any particularly strong libation, but because it had soda in it, and he needed to be careful about his sugars so late in the day. Most of the time he just drank the tea he loved making, so his body wasn't really used to soft drinks or caffeine. If he didn't want to be bouncing off the walls or getting up every two hours to relieve himself, it was best to be moderate.

While he was just about as enchanted with the effervescent little Savannah, he wasn't exactly planning to stay around for long. Just enough to check out this supposedly handsome doctor.

But Papa wasn't too worried. After all, if Cass liked him, he had to be a fairly good person. She was an excellent judge of character. Or at least she was before the accident. He hadn't missed how his daughter's demeanor had soured and her optimism had taken a decidedly pessimistic tilt.

Oh well. She deserved the right to feel a little sourness if that was what she needed to recover. Goodness knew that she hadn't exactly been dealt a fair hand.

Scanning the house again, he saw Charity interacting with that handsome doctor fellow who had visited a couple of times. He seemed like a nice enough man and had an excellent daughter, that was for sure. Cass had definitely been right about the chemistry of it all because he could see it from all the way across the room.

But he could see some fear there, the hesitance in Charity, the way her shoulders tensed. After what happened with Eric, he couldn't exactly blame her, but he didn't want her to be held back by that worm of a man.

The two of them talked for a minute, then separated, and Papa saw his moment. He knew his children were all far too old for him to play matchmaker, but there weren't any rules in the parent handbook about a little good-natured... investigation.

As he approached the doctor, the man looked like he was deep in contemplation, his eyes glassy as he looked after something not in front of him. Clearing his throat, he decided to dive right in.

Actually, he finished his soda and grabbed one of the bottles of beer from the fridge. Maybe a little bit of liquid courage wouldn't hurt.

"You look like you're thinking about something serious."

The man jolted and whirled, barely schooling his expression after a beat. Papa might have felt bad if it wasn't so humorous. The man was certainly jumpy.

"No. Nothing really."

Was he a grown man, *blushing?* No wonder Charity liked him. She needed a little softness for her harder edges. Not that she needed a sadsack or a wimp, just someone who could help temper her. Sometimes Charity got so into taking care of others, she pushed herself far beyond what any reasonable person could expect of themselves and still wouldn't be satisfied with her own performance.

Eric had been deceptively like that at first. All romantic and respectful of feelings. But after time it became clear that it was just a façade, and he hardly cared about anything outside of his own needs and wants. For what it was worth, from the couple of dinners they'd had together and their few conversations, Alejandro seemed much more genuine.

"Aw, is that so? And here I hoped maybe you were thinking about Charity."

The young man practically choked on his beer, swallowing hard and coughing. It definitely took quite a bit of willpower to not chuckle at the doctor, but somehow, Papa managed.

"Come again?" he sputtered once he was mostly recovered.

Papa thought about what he was going to say for a moment. He hadn't really planned any sort of grand speech to the guy who was maybe or maybe not courting his daughter. He'd just seen the uncertainty in her eyes and had wanted to make sure that uncertainty didn't cost her something amazing.

"I love my girl, I do, but the truth is she's gone through some things that have hurt her. Real bad. She tries to hide it, pretend that she's alright, but a father knows, you know?"

"Uh-huh," the doctor responded, taking another long drink. Noncommittal, but that was alright. Papa realized how intimidating it could be to be confronted by the parent of someone you were interested in, even if everyone involved was technically a grown-up.

"But when she's around you and your little girl, she lights up. She laughs and smiles, even if she's not taking care of someone. It's nice to see my girl back." Papa sighed and sat down next to Alejandro. Sure, his words were unplanned, but they were true. Charity had dedicated herself to the family for most of her life, and that had only increased tenfold since Cass's accident. She needed something for her. Something lovely, comforting and joyful.

"Pardon an old man for meddling, but I just can't help but think... well, that you two have some things in common that most people don't."

"Do we?" Alejandro asked, sounding genuinely surprised. Papa was fairly certain that he wasn't being sarcastic. From what he'd observed, the doctor wasn't the type. Sarcasm was definitely more of a Cass and Charlie thing.

"I don't know your exact story, but it's clear you lost someone." Papa remembered overhearing something about "tragedy" and "wife." It didn't take a genius to figure out that if Cass was pushing her older sister towards the doc, that his wife wasn't in the picture any longer.

"And Charity just about had her heart ripped out and stomped on. At first, I thought maybe you were just enjoying someone taking your girl off your hands for a quick rest, but then I saw how you looked at Charity at the corn festival. And I started to get an inkling maybe it wasn't just the free babysitting."

Papa wasn't sure what he had expected, but it wasn't for a storm cloud of emotion to cross the man's face. Once again, his eyes zoomed off far beyond Montgomery, seeing something that he couldn't. Papa waited another moment, hoping the man would respond, but the doctor seemed thoroughly lost in thought yet again.

Had Papa crossed a line? He didn't think so. But he was definitely right about the wounded thing. The pain within the man was practically radiating out from him, driven by a hurt that was clearly deep within him. He'd seen the same thing on Charity many times, back when Eric's awful deeds had been revealed one by one.

"Again, hope I wasn't butting in, but you seem like a decent man, and I just wanted to let you know—in case you were stuck in your own head—that you aren't imagining the chemistry between you two. Cass has been going on about it since the second time she met you, although she'd probably kill me for mentioning that."

"She what?"

Alejandro's eyes went wide yet again at that, and Papa suddenly remembered just how dumb he had been about such matters for most of his life. Sometimes Mama would just shake her head and explain to him matters of the heart like it was the simplest thing in the world. After he'd lost her, he was worried he'd never be able to manage on his own. But... eventually, he got good at watching people, on figuring stuff out on his own.

If Alejandro had lost his wife as well, maybe he was in that same sort of state. It was a strange transition to go from being secure in a relationship with the love of his life to being thrust into the dating world again. Papa certainly hadn't ever rejoined that particular slice of life.

"Ah, I've said too much," Papa muttered, getting back to his feet. He needed to clear out before either of his daughters spotted him, because he was sure they'd have plenty of questions if they did. "If you don't mind me, I'm going to go pretend I didn't meddle."

Whew, that was certainly a conversation. Although Papa didn't quite rush away, he definitely didn't idle either. He needed a break from all the socializing and hubbub and trying to maintain the proper balance between guiding and invasive.

It wasn't that he was anti-social. It was just that he was more of a sprinter than an endurance conversationalist. He found himself getting tired easily, conversation turning into a low hum that his mind dismissed rather than something to actively participate in.

And then he spotted it, a chess set sitting in the corner of the dining room, small chairs on either side of it. It was a small space away from two older women who were playing cards, but it was far enough that Papa most likely wouldn't have to engage with either of them.

Perfect.

As he grew closer to it, he realized that it wasn't just a wooden chess set, like the one he'd carved for Mama back when they were young. No, it was made entirely of stone, with pearlescent alabaster for the white and the inkiest, shiniest onyx that he'd ever seen. Papa couldn't help but whistle lowly to himself.

"This is something else."

Papa knew that he could easily have bought such a set; he was rich after all. Thanks to his family's inheritance, he could try very, very, *very* hard to spend all his money and likely still end up with plenty to live comfortably. It was just that throwing so many dollars at something he would only touch once or twice a year seemed sinfully wasteful.

Actually, if he was being honest with himself, his family's whole situation seemed kind of wasteful. While his two brothers were building empires of their own to grow their wealth, Papa just didn't see the point. They had far too much money as it were. He needed to do something about that, but between his garden and taking care of his family, it always seemed to get pushed to tomorrow.

And there had certainly been a lot of tomorrows since he'd first thought about the whole thing. Hadn't he learned from Cass that tomorrow was never guaranteed? Apparently not.

The sound of laughter drifted across the room and Papa looked up from the hole he was staring into the floor, his eyes automatically scanning for his children. When was the last time he'd played chess with any of them? They used to all the time. Until...

Well, until Mama died. They hadn't meant to, but they'd all stopped once she passed. It hadn't been purposeful, not really, but between the mourning, and the catching up, it kind of just... happened.

"Are you up for a friendly game?"

The query was so quiet that Papa wasn't actually sure that he heard it. Turning, he saw a woman standing a short way from him, her own cup of soda gripped tightly in her hands. She was one of the card players he'd spotted earlier. So much for not having to interact.

She was cute, in an austere sort of way. Her hair was pulled back neatly into a bun, and she wore mother-of-pearl horn-rimmed glasses. Her lips were cherry red, and her face had the warmth of laugh lines, while the crow's-feet at the corner of her eyes spoke of thousands of smiles.

"Um..." His first thoughts was to say no, that he'd simply wanted to stare at the set and remember simpler times. But something stopped him. Maybe it was the nervous rock to the woman's stance. Maybe it was the hopeful look in her eyes. Maybe he was just lonelier than he thought. "It's been a long while since I've played. Don't know if I'll be much fun."

"Oh, that's alright. I won't trounce you too hard." She hurried to sit across from him, a broad grin breaking across her pleasant features, showing exactly how she'd gotten the lines across her visage. "I try to practice good sportsmanship. At least most of the time."

"I hope you see fit to have some mercy on me then."

"Just to show you how charitable I am, I'll let you play white."

While Papa was rusty at chess, he still knew that was definitely an advantage. "Your graciousness knows no bounds."

"Oh, it has many bounds. I just work with children, which has taught me a type of patience I didn't think possible."

He couldn't help but share a chuckle at that. "They really are something else, aren't they? The next generation, and the next."

The woman paused in her settling down, a sweet smile across her amiable features. "Why yes, I certainly think so. I'm just not used to hearing other folks my age think that."

"Ah, yeah, I know folks like that too. Sometimes it can be hard to understand our children, or our children's children, but they're living in a world that's very different from the one we grew up in. They have more information at their fingertips than we could have ever even dreamed of. They see things in a way we'll never understand, and that's okay, because it's not our future they're building. It's *their* children's future they're creating."

"That's certainly a refreshing view to have. I should admit that I'm awfully tired of all the young-bashing that seems to pass as news or media fodder lately. I work with these children every day and I can tell you, they're utterly amazing, even with all their flaws and apps."

"I find most of that generational tension stuff fairly contrived. Not all, but most, to keep us divided instead of working towards one goal."

"Oh, and what should that one goal be?"

"To make the world a better place than when we came into it."

"I think that's a lovely goal." It didn't seem possible, but the woman's grin grew both softer and warmer. "But perhaps an even more reasonable one would be to move that rook you've had in your hands for several minutes."

"Huh?" Papa looked down to see that he was indeed holding the rook in his hand, completely unmoved. "Oh, I suppose that would help to start the game, wouldn't it?"

"I would imagine so, yes."

Montgomery tried to consider the board for a long moment, but he kept feeling the woman's eyes on him and his concentration would slip ever so slightly. He wasn't really worried about winning or losing, but he didn't want to seem like a total moron.

Finally, he moved the first piece, glancing up to the woman. While her appearance had seemed easy-going and relatively benign at first, Papa suddenly realized that he was in the presence of a shark.

How *fun.*

"Interesting opening," she remarked cheerily, moving her own piece. Not a knight, like he did, but a pawn instead.

"Interesting bad or interesting good?" Papa murmured, looking over the board again and trying to figure out what moves the woman might make.

"Some might argue that any sort of interesting is good."

"Sounds like someone who's never gone through actual 'interesting' times."

She chuckled lightly, a repeat of the same sound Papa had made earlier, but he found he liked it from her mouth more. There was a lower, almost raspy undercurrent to her voice, one that spoke of a full life with plenty of shouting, singing and laughter. Like smokey honey, soothing in its tones.

"And you sound like someone who's stalling from making their next move."

"Pffft, stalling?" Papa shot back. "Hardly."

"If you say so."

Montgomery shook his head but moved his next piece, nonetheless. His opponent didn't even look at it, just idly moved another pawn without even missing a beat.

"You know, a less confident man might say that you were just trying to intimidate me."

"Is that so?" she answered, looking incredibly amused.

"Yup."

"But you're not a less confident man?"

"Nope. I think you're exactly as good at chess as you're acting and that I've already lost."

She regarded the board carefully, that smile still on her face. "No. There are a few ways you could win."

"A few? And how many of those are likely outcomes for someone of my skill level?"

"Hmm... far fewer."

"Alright then." Papa moved another piece, and she responded with another pawn. Papa thought for a couple minutes, then moved his bishop.

And that was the wrong move.

Suddenly it was her bishop streaking all the way across the

board, taking his first casualty. She didn't say anything, just set it to the side without comment.

"Right, well, blood will be spilled, I suppose."

"That is generally the way of war."

"And this is war?"

"A war, a dialogue, a game. Whatever you need it to be, I suppose."

Papa reached for that beer he'd grabbed to talk to Alejandro. He certainly needed it. "Whatever I need it to be, huh?"

She didn't reply to that, instead waiting patiently for Papa to make his move. And she certainly had to wait, because he had zero plans in his head. He tried to recall the moves and strategies he used to employ, but they were all buried far too deeply into his memories that were tied to Mama. Memories he didn't want to approach in the middle of a party.

Eventually, he did make a move, and she responded just as quickly, with yet another pawn.

Papa moved. She moved. Papa moved. She moved, and he lost another piece. So on and so on it went, and on the rare chance that he took one of her pieces, she would respond with more moves that absolutely massacred him.

Eventually, it was inevitable; she had him in a checkmate.

"Good game," Papa said, letting out a long breath. "But why do I get the feeling that you could have won that a lot sooner?"

"Probably because I could have," she admitted blithely. "I guess I just wanted to enjoy your company a bit longer."

"You wouldn't be trying to pull my leg would you?"

She laughed outright at that, her hand going to cover her mouth. "Hah, I assure you, it was nothing like that. It's been a while since I've had such a fun chess game and I didn't want it to end."

Oh. Well that was quite the compliment. Papa felt his face flush ever so slightly, which was surprising enough to make his cheeks color that much more.

"Glad to have been entertaining."

"Thank you for the lovely game. I suppose I should go help myself to some of those wings before they're all snatched up."

"I reckon you're right. Everybody loves wings."

"Everyone with sense, at least."

With a nod of her head, she stood and wandered deeper into the party where many of the guests were gathered around the food table. It wasn't until someone walked in front of him and cut off his line of sight that he realized he'd never even asked her name.

Too late now, he supposed.

5

———

*J*eanette looked up at the sky, hands on her cheeks as she willed the burn in them to go down.

She had been planning on canceling; she really had. But when she'd called and Savannah had answered, gleefully excited at hearing Jeanette's voice, she'd caved. So, she'd found herself at her first party in years, clutching her soda like it was her last lifeline.

Thankfully Mrs. Whittaker, the lovely receptionist of the local clinic, had been there as well and looked absolutely exhausted. While Jeanette wasn't close with her, they were at least friendly acquaintances and she felt comfortable approaching the other woman and asking if she was up for a card game.

That was how Jeanette ended up playing about three games

of war, four games of go fish and one of rummy 5000 until Mrs. Whittaker finally said she was ready to mingle and be social.

Which had left the librarian far too alone.

She'd sat there, panicking for a moment, dreading actually having to interact with such a large group of people. She didn't know why she was so anxious about the idea. It wasn't like anyone expected an incredible social performance out of the school librarian, but the panic was there nonetheless.

Until she spotted someone sitting at the chess set.

She didn't recognize the man from the back, but she could tell from his salt and pepper hair that he was someone at least somewhere around her age, and that's all she needed. Playing a game with a stranger was much more appealing than having to try to participate in a conversation with more than four participants.

So, she'd gone over, asked him for a game, and then promptly recognized exactly who she was talking to. None other than Mr. Montgomery Miller, of the Miller Ranch. The auditorium of the school was named after his late wife, and his booth at the corn festival was infamous for selling out of his strange and fun produce.

They were filthy rich, far richer than any one rancher would normally be, but he came from an actual dynasty that went back to when the West was still the great frontier. Their influence stretched far, all the way to Montana and even Texas, where she heard the mega-corp part of their family lived.

And, if that weren't enough, he was devastatingly handsome. She hadn't expected that. Sure, she'd heard plenty about the Miller clan since she'd moved to the town nine years earlier, but she'd never really interacted with him. Really, she'd only ever seen him at a distance, seeing how she wasn't exactly keen on going to the corn festival on her lonesome. A bit too much noise and bustle for her hermit self.

"Oh, sorry, I didn't know this was occupied."

Jeanette started, whirling around to see that it was none other than the very man she was thinking of, Papa Miller himself. Perhaps it was weird to think of him as "Papa," but that was what she heard him called more often than not.

She was about to tell him that was fine, that she could leave, but then he was talking again. "But I'm glad to see it's you out here."

"Y-you are?" she blurted, almost cringing at how shocked she sounded. Goodness, she knew students with more tact.

"Yes, after such a fun game, I wanted to introduce myself properly." Oh, how funny that he thought she wasn't already very acutely aware of exactly who he was. "My name's Montgomery. Montgomery Miller."

"Jeanette Edalira. Thank you again. It was a very fun game."

"I was certainly entertained."

His hand was warm against hers, large and rough. Enough to completely dwarf her fingers in his, and that thought made goosebumps rise along her arm in a tingling sort of ripple.

Goodness.

"So," he said, letting her hand go. She almost wanted to keep touching him, the warmth of his hand a direct contrast to the cool night air around them. "Why aren't you in there bumpin' and grooving?"

She chuckled again. "Yes, because a small town doctor's birthday party is certainly a place where there will be much bumping and grooving."

"Fair enough, but still, thought I was the only hermit around here."

Jeanette had to raise an eyebrow at that. Sure, she was aware of the comments that the Millers tended not to participate in most social stuff outside of the corn festival, Cinco de Mayo and Christmas festivities, but she figured that was because the Richie Richertons just thought they were too good for most of the poorer townsfolk. But in actually meeting the patriarch, Jeanette was fairly certain that wasn't the case.

"I'm not exactly one for loud spaces or lots of people," Jeanette admitted. "Unless they're under four feet and sitting cross-legged on the floor for reading time."

"Hah! That sounds like it would be some kind of party."

Jeanette found herself grinning despite herself. She didn't want to appear over eager or even easily buttered up, but she would be lying if she said she wasn't attracted to the man.

Right, her and just about every other single woman in town over the age of thirty-five. All that money was a draw for plenty of them, and his dashing good looks didn't hurt.

But he wasn't like some movie star silver fox, impossibly handsome and groomed. No, he was more realistic in a way that was hard to explain. His skin was tanned and wrinkled, but in a way that made his striking bone structure that much more emphasized. His eyes were kind, but there was a sort of intensity to his gaze. Another thing that she'd heard of with the Miller clan. They were all known for their particularly... intimidating gaze, for the lack of a better term.

"So, a hermit, huh?" she asked, clearing her throat slightly. Her mouth was so dry, she wished she had more of her soda, but it was awfully late to be ingesting that much sugar. "I have to admit, I'm surprised to hear that."

"Are you? Why?"

Wait, she couldn't admit to why without revealing that she

did indeed know who he was, and she had a feeling he was enjoying the fact that his reputation didn't proceed him for once. For some reason, even though she hardly knew him, she didn't want to burst that bubble quite yet.

"I just figured a dapper young man such as yourself would love being the life of the party."

"Oh, I am many things, but a young man isn't one of them. I don't think I've been anything near young for about forty years or so."

"You and my knees then, apparently."

"It's the hips and back for me. They went on strike when I was forty and they're very resentful that I still use them." He grinned ruefully at that, and goodness, if that didn't make her heart do strange things.

What was going on with her? She hadn't felt such strange rushes of twitterpation since she was a young woman. She was far too old and far too tired to have butterflies trying to invade her stomach.

"I hope your negotiations with their Union went well."

"It's an ongoing process."

They both shared a laugh, and it was just so *nice*. Jeanette still felt a slight sting of wariness considering he was a millionaire and possibly the most eligible, silver fox bachelor in their entire town, but that was easing with every moment. Because, as far as she could tell, Papa Miller was *funny*. And genuinely so. His humor didn't involve insulting people or picking at their insecurities, like some people's did. Jeanette could never stand folks like that, especially when they would complain that everyone around them was "sensitive."

But once their laughter faded, the conversation did too, and she found herself looking up at the stars.

"They really are beautiful this time of year, aren't they?" Montgomery Miller's voice was a low rumble behind her, and it made goosebumps rise along her skin in waves. Goodness! What was going on?

"I think they're beautiful year-round," she murmured. "The only difference is whether we can see them or not."

He didn't answer for a moment, and she wondered if he thought she was being needlessly pedantic, but then he cleared his throat and spoke.

"I never thought of it that way."

"You sound like you don't agree."

"No, I do. I really do." There was still emotion in his voice, however, something thick and very weighty. "The idea that their beauty isn't diminished just because we can't see them just... hits me in a certain way I didn't expect."

Oh, Jeanette hadn't anticipated an answer like that, and she swallowed hard. "It's easy to get into the mode of believing how we perceive things is everything. I find it helpful to remind myself that things still exist even if they drift out of my periphery."

"I don't know if I've ever agreed with a sentiment more."

Oh. He said it so casually, like he was just talking about the weather. But he wasn't just talking about the weather. He was agreeing with one of her many philosophies, one she rarely shared because how often did she have a chance to have a serious conversation about such things with middle schoolers?

"You're too kind," Jeanette muttered, not sure what else to say. And if she was being honest with herself, she was afraid that she'd let out something foolish that would ruin whatever impression he had of her.

"Considering the world we live in, I figure that every bit of kindness is needed."

"I can't argue with you there." It was true. Sometimes, if Jeanette thought about all the bad in the world too hard, it was incredibly difficult not to just sink into depression.

She looked up to the stars again, twinkling like individual promises of everything that could be in the inky velvet of the night sky. When was the last time she'd just stopped and allowed herself to revel in such natural beauty? It felt like ages. Usually, she was tucked into bed and sipping at her chamomile tea.

Wait a minute... what time was it?

Pulling out her phone, with its intense case on it to protect it from how often Jeanette dropped it, she saw it was actually an hour past her bedtime. No wonder her emotions were being so silly! Her body didn't like it when she interrupted her routine.

"Have an appointment you're missing?" Montgomery joked beside her.

"Yes, actually," she answered, enjoying it maybe a bit more than she should when he looked surprised. "I'm prepping for a contest at the school called Battle of the Books, so I have to get to the school before six am. I should be in bed already!"

"It's the weekend."

She just gave him a look. "Are you telling me that you don't maintain your sleep schedule on the weekend so Monday doesn't come around and take you out at the kneecaps?"

He laughed again, and it was just as pleasant as the first time. "You have a point. Could I walk you to your car?"

For some reason that seemed like too much. Jeanette wasn't some ingénue or young and supple second wife. She was just a little hermit of a school librarian, as plain as plain could come.

"No, that's alright. I can manage myself. You go enjoy the

party! I think the birthday doctor might have a thing for one of your lovely daughters."

"It's that obvious, huh?"

"No, but Savannah does love to talk."

"Hah! That she does. Have a good night, Jeanette."

"You too."

She hurried off, feeling his eyes on her as she went down the porch steps and hurried to her car down the street. But as she drove off, she couldn't help but wonder what would have happened if she had stayed.

6

———

Papa

$\mathcal{P}$apa Miller finished signing in at the office and headed towards the library, the Vice Principal chatting nonstop. It was far too early in the morning to have someone chewing his ear so emphatically, but he still had enough good sense not to tell her so.

"It really is lovely that you're willing to help us out with this new project. One of our sister schools in the city had immense success with it, and we weren't sure if it would work for a small school like ours, but so far the kids are quite enthusiastic!"

"Glad to hear it," Papa said, keeping his voice neutral. "It sounds like a fun way to motivate them to read."

"It is! I have to say, our Librarian is just *wonderful*. She was the one that made us aware of the whole thing at all. I know that they're often an overlooked part of faculty, but our Librarian really goes above and beyond."

Papa was inclined to agree. That was why he was at the middle school before seven am on a Monday.

Part of him wondered if he was being creepy, if he was crossing some line. But it wasn't like he showed up at her house or anything, and it wasn't completely unusual for him to volunteer to help with school events. Sure, normally it was just running the ticket table for their school plays or sports fundraisers, but that didn't mean he couldn't branch out.

And if branching out meant that he got to enjoy the company of a lovely woman, well that was a bonus.

...he was being creepy, wasn't he?

He hoped not, but Papa did have to be honest that half the reason he was at the school right after he finished his morning chores was because the librarian had left an impression on him. An impression that he couldn't quite put words to.

She was interesting, that was for certain, and obviously as sharp as a knife. She'd surprised him several times, and a few of the things she said poked at a part of Papa's brain that he felt he didn't use very often.

Like that beauty still existed even when not being perceived. Just because he wasn't aware of something truly wonderous didn't mean that it didn't exist. It was just as real even if it wasn't a part of his perception, and that... that made him think alright.

He just hoped she wasn't upset that he showed up.

"Ah, here we are! I see the lights are already on. No surprise there. Our Librarian loves to burn the candle at both ends. She really is dedicated. We are so lucky to have her."

"I'm in the position where I'd agree with that."

The Vice Principal nodded enthusiastically, then opened the

door, ushering the two of them in. Sure enough, there was Jeanette by a printer, a steaming mug in one hand, a stack of books under her other arm and tapping her foot gently.

Funny, Papa had never seen someone gently tap their foot. It was usually a sign of impatience. Instead, hers seemed to be thumping along to some song that only the librarian could hear. It was endearing, much more than it should have been, as was the little jump she gave as the Vice Principal cleared her throat.

"Goodness, Xiomara, you scared m-me." Jeanette sputtered to a stop as her gaze landed on Papa and her eyes went wide. "Montgomery! What on earth are you doing here?"

That worry about being creepy surged back up on him and Papa quickly tried to explain himself. "You mentioned that whole Battle of the Books thing, and I volunteer fairly often here, so I figured I would swing by if an old man like me could be any help."

"Oh yes," the Vice Principal said, or Xiomara, apparently. "Mr. Miller is one of our most reliable volunteers. He's been running our ticketing booths and helping clean up after dances for years now. I know you don't attend many of our social events, but we all adore him!"

Goodness, that was a bit heavy on the praise. Papa did like to help out at the school because it felt like paying back some of the blessings he'd been born into, but he wouldn't consider himself a star player. He liked being a helper, that was all.

"O-oh, well, uh... yeah, I could use some help. If you don't mind."

"I don't mind at all. Please, put me to work. I'm sure my kids will be happy to have me out of their hair for a change."

That wasn't really true, but it seemed like something a regular person would say. Papa was very lucky that all of his children liked to hang out with him... when they had time. The only one who regularly needed space was Cass.

"Well, I'm finishing up printing the rules, book list and practice questions for all the students. It's too much for this paper tray, so would you mind grabbing it every twenty pages or so?"

"I can do that."

"Perfect! When it's all done, if you could sort them all into different stacks, then assemble the packets, that would be a dream."

Papa felt that familiar warmth in his chest. It definitely seemed like he was going to be able to legitimately help the woman.

"Oh! And then staple the corners?"

"I have been known to wield a stapler or two in my life."

"Fantastic! Thank you! This means I can get a jump on clearing off one of our shelves and dedicate it strictly to Battle of the Books reading."

She sounded so happy and hurried away to the opposite wall of the library, where there was a low shelf almost as tall as her with some beanbags and small chairs arranged around it. A reading nook, if Papa had to guess, and a cozy-looking one at that. He didn't remember anything like that when he last visited the library, but that had been about a decade or so earlier.

It was simple work, basically standing by the printer and making sure it didn't overfill its output tray, but Papa didn't mind. He liked feeling useful. He wished that he could start up a conversation with Jeanette, but she seemed to be concentrating very hard as she took an armful of books off the shelf only to do a circuit around the library until her arms were empty and all the books were safely reshelved.

She was like a machine, muttering to herself slightly and

always moving. For all her jokes about her knees, she certainly was spry. Papa was certain he could keep up with her and wished she would let him carry those heavy books for her.

But his job was the papers, so he waited dutifully until the printer let out a relieved sounding beep, then headed over to the closest table to sort them out. That didn't really take concentration, but it also did, and time began to slip away.

It was reassuring, the repetitiveness of it, and it reminded him of up-potting his tomato starts when they grew too big for their container. Soothing, in a way, and before he knew it, he had all the papers sorted into individual stacks.

"Now, where is that stapler?"

Papa looked around himself, figuring it was already on the table, but no. Nothing. Getting up—with a very unhelpful crack from one of his hips—he went over to Jeanette's cluttered desk but didn't spot it there either.

It probably was just in a drawer or something, but Papa wasn't about to go rooting around in her personal space. He was a guest, after all.

With one last look over the computer area to make sure that it hadn't been tucked some place, Papa went to find Jeanette. If anyone knew where the stapler was, it was obviously her.

He spotted her between two tall shelves, a pile of books at her feet and two large tomes in her hand. She was staring studiously at them, like they had personally offended her, and for a moment Papa didn't want to say anything. She looked so in her element that it seemed wrong to interrupt her.

"Something the matter?" she asked after a long minute. Because of course she knew he was there.

"Uh yeah, I was looking for the stapler."

"The stapler? It wasn't on my desk?"

"Not that I could see."

She frowned, putting the two books on the shelf. "I'm almost positive I left it on my desk." Expression clouded, the woman strode past Papa and back to the front area of the library.

"You looked like you were concentrating."

"I was reshelving the books on my suggested reading list to make room for Battle of the Books, but I seemed to have an extra volume of one of the bigger books, and it threw off my math on how much space I had."

"An extra volume? How does that happen?"

"A couple of different ways. A kid returns it and I didn't scan it back into the system like I thought I did, or a kid checked it out but then left it behind, and it accidentally got put back on the shelf. Maybe it slipped through the cracks."

"I didn't realize there could be so many possible pitfalls in the library sciences."

"Well, it did take me four years to earn my degree."

"Four years? I had no idea."

Papa didn't have any sort of degree himself. His brother McLintoc had gone to college and gotten his degree, but it certainly hadn't made him any happier. Not that Papa was against higher education; he wasn't at all. But he hated how it was forced on people as a matter of course. There were some people it was for, and some people it wasn't. That was why he supported Cici's college career just as much as he supported Charlie for deciding it wasn't for him.

"A lot of people don't. Ah, here it is!"

Jeanette hadn't gone to her desk, but rather to a shelf behind it, reaching around a glowing globe to grab a neon green stapler.

"I didn't know they came in that color," Papa said, chuckling slightly.

"They don't normally, but I work with young ones. I've learned that the only way to not lose small stuff like this is to make it as vibrant as possible."

"That's a strategy I wish I knew about when my children were younger."

"Yes, I imagine that was a lot, being a single father and all."

Wait, had he told her that? He was pretty sure... Oh. She knew who he was. He supposed it was silly to expect her not to, but he would be lying if he didn't admit that he enjoyed the novelty of thinking she didn't know.

"What about you? Any children to speak of?"

Maybe that was far too personal of a question, but Papa couldn't help himself. He didn't see a ring on her finger, but that didn't always mean anything.

But it was that very spot that stopped him in his mental tracks. Since when did he care about wedding rings or not? He hadn't been interested in anyone romantically for over ten years. He shouldn't be concerned about her marital state at all. Yet the question was already out of his mouth, so it wasn't like he could take it back.

"No, no children for me. Just wasn't in the cards."

He could tell she was aiming for casual, but there was a strained sort of sadness to her words. He didn't need the details to recognize mourning when he heard it. Whatever Jeanette had gone through, it obviously still wore at her.

The warmth and happiness that had been growing in his chest shrunk slightly, feeling rankled that something had hurt the librarian. Which was certainly a weird reaction to feel about a woman he'd only talked to twice.

Huh. It was a very strange day.

"Anyway, here's the stapler."

It wasn't the smoothest way to break the sudden silence between them, but it worked, and Papa took it gratefully. Retreating for the moment, he went around stapling together all of the packets.

Unfortunately, it wasn't enough to occupy him for long. Less than twenty minutes later, he was staring at his finished pile and wondering if he should bug Jeanette again.

Because he didn't want to be a pest. In fact, that was just about the last thing he wanted to do. But he also didn't want to just sit around and do nothing. That negated the entire purpose of him being there. He was supposed to be helpful, not a bump on a log.

So, heaving a deep breath, he went to find Jeannette again.

This time she wasn't in the shelves, but instead lying under a table. Papa found her by almost tripping over her shins, the rest of her body covered by the wooden surface.

"What are you doing down there?"

"Cleaning," her muffled voice drifted up, sounding quite pleased. "Thanks to you handling all that paper stuff, I'm ahead of schedule. I haven't had time to scrape these for a least a month, and *whew*, there's a lot of buildup down here."

Papa had plenty of experience with all the cleaning that came from having children, but her lying on the ground and scraping a table wasn't in his repertoire. "Why... I'm sorry, what's built up under the table?"

"Right, I forget that it's not a common worry. But Gum. So much gum. Occasionally other candies, but it's almost exclusively chewed gum. The stuff is like cement, so it's really time-consuming to get at it."

"Are you serious?" Montgomery asked, eyes going wide.

"Unfortunately, yes. It's a real problem. So really, your help has been amazing already."

She was sweet, but it didn't sit right with Papa for her to be doing such intense work while he just stood about.

"Why don't you let me handle that and you take a break."

"Oh, I'm fine."

"I figure, but I've finished with the papers and I wouldn't mind something more physical. Gotta stay moving, ya know, otherwise I might turn to stone."

The woman scooted out from under the table and if she didn't look absolutely adorable with her pink cheeks and hair falling out of her bun slightly to frame her face. "Are... are you sure?"

"Yeah, absolutely. Sitting still has never been a strong suit for anyone in my family."

"Well... I suppose I wouldn't mind having someone tap in. This really does a number on my wrist." With a huff, she was about to push herself onto her feet when Papa extended her a hand to take. She gladly accepted, then handed Papa both a paint scraper and a plastic trash bag when she was on her feet.

Sure enough, when Papa looked into it, he saw various dull shades of very much masticated bubble gum.

"That is disgusting," he remarked grimly. If he ever found out that any of his children stuck their gum to the underside of school tables, he'd have them on community service until they learned to respect their peers better. There was nothing worse than accidentally touching someone else's wet, slobbery gum.

Something about his expression must have been amusing, because Jeanette gave out a genuine laugh. "I suppose it is! It's easy to forget when I've been so desensitized to it."

"I appreciate your sacrifice for the future generations of America."

Another laugh from her, and it was such a pleasant sound. Papa certainly didn't consider himself a comedian, but he liked that he could amuse her. "Remind me to keep you around every time I'm feeling like my job is a little thankless."

"You got it. I can be your own personal..." What did Cass say the young kids call it? "...hype man."

This time she actually cackled, tilting her head back and just letting her peals of mirth fill the library.

"Goodness! You keep that up and I'm going to need an inhaler. You are too much!"

"I do try."

"You succeed." She drew in a breath, recovering, before straightening. "Alright, I'll go get us some drinks and snacks. Any requests?"

"Just some water. I've got my tea on me if I want something flavored."

"Sounds good. I'll be back before you know it."

Papa nodded and then got onto the ground, sliding under the table where Jeanette had been. He could still faintly smell the light perfume that she wore clinging ever so slightly to the carpet. It wasn't strong enough that he could pick out exactly what scent it was, but it was lovely.

"Concentrate, you oaf," he murmured to himself, bringing the scraper up and going for the closest wad of mauve-gray.

Ugh. She hadn't been kidding about it being almost like cement. For being such a tiny thing, it sure had plenty of grip. It was a wonder it didn't pull kids' teeth out of their own mouths.

When Papa finished the first table, Jeanette was still gone, so he just went over to the closest table and slid under that one next. His shoulders and upper arms weren't exactly happy with the situation, but there was something nice about doing manual labor that didn't require a ton of brain power. Although Papa enjoyed seed starting and working in his garden, it all required some thought and planning. But scraping gum off of some wood? Not so much.

"Hello? Montgomery? Are you still—Oh! You're under another table."

Papa was tempted to stay under the dark wood and finish the task, but his body certainly wouldn't mind a break, so he rolled out and sat up. "Finished up that last one and figured I might as well keep my streak alive."

"I can't believe it. That table is the farthest from my desk, so I'd be willing to bet it has the most gum out of all of them. I would have been at least another hour under there."

"Glad I could save you the time."

"That's an understatement if there ever was one! Makes me wish I had you around every day!"

Wouldn't that be something?

"Anyway, the busses will be arriving soon and there's always a couple of children who file in to grab a book for their school day or return one from the previous day, but it doesn't really get busy until around nine, when the first homeroom class happens for the sixth graders."

"Do you want me out of here by then?"

"Well, if you want to stick around, I do have a back room over in the corner there."

"Back room? Sounds nefarious."

"Hardly. But it's where I have the Battle of the Books orders, more books that either need to be shipped off or entered into the system. Damage write-offs... the list goes on."

"Right, and I could be of help back there?"

"If you don't mind a little more of that manual labor. I'll be able to visit you on my breaks and lunch, and the gaps between classes. After lunch, my assistant librarian comes in, so I'll have more time to help."

"How long would this take you?"

"Oh goodness, maybe a week or two? It's heavy stuff and I only have a few minutes at a time in the first half of the day."

"Then I'd be happy to help." The idea of saving Jeanette an entire week of hard work made it hard not to grin widely. "Just tell me what to do and I'll do it."

"Goodness, where have you been the past nine years I've been here?"

Lost, apparently. "Well, I do have this sizable ranch that I tend to hang around on."

"Hah, well I can't blame you for that!" Although Papa was trying not to grin like a maniac, Jeanette was certainly wearing a wide grin. "Alright, let me get you set up. You really are a lifesaver."

"I don't know about that, but I'm glad I could be of help."

"You certainly are, more than you know."

IT WAS HARD WORK, sorting the boxes into piles. He had no idea how Jeanette was expected to do all of it on top of all her other duties. Because every time he looked out the window set in the door, she was running around or helping students or otherwise being quite busy.

But even though it certainly wasn't easy, every time Jeanette popped in only to gawk in wonder at all he'd done, Papa felt rejuvenated all over again. It was like he was ten years younger, and even though he knew he was going to pay for it the next day, he was happy to work for as long as she needed him.

But the highlight of his day was definitely lunch. He hadn't brought anything to eat, sure Jeanette wouldn't want him around that long, only to be surprised when she showed up with a platter full of food.

It turned out she had an in with a couple of the cafeteria ladies and it was their lauded chicken tender day. Although Papa had tasted better, especially considering Clara's exceptional cooking skills, but they were delicious, nonetheless. Or maybe that was because of the conversation. Papa had certainly heard stranger theories.

Much like the rest of the day, the forty-five-minute lunch passed far too quickly, and then Papa was back to the grind. He probably never would have made it without the water bottles that Jeanette had given him, and she showed up with more when the assistant librarian finally arrived to relieve her.

"Oh, would you listen to that? That's the last bell."

Papa wiped his forehead with his handkerchief. "What, already?"

"Not quite sure what you mean by 'already.'" Jeanette chuckled. "You've been here for hours. Goodness, I'm beginning to think you're secretly a thirty-something who just has a penchant for gray hair."

"Thirties were a long time ago for me." Papa thought back to how his life was when he was thirty. He'd still had the love of his life, for one, and his children were just beginning to fall into their own personalities, and they hadn't experienced the worst trauma of their lives yet.

"Right, well, if you want to escape this prison you've found yourself in, you can head home."

"Are you heading home yet?"

"No, not quite yet. I stay here until the late bell for students who come here to read, pass the time until their parents pick them up, or do computer work because they don't have one at home."

"Wait, there are students who don't have computers?" Papa wasn't the tech savviest himself, but he knew he lived in a technological world. The idea of students in this day and age not having access to a computer to do all their work at home was hard to imagine.

"Not many, but certainly a few. And there's a handful more who don't have internet. It works well enough for them typing up essays but not so much for any research work."

Huh, that got the wheels in Papa's head turning, but that was a matter for another day.

"Ah, when's the late bell?"

"About another hour from now. Then I clean up, pack up, and otherwise lock up."

"I don't mind sticking around, unless it would make it easier for you if I departed."

"O-oh, no, I don't mind. If you're sure? You've been working so hard all day."

"It's just another hour or so. It'll give me a chance to lug all these Battle of the Books boxes out into the main area."

"I... I would appreciate that very much," Jeanette answered, her voice soft and her gaze going a bit... well, Papa didn't know how to describe it, but there was certainly a change in it. "Thank you, Montgomery. I can't even imagine how far you've put me ahead. I might actually be able to show up for work at reasonable times for the rest of the week."

There it was, that happy, blooming warmth in his chest. The one that made it easier to forget about all the dark things in the world, the ones that liked to hide behind corners and pop out at the worst moments.

"I'm just happy to be useful."

She gave him a little nod and opened the door, heading out into the main part of the library. Papa looked around at the closest box he had ready to go and followed her, setting it next to the empty bookshelf.

One after the other, he trotted them out. His mind narrowed through to a singular focus, like he hadn't had to in years. Sure, there was plenty of manual labor to do on the ranch, but his children took care of most of that.

Well... they did before Cass's accident. There was a lot to catch up on, and they were still trying to figure out the proper efficiency to divide up the chores without her.

Once again, time passed far too quickly, and before Papa knew it, Jeanette was clearing her throat behind him.

"Alright, time to go."

Papa pulled out a handkerchief from his shirt pocket and dabbed at his face, suddenly feeling a bit grubby and gross. He normally didn't mind a good, hardworking sweat, but some part of him wanted to look nice for Jeanette. Put together. Like the type of man that a demure, intelligent librarian might want.

...why was he worried about what a woman would want?

"Want to walk out together?" Jeanette continued, completely unaware of the whirlwind of thoughts in Papa's head.

"Sure, ma'am, I'd like that. I do have to sign out at the office, though."

"Oh, right. We'll stop there first."

They didn't say much as they walked to the office, signed Montgomery out, then headed to the parking lot. Papa had completely forgotten where his spot was, but thankfully his dark green vehicle stood out plenty. Jeanette's, however, was not so easy to spot.

Papa had watched her drive away in it once, but when he looked over the dozen or so cars left, none of them were particularly noteworthy.

"This way," she said, gesturing for him to follow. Papa did, and it turned out she was parked all the way on the opposite side of the parking lot.

"Why so far?"

"Have to get my cardio in where I can. I expected a much longer day, you know, one where I wouldn't have the energy to walk around the block when I get home."

"Ah, well, I'm glad that I could provide you with that."

"Me too."

There was that soft voice again, sweet and yet somehow scared. Like if Papa moved too fast that she would bolt at any moment. But Montgomery didn't like to be frightening, imposing or intimidating. While McLintoc might have been about power and being perceived like that, it had never been Papa's thing. He wanted to be a source of protection, comfort and strength.

"Well, here's my ride."

"There it is," Papa said, not sure what else to say. "Thank you for letting me help you today."

"Thank *you*! I really cannot express how grateful I am."

"You don't have to."

There was a moment where they both hesitated, like they

weren't sure of something, but it was gone almost as soon as it was born. Jeanette cleared her throat and got into her car, while Papa backed up a few steps, allowing her to pull away.

He watched her go until she turned the corner, a strange sort of feeling churning in his gut.

"Pull yourself together, Monty," he grumbled to himself as he strode to his truck and hopped in. "You just need to get home."

His world grew kind of hazy as he stuck his keys in the ignition and made his way home. But it wasn't until he drove under the welcome sign to their little ranch that he realized it.

Was it possible... possible that he had a crush on the school librarian!?

7

Papa

They hired a new ranch hand.

Papa Miller hadn't quite been on board when Cass brought up the idea of hiring someone to take over her chores. Between the other members of the family, they surely had enough people to cover any gaps.

It was Charlie, actually, who convinced him in the end. He'd mentioned how Cass had always been a responsible one, a gap-filler, and her seeing her family struggle to take over those spots made her guilt that much worse. So Papa had signed off on it, and the next thing he knew, Clara was dragging a random stranger onto their ranch.

He was a tall, quiet man, with dark skin and an impressive frame. Papa wasn't sure what to think of him at first and kept a solid eye on him, but he turned out to be a nice, quiet fellow.

With one magnificent horse.

Papa wasn't sure he'd seen a horse so tall, wide, and utterly majestic. Seriously, the mane on the mount alone was something for the record books, thick and long, with ever-changing braids in it. To be honest, it was the guy's tender treatment of his animal that helped sway Papa's opinion.

"Hey Papa, you spying on the new guy again?"

Montgomery turned to see Clara putting on her pair of shoes in the kitchen doorway, a wry grin on her pleasant features.

"Don't you have a grumpy man to go help?" Papa shot back.

A lot had changed since his last time at the library. Alejandro and Charity had gotten together. And Clara had rejoined her volunteer efforts with the church and ended up delivering meals to a man who had been struck by lightning.

Oddly enough, he'd been struck the same night that Cass's accident had happened. Normally Papa wouldn't be comfortable with one of his daughters going to an unknown man's house, but some part of it felt... fated.

Maybe that was silly, but what were the chances that his daughter would get wrapped up with another person affected by the same storm? Sure, Papa lived a somewhat serendipitous life, but that was pushing it, even for him.

"Papa, I told you, he's been trying. He's doing much better."

"You are ever the optimist," Papa remarked, looking out the window again.

"Hey," Clara said, crossing to him and placing a hand on his shoulder. "This Mick guy is helping Cass a lot. It's gonna be okay."

Okay, so maybe he was a little prickly because he'd almost lost her once. Could anyone blame him?

"By the way, Savannah texted to say she'd be popping by after school. In case you want to make her a little snack."

Papa grinned at that. Since Charity and Alejandro had officially started going out, the young girl had basically become his unofficial grandchild. And he didn't mind at all. She was a fun kid, full of questions, and she *loved* the ranch. From the garden to the goats, and even the more mundane chores, she always treated everything like an amazing secret that she was being let in on. Papa would be lying if he said he didn't enjoy her youthful energy. It had been quite a long time since a little one had been on their land, and Papa hadn't realized how much he missed it until Savannah was doing handstands and somersaults while asking the differences between winter and summer squash.

"Thanks for letting me know."

"You know, if you gave her your number, I'm sure she'd text you too."

Papa considered that. He liked the girl, but he wasn't sure that he could keep up with a younger person's texting rate. Although Savannah didn't seem phone-obsessed, she still was probably much more adept at the short messages and memes than Papa.

Instead, he let out a noncommittal noise. "You have a good day with Mr. Westbrook."

"I'll do my best."

With a nod, she headed out the door, leaving Papa to make that snack. And he definitely needed to. Savannah was still growing, becoming a tall, reedy thing that looked older than she was, and she ate as much as any of the Miller children did when they were young.

Of course, Savannah would never just admit to being hungry,

and would let herself do without until she got home, so Papa always made sure she had plenty of food options available.

Soon, Savannah showed up in Charity's car, bouncing and ready to visit all the animals. Thankfully, the eldest daughter knew better than to let her run immediately into tasks, bringing her inside to do a half-hour of homework and eat.

"Charity, why don't you go catch a shower and I'll hang out here with Savannah?"

"Oh, are you sure?" his daughter asked, looking quite relieved. Normally, they all tended to shower at night after a hard day's work, but he was pretty sure Charity had passed out early and missed her usual chance.

"Of course. You're cool with this, right, Savannah?"

"Cool as a cucumber!" she replied, already pulling her math books out. Papa wasn't a fan of how much homework was usually given to kids, but at least Savannah always seemed to work through hers quickly.

"There you go. See, at least someone still thinks I'm cool."

"I didn't say that."

"Thanks, Savannah," Papa responded, chuckling.

"Alright then, I'll go wash up and change. And then we'll go see if the goats need anything."

"Awww yisss! I love my jumpy boys!"

Jumpy boys? Papa mouthed to Charity, but she just shrugged. Slang, it always kept going. Language was both amazing and exhausting in that way.

Sometimes, it was better not to ask, however, and instead he went about grabbing the sandwich and little veggies he'd cut up for her. Nothing fancy, but Savannah ate it up like it was the best thing in the world. Granted, she seemed to eat everything like it was the best thing in the world.

Ah, the life of a teenager.

"Hey, Papa Miller."

"Yeah?"

"My team is doing great in Battle of the Books! We made it to the semifinals."

"That's terrific, Savannah. I bet your dad is proud of you."

"Oh yeah, he totally is. But I wanted to ask you if you'd come watch."

Papa paused for a moment. "It's going to be its own event?"

"Yeah, that and the finals. After school in the auditorium. Dad's gonna be there, and Charity too, but I think it'd be cool if you wanted to come too."

Papa hesitated for a moment. He wanted to go, to support Savannah, but he wasn't naïve enough to think that he wouldn't run into Jeanette there, and ever since his personal revelation that he had a crush on her, he wasn't sure how to act around the woman.

"But you don't have to. I know you're busy."

And that was what sealed it for him. He'd been a father long enough to tell when a child was trying to play it cool, and while Savannah had many, many skills, "playing it cool" was not among them.

"I'll be there," he promised, sending her a wink. "Wouldn't miss it for the world."

"Awww yisss! You're gonna see me absolutely crush it. Next year, they're probably gonna have to add some new game mechanics to make sure one team member can't carry the entire group to the top."

Papa understood... most of those words. "Game mechanics?"

"They're like, uh, the rules of the game? Like, a game

mechanic would be when you're playing solitaire how you can double click a card to make it go where it's supposed to?"

"Ah, I see. I have to admit, I'm surprised you know what solitaire is."

"*Pppft,* of course I do. All the dinosaur computers in the English rooms have that game on them."

Right. She was talking about the computer program. Now the comment about double-clicking made sense. "Naturally."

"But thank you, really. I'm excited for all of you to be there. You're basically family."

Now it that wasn't enough to make Papa's heart squeeze warmly in his chest. "I'm honored."

"Aw, it's nbd."

Papa didn't even bother to ask about that one. He just returned to the fridge and went about making Savannah another sandwich. She was a growing girl, after all.

And maybe it was also to distract him from the fact that he was going to see Jeanette again, and he'd have to face the fact that he couldn't get over his feelings of guilt and betrayal whenever he thought of her. Was he breaking his marriage vows to Mama by thinking good thoughts about the lovely librarian?

When did his life get so complicated?

"WHAT DID Charlotte Doyle do with the whip she took from the Captain?"

Papa couldn't help it as his leg bounced, his rear all the way on the edge of his seat. Charity, Clara and Charlie were all similarly perched beside him, with Cass at the end in her motorized chair.

It was the last round and although Savannah's team was well ahead, it was clear that she and a girl on the other team were both gunning for the most individual points of the night. Papa wasn't exactly sure why, but he did remember Savannah mentioning something about an MVP award.

"She used it on him!" Savannah said, practically jumping out of her seat.

"Very good! She did exactly that. Now, Team Artichoke, your question."

The way it worked was that each contestant was asked a question, from right to left, and if they couldn't answer it, it would go to the opposite team, who had half the time to steal the question. It was certainly very lively and competitive for being a kid's scholastic event, and more than once Papa found himself cheering perhaps a little too loudly.

Oh well. So, he was enthusiastic. Surely no one could find fault with that. Savannah certainly didn't mind, grinning from ear to ear and waving whenever she heard him root for her. And Papa had to admit, that smile was something he would never get tired of. There was something magical about the genuine, unfiltered happiness of a kid, and he was glad that it was back in his life.

The rest of the round seemed to fly by, and before he knew it, Savannah and her crew were awarded the win. There was more cheering, and then the announcement of when the finals were, and that was it.

Too bad it couldn't have been that simple. If Papa had his way, he would have hightailed it out of there, grateful he hadn't been forced to speak with anyone that he didn't want to. But Savannah was practically mobbed by her teammates, her friends, and anybody else who wanted to congratulate her, and he knew he couldn't split without giving his own praise.

Well, he could, but it would definitely hurt her feelings, and Papa wasn't about to do that over him having butterflies about a nice librarian.

He waited for a clear moment before stepping up to her. And he was instantly rewarded for his decision. The second her eyes locked onto him, she raced forward, throwing herself into his arms.

"Thank you for coming!"

"Of course. I wouldn't miss it for anything."

"I know you said that, but usually when people do, they don't actually mean it."

"Well, I try to be a type of man who means what he says."

She nodded gravely. "Papa is the same way." But then her expression instantly brightened. "So what did you think?"

"I think you're an absolute shark. No wonder you're so good at Speed."

She laughed at that, cheeks bright with her happiness. "Thankfully I win more at Battle of the Books than Speed. I don't think that we'd be in the semifinals with a win percentage just barely higher than fifty percent."

"No, probably not," Papa agreed, thoroughly amused by her matter-of-fact response. That was his Savannah.

"You did amazing, *mija!*" Alejandro said, cutting in. But Papa was grateful for the interruption as he realized just what he'd thought.

It was small, and yet something he hadn't allowed himself before. But he'd thought of Savannah as *his* granddaughter. Not just a young girl who hung around. Or the daughter of the man his eldest was dating. In that moment, with his nervousness and worry set aside, his mind had unabashedly labeled her as family. No ifs, ands or buts. And now that he thought about it, it seemed *right*.

Which was certainly something indeed.

Emotional revelations were definitely thirsty work, so Papa headed for one of the vending machines he knew were just outside of the cafeteria. He wouldn't have many options he could drink, but if he recalled, there was a green tea sort of thing that could get him through until he got home. He had a lovely pitcher of honey-ginseng tea waiting for him, but his mouth was far too dry to wait that long.

Thankfully, the green tea was in stock. Papa quickly bought some, then headed back into the auditorium only to nearly run into the very person he was trying to avoid.

"Mr. Miller!" Jeanette said, clearly surprised to see him.

Papa felt a bit bad about that. He'd spent a whole day with her, helped her get ahead, then disappeared. He hoped she didn't think it was anything that she did, because it really wasn't.

"Please, it's Montgomery."

She just nodded slightly, looking like she didn't quite know what to do with her hands or arms. She could join the club. "Right. It's good to see you again. I'm glad you got to see the fruit of some of your hard work."

"My hard work? The credit is due to you. I was just your dumb muscle for a day."

"Well, I wouldn't exactly call you dumb," she said, trying to laugh, but the sound was just a hair shy of being normal. "I hope you enjoyed yourself?"

"Yeah, of course I did. Savannah asked me to come so I had to be here."

"Savannah, right. She's why you're here. That makes sense."

Jeanette looked behind him then back, like she was looking for an escape route. "I'm in dire need of something to drink, so I'm going to treat myself to a soda. You have a good night, Mr.—I mean, Montgomery."

"Yeah, you too."

She hurried away and Papa had the urge to go after her. To tell her that she hadn't done anything wrong and he was just completely caught up in his own issues. But he didn't do any of that. He just turned around and went back to his family, heart heavy in his chest.

8

Jeanette

eanette loved kids, she really did, but sometimes they really seemed to be agents of chaos and disease. Equipped with super germs and mega-hormones, their bodies were sometimes ground zero of the worst things.

And currently, she was down for the count with one of those things— a respiratory infection that was bad enough to knock her off her feet and have the doctor forbidding her to return to school without antibiotics and some serious rest.

She was going to get better. And honestly, she had been trying to ignore not feeling well, but her cough had been so loud that it was bothering the students, and that had turned her in.

That was probably for the better, however. She was utterly exhausted in a way she hadn't been in years. Maybe she was just getting older, or maybe Battle of the Books had taken more out of her than she thought. Either way, she was laid up with barely enough energy to warm up canned broth.

Still, it wasn't so bad. She couldn't remember the last time she'd slept in so much, and it was certainly getting the assistant librarian more hours. Goodness knew Bella could use the extra in her paycheck with her little one on the way. But—as much as Jeanette joked about being a hermit—being stuck in her house for four days straight was a little lonely.

Actually, a lot lonely.

She didn't think it would be, considering she was unconscious most of the time, but it was. She woke up, quiet and alone. She slowly sipped her broth, quiet and alone. She slept, quiet and alone. There was no one to check her temperature. To watch television with her. To help her change the sheets.

Just her, and her mean old respiratory infection.

So, when a sharp knock sounded on her door, Jeanette nearly launched herself out of her own skin.

"Hel—" Her body cut her off, wracking her frames with coughs. *Ow.* That hurt. "Just a minute!"

Regaining her breath, Jeanette got up from the cushy chair she liked to watch TV in and hobbled to the door. Despite being mostly flat on her back for the past few days, her muscles were sore and aching, like she'd run a marathon.

She had no idea who was on the other side of the door, but she largely wasn't worried. In the small town, most people knew each other, so it was probably just someone from the church or school coming to check on her.

"Mr. Miller!"

Somehow, she didn't expect it would be the one man who'd been on her mind constantly.

"It's Montgomery, please."

He looked just as handsome as ever, salt and pepper hair and a blue and purple plaid shirt tucked into his jeans. What was he doing, showing up at her door looking so alive and healthy and also did she mention handsome?

"You shouldn't be here. I'm awful sick—"

"I'm sorry for showing up without permission, but Savannah mentioned you were sick and so I brought you over some of Clara's certified sick food. Guaranteed to cure what ails ya."

That was so incredibly sweet, but all Jeanette could think about was how she hadn't brushed her hair in three days, how she was covered in sweat, and she was pretty sure she had broth stains on the front of her gown.

Oh dear.

Why did Montgomery have to see her like *that?*

"Well, I can take that to the kitchen then. Thank you. You didn't have to do this."

To be truthful, what little she could smell was absolutely delicious, warm and comforting in all the right ways. Jeanette bet a good meal of whatever that was would leave her belly nice and contented while also clearing her nose right up.

"If you don't mind, it's a little heavy. I can carry it for you. Unless you prefer your privacy, in which case, I completely understand."

Jeanette paused for a moment, feeling incredibly self-conscious. But her arms did feel like noodles, and the idea of carrying the bags of food he had seemed nearly insurmountable.

"Alright. I'd certainly appreciate the help."

"Glad to be of service."

It was a nothing phrase, another way to say "no problem," but when Montgomery said it, it seemed oh so genuine. He was so sweet in ways that she didn't think were real. The kind of sweet kindness that made her toes curl in her shoes and her heart beat faster in her chest.

"Right this way."

He followed her to her kitchen, which was remarkably unused compared to how she normally made her breakfast and dinner every day, and began taking out thermoses and fancy-looking containers.

"If you tell me where your bowls and plates are, I'd be happy to serve you."

Jeanette did just that, and that measly effort was thoroughly exhausting to her, leaving a new layer of sweat on her forehead. "I'm going to go sit down, if you don't mind."

"Please do. I'll have this ready for you in a jiffy."

Jeanette tottered to her living room but paused in the doorway. "Aren't you worried about getting sick?"

"Oh me? Not so much. I've got a pretty strong immune system. Besides, if I do get sick, I've got my whole family to take care of me."

"...right." The thing he wasn't saying was that Jeanette had nobody. She was alone. "Thank you, then."

"It's no problem, really. Why don't you make yourself comfortable and I'll take care of this."

Jeanette used the last of her energy to give a little nod and then made her way to her chair. She sank into it, still feeling embarrassed and thoroughly drained, but there wasn't a ton she could do about it. She was sick.

It felt entirely alien to hear someone puttering around in her kitchen while she was in a different room. The last time she'd had anyone in her place was a small church brunch with two ladies from Bible study and that was five years ago.

But the thought of real food besides reheated broth was enough to slake her growing discomfort, especially as the scent grew. It didn't take long for Montgomery to enter the living room, a bowl in one hand and a steaming mug in the other.

"This is the soup Clara made, and here's some tea. There's also some roast chicken, but I wasn't sure if your stomach could handle it, so I figured we'd see how you did with the soup?"

"That sounds good," she rasped, only just noticing how rough her voice sounded. Did she always sound so croaky?

"Do you have a tray I can put this on?"

Jeanette nodded, pointing over to a foldable TV tray she had in the corner. Mr. Miller placed the food down on her coffee table, set up the TV tray for her, then carefully placed the food and drink in front of her.

It was just so... lovely. She didn't have any other words for it. His actions were simple but made her feel valued. And when he looked her over, she felt like he truly cared about her health.

Which was silly. She was a nobody to him. A stranger. During his whole day volunteering at the library, she had thought that maybe, just maybe that something was there, but then he'd utterly disappeared for over a month. No word. No trying to get her number. No more volunteering; he was just gone.

So, it didn't make sense that he was in front of her, looking at her like *that*.

Maybe she was sicker than she thought and just hallucinating about how kind he was being to her. But she didn't know what it said about her that she was fantasizing about being nursed by a man she hardly knew. That wasn't like her at all.

"Looks like I forgot about a spoon. Don't suppose you got any of those around here?"

Jeanette managed a very weak chuckle. "I suppose I might."

She told him where they were and soon, he was back with one, brandishing it like a grand gift. It was enough to get another bit of mirth, but Jeanette was tapped out. She needed that delicious-smelling soup inside of her STAT.

Taking the spoon with a trembling hand, she managed to get a steaming helping into her mouth. Just like she'd expected, it was *perfect*. Hot like a steamy bath, it warmed her from the inside out, spreading through her like the world's most comfortable blanket. It was full of savory flavors, with just enough spice to make her nose run. Of course, that just helped her smell the delicious food that much more, and her sinuses slowly began to unclog.

"Good, isn't it?" Mr. Miller asked, grinning broadly.

Jeanette could only groan in response before taking another spoonful. It also coated her throat, soothing the irritation that had been there.

"It reminds me of tortilla soup, but homier somehow?"

"It's inspired by that, I think. Clara said it's her own personal mash-up of chicken dumpling and tortilla soup, but with fewer carbs. Something about... bacteria or sickness feeding on sugars?"

Jeanette nodded. "I'm fairly sure viruses have some extreme reactions to sugar as well, although they don't feed on them, per se."

"Sounds very complicated." Montgomery laughed gently. "All I know is that her soup works." He paused, his smile fading and a more awkward expression crossing his handsome features. Or maybe she was imagining that too. It was hard to tell.

"It's amazing," was all Jeanette could supply before needing to take another spoonful.

"Don't forget the tea too. It's supposed to work as a one-two punch."

Jeanette nodded, picking up the mug and gulping down a good amount. Like the soup, it was warm and soothing, coating her throat and soothing all that irritation. It wasn't like she was about to roll out into the street and start singing, but her body certainly felt less ragged.

Maybe later she could handle a shower.

"Well, you can tell that Clara of yours that I'm giving her a rave review," Jeanette said after a few more spoonfuls. "Thank you for sticking around to set all this up for me."

"Well, I don't have to leave right away, if you'd like some company. I figure you probably haven't had many visitors as of late."

"You're not exactly wrong about that." Jeanette thought for a moment. He'd already seen her at her worst, and it *was* nice to talk to him, even if he sometimes made her feel like she had all the social skills of an especially stressed hamster. "I suppose I've already infected you, so you might as well stick around, if you don't mind."

"I don't mind at all."

If it were anyone else, she probably would have doubted it, but there was just a certain guilelessness to him that made everything he said seem more genuine. She'd noticed that before, but it still surprised her every time.

Jeannette made an attempt at conversation. "How do you feel about some TV classics? I've been rewatching *Little House on the Prairie* lately." Jeanette raised an eyebrow when Papa chuckled at that. "Not a fan?"

"Oh, I never felt one way or another about it, but Clara was obsessed with the books when she was younger. She was thrilled when she found out there was a whole show about it, but then when it started to go off-script, she got upset and never touched it again."

Jeanette had to chuckle at that as well. "Children and their particularities. I can understand how it might be confusing to her. It's hard to separate different forms of media when you're that young."

"Honestly, I know plenty of adults who are terrible at it too."

"I know people exactly like that, but I try to avoid them as best I can."

"Why do you think I rarely ever leave the ranch? Best way to avoid them all, if you ask me."

Jeanette nodded absently, slowly sipping more tea, then spooning more soup into her mouth. "You just leave to help little ol' librarians and run ticket booths for sporting events."

"And don't forget selling specialty produce at festivals."

"What a wild life you lead." They both chuckled.

It was the most she'd spoken since she'd gotten sick, and although her body was feeling better, her energy was quickly fading. It didn't help that she was feeling so syrupy warm and contented from the good food. Carefully, she managed a couple more spoonfuls and maybe about half of her tea before the world got a little softer, a little fuzzier, with Monty's words blending together in a comforting rumble.

And that was how she slipped away into a nap, feeling better than she had in days.

JEANETTE DIDN'T REALIZE she'd even fallen asleep until she tried to open her eyes and the crust stopped them. Ew.

Rubbing at them, she slowly came to, feeling better than she had in days.

Wait, she hadn't been alone! She'd been in the middle of a conversation with her guest, who just so happened to be a very handsome and eligible bachelor who dropped by to take care of her.

Oh no. Had... had she *snored!?*

"Montgomery?" she called out, realizing that the TV had been turned off and she had a throw blanket placed over her. "Are you there?"

No answer. Getting up as best she could—which certainly was an effort even with how much better she was feeling—she made her way toward the bathroom. On the way there, she saw a note in the kitchen, written with surprisingly neat handwriting.

I wanted to say goodbye, but you were sleeping so soundly it seemed a shame to rouse you. I hope the food does you well. I put the roast chicken in the fridge. I wrote my number below. Please text me if you need anything.

—Montgomery *Miller*

Her heart skipped a beat. She folded up the note and placed it in the pocket of her house robe. It was something for her to ponder over, later.

She realized that she finally had enough energy to take a shower. A quick shower, but a wash nonetheless.

The warm water felt wonderful on her skin, as did the soap that added some aromatherapy to the task, and by the time Jeanette stepped out of the shower, she was one step closer to being human. Instead of feeling like she was stuck at the bottom of a pit of misery and despair, she felt like she could probably be back to full health in another day or so.

While it was hard to believe that some soup and tea could make such a difference, she supposed she had been both a little dehydrated and malnourished. Maybe her body had desperately needed the nourishment, and now that it had it, she had enough energy to get her through the day.

Still, she would definitely need to make a thank you basket for Clara. That girl certainly had a gift.

...but maybe another nap first.

Although Jeanette was feeling like the respiratory infection was slowly losing its grip on her, she wasn't exactly fully cured, and her body still needed rest, or she'd be back in the same boat all over again.

Granted, if she was in the same boat, maybe Montgomery would visit again?

Jeanette caught herself in her own thoughts, shaking her head. But her mind refused to reset itself, playing the man's visit over and over again in her mind. The rumble of his voice, the gentle look in his eyes, the stubble on his chin. All of it.

It was hard to remember a time when she wasn't alone. It was a solid part of her life, the peace and stillness that she told herself she loved. And yet Papa Miller being at her place wasn't a disruption. No, far from it. He was a comfort that filled the space and made it that much more welcoming. Like a missing puzzle piece that she hadn't been aware was even gone.

Or maybe she was still sick.

...she should probably have some more soup.

Grabbing a pot, Jeanette set it on the stove and started

heating up some food. She didn't have enough energy in her for the roasted chicken, but she could stay awake for a little longer.

But as she stood at the stove, stirring idly, her mind kept returning to Montgomery. It was impossible to deny that she liked his company. That he made her feel the way she hadn't felt in years. As strange as it was, it wasn't like she was cheating on anyone. Why was she acting so guilty?

It was silly. If her husband was still here, he would just give her a curious sort of look and ask why she was complicating things that didn't need to be complicated. She liked interacting with an eligible man. So what?

She'd always been a go-getter kind of woman, independent to a fault. If she wanted to spend time with Mr. Miller... she should just do it.

Yes, it was that simple. She just had to call the number on the note. Just ten little numbers that she had to punch in so she could talk to him.

Well.

Maybe when she was feeling a little better. She didn't want to push herself too hard, after all.

9

Papa

It had been a few days since he last visited Jeanette, and Papa couldn't figure out if it was too soon to visit again or if he could drop by twice without asking.

Every time he tried to put her out of his mind, she'd pop right back up again. Tending to his garden? He'd wonder if Jeanette had a favorite flower. Taking care of the chickens while Clara was helping Mr. Westbrook? He wondered if Jeanette liked chickens at all. Cooking, he wondered if she was eating, drinking tea; he wondered if she was hydrated. So on and so forth, until it seemed like a futile effort to try to shove her back out of his mind.

But whenever his thoughts lingered on her, he couldn't help but recall her home. It was lovely, really. Clearly painstakingly decorated and filled with so much detail. But at the same time, it was so empty, and that made him feel sad.

Jeanette didn't deserve to be alone. And it would be one thing if she was content with it, but to him, it didn't seem like she was.

And that wasn't fair.

"Hey, Papa! I'm home early!" Clara called as she came into the house.

Monty started from where he was sorting out his seed packets. In reality, he had them all meticulously ordered in his filing cabinet, but he'd decided to go through and weed out any that were older than five years, as their germination rate was much lower than newer seeds. He was still planning to use them, of course, but in a new bed that he had mentally dubbed his "wild bed," back by the goats.

Sure, he had the front garden, which was half ornamental, and the garden in the backyard that he and Mama had built together, but after so many years he felt like he could use a little more space. Especially considering all the extra mouths that were around. Between Alejandro and Savannah's visits, and Mick being around full time, the family was going through fresh produce much more than usual.

Which Papa didn't mind at all. And maaaaybe he was using their presence as an excuse to make more growing space, but there were worse reasons for a little bit of self-delusion.

"Hey there, Clara. Mr. Westbrook get under your skin a little earlier than usual?"

"Hah! No, not quite. He just was very tired and needed to lay down, so I finished up some chores and cleared out." Clara finally rounded the corner of his office, a sly grin on her features.

Papa was immediately suspicious, but before he could ask, she was speaking again.

"You have a visitor, by the way."

"A visitor? Who?"

But Clara just shrugged and practically pranced off. "They're waiting outside! You better let them in if you want to be a good host."

"She seemed pleased as punch with herself," Papa muttered to himself, setting his seeds aside and getting up.

He wasn't quite sure who would be visiting him without a call. While he tried to be friendly with everyone, he wasn't exactly *friends* with anyone. Maybe someone from church? Or a surprise visit from one of his nephews?

No, Clara wouldn't have looked so smug about that.

But then Papa opened the door and he saw exactly who it was, his heart doing a little leap in his chest.

"Jeanette!" he said, unable to hide his shock.

"Oh hey there," she said, a shy grin across her pleasant features. "I hope you don't mind that I stopped by."

"U-uh, no! I-I-I... I just..." Papa realized that he was stuttering and took a breath. "Why are you here? Is everything alright?"

"Yes. I wanted to bring your containers back, and I wanted to thank you for helping me."

Right. He had left the soup thermos, the tea thermos, and Clara's special container for transporting her roasts and other hot foods. Quite a bit to just leave behind. Of course, someone thoughtful like Jeanette would return them.

"You didn't have to do that. I could have stopped by. Shouldn't you be resting and recovering?"

"Nah, I figure a week off my feet was plenty. Don't worry. I'm feeling almost one hundred percent back to lil' ol' me."

"Well, I'm glad to hear that. Not to be rude, but you did look a little rough around the edges the last time I saw you."

"Trust me, I felt a little rough, if I'm being honest."

Papa nodded and took the bag she held up, but he didn't want her to walk away. "Since you're already here, would you like to come in for some tea?"

The grin that spread across her face was absolutely enchanting. "Sure, I'd love that."

Papa stepped aside, opening the door for her to enter. She did, looking around with an impressed expression. Papa was so used to his home he sometimes forgot that it looked quite large compared to Jeanette's place.

"Wow, this is lovely!"

"It's alright," Montgomery said, not sure how to reply. "We do well enough by ourselves."

"That's putting it lightly."

Papa didn't normally feel self-conscious about his family's wealth, but he couldn't help but wonder what Jeanette thought about it. Did she think he was selfish? Hoarding resources when so many people were doing without?

He supposed it was true that he could be doing more for the community, but it was hard not to feel overwhelmed sometimes by it all.

"The kitchen is this way," he said instead, gesturing. Once again, Jeanette followed him, perching on one of the stools around the kitchen island as Papa put a kettle on to boil. It was only when he was reaching for one of his tea pouches that he remembered he had a pitcher of peach-honey tea in the fridge.

"Would you like something warm or cold?"

"Ooooh, what do you have that's chilled?"

"Some peach tea that I made yesterday. It usually goes before night hits, so I forgot about it."

Jeanette chuckled lightly. "What, was it a bad batch or something?"

"Hah! Tasted alright to me. I just forgot that Charity is up at her cousins', Cass has been spending most of her time helping our ranch hand recover, Clara was doing her charity work for the church, and Charlie's helping the fall rodeo about three hours away."

"Goodness, you're practically all alone. You're lucky I came by. Otherwise you might have just perished from the loneliness."

"A truly desolate fate."

Her tone was light and teasing, but there was a hint of truth to it. When the ranch was full, it was full, with Savannah bouncing around adding more life than ever. But it seemed that each of his children were starting to branch out, finding more and more valid reasons to stay off the ranch.

And he didn't resent them for it. He knew it was healthy, and he honestly loved hearing how excited they were about the new developments in their lives.

But, as he watched Cass and Mick grow closer, as he watched Charity and Alejandro walk hand in hand, as he greeted Clara when she returned home only for her to shower and pass out in a nap, it was hard not to feel... left behind.

"Ice or no ice?" he asked, choosing to change the direction of the conversation.

"Ice, please."

Papa nodded and filled a tall glass for her. He probably watched a little too intensely as she took a long drink, but the smile that she flashed him at the end was totally worth it.

"Wow! This is delicious! It's so sweet but not overpowering.

Any chance you've got this bottled up somewhere, cause I have a pantry I wouldn't mind stocking."

"Really? You like it that much?"

Papa didn't know what it was about talking to Jeanette that made him lose the normal assuredness he usually had, but it was getting old. He had been out of high school for decades. He had no desire to go back.

"Yes, this is fantastic! I wouldn't be able to drink it after three or four in the afternoon, I think, but it sure would be a temptation."

"Hah! I understand that. That's when I switch to my chamomile-blueberry blend."

Jeanette's eyes went wide at that. "You can't just mention that and not let me try it."

Papa's chest felt all warm again. "It's pretty potent. Why don't I give you some to take home so that you don't pass out at the wheel?"

"You know what? That sounds like a plan. I've always valued being able to stay awake while I drive. I'm just crazy like that."

"What a peculiar preference."

They both laughed lightly together, and it was such a *nice* feeling. Papa was blindsided by it, which felt just about as ridiculous as everything else, so instead he busied himself with pouring himself his own drink that he hastily gulped down.

He had no idea what to do or say once he finished swallowing, however, and apparently Jeanette didn't either, because they just stood there in a rare moment of silence on the ranch.

Papa never thought he would be grateful for a particularly mouthy chicken, but a sudden flurry of *very* opinionated clucks and calls broke the suddenly intense quiet between the two.

"Goodness, what is *that?*" Jeanette asked, cackling practically as loud as the hen.

Papa felt relief roll through him and said a silent thank you to Clara for raising such characters.

"One of our feathery divas, as Clara calls them," he answered simply. "Would you like to meet her?"

"Would I? I feel like I'd be missing out if I didn't."

Happy to have a reason for her to stick around, Papa showed her to the coop. He wasn't entirely sure how she would respond —towns folk could sometimes be so weird about farm animals —but he was pretty sure that she'd be fine for the most part. She didn't seem like the type to forget that animals had to relieve themselves and sometimes that stunk up the air. Although Clara's deep litter method was fairly good at keeping everything fresh.

"Goodness, divas is right!" Jeanette exclaimed almost immediately when they arrived at the fence. "Look at these ladies! That one even has feather britches." The woman sounded so downright amused that Papa couldn't help but grin along with her. "She's out here wearing fancy pantaloons and I showed up to meet her in jeans."

"That's Scheherazade. She's a white sultan chicken."

"Oh my, Scheherazade? Are you kidding me?"

"Nope, I'm completely serious."

"That's amazing." She pointed to another. "Why does that chicken have fur?"

"That's a black silkie chicken, actually. It's not fur, but it certainly does look like it, doesn't it?"

"I had no idea there were so many chickens that look like someone tried to draw a chicken but didn't know quite what a chicken actually looked like."

The chuckle burst out of Papa without warning, and it quickly led into startled laughter. "In all my years, I've never heard anyone describe it like that."

"Well, you haven't been hanging out with the right people then."

"Apparently, I'm finding out."

"Okay. What about that one? You can't tell me that's not secretly an alien masquerading as a farm animal."

"That's a Polish chicken."

"Their hair makes them all look like Albert Einstein."

"That's from an extra bone on their head making a sort of dome crest."

"This is insane. I love it. Tell me more about these wonderful little ladies. Where's the mouthy one? I don't see any of these cluckers losing their mind."

How could he say no to a request like that?

One by one, he introduced her to each of Clara's flock. Technically, the coop belonged to the whole family, and everyone enjoyed both the eggs and meats that they provided, but Clara had a connection to the furry little divas more than anybody else. The girl just loved animals, and Papa loved that about her.

But eventually, they did run out of chickens for Papa to tell her about, but he found himself not wanting her to go. Jeanette's smile was huge and her jokes were spot-on, leaving Papa feeling more seen than he had been in years.

Strange, he had such amazing relationships with his own children, with Savannah, and he was getting to know Alejandro and Mick pretty well, but he didn't have any friends or connections his own age. That... that probably wasn't very healthy.

But talking to Jeanette? That certainly felt healthy. Or at least healthier than anything that he'd been doing. Sure, sometimes it felt awkward or nerve-wracking too, but maybe that wasn't the worst thing.

"Would you like to see my garden?"

He tried not to hold his breath, but he still found himself waiting on pins and needles for the few seconds it took Jeanette to respond.

"I would *love* that!"

"Then right this way."

Papa started out with the front garden, not wanting to overwhelm her. He kept expecting her to eventually slide into polite disinterest. After all, not everyone was a garden enthusiast like he was, but she seemed entirely into all of it. Especially when it came to his bean collections.

But perhaps that was because he kept picking certain ones off the vine and handing them to her to snack on.

"I can't believe this! It tastes so fresh, almost like a cucumber. How interesting." She hummed happily to herself as she chewed a greenish bean with speckles of purple throughout it. "What is this again?"

"Rattlesnake pole bean."

"Fascinating. They look so similar to the other ones, uh... What were they again?"

"Dragon tongue bush beans."

"Right, that! They look similar, but they taste so different. The texture's different too."

"Yeah, the Rattlesnakes are one of my favorites to eat raw, but I prefer the blue lake pole beans and dragon bush beans cooked. Charlie will just come through and eat all of them raw, so it's really each to their own."

"This is incredible. I can't believe you have basically a food forest right around your house. I wouldn't think that most of these things could even grow here. New Mexico isn't exactly the best place for gardening."

"Honestly, as long as you pay attention to the plant's needs, it's easy to shift when you plant around the calendar to make sure it can thrive."

"Amazing. I can't believe it. And I didn't even know that there were so many kinds of kale. I thought, you know, kale was kale."

"Well, just don't put too much stock in that one. It's on its way out since it's really too warm for it right now, but during the winter, the stuff is really amazing."

And so it went throughout the entire tour. They never really got beyond his garden and he didn't tell her his plans for a new garden, and it still took about two full hours before they headed back inside. It seemed like Jeanette was going to ask to see more, but Papa didn't miss the slight tremble to her hands or the paleness to her face.

As much as he wanted her to stay, she was still recovering from a pretty bad sickness. It was easy to forget that, with how enthusiastic and lively she had been, but she needed her rest.

"Hey, why don't you sit and drink another glass of tea while I pack up that chamomile blend for you?"

"You don't have to do that. I've taken up so much of your time already."

"Please, I'd be happy to. I make far too much tea for us to ever go through."

"Well... alright. I suppose I could catch a breath before heading out."

"Great."

Papa got her another glass of peach tea and took his time with grabbing his chamomile-blueberry blend jar from their pantry and scooping some into one of the smaller jars he liked to give out. It wasn't that he was procrastinating—he wasn't! He just wanted to make sure she well and truly rested before heading immediately out the door.

Yeah, that was it. He was just being *courteous.* Really.

But no matter how courteous he was, he could only dawdle for so long. Eventually, Jeanette's glass was empty and the jar he gave to her was full, sealed, and tied with an emerald ribbon.

Drat.

"Thank you for stopping by," he said, holding the door for her. "We should do this again sometime. I'm sure the goats would love to meet you."

It was just an invitation, but it was also a risk. She could say no. Or she could say yes, and Papa wasn't sure what to think about that yet.

"That sounds lovely. We'll have to make plans. I'll call you?"

Papa nodded, excitement sparking in his chest at the same time his stomach dropped. It was quite some complicated organ-based choreography.

"Yes, please."

She gave a little nod and that was that. Papa walked her to her car, and he couldn't help but think it almost felt like the end of a date. Which was ridiculous, because she'd just dropped by to return his things. That wasn't exactly a romantic overture.

Clearly, he'd been out of the game for far too long. The last time he'd been on a date had been far more than a decade ago.

"You be safe now," he murmured as Jeanette slid into her car. It was an older thing but looked well cared for. "Make sure to stay hydrated."

"Oh, don't you worry about that. And I can't wait to try this tea tonight!"

That warmth in his chest again. "I look forward to hearing your review."

And then she was driving off, leaving Papa standing in his driveway, wondering at the complex bundle of emotions churning through him.

Oh well, no matter what happened and no matter what he figured out, he was pretty sure that he was at the start of a wonderful friendship.

10

Jeanette

Things were going great!

Jeanette was able to tackle her work with renewed energy. With Battle of the Books over, she suddenly had a lot more free time, which she definitely appreciated. She hadn't realized just how much she'd dedicated to that whole endeavor until it was over and she was able to clean up all the fallout.

But she was grateful for the reprieve, because it was the end of the school year and Jeanette was closing up the library for three weeks. She never got a full summer break, but that was alright. Jeanette didn't mind. It gave her plenty of time to prepare for the next year and make sure she had all her ducks in a row.

So yes, the extra time was nice, but the real gift was Montgomery and his whole family. They hadn't gotten together much, at least by some people's definition, but they saw each other at least once a month and that was lovely. Jeanette had toured all over the ranch, and it truly was a wonderous place. The little goats were mischievous and far too smart, one who seemed to have a keen love of knocking Jeanette off her feet. He never hurt her, but he always tried to sneak up in her peripherals or behind her to get a good headbutt right to her rear end.

But besides the goats, there was the waterfowl, Charity's workshop, and the *family*. Jeanette had heard many things about the infamous Millers. From the eldest starting a fight at a town festival, to the next oldest almost dying in a terrible accident, to the young man being quite the handsome bachelor but having seemingly no interest in dating any women.

Yeah, there were a *lot* of rumors about that one.

As far as Jeanette could tell, however, they were all lovely people. Very different from each other. But lovely. Charity could be a little intense, but she was funny, loving and quite protective. Cass was... prickly, the poor thing. But Jeanette didn't exactly blame her. Her situation wasn't the easiest road to walk down.

As for Clara, she was warm and always full of energy. She wasn't around very often, considering all the help she was giving that Nathan fellow, but delicious food was always involved when she was.

Lastly was Charlie. He was just as charming as she'd heard, and he could crack jokes like no one else, but there was a certain sort of apprehension about him that she just couldn't put her finger on.

There was one Miller left, the youngest, but she was off at college. She was supposed to arrive for a couple of weeks in the middle of the summer, and Jeanette was very much looking forward to meeting her.

Maybe Jeanette was getting a little ahead of herself, but it felt like she had suddenly fallen into something similar to a family without having to do all the legwork of actually trying to have a family.

Yes, definitely getting ahead of herself.

But that was okay, because it was in her own head. Nobody else had to know how hard she was bonding with the Millers while they were just being friendly. And there were no rules that she couldn't enjoy their company as well as all of the warm fuzzies they gave her.

Because it was nice not to be alone for once. *So* nice.

Jeanette had thought she'd liked being alone. That she preferred it. But the more she hung around with the Millers, the more she realized that she hadn't liked it at all. She'd just settled.

It was a shame, really, how much time she'd wasted, thinking she was happy when she'd barely been existing. But she supposed it was easy to think things were good enough when she was too scared to try for anything else.

Oh well, no use crying over spilled milk. What's done was done, and Jeanette liked to think that she was on a better road.

"Bigger and better," she muttered to herself as she locked up the library doors and headed to the parking lot. From there, she headed into town to one of the two restaurants they had.

It was something that she wouldn't have normally done, but she had someone to meet up with.

"Hey there," Papa said once she spotted him and crossed to the table that he was already at. "How was school?"

"Fairly innocuous, believe it or not. No drama or last-minute emergencies."

"Wow, that's pretty rare."

"You have no idea. But how was your day? I know you're ramping up for the worst of summer, right?"

"That I am. It's funny, occasionally I talk to my brother up in Montana and he complains how they're hitting unbearable highs of mid-nineties."

A startled laugh burst from Jeanette at that. "Goodness, mid-nineties? I wish that was our hottest temps. What was our high last year? One oh seven?"

"About that."

"At least it's mostly a dry heat."

He nodded, but the conversation was interrupted as their server swung by, taking their drink orders. Jeanette decided to treat herself to a soda, even though she didn't need it. But something about being around Monty made her want to be more alive. More... *more.*

Papa ordered himself a single dark draft beer and an appetizer sampler for them and then the conversation was back.

"You know, I really appreciate you meeting me out here. Most everyone is out of the house and for once I didn't feel like cooking."

"What? Mr. Montgomery Miller not wanting to cook? Have I stumbled into an alternate dimension?"

"Maybe. Stranger things have happened."

"I suppose so." After all, she was a small-town librarian at dinner with an eligible multi-millionaire. Jeanette wouldn't be surprised if her car suddenly turned into a pumpkin at midnight.

Their drinks arrived and then it was time to order. Jeanette had forgotten to even look at the menu, but a quick, panicked look to Montgomery and he gave her a gentle suggestion of asking if they'd like to share a family meal.

Thank goodness.

An unexpected side effect of being a hermit for so many years was that she seemed to have forgotten entirely how to exist like a normal human adult. People probably thought she was halfway into dementia with how she got flustered with something so simple as ordering food.

"So, anything new and exciting going on? A new wave of summer pests?" Jeanette asked once the server was gone.

"No, actually. Things are fairly quiet now. Once Cici's back, things will pick up again, but with Clara busy, Charlie at the rodeo, and Charity spending most of the summer with Alejandro and Savannah, I actually have some free time."

It was a good thing, or at least it was presented that way, but Jeanette didn't sense his normal genuineness about it.

"That's, uh, that's why I asked you here." Suddenly his tone was nervous, and he started fiddling with his napkin. It was interesting to see him transition so swiftly from his easy-going, confident nature to being so uneasy.

"Oh? Are you okay? Is something wrong?"

"No, nothing's wrong! I uh, I just..." He took a deep breath. "I'm going camping this weekend. Fishing too."

"Camping? How nice! I can't remember the last time I went roughing it. Maybe over a decade ago?" She didn't know why he seemed so nervous about something as simple as camping. It wasn't particularly scandalous or surprising.

"Well... if you were free at all, you're more than welcome to, uh... come along. If you wanted, that is."

"Are you serious?" Jeanette couldn't help but stare, her eyes going wide, as her brain tried to keep up with what happened.

Montgomery Miller, multi-millionaire and silver fox, wanted her to go on a camping trip with him.

What.

What?

That didn't compute. Sure, they'd been hanging out more. And yes, they were two grown adults who could do what they wanted. But they weren't even dating, so going somewhere alone with a man seemed so... *scandalous.*

"You don't have to answer now," he said quickly, clearly able to pick up on Jeanette's trepidation.

But, as the shock ebbed, Jeanette started to think about it. It was camping. They'd have separate tents. Sure, maybe some people would think it was odd that a spinster librarian was going on an excursion with one of the town's most eligible widowers, but what did they matter?

What did *any* of it matter?

The only thing that was important was that she was friends with Montgomery, whatever that meant, and she liked spending time with him. And the more she thought about it, the more she realized that *yes,* she did want to go camping with her closest friend.

"You know what? You're on."

A truly brilliant grin spread across his features, and goodness, if that didn't make her feel all warm and bubbly inside.

"Really? You sure that'd be something you'd enjoy?"

"Yes. I would. The only thing is I might need a little help with purchasing the proper equipment. I think I got rid of most of mine in a yard sale years ago."

"Don't worry about that. With five kids, I've got plenty I can loan you."

"Fantastic," Jeanette said, grinning dopily at him. "I can't wait."

11

Papa

*P*apa had been camping plenty of times. Ever since his kids had graduated high school, he'd done his best to take a weekend trip just for himself to be alone in the woods. It helped him keep connected with himself, and sometimes, it was nice to just be quiet.

But this camping trip was nothing like any other, even the ones he went on with his kids. And that was because he was with none other than Jeanette.

When he'd first asked her, he was sure that she'd say no. But somehow, she'd said yes, and then he'd had two weeks to plan a trip for the two of them.

Not a romantic trip, of course. Just as friends.

They were just friends.

That was it.

...or at least that was what he told himself.

"Okay, so this diagram is really faded. Where do I put this bendy thing?"

Papa's attention was brought back to the moment, where Jeanette was dutifully separating all the pieces from the tent bag he'd handed her. It was a truly neat arrangement, and Papa wasn't quite sure how she'd done it so fast.

"I didn't even know that diagram was still in there. Here, let me show you how this goes. I made sure not to get any of the finicky ones."

"You have finicky tents?"

Papa paused for a moment, realizing the silliness of that statement. "Yeah, we definitely do."

"Why keep them then? Pardon me in thinking that you could afford to replace any, uh, finicky tents."

That actually did make Papa stop and think. She had a point. If he wanted, they could buy some sort of super mega destructo tent that most people could never hope to afford.

But he didn't want that. And he didn't think any of his kids did either.

He'd never stopped to think about why that was.

"I guess we just like their character."

"Character, huh?" Jeanette's voice was lightly teasing, but there was a tenderness to it. A tenderness that Papa didn't realize that he was missing so desperately. "Is that the word we're using?"

"Yes, we most definitely are."

She nodded, her hands running along the sun-faded fabric of the tent shell. "I think I can get that." Her gaze locked with his and there was that undercurrent of tension that would occasionally crop up between them. In the months that they'd been casually interacting, it wasn't a constant, but every now and then it would rear its head when he least expected it.

But it caught him every time.

"These tents are lined with your memories. Special moments that you and your children made together. You could buy the newest, fanciest tent, but it'd be empty in a way these aren't."

Papa's heart squeezed in his chest. Funny, how viscerally his body reacted to a woman he'd met less than a year ago. "Yeah, something like that."

"Alright then, tell me a story while you teach me. I want to know what these tents are made of."

So Papa did.

He always had the memories in his head, but it was something entirely different to tell those stories to someone who looked at him like he was nearly the center of the world. Because that was exactly how Jeanette gazed at him, her keen eyes kind and earnest in their interest.

He told her about the time he'd taken Charity out with him because he'd sensed she was getting overwhelmed with trying to take care of the house and all of her siblings. It'd been a time where he'd wanted her to have time for just her, to do whatever it was that she desired just because she desired to with no other reason. He wasn't sure if she ever truly internalized the effort, but after that she had started doing things just for her.

He told her about the time he brought Clara and Charlie, with Clara spending almost the entire day foraging for food and sharpening a stick to try spear fishing, while Charlie climbed just about every tree he could until he fell out of one and nearly knocked his front teeth out.

And Jeanette listened to it all with enthusiasm, and before he knew it, the tent was set up and they'd built a fire circle.

"Look at that! That normally takes a lot longer."

"Many hands make light work, or something like that. Now let's get your tent set up and you can tell me more stories."

She was incredible.

It wasn't the first time he'd been struck by that thought, but it was one of the first times that he didn't feel guilty about it. Maybe he just needed to get away from the ranch and all of its mires to appreciate just how much light Jeanette brought to his life. Was it so wrong that he had a friend? And a good friend at that?

...maybe. But he wasn't going to worry about it for the moment.

But his tent was the one he was the most familiar with, so it took them just a few minutes to get it set up. Jeanette almost looked disappointed that it was over so fast.

"Well, what now?"

"We're pretty far ahead of schedule. I guess the best thing now is to go dig our bathroom ditch, then we can go fishing."

"Bathroom ditch?"

Papa didn't miss the alarm in her voice. "Sure, where else would we take care of our business?"

"I guess I didn't think about it. Most of the campsites I stayed at either had a bathroom cabin or a port-a-potty."

"Ah, nothing like that here. I can go do it on my own, if you want."

"No, I don't mind. I want an authentic camping experience, so by all means, lead the way!"

"You sure?"

"Oh yes, I am." She gave a resolute sort of nod and Papa couldn't help but think that she was addressing something more than just digging a toilet ditch. "It's practical and valuable information."

"Alright then."

Grabbing the needed supplies from the back of his truck, Papa led her out into the woods. Not far enough away to be dangerous if one of them needed to get there in the dark, but far enough away that there wouldn't be any unpleasant smells in their camp. Thankfully, it went smoothly, and before he knew it, it was handled.

"Fishing time?" she asked hopefully.

"Fishing time," he confirmed, grateful for her enthusiasm. He thought that he would have been overwhelmed by having a stranger he had to take through the camping process step by step, but he was quickly finding that he enjoyed it.

But maybe that had something to do with who he was explaining it to.

"So, I hope you don't mind, but I brought one of the rods that used to be Clara's favorite."

"Oh, is it so different from yours?"

"Yeah. I can explain how but—"

"No, you're right on that one. While I'm loving this refresh on camping info, I can't say that I'm entirely enthused about learning the difference between fishing equipment."

"Glad to know I guessed right on that. Have you fished before?"

"Ages ago. Almost feels like another lifetime."

That was a feeling Papa understood. "Alright, once we get our stuff and find a spot, I can walk you through the basics again. A nice refresh, like you said earlier."

"Yes, a nice refresh."

She was looking at him in *that* way again. The one he didn't quite have words for. Sometimes it felt like it was just the happy gaze of friendship. But sometimes it felt like more.

Maybe he should focus less on that look and more on actually fishing.

Right.

Once more, Papa grabbed everything they needed and set it on the ground. They were about a four-minute walk from his favorite fishing spot, which wasn't bad, but he usually had to take two to three trips to have everything he wanted.

"Goodness, what's this whole pile?"

"Our fishing supplies."

"Are we going on some sort of fishing cruise I'm not aware of?" Jeanette joked, bending down to examine the pile.

"Hah! I'm not sure what that would look like, but it certainly sounds fun."

"I'm sure it would be. But seriously, are you being serious with this?"

"I am. Not all of this is necessary, but it's what I like to be comfortable. I have camping chairs for me and you. I have my drink and snack cooler. We've got our bait cooler—that's the very small one—which will hopefully become our catch cooler. Both of our rods, my fishing kit, sun screen, bug spray and mud boots in case I want to stand in the water. And a picnic blanket, just in case."

"Wow. I never would have thought of all that. When you say it, all of those seem necessary though."

"Some people have much simpler setups, and some have more complicated. You keep doing this, and I'm sure you'll develop your own preference."

"Well, I'm not sure how often a middle school librarian will have time to pack up and go fishing, but that's good to know. But here, let me grab some of this and you can show me where this magical fishing spot of yours is."

Much to Papa's chagrin, her hands instantly went for the heaviest things, the coolers. While Papa believed in equality, sure, he also believed that being a proper host to his guest meant not letting her carry the worst of the pile.

"I got those; don't you worry. If you could grab the chairs and rods, that would be great."

Her eyes narrowed in suspicion, but thankfully, she did as he asked, and they trudged through the thinning trees that led up to the creek.

"Wow, this really is beautiful," Jeanette said about halfway there, looking around with a new sort of wonder. It was certainly cuter than it had any right to be.

"It is, isn't it?" Papa asked.

It was also one of the few places that he frequented that Mama had never been to. He'd discovered it after her death, in that aforementioned getaway once his kids started graduating high school, and it was his place to get away from all the ghostly shadows of past trauma.

He loved Mama; he did. And he would carry her forever in his heart. But sometimes the weight of everything he'd lost and everything they could have had together was just too much for him to bear. It made his heart hurt in a way that never dulled, even all these years later.

"Here we are," he said, recognizing the spot he'd come to love. His home away from home.

"My goodness, Montgomery, you didn't tell me it was so *beautiful.*"

No, he supposed he hadn't. But when he looked over the small spot, he couldn't help but agree. There was an old weeping willow that was leaning impossibly over the water thanks to being hit by lightning long ago. The char mark was still there, black with tiny scorches branching out like veins, and it split the tree in two. One went slightly to the left but mostly stayed erect, while the other bent, bent, *bent,* until its main branch was only a foot or so above the water.

"It provides a lot of shade, which I like, and the fish sure do too. A lot of them come up much closer to the surface than they normally would for caterpillars and other wormy things."

"Amazing. Now I'm *really* excited."

"Glad you approve."

"Approving is putting it mildly. I have to say, I think you're ruining me for any future camping I might do."

"I believe this is where the children might say sorry not sorry."

"I do believe I've heard that before," Jeanette said, a smile across her entire face as she started setting up the chairs. "And then they break either into a strange dance or do something called 'dabbing.'"

"What on earth is dabbing?"

"There are some things better left unknown," Jeanette replied sagely, finishing up with the chairs. "Alright, I'm pretty sure I remember how to add the hook and get my bait on there. You want to observe?"

"Let me just finish with the coolers and whatnot over here, then you're on."

"Fantastic!"

Yeah, it really was.

True to her word, Jeanette was pretty much able to handle herself on getting her rod ready to fish, then casting and reeling it in both easily came back to her. Papa almost wished that she'd had more trouble, because it would have been more of a reason to stay close to her. Unfortunately, her proficiency meant she was sitting in her seat far too soon, casting out into the gently flowing creek.

Except he shouldn't care about being close with her at all. They were just friends.

That was it.

Friends.

They were two adults who enjoyed each other's company, sure, but Papa had never believed that just because a man and woman were close that it meant things had to be romantic between them. Platonic relationships were just as important.

...but still, it would have been nice if he could have shown her how to attach her hook one more time.

"You know, I'm not entirely uncertain I won't fall asleep like this."

"I won't lie to ya, I do more often than I don't. Fishing is a nice dozin' sport, if you ask me."

"Finally, an athletic endeavor where I can participate but also sleep at the same time. Why have I never realized this before?"

Papa chuckled at her humor, plenty amused. Jeanette tended to present herself as just a little ol' librarian from a small town, but she was always so witty and hilarious to him. In his eyes, there was nothing little or ol' about her at all.

She was amazing.

He caught himself looking at her more than once, watching the occasional ray of sunshine make it through the tree to dapple her face with leafy shadows. Thankfully, a tug on his line got his attention, and he stood to reel it in.

"You have something already? No fair!" Despite her exclamation, Jeanette was clearly thrilled as she launched herself to her feet and stood right beside Papa. "Does it feel strong? Can you tell if it's a big one?"

"I have no idea, but I gotta concentrate."

"Right, I knew that."

She quieted, but he could feel her reverberating beside him, and he couldn't help but feel he was making an impression when she gasped or held her breath. She certainly was making the whole process more exciting.

It would have been embarrassing if he lost the fish, so Papa was very happy when he managed to bring it up onto the shore.

"Would you look at that?" he asked, turning to Jeanette.

And just like he hoped, she was looking at him with wide eyes, a wide grin, and that look he enjoyed so much.

"That's amazing! What is—"

She was cut off as a huge, particularly fuzzy bee crashed into her face. Clearly startled, she yelped and took a step back.

The only problem was that there wasn't any ground for her to step back onto. Instead, there was just the drop-off that went right into the creek.

"Montgomery!"

Her arms flailed and Papa reached for her, but she was too far, and the next thing he knew, she was falling butt-first into the creek.

It wasn't particularly deep along the bank. Maybe mid-shin level, but it was enough to get the librarian plenty wet when she landed, giving quite an impressive splash.

"Jeanette, are you alright!? Were you stung?"

He rushed to her, alarm sending his blood pumping through his veins. The woman had a shocked sort of expression on her features, her mouth still open in a gasp.

He was expecting the worst, but he certainly wasn't anticipating for Jeanette to burst out into peals of laughter, shaking in the water.

"Are you okay?"

"I'm fine, I'm fine. I just... I'm just a little wet is all."

Papa chuckled weakly, happy that she was alright. "Here, let me help you out."

Stepping closer, Papa offered his hand. But what he didn't count on was for the lip to crumble below his foot, pushing him entirely off-balance.

"Whoops!"

He tried to catch himself, he did, but when he placed his foot down for stabilization, it landed in mud and suddenly he was doing a very unplanned split.

"Yikes!"

Thankfully, he was able to throw himself to the side, saving himself from a terrible pulled muscle injury in his groin. But that meant he landed horizontally in the mud and water, nearly coating his entire body in the grime.

It filled his mouth, though, which was less than pleasant, and when he sat up, he was sputtering in a less than impressive way.

But that just made Jeanette laugh harder, and then Papa was laughing with her.

Jeanette tried to talk through her laughter. "I'm sorry, it's not funny, but also, it's *so* funny! When was the last time I even fell? And it had to be in *mud!*"

Papa nodded along, the slapstick of the situation getting to him. He felt like someone had dumped glue over his head, and he was sure once he got out of the water, he would look like a real fright.

"Come on, let's try to get out of here."

"Something tells me that's going to be much easier said than done."

Papa couldn't help but agree. Suddenly his clothes were ridiculously heavy. He was relieved that he didn't stink. While the creek was lovely and good for fishing, the bank was full of plants, mud, and algae. Not exactly the ingredients for a pristine experience.

It took quite a concentrated effort, but eventually he managed to get to his feet. He tried to pull Jeanette up, but her hands slid right out of his muddy ones, splashing little flecks of wet, sticky dirt across her face.

So naturally, she broke into laughter again.

"I'm sorry. I know it's not funny. I know it." But she continued to laugh, nonetheless. "Once we get on shore, I'm going to take a photo of this."

Not for the first time, Papa was glad that he tended to leave his phone on top of the cooler whenever he went fishing. Not that he normally planned on being upended into the creek. But he'd dropped the device in far less inconvenient situations, so he figured it wasn't a wise idea that he hold it around a source of moving water.

"We've got to get to shore first then."

"Just give me a second to catch my breath. I go a little boneless when I get the giggles."

"Oh, I think you've gone far past the giggles. You're in outright howling territory."

But that just made her belt out another round even louder. Papa liked to think he was clever, but he didn't feel *that* funny. "Howling feels about right. I just—" She cut herself off, laughing some more, before slowly containing herself. Once she was more settled, Papa offered his hand again, and this time it didn't spray her in the face with more creek schmutz.

It took some effort, but he managed to get her to her feet, and they both schlupped their way to the shore. It was only a couple of feet away, but with how deeply their feet sank into the muck, it took a lot of effort. When they did finally get on land, Papa sat right then and there, breathing a little harder than he would have liked. Jeanette flopped next to him, and he laid back too.

They both said nothing for a moment, just breathing hard, before she spoke again.

"Did that really happen?"

"Yeah... yeah that did."

They exchanged a look and then they were laughing again. Long, loud and unabashed. Papa laughed so hard his stomach hurt and his legs went "boneless," as she had called it earlier. And Papa didn't rush to end it either, letting himself enjoy it without holding anything back.

Eventually, however, they did wind down, and he found himself staring up at the sky, just enjoying the clouds as they drifted by. He felt so at peace. More than he had in a long while. Tearing his gaze away from the sky, he looked over to Jeanette.

"Hey, you wanna go cook up some chow?"

"Yes," she said, voice soft. "Let's do that."

12

———

Jeanette

Jeanette never thought that she would think of camping as *magical,* and yet that was exactly the boat she was in.

Sure, she'd been nervous at first—how could she not? But that had quickly faded as they got the camp set up and went fishing. It had been years since she had tried using a pole, but it came back relatively quickly to her.

And then there was Montgomery Miller himself.

It wasn't fair how he stood there, the sunlight streaming behind him, highlighting him on a holy sort of silhouette. He'd been radiant, shining in the backdrop of the beautiful scenery, and for a long moment he seemed so untouchable. Like she was from a different world and he was something apart, something too good for her.

It had been a sort of uncomfortable feeling, but it also drew her in, and she'd grown closer to him in the effort to figure out how she felt.

But then there'd been a bee in her face and she'd fallen into that water, and the tension inside of her broke. All the worry, all the uncertainty faded, and she'd been able to enjoy the moment.

And that moment led to another, and another, until they'd cooked dinner together from the coolers Papa had brought, and she was sitting contented and full, watching the sun slowly set.

It was lovely. She wished that she could bottle that moment and keep it with her forever. It would certainly come in handy, especially during new school year prep and next year's Battle of the Books.

"Hope you don't mind; I like a little music."

She didn't have time to respond because Montgomery was already walking to his truck, and he pulled out a real, actual *mandolin.*

Jeanette blinked twice, wondering if she was imagining it, but no, he certainly had the classic instrument in his hands.

"O-oh, I don't mind. At all. By all means, serenade away."

He smiled gratefully, and Jeanette's toes curled in her shoes. *Goodness*, he was just too much for her sometimes, but all in the best way possible.

"I haven't played this in six months, I think. Cass's accident got me real offtrack."

The back of Jeanette's mind darkened. Sometimes it was easy to forget that horrific accident that had happened during that terrible storm a few seasons back. She'd come a long way, or at least that's what Jeanette had heard from Montgomery and

Savannah, but the librarian hated to think of all the scary and awful times the Miller family had had to go through.

"I'm delighted to be here for your grand return, then," she managed to say, hoping she sounded casually enthused. But it was so hard to be casually anything with Monty. Everything she felt around him was so much stronger, so much sharper than she was used to.

She'd been living a quiet life, a nearly silent life for so long, that sometimes Montgomery Miller was like a thunderclap of experience. Happiness, uncertainty, attraction, distrust, laughter, fear, the list went on and on. It was a litany of emotion, and borderline overwhelming, but she also didn't want to give it up.

Strange. So strange.

But then Monty began to play, and all of that maelstrom of sensation quieted.

The music was *beautiful.*

His fingers plucked at the strings, slow and steady, and a beautiful melody began to slowly trickle out, spreading over their little campsite in a peaceful wave. Jeanette thought that she could sink right into that without a care, but then his voice joined in.

Oh.

Oh *goodness.*

That just wasn't fair.

Low, layered in a way that didn't seem possible, with an earthen sort of rumble to it, he sang of the sun through the trees and the green of the leaves. He sang of seasons changing and those very leaves falling, littering the ground.

It wasn't a quick song, not by any means. But it was over far too soon, faded into only Jeanette's memories.

She wanted him to sing again.

Mercy, did she want him to sing again, so much so.

But she couldn't bring herself to say anything. Instead, she only sat there, watching as Monty chuckled lightly to himself and set the instrument aside.

"Seems I'm a bit rusty."

That was rusty? Jeanette couldn't even imagine. That had been so good, like she was taken away to some world where anything was possible. A world where she wasn't an old widow who'd spent so much of her life locked away.

One where the love of her life hadn't been taken away without warning and she'd been so scared of the world that she shut herself away from it.

"Penny for your thoughts?"

Jeanette pondered a moment, wondering exactly what to say. "Just thinking about life and time and just about everything."

"Ah, so just some light wonderings."

"Yes, exactly that."

He nodded along, grabbing his mandolin and walking it to his truck. "It's a lot, isn't it?"

"What is?"

"Life sometimes. It's so much. Sometimes it feels like too much. And sometimes not enough."

Jeanette hadn't been expecting that, and she stared a moment before agreeing. "Yes, that's pretty much the long and the short of it."

Montgomery returned, building up the fire a bit. "You wanna talk about it?"

She hesitated a long moment again on that, her mind still trying to catch up. The moment almost felt too vulnerable to be real. And yet it was as real as anything else that she could perceive.

"Sure."

And so, they talked. It wasn't anything too deep, nothing so philosophical that she felt like she was taking a college course. Instead, it was just casual but comfortable conversation that covered just about anything that popped through their minds.

It wasn't anything particularly charged, but Jeanette felt like she was learning so much about Montgomery, and it wasn't something she had to pry out of him. They talked about gardening, and what he hoped for his children. They talked about Savannah and what she wanted to do with the library. They talked about their favorite seasons, their favorite foods, even favorite animals. Then about the state of the world, nature and how everything kept getting faster and faster.

Before Jeanette knew it, Monty was lighting one of those citronella torches and they were watching the sun set together.

And that was beautiful too.

"If every day was like this, do you think we'd be desensitized to it?" she murmured, staring as the burning coral of the sky bled into lavender and then the royal blue of the oncoming night. It was hard to think that the peace around her, the stillness in the air would ever be anything but incredible, but she knew that humans were a fickle sort of creature. And she was oh so very human.

"Perhaps. I think it would be easy to. But as long as we put the effort in not to become ungrateful, I think we could hold onto the blessing."

Jeanette didn't miss that he used the word "we" or that he'd described it as a blessing too. It was like the two of them clicked on things that most people would call cheesy.

"Yeah, I never want to let this kind of blessing go."

"Me either."

They sat a bit longer, until the multicolored night sky slipped all the way down into onyx velvet. Stars twinkled into vision, winking up above like all those little promises that she was too scared to grasp.

"We should turn in for the night," Monty said eventually.

Part of her was ready to nod along and disappear into her dreams, but another part of her was brave enough to ask for something else. "Before we do, could I have a lullaby?"

"A lullaby?"

She nodded. "I usually have a white noise machine, but some gentle music would be nice."

"I can do that. Why don't you head to your tent and I'll play ya off."

"You certain? I don't want to keep you up."

"Nah, I gotta watch the fire until it's out and put some water on it. Don't you mind it now. Just get some rest."

Well, she couldn't argue with that. "Thank you, Montgomery, for everything."

"Thank you too."

She couldn't imagine what he was thanking her for, but instead she just ducked her head and went into her tent. Settling into her bedroll, she heard the first gentle notes of the mandolin drifting through the vinyl, soft and soothing.

It didn't seem real, any of it, and yet she knew it was as she fell asleep to the soothing timbre of his voice.

13

———

Papa

A gentle chorus of bird chirps roused Papa, warm and cozy as he was in his tent. Well, it started as a gentle chorus, until a group of the birds got into a very heated argument about either food, mates or shiny trinkets and it turned into a whole cacophony.

Papa tried to move about quietly, seeing that Jeanette was still in her tent, most likely asleep.

The day before had gone so much better than he ever could have imagined. He didn't know what possessed him to pull out his mandolin and start playing, but Jeanette's face when he started told him that he'd chosen right.

It didn't matter that their muddy clothes were in bags, sitting in the bed of his truck. They were in new clothes that were warm and comfy while their bellies were completely full.

It was nearly a perfect night, and he hadn't thought that was possible.

Might as well follow up such a perfect night with a good breakfast.

Careful not to make too much noise, Papa got to cooking. He couldn't exactly make a whole spread while roughing it, but he packed enough eggs, bacon, and hash browns in one of his coolers to make sure they had plenty. Probably too much, but Papa was used to making food for five to eight people per meal.

Humming quietly to himself, Papa cooked the eggs and hash in one skillet with the bacon and some sausage he forgot he packed in the other cooler. He was about halfway done when the sounds of Jeanette rousing herself drifted over to him, and a few moments later she was unzipping her tent flap.

"Oh, hello," she said, looking at him from under those pale lashes of hers. "You're up early."

"This is actually sleeping in for me," Papa answered with a wry grin. "I normally get up anywhere from four to six am depending on the season."

Jeanette's eyes went wide and she let out a shocked sort of sound. "And here I thought my six-thirty am wake-up time was early. What time is it, anyway?"

"About eight, I reckon. Haven't checked my phone since I started cooking."

"Goodness, well, I'll go freshen up, then I'll be right back. It smells amazing, by the way."

"Glad ya think so."

Jeanette went off to do her thing, but the more minutes that passed, the more a growing sort of nervousness began to build in the back of Papa's mind.

He hadn't been sure what to think when Jeanette asked him

to serenade her to sleep. It seemed so intimate, in a way that it probably wouldn't be to anyone else. He'd played for nearly an hour while watching the fire burn down to nothing, then went to his tent and continued to strum away absently until he fell asleep himself.

Jeanette returned, their eyes locking, and he couldn't help but feel that something... *shifted* between them. Not in a bad way, but not necessarily in a good way either. There was an intensity that crackled in the air, and he didn't know what to do about it. Did she feel it? Was it all in his head?

"Still smells amazing here," she remarked, awkwardly shuffling to her seat from the night before. "Need me to do anything?"

"No, just gotta plate this up. Don't you worry."

She let out a nervous sort of laugh. "I'm not worried. Just, uh... I'm just waking up."

Yeah, she definitely felt it too.

"I hope you enjoyed the music last night."

"It was lovely," she murmured, a small flush to her cheeks. "Thank you for the lullaby."

"Of course, anytime you need."

He passed her a heaping plate of food, then prepared his own before sitting in his chair. They ate silently, the mood flickering between quiet and serene, then silent and intense. Just when he thought he found his footing, it would shift again.

"So, when should we pack up?" she asked about halfway through the meal.

Oh right, he forgot. Unlike his usual week-long trip, they were just on a weekend excursion. It was Sunday, and they'd be heading back just before dark.

"I would say just about when afternoon starts. I don't like to rush."

"Me either." There was a lengthy pause and Papa assumed she had said all she needed to say, but then she spoke again. "I almost wish I could stay here for months."

"Do you?"

She nodded. "I'd miss the kids eventually, and my home, but it's nice to imagine."

Papa grinned, his heart thumping in his chest. "I'm glad you've had a good time."

"I have. I really have."

"Me too."

"Thanks for bringing me here, really."

"Thank you for trusting me."

And then they went quiet again, finishing their meal at a leisurely pace. From there, they did another spot of fishing. There were no falls into the water this time, or any other eventful tumbles, and Jeanette did manage to catch something. It was a small little thing, and they had to let it go, but the librarian was pleased, nonetheless.

Papa watched her as she laughed, emotion flowing through him. The hours were going too fast and their departure was rushing ever closer. He too wished they could stay for longer, that Jeanette didn't have to go to school and the real world.

But at the same time, that growing nervousness was making him feel unsettled. Like he was going too far, too fast and there were no brakes he could slam. He hadn't paid attention to any women since Mama, and he hadn't intended to. She'd been the love of his life, and he only ever got one.

If that were the case, why was he spending so much time with Jeanette? Why was he feeling the things that he was feeling? It was a betrayal of his wife. Sure, she had been gone for ten years, but that didn't mean anything.

...hadn't he promised her that he'd move on? That he wouldn't trap himself in his mourning? Yeah, maybe he'd said as much, but that had been before she was gone. Before his heart was ripped out and he'd had to sew together all the pieces.

That circle of emotions went through his head over and over again, occupying pretty much all of his thoughts as they went about cleaning and packing up.

At least that went according to plan, with no surprise bee stings or snake bites, and far too soon, yet not soon enough, Papa found himself face to face with Jeanette, saying goodbye.

"I'll see you again next week or so?" she asked, face tilted up towards him. Her lashes framed those doe eyes of hers, and her cheeks had a serene sort of blush. If it were any other situation, with any other people, it would have been an opportunity to kiss.

And for a moment, Papa very much wanted to.

It would have been so easy to just dip his head down and press his lips to hers. He could wrap his arms around her waist and pull her to him. It had been over a decade since he'd even held a woman his own age, since he'd had any romantic overtures at all, and his entire body cried out for it.

But only for a moment.

Then the guilt rushed in, as biting and vicious as it always was, snuffing out all of those feelings in just a blink.

So instead, he offered her a handshake.

"See ya round," he said, voice sounding lame, even to himself. What was he doing? He had a family to take care of. He didn't need anything outside of that. Besides, his family was still recovering from everything that happened with Cass. This wasn't the time to be having his own silver-age romance with the school librarian.

"Uh, yes. I'll see you around, then."

With that, they went into their two cars and drove away, Jeanette following him until they reached the main road. Papa watched in his rearview mirror as she eventually turned to go into the town while he continued on to the ranch. But as he drove, he couldn't help but feel torn between keeping things as they've been since his wife died or allowing himself to fall in love again.

14

---

*I*t had been a month since she last saw Montgomery, and Jeanette didn't understand what on earth had happened.

They had been doing so well and it really seemed like they had such a connection. The camping trip had been magical, impossibly so, until the incredibly awkward goodbye.

And for the second time, Jeanette found herself ghosted. He'd stonewalled her, point blank, and she was a combination of angry and embarrassed.

Was he purposefully playing her? Laughing with his friends about the pathetic school librarian who thought she had a chance with him? Did he just get a kick out of being hot and then cold?

Or was it something else?

Jeanette could understand if he had some lingering issues because of his wife. She had similar ones from her darling husband. But if that were the case, why couldn't he *talk* to her? She was fine being his friend if all they could be was friends. Jeanette enjoyed his company even if it was platonic.

But she hated being cut off like she didn't exist. Like she hadn't been anything and hadn't shared any sort of connection with Monty. It hurt. It made her not want to trust him.

Her heart ached.

She supposed that she could just call him, but after a month of him replying to her texts with single words, she already felt so foolish at his rejection.

So instead, she just dedicated herself to her work.

Which wasn't a bad thing, considering it was a new school year and there were plenty of things all the kids needed.

Like the school play.

Jeanette usually helped with the audition process and would run lines with children if they wanted during their study halls, but she decided to take a much more active role. She signed on for helping with wardrobe, set design and even printing. She didn't know there was so much printing needed for a simple school play, but between the flyers, the scripts, and the programs, it was a lengthy list.

Plenty to keep her occupied and her mind away from dwelling on how she was pushed aside like last week's trash. What was wrong with her? Maybe she was right to hole herself up in her house for years. Over time, she'd just become something that didn't quite fit into human society. And somehow, Montgomery had been able to sense it. Could she blame him, then, for tossing her away?

Perhaps not.

Of course the whole distracting her thing only worked when the Millers weren't directly shoved into her face.

"Hey there, Miss Edalira!" Savannah said, bouncing up to her. The girl always had so much *energy*. It was astounding, really.

"Hey there, Savannah. How're you today? I didn't see you during your study hall." Or her lunch. It seemed that the new school year had brought the girl new friends, which pleased Jeanette to no end. Sure, she loved having Savannah around, but it had worried her how the young girl hadn't had any friends to spend time with. Clearly, that was no longer the case.

"I was running lines with Juliette! We want to be off-script by the end of the week."

"That's very ambitious. You know you have until the end of the month, right?"

"Yeah, but I'd rather be early than procrastinate and not hit the deadline. You know how it is."

Goodness, no wonder people were constantly mistaking Savannah for older than she was. Sure, she was quite tall for her age, but sometimes she had a way of speaking that made her seem like a teenager in the middle of realizing how the world worked instead of a twelve-year-old kid.

"Well I admire your determination. I'm sure you're going to be absolutely amazing."

"I hope so! I'm inviting everyone I know to come see me. Daddy says even some of his friends from California are coming too."

"Goodness, is that so? I hope we don't run out of seats."

"If we do, we'll just duct tape them to the ceiling."

And there was the childlike part of her. Jeanette laughed,

picturing it all. "That would certainly make for an interesting experience!"

Savannah nodded before her gaze caught on something behind her. "I'm gonna go talk with my stage-mom," she said, bounding off before turning on a dime and jumping right in front of Jeanette again. "Btw, I brought a couple of the Millers along to help with set design so you can finally take a break."

"You what?"

"They're good listeners. Just tell them what to do and they'll get all the grunt work done while you direct."

"You really didn't have to—"

"Gotta go! Talk to you later, Miss Edalira!"

That was just about the last thing Jeanette had expected, and she found herself looking around, as if Montgomery Miller was going to pop out like the boogeyman. Instead she just saw the normal children and volunteers that were always there.

Curious.

She got her answer, however, when she went to refill her water bottle at the fountain and saw none other than Charlie, Charity, and Montgomery Miller standing by the door, talking to the Vice Principal again.

Great. Just great.

Jeanette gave up on her water and tried to hurry back into the theater, but she was spotted. Much to her chagrin, Montgomery Miller raised his hand in a wave and started walking towards her. Jeanette could continue hurrying off, but that would be even more dramatic and awkward, so instead she rooted herself in place.

"Jeanette, hi, how are you?"

Part of her very much wanted to snap at him, to ask how he

dared to talk to her after giving her the cold shoulder. But, while Jeanette's temper was flaring, she ultimately hated drama and fights. So instead, she took a deep breath and gave him a level look.

"I'm doing well, Montgomery. Savannah told me some of you were coming to help." Jeanette answered. "I'll be honest, I'm surprised you would want to come here considering that you've been doing your best to avoid me for the past month."

To her satisfaction, Monty's cheeks flushed with embarrassment. Jeanette didn't hate him, but she certainly wasn't pleased with the man either.

"Yeah, about that," he muttered, his eyes not quite meeting hers. "I suppose I owe you an apology."

Oh? That hadn't been what she'd expected.

"Alright," she hedged.

"I, uh, I'm struggling with some stuff. And I'm afraid that stuff has caused me to maybe, well, mistreat you a little."

"...uh-huh."

"And I'm sorry for that. I would hate to be treated like that, so I shouldn't go around and treat other people like that. Especially people as wonderful as you."

"It does feel rather awful."

"Yeah, I can imagine. And I regret it. I... I shouldn't have been avoiding you."

Jeanette drew in another shuddering breath, wondering if she was too willing to forgive far too quickly. "Why didn't you just talk to me, Montgomery? I understand your family has a lot going on, and I lost my partner too. I know that grief comes in waves, and sometimes it feels like it's impossible to keep swimming, but why did you have to cut me off?

"Did I do something wrong? Cross a boundary? Because I'll be honest, I have a hard time trusting anyone, and you dropping me at a moment's notice is wreaking havoc on my trust."

He seemed to shrink further at that, and while it almost made her feel guilty, it also made her feel better that he was indeed listening and cared about what she thought.

"I know. And I'm sorry. I will try my best not to repeat my mistakes." He rubbed his face, and she watched his Adam's apple bob as he swallowed. "I understand if you never wanna talk to me again, but I was kinda hoping that maybe we could still be friends."

"Friends? Is that what we are?"

Disappointment rose, acrid and bitter on the back of her tongue, at the same time as relief rushed through her. She had… she had hoped that maybe there was something more between them. That she hadn't imagined the connection she'd felt earlier. But like she'd thought before, if all he wanted was friendship, she was good for that. She could be plenty happy with that, as long as she could actually trust the friendship.

"It's what I'd like us to be. You're an amazing person, Jeanette. And I enjoy spending time with you. You're more than welcome on the ranch; everyone loves you."

Jeanette didn't answer right away, thinking about it. Montgomery was the first person she'd truly connected with since her husband died, and she didn't want to continue a hot and cold relationship. It wasn't good for her.

"Alright, but on a trial basis. You disappear again, and I'm out."

"I can understand that."

There was another charged moment between them, like both

of them were waiting for something else to happen, but it passed before she could figure out what exactly it was.

Eventually, the quiet was too much and she extended a hand. He took it, and they shook just as awkwardly as they had at the end of their camping trip.

"Thanks for the second chance," he said, still looking sheepish.

"Third try," Jeanette corrected.

"Right. Third try."

"Now, how about we get to painting?"

To Montgomery's credit, he did really turn it around. Granted, it was the second time he'd done as much, but she hoped it was going to stick.

But, even if it didn't, it certainly helped with all the set work they needed for the play. Normally it wasn't until tech rehearsal week that they were anywhere near that level of completeness, and it took plenty of pressure off to be so far ahead.

Her weekly dinners picked back up, and while he never suggested camping again, they still played chess, cards, and even went to the movies every once in a while. It was nice, not as nice as before, but still... *nice.*

And so her days went, one after the other. The school play was marching ever closer, the warmth of summer long gone and fall making itself at home. It was an easy routine to fall into, one that made the days slide that much further into an unremarkable pattern.

"Hey, Jeanette."

The librarian looked up from the script she was highlighting with tech notes for the sound crew after two of them had lost their own copies. Monty stood at center stage. Rehearsal had ended about forty-five minutes earlier and almost everyone had already headed out.

"Yes?" she asked, giving him a quick look over. He was wearing his usual ranch casual wear, but there were some paint spatters in his hair and a streak down one side of his face. It was cute in a way it shouldn't be, and she hated the way her heartbeat picked up at the sight.

They were just friends.

They were just friends.

Yet no matter how many times she reminded herself, there was a part of her that wanted... *more.*

But she did her best to shove those feelings down. Montgomery said he was available for friendship, and that was all she would expect. She knew that some people would pine over a potential crush, but she wasn't like that. Either she needed to value what Monty was offering or she needed to distance herself.

"I was wondering if you'd want to go to the fall festival with my family?"

She blinked at him, like his words weren't translating.

"Pardon me?"

"I'm sure you've seen the booth I usually run. Well, my daughters are saying that I spend too much time stuck behind it, and they want to split up the hours better. So, I could use someone to walk around with."

That sounded a lot like a date.

But it couldn't be a date. Because they were just friends.

Right?

"I... I usually don't go to the festival." Suddenly, it felt like the world was closing in around her.

"It would mean the world if you'd make an exception for me."

"I... I suppose I could do that."

Oh my... What had she just agreed to?

15

Jeanette

"Wow, this certainly is quite the display," Jeanette said, grinning broadly as she looked over Montgomery's booth.

She supposed booth wasn't quite the right word considering that he had a whole tent, but she wasn't really familiar with small-town fair terminology. What was clear was that the tent was lovingly prepared by him and his family, with plenty of unusual-looking produce piled in meticulously decorated baskets.

"Thanks. We've had a really good year. Normally the powdery mildew kills off a lot of my more exotic melons before they can produce much."

"Powdery mildew?"

"It's a blight, basically. Vicious little thing."

"Oh, okay. Sounds pretty bad."

"It is. I can't tell you how many wonderful plants it's killed in a matter of days."

"That's so sad!"

"More like infuriating." He clapped his hands, however, clearing his throat. "But, like I said, we're very grateful it gave us a break this year. You know, with everything going on."

"It's been a lot, hasn't it?" Jeanette agreed. For all their money, the Miller family certainly didn't have it easy.

"It certainly has."

"Did you want me to grab you anything while you're trapped behind here?"

He chuckled. "Well, I wouldn't call it trapped, but it'll be a few minutes before I'm free. I wouldn't mind some of that *elote* from the booth round the corner."

Jeannette's stomach let out a rumble at that. "I can't remember the last time I've had that; good idea!"

"You live in New Mexico and don't eat *elote* every summer?"

"I guess I don't get out much."

"Well, Guadalupe makes some of the best around. Tell her to just put it on my tab."

"You have a tab with the *elote* booth?"

"I have a tab with all my favorite booths. I *love* the fall festival."

"Apparently."

With a chuckle, Jeanette hurried off to get the corn treat. Once she was there, she also might have gotten two steaming mugs of *horchata* and some fresh fruit with *taijin* on it. It was quite a bit to juggle, but she managed, and the look on Montgomery's face when she arrived in front of his tent was priceless.

"Whoa, that's quite the spread you got there!" he said,

rushing forward to help her set it down. Somehow, she managed not to spill anything on herself, and soon they were both seated behind his display, eating and drinking the delicious food. Montgomery was halfway through his fruit before he paused, eyes going narrow.

"You paid for this yourself, didn't you?"

Jeanette just took an especially large bite of her *elote* and shrugged.

"You're incorrigible, you know that?"

She just batted her eyes at him, trying not to laugh when her mouth was so full of food. The last thing she needed to do was spray her chewed bits of corn all over Monty's lovely tent. That would certainly make an impression, but that wasn't the kind of impression she wanted to make.

It was a lovely way to spend time, however, and none of that tension that used to make her blood boil or nerves that made her stomach twist.

"Miss Edalira!"

Jeanette set her food just in time for Savannah to launch herself over Papa's table and land right in front of her, arms wide for a hug. "You came!"

"I did," Jeanette said with a chuckle, standing so she could return the young girl's embrace.

"Have you had a chance to walk around yet? I'll take you!"

Alejandro put a hand on his daughter's shoulder. "Hey, *mija*, I think Papa would like to take Jeanette on a tour of the place."

The girl paused for a moment, her eyes narrowing as her gaze flicked from Jeanette to Papa.

"Is this a romantic thing? This feels like a romantic thing."

Out of the mouths of babes and fools...

Jeanette had to admit, it was pretty amusing to see Monty

practically choke on his *horchata*. She had to hide her mouth behind her hand, trying not to laugh. The last thing she wanted Savannah to think was that she was being made fun of.

To his credit, Montgomery Miller managed to recover after a few moments, but it was quiet Alejandro who swept in to save the day.

"Savannah, remember what I told you about men and women being friends."

"Uh..." She seemed to ponder for a moment. "That it's normal and it makes them uncomfortable when people force romance on them."

"Yes, very good, *mija.*"

"Oh, I just did that, didn't I?" Savannah heaved a sigh and shot Jeanette a bashful look. "I'm sorry. I didn't mean to."

"It's alright, dear. I know you didn't."

Thankfully, Charity rounded the corner, both her hands full of large snow cones.

"Hey there, ready for your break?"

"Sure am," Montgomery said, jumping to his feet. "How about you, Jeanette?"

"Oh, I dunno, I'd like to finish my *horchata.*"

"...you sure?"

The look on his face was so pleading that she couldn't help her chuckle. "I can always come back to it."

Thank you, he mouthed, and Jeanette had to repress a chuckle again. It was just too funny to see him be sheepish about ultimately harmless things.

So together, they left the booth, Monty only looking behind him twice in concern.

"I get the feeling that you don't leave your booth very often."

"Usually only once a day outside of bathroom breaks."

"Whew, no wonder your kids wanted you to take more breaks."

"What can I say? I love my produce."

"Hah, believe it or not, I did figure that out already."

"Your powers of observation and drawing conclusions from that data are truly exemplary."

Jeanette snorted, surprised by his dry quip, and the snort just made her laugh harder. There would have been a time when she was much younger that she would have been mortified at the unflattering sound, but she was far too old for that. Hiding mirth and laughter was for the young and insecure.

And Jeanette was very done with being insecure.

"So, where's our first stop?"

"Since we just ate, I thought we'd check out some of my other favorite food booths later. How about some ring toss and other games that are most certainly rigged against us?"

"Sounds amazing. Let's go lose way too many of our singles."

"Now you're speaking my language."

They went to the center of the fair where the games were kept.

"I haven't done this in ages," Jeanette said.

"Is that because you spent nearly ten years going only from work to home?"

"Goodness, way to 'call me out,' as some of my students might say."

"Hah! I suppose I am being a little smart. I think you're different, though, because you do so much outside of just being a librarian." It was like he sensed Jeanette rankle at that, because he hurried on. "Not that there's anything about 'just' when it comes to being a librarian, but you also help with plays, and then there's the Battle of the Books thing."

"Fair enough. Those do add plenty of spice to my life."

"And stress?"

"And stress. Most definitely." She shook her head, quickly recalling several memories of the last year when she'd first been putting that whole competition together. "But it's all worth it."

"And I believe that. I've never seen someone so dedicated to so many children that weren't theirs."

"Sometimes, it feels like they are my children, in a way."

"...that's real lovely."

The way he said it, so soft and gentle, almost made Jeanette miss a step. Those feelings that she dismissed out of her respect for Montgomery swelled for a moment, threatening the peace she had been feeling.

Come on, Jeanette. Get yourself together!

She truly appreciated Monty's friendship. She did. If he wasn't able to give more, she respected that. Friendship was not a consolation prize.

Thankfully, the games proved to be a fun distraction. The sudden conflict building in her chest fizzled out, and once again she was able to enjoy the situation for what it was.

And, much like she'd expected, they lost an inordinate amount of money. But she didn't mind. Half of the proceeds of the booth went to the town's small park, theater and town hall, while the family that ran the booths got to keep the other half. Besides, with her stunt of paying for the food, Montgomery insisted he pay for all of the games.

"Well, all that losing worked me up an appetite. How do you feel about doin' a snack circuit?"

"I don't know how much more I can eat. That *elote* was amazing."

"Aw, come on, you gotta have at least a bite of things."

"I'll do my best."

She did indeed do her best, but even with all the walking around to work up her appetite, she still couldn't keep up with Montgomery Miller. It made sense, considering he had nearly a foot on her and was corded with hard-earned muscle, but it was still certainly impressive. Thank goodness he was rich, because otherwise he'd go broke trying to feed himself.

They took their time, wandering about for at least an hour after their gaming session before returning to the booth. There, they sat back in their chairs, relieving Charity, Alejandro and Savannah—who took off like a streak of light—and enjoyed the night.

Jeanette was surprised that she didn't feel her normal anxiety creeping in at needing to have small talk with so many of the townsfolk. Maybe it was because she wasn't alone, or maybe it was because Monty's booth was mostly the center of attention, not her, but either way she was grateful.

They stayed there for another hour or so until Clara flounced up with her brother Charlie, both of their cheeks red.

"Hey, you two weren't off getting in trouble again, were you?"

"Depends on what you call trouble," Charlie responded, winking. It was easy to imagine Montgomery at his age, full of boyish charm and far too much charisma.

"*Charlie.*"

"We got kicked out of the fake bull-riding challenge," Clara blurted before clapping her hands and breaking out into a cackle.

"Wait, they let you on in the first place?"

Jeanette looked between them. "Am I missing a joke?"

But Montgomery just let out a rueful sigh. "Every year there's this unit that comes from the next county over that has a mechanical bull. Our clan generally gets banned from it every time a new showrunner takes over."

"It was a new guy," Clara said, grinning broadly. "You should have seen the look on his face when I hopped on."

"It was great," Charlie said. "He started out with a crack about needing to be careful. And then he made a crack about weight capacity."

"What?" Jeanette asked, shocked. "You're kidding?"

"Oh, don't worry about it," Clara said, grinning. "He's got plenty of egg on his face. I lasted two songs before I won the prize and he was all sour, so I challenged him to last as long as he could and I'd beat it."

"You should have seen it!" Charlie said. "It was worth giving up my turn. Guy was *crimson* when he couldn't even last half as long as Clara. Everyone was laughing so he shut the thing off and stormed away in a huff."

"He definitely will not be coming back next year," Clara added. "Hopefully whoever they get then will have some better customer service."

"Well, you wanna do another walk? See if there's anything you wanted to buy? Gotta admit, there's some great salsas, preserves and other great treats you can only get at this time of year."

"Sure," Jeanette said, grinning herself. "If you young ones are sure you don't mind watching the booth?"

"Not at all. We got our rowdy time. We can be responsible for a bit."

"So it's settled. Let's go."

They walked again, the sun having set and the many lights of the festival twinkling invitingly. It was an enchanting sort of backdrop, and it was hard not to stare at Montgomery as they strolled.

He wasn't kidding when he said there were treats to buy. It seemed the next thing Jeanette knew, they were rolling around a cart full of kitchen goods and other items. Where the cart had come from, she had no idea, but it was definitely there.

Sure, there was some melancholy in the back of her mind that came from wanting Montgomery so very much and knowing it was futile, but it was a small voice. One easily ignorable when she was having so much fun.

After all, they were just friends.

And she could live with that.

16

Papa

apa couldn't live with being just friends with Jeanette.

The more they spent time together, the more he realized how much he liked her. It wasn't exactly how it had been with Mama, but that was alright. It didn't need to be. It was something different, something warm and wonderful, something that he enjoyed without a doubt.

Every time he started to come to terms with it, his fear would rear its head. That little voice that said he was violating his vows to Mama certainly was insidious, but the more time he spent with Jeanette, the quieter and quieter it got.

...but never quite silent.

He felt caught yet again, torn between his loyalty to the original love of his life and his desire to explore his feelings with Jeanette.

But it was more than being just attracted to her. He wanted her to have nice things. He wanted to sit on the porch swing and drink lemonade with her while watching the sun set. He wanted to paint all of the drama sets for her, organize all of her library shelves, and make sure she was never alone again unless she wanted to be.

He wanted a lot of things.

And it seemed like he couldn't have both. He was stuck at an impasse, wanting more, watching life pass him by while not seizing everything that he could. It was frustrating, but it was safe.

And that was the limbo he was stuck in.

Until Savannah dropped an absolute bomb on him while she was visiting on a Wednesday.

"Hey, what should I get Miss Edelira for her birthday?"

"Her what now?" Papa asked, mid-step in taking a fresh harvest of greens to the sink.

"Her birthday. She's so nice, but I don't know much about her besides she likes books. I don't want to be lame, though, and just get her a book. That seems like a cop-out."

"Jeanette's birthday is this weekend?" he repeated, feeling like his mind had suddenly come to a grinding halt.

"Yeah. I figured you two were gonna do something. You know... cause you're... *friends.*"

It was a strange sensation, being called out by a preteen, and Papa wasn't sure what to do about it.

"We are friends, yes."

"So you have plans then?"

"She's been busy. Maybe it just slipped her mind."

"How can someone's birthday slip their own mind?"

"It's a strange world being an adult," Papa muttered. "Sometimes what's important changes."

"Daddy says that birthdays are a celebration of life. I can't imagine ever being so old that I don't want to celebrate the fact that I'm alive."

"Oh, goodness, lil' sparker, that's a beautiful way to look at it."

"Uh-huh," she chirped before that too-clever expression crossed her face again. "Anyway, this part of my homework needs a lot of concentration. This would be a good time to go talk to a friend if you wanted to, 'cause I'll be too busy concentrating to eavesdrop."

"Alright, point taken, Savannah."

Sometimes she was far too clever for her own good.

Heading out onto the porch, Papa paced for more minutes than he would have liked to admit. He recognized that he was building up asking her far too much in his own head, but he couldn't help it. He'd spent far too long taking comfort in his own rut. It seemed impossible to climb out of it and risk the change.

But at the same time, he couldn't miss Jeanette's birthday. And he definitely was worried why she hadn't told him about it. It seemed like something she would confide in a good friend.

...unless he wasn't a good friend?

He had been selfish twice. Disappeared at the drop of a hat. But he'd apologized and it seemed like they'd been going well from there.

What if he thought wrong?

Well, he wasn't going to figure anything out while walking

back and forth on his porch, so eventually he gave in and dialed her number.

It felt like his heart jumped each time it rang, and that he wouldn't survive the third and final shock, but thankfully, Jeanette answered.

"Montgomery, hi! I'm still at school. Did you need something?"

"Uh, yeah, a little birdie told me it was your birthday this weekend."

"Huh? No, it's not…" He heard the sound of shuffling, then a disbelieving sigh. "Oh, would you look at that? I guess it is."

"Did you forget your own birthday?"

"Of course not. It's almost impossible to forget your own birthday." There was a *very* pregnant pause before Jeanette cleared her throat. "I just might have forgotten what month we were in."

"School that hard, huh?"

"It's been a busy month." She let out a soft gasp. "Goodness! This means the play is in less than five weeks. I thought we had at least seven."

"Hey, before you get caught up in all that, I wanted to ask you what your birthday plans were."

"Well, considering the revelation of where in time I actually am, I can't say I rightly have any besides making sure we stay ahead like we are now with the play. I've been trying to get the jump on Battle of the Books as well since we're expanding."

"Jeanette, that's unacceptable."

"Getting ahead?"

"No, not doing anything for your birthday!"

"It's just a day like any other, Montgomery."

That simple admission made his heart ache much more than

it should have. "No, it's not Jeanette. It's a celebration of your life. That you've been here another year and that the people around you are lucky enough to celebrate that."

"Oh, well when you put it like that..." He could almost see the blush on those rounded cheeks of hers in his mind's eye. She was too adorable.

"Come on, there's gotta be something you wanna do, a place you wanna go? Something you had in your back pocket for some nebulous date in the future where you had enough money and time."

"Well..."

He could also hear her internal debating despite it being utterly silent, so maybe he put a pleading tone in his voice. "Jeanette, please. I'd love to celebrate your birthday with you. You mean a lot to me."

Because she did. Whether they were friends only or if Papa was trapped in his emotional crisis, he knew without a doubt that Jeannette mattered to him more than he could put into words. She was his first close friend in a decade, and he trusted her like he didn't anyone else outside of his family.

She didn't mind that he was quiet, or that his humor zipped between cheesy and dry. She didn't mind that he was a homebody who loved his garden and was content to weed in it silently while she read a book a few feet away from him.

"Alright... well, there is this crazy place I've heard of in the city with all-you-can-eat steak and other prime cuts. I've always wanted to go, but it's pricy and I've never had anyone to go with. Seems like the kind of thing you'd want to share."

"It's a date then. This weekend, you and me at this fancy place. Don't worry, I'll set everything up myself."

"O-okay..."

"Thank you, Jeanette."

"Shouldn't I be thanking you?"

"Hopefully you will after the best birthday night you've had in years."

"It's not a very high bar to beat, if I'm being honest."

"Good to know. I'll message you later to arrange the details. Savannah's inside right now and I should probably go check on her before she solves theoretical physics or something."

"That would be something she would do. Goodbye, Monty."

"Talk to you later, Jeanette."

It wasn't until Papa hung up and was halfway inside that he realized what he said.

It's a date then.

Huh, that was certainly something.

17

Jeanette

*I*t was her birthday, and for the first time in years, Jeanette actually cared about it.

Normally the day was just a sort of enhanced school day. Some students would bring her nice treats or a gift, the faculty would give her cupcakes and the lunch ladies almost always made sure they had her favorite pizza ready on that day. Once school was over, she'd go to the bakery and help herself to a cheesecake, which she took home. From there, it was snacking on that and a nice meal she'd cooked up while watching some of her favorite classics.

And that was pretty much it.

She would go to bed on time, without any fanfare, and go on to the next day as if it were like any other. If her birthday fell on the weekend, well that usually meant ordering some food and still getting the cheesecake, but that was pretty much that.

Of course Montgomery Miller had to turn that on its head too.

She only had two and a half days to wait after his announcement over the phone that he was going to take her to the grill place she'd wanted to visit for years, and yet she'd still been thinking about it pretty much non-stop. As much as she tried to tell herself that it wasn't a date, that it was just Monty being a good friend, his words kept playing over and over again in her head.

It's a date then.

It was a common enough phrase. In her mind, she knew what he meant. But her heart... it did hope every now and then.

So maybe she spent a bit more time than usual getting ready. Maybe she did her hair up in a special style and put on one of her favorite dresses. Who could blame her? It was her birthday, after all.

Jeanette checked her watch. It was still about a half-hour before Montgomery said he'd pick her up, but he always had a penchant for showing up a little early. Her stomach was so full of butterflies that she hoped she'd actually have room for some of the delicious food they were headed towards. It wasn't every day she could eat herself silly on prime cuts.

Although... Montgomery probably could. It still boggled her mind sometimes when she remembered just how rich he was. He really came across as a down-to-earth, lovely man who had his feet on the ground—if not his hands in the dirt.

Her musings helped her pass the time, and not too much later, Montgomery was pulling up. Jeanette hurried out to him, pausing to lock her door since she was going out to the city.

When she turned around, she was surprised to see Montgomery standing at the base of her porch, flowers in hand.

"What's this?" she asked, gingerly taking the bouquet from him.

"A birthday present for a beautiful lady." He was grinning at her like everything was completely normal. Did friends just give each other flowers? She wasn't sure. Montgomery said it like it was perfectly normal, but the way he looked at her...

Was less than normal.

Or maybe she was seeing what she wanted rather than what was actually there.

"Well thank you. These are lovely."

"Glad you think so."

"I'll pop inside and put them in water before we go. Be right back."

When she returned, he was waiting patiently where she'd left him.

"Shall we?" he asked.

He offered his arm and Jeanette paused a moment before looping hers through it. Together, they walked to his vehicle. Monty let go of her, but only to open her door for her, and Jeanette couldn't help but feel pampered.

Was he always like this? She didn't know. It was his first time driving her anywhere. Normally they just met up wherever they were going.

Like friends did.

She needed to crawl out of her own head before she ruined her birthday for herself. She was about to have a lovely time with a friend and that was enough. She didn't need to get greedy.

"Go ahead and put on whatever you like. I have that satellite radio."

"Oh really? And here I thought you'd be a cassette sort of guy."

"I am, but this was a treat from Cici. Gotta admit, I like a lot of the channels."

"I've heard they've got an Elvis only channel and a Johnny Cash channel."

"Just to name a few. I like the mixes more. It gives me variety."

Jeanette nodded and began to churn through the channels. When she found one she liked, she still turned it down, happy to listen to Montgomery as they drove. After all, it was a lengthy drive to the closest city to the west.

"So, how did you find out about this place? It's kind of far."

"One of my coworkers went there with her husband for their anniversary. She absolutely loved it."

"Huh, so it really made an impression then?"

"Yes. And it's so funny, because she's this tiny little thing. A few inches shorter than me and as thin as a wisp, but her talking about how she went to town on the most steak she'd ever had landed somewhere right between amusing and intriguing."

"I gotta admit, I've been fairly careful about my red meat intake these past couple of years, so I'm excited to utterly ruin that."

"Hah! Oh goodness, what a streak to lose. But I'm sure you can make up for it with good behavior and lots of greens from your garden."

"It is a good thing ranchin' keeps me so active. Otherwise, I wouldn't be able to eat like I do."

"You do have an impressive skill for putting it away."

"It's impressive, now, huh? I gotta admit, that's one of the nicer things the ol' Miller black-hole stomach has been called."

Jeanette recalled the couple of times she'd seen the rest of his family eat, and they all tended to ingest just as much if not more than their patriarch. "You know, now that you say it's a family thing, it all makes sense."

"If you think it's bad now, you should have seen them all through puberty. One of the reasons all of my kids know how to cook is because I just couldn't keep up with them."

"Really? They all do?"

Jeanette had seen Clara cook plenty of times, and to be honest the young woman's pot roast, ribs and soup were legendary, but she'd never really witnessed any of the others get close to the stove.

"Oh yeah. I'm a firm believer in making sure all my kids have the skills to provide for themselves. Cici's the only one who's not really that great at it, but they can all hold their own." He glanced away from the road a moment then chuckled, no doubt at Jeanette's confused expression. "Clara and I do most of the cooking because that's where we find our joy. But if for some reason we couldn't, the others would step in without a problem."

"I understand. It's lovely that you all have each other's backs like that." It certainly wasn't that way for Jeanette. If she didn't cook, she didn't eat, unless she spent some of her scant extra money on ordering in. Strange to think about having someone she could just turn to and ask to make her a meal.

"Hey, you like to cook, right? What are your favorite meals to make?"

"I don't know if I like to cook so much as it's always just been a matter of course."

"What do you mean?"

"Cooking is a necessity. That's all."

Fortunately, Montgomery didn't press it, and instead rolled into his favorite things to cook. Jeanette loved listening to him when he was being himself, and as soon as he was done, she prodded him into sharing his favorite teas to make. Then what got him into tea-making to begin with. And whether he was humoring her or not, he answered whatever questions she had in depth.

It was lovely. Once again, she felt closer to him, like she was a valued confidant let into his inner circle that most people never got to. Internally, she swore to always protect what he told her with all that she had.

Naturally, Montgomery didn't let her always keep the conversation on him. He would draw her in, asking her questions that showed he kept closer track of her life than she thought. He asked about her move to town, and her dream for the library. He asked if she ever had pets or if she had an ideal one. It made her feel seen in a way that she wasn't used to.

...but in a way she wouldn't mind getting used to.

Living on her own for so long, slipping into hermit-hood ever since she'd moved to New Mexico, that she'd developed a certain sort of aversion to being seen. She did her best to stay out of the limelight and not take up the attention of anyone besides the students and school staff. But when Monty looked at her like she was the most interesting thing in a twelve-mile radius... it was different. It wasn't threatening. It was welcoming in a way that she didn't quite know how to parse.

So they talked, and talked, until Jeanette's throat was scratchy and her mouth was dry. She was more than happy when they pulled up to the restaurant, Monty going around to help her out of his vehicle. For a moment she was confused because they were parked right in front of the restaurant, but then Montgomery handed the keys to a man in a vest and she realized that he was the valet.

Wow, she was over fifty years old and had never used a valet before. How fancy.

For a moment, she was worried that she would feel out of place, but once she got inside, those concerns faded. It was a balance between high-end and kitschy that she could get behind. But it wasn't until they were being led to their table that she realized, although the restaurant was an incredibly expensive place for her that she'd have to save a little extra money to go to, it was nowhere near a five-star restaurant. To Monty, it was most likely a cheap, themed restaurant with an emphasis on red meat.

But he'd still been so excited to go.

That made her heart bubble with warmth, spreading out through her body until her toes were wiggling inside of her shoes. Her mind couldn't help but infer that he was excited because the restaurant didn't matter. It was *her* who made the difference.

Or maybe she was being a touch egotistical.

Whatever, it was her birthday. She could be a little self-centered if she wanted to.

"Thank you for bringing me here," she said, grinning moonily across the table at him. She knew she should probably pull herself back a little, but she was too excited, too happy, and *very* hungry.

"Thanks for sharing this day with me."

Of course he would say that. "I'm just glad that you didn't try to convince me to have a whole party. I like you, Montgomery, but that would be too much for me."

"Nah, I'll leave the parties to my children. It's harder to duck out when you're the host or the main event, far too much pressure for me."

"Finally, someone who understands the value of having multiple escape routes at a social gathering."

"Wouldn't survive without them."

The conversation naturally shifted into some of their horror stories from different social events through the years, and time flew. Before Jeanette knew it, they had ordered their drinks, got their drinks, and the first round of their experience was delivered.

"I thought we would be waiting longer," Montgomery remarked, picking up his fork and knife.

"Me too. But I'm not exactly complaining when the interruption is all this." Jeanette cut herself a piece and popped it into her mouth. Almost immediately, it began to melt across her tongue, buttery rich and fat in all the right way. Was this what expensive cuts of meat tasted like? It almost made her want to drive to the city every week and buy something from their expensive specialty boutiques. She'd go broke in a quarter or so, but what a way to fall into bankruptcy.

"Oh my goodness gracious," she remarked before hurriedly cutting herself another piece.

"That good?"

She made affirmative noises while she chewed the next piece, her eyes sliding closed. She was on cloud nine, that was for certain. Well, if cloud nine was made out of deliciously seasoned and grilled meat.

"This is the best birthday ever."

"You're right. Your bar might be a little low."

"Taste the meat and you'll understand."

Chuckling, he did so, and he nodded along. Although it was clear he wasn't having quite the rapturous experience that Jeanette was, he definitely looked to be enjoying himself.

And so their meal went on, in rounds that were barely spaced out from each other. They talked, they ate, they laughed and otherwise had an amazing time. It was like the camping trip, but without any of the strange tension that had made her anxiety spark. Just the two of them, having a blast and eating delicious food.

Thankfully it wasn't *just* meat. There were servings of salad and citrus fruit to help break up the richness of all the different cuts. It helped Jeanette pace herself and not get completely caught up in the rush of meat-phoria.

At least they were able to take their time, the dinner spanning over two hours. No one tried to rush them, and with frequent breaks to stop and chew, they never ran out of things to talk about.

It was perfect.

Or at least it was until several staff members came forward with a truly impressive prime rib cut, a single candle in it.

"Montgomery..." she murmured, eyes wide. "Please tell me they're not about to sing to me."

He didn't say anything, giving her a sort of coy shrug.

"*Montgomery*, they had better not be about to sing to me."

But then they were all at the table, and their leader was setting the plate in front of her.

"Happy birthday," the server said with a smile. "Thank you for choosing our place to celebrate your big day."

"Happy birthday!"

"What better way to spend the day than stuffing your face!"

The three servers gave a quiet and short thank you all together, before quickly hurrying off.

"Oh."

"See, that wasn't so bad, was it?" Montgomery said once she had a chance to recover.

"I have to admit, that was the most pleasant birthday greeting I've ever had at a restaurant."

"I thought it might be low-key enough for you. Besides, who in their right mind would ever pass up on a birthday prime rib?"

"Not me, that's for sure."

Jeanette dug in, savoring every bite. Although she took a good long time to finish it, she was most certainly full when it was gone.

But just because she was full didn't mean the meal was over. She continued to sit and digest while Montgomery ate away, and then when he was done, they talked some more.

Somewhere around the three-and-a-half-hour mark, Jeanette remembered that they were probably hogging the server's table.

"We should probably head out," she murmured, not really meaning it.

"Probably," Montgomery remarked, sounding equally unenthused.

"I... I don't really want to go home yet."

"Me either."

They both sat there, looking at each other from across the table, until Montgomery cleared his throat.

"I think there's a park nearby. Perhaps we could go on a post meat-coma walk?"

"Yes, I'd love that."

His grin back to her was genuine in all the ways that never failed to make her heart pound. "Alright then. It's a plan."

He went through the process of telling the server he wanted the check, paying, then heading back outside. He didn't gather his car, however, and when Jeanette asked, he assured her that as long as he came back before close, it would be fine.

The park turned out to be less than a five-minute walk away, which they traversed arm in arm. It was so peaceful, and it did help with her digestion.

"This might be the best birthday I've had in ages," she murmured, leaning her head against Monty's arm.

"It has been pretty lovely, hasn't it?"

"Hah! You could at least try not to sound so pleased with yourself."

"That'd be hard, because I'm very pleased with myself."

"Hah! You're incorrigible."

"I'm many things. But mostly I just like to see you happy."

There it was again. Jeanette was mostly good with respecting their friendship boundary, but sometimes he said something like that and it was hard not to think there was... well, *more*. They were arm in arm after a dinner just between the two of them, and he'd brought her flowers. With that added onto such romantic overtures, it was hard not to get her lines crossed.

Jeanette wasn't exactly a spring chicken, but even in her hermitage, she knew that if she didn't address the conflict in her, it would fester and she'd either hurt herself or Montgomery. And she didn't need to do that. She needed to be honest about her feelings and place her own boundaries if she needed.

...maybe in a few minutes. She didn't want to ruin the mood.

They strolled along until they reached the artificial pond

near the center of the park, where they stopped and looked over the wildlife and flora. It was beautiful, truly, and Jeanette couldn't help but muse at how many beautiful things Montgomery had brought into her life.

She owed him so much; she really did. Did he realize how he'd pulled her out of the hole she'd allowed herself to sink into? Or did he just assume that she'd always been somewhat active? She didn't know, but she had far too much on her mind to ask about that particular topic.

"You ever wish you could stop time?" Monty asked, pulling her out of her thoughts.

"More and more as of late." How many years had she wasted sequestered in her house? Too many. She would kick herself, but she was pretty sure she hadn't been ready before. Or maybe that was just her fear talking.

He turned to her, letting go of her arm but only to grab her hand instead. Jeanette felt like she was back in high school, just holding hands making her skin warm up.

"Sometimes, when it is just the two of us together, it's easy to forget the rest of the world outside of us."

Why was he saying such things!? Surely he had to hear himself. But when she gazed up at his handsome face, she didn't see any manipulation. Or even expectation. It was just Monty being his earnest, beguiling self.

She wished she could raise her free hand and trace the lines on his face. She knew some of their stories. The smiles, laughter, pain, and frustration that had carved their own paths into his features. But there was so much more to know. She wanted to hear all of them, one right after another, until she knew him better than she knew herself.

She wanted *so* much, but at the same time, she knew that

Monty didn't feel the same. He had limits. He had old wounds that weren't healed. He dealt with the death of his spouse very differently than how Jeanette did, and she needed to accept that.

Easier said than done.

"Funny," she murmured, throat constricting around her words. Why was her tongue suddenly so heavy in her mouth? It was awfully inconvenient. "When I'm with you, I'm reminded of so much of the world and all of the amazing things in it."

"You make me sound way more important than I am."

"I don't think you have a very accurate idea of how important you are at all."

"Jeanette..."

The way he murmured her name, all low and just barely audible, had goosebumps rolling along her arms in a wave. Goodness. *Goodness!* He just wasn't fair.

"Monty," she answered back, squeezing his hand. She needed to find the bravery to say what she needed to say. Being a coward would be a disservice to them both. "I... I need to tell you something."

He immediately stiffened. "Yeah?"

It wasn't too late to back out. She could just say a non-sequitur and that would be that.

No.

She needed to be brave.

"Look, I love spending time with you. I love our friendship. But I need to be honest with you."

"...yeah?"

"I have feelings for you, Montgomery. And I don't want to hide them anymore. I can accept that you only want to be friends if that's what you wish, but sometimes, you send me these mixed messages.

"I'm not making an ultimatum right now. I'm not even saying that you have to have feelings for me. But I need you to know how I feel, and I need clarification from you."

He didn't say anything for a moment, and Jeanette found herself holding her breath long enough that she got a bit dizzy. She did remember to drag a breath in before she passed out, however, and eventually, Monty did speak.

"I... have feelings for you as well."

"Oh?"

Oh? What a silly thing to say to the man she was falling in love with who was confessing his own feelings.

"If you have feelings for me, why have we been dancing around each other so much?"

"Because I'm... I'm struggling, Jeanette. I feel for you like I haven't felt for another human since my wife passed. And when she left us, I thought there would never be anyone else who could make me feel the same way."

Jeanette wanted to tell him that wasn't how humans worked. That there wasn't anything wrong with healing and moving on when the people they loved passed. But she could tell that Monty was still thinking and trying to find his words, so she kept quiet.

"I'm scared of these feelings, but I want to pursue them. I want to be not scared. But I also feel like I'm betraying my wife. I know she's been... gone for so long. But so many times it feels like it was just yesterday."

"I'm so sorry, Monty, I am. I wish I could tell you exactly how to deal with all of that. And if you don't want to pursue what's happening between us, I understand that too.

"*But*, if you wanted to try things, I'd understand if you falter. All that matters to me is that we're on the same page."

"Really? It's just that easy?" He sounded skeptical and she couldn't help but let out a small, dry laugh.

"Monty, I never said anything about it being easy. It won't be. You know from experience that there will be waves. That some days will be better than others. But as long as we're on the same page, we can help each other. We can *communicate*."

"You'd be willing to go through all that?"

"There's a lot I'm willing to do for you, Montgomery Miller. Talking to you is not exactly a trial."

"You deserve something so much easier."

"I don't care about easy, Monty. Our lives weren't made for that. And easy isn't fulfilling. Trust me, I chose the easy option for the past ten years and it had me sequestered in my house, alone with no prospects, friends or anything."

Tears pricked at the corner of his eyes and Jeanette wanted to wipe them away so much. But she wasn't sure it was time yet.

"I..." He heaved a breath, and then his arms were around her. "You sure you want this? I... I will try so hard, but I can't lie and say that I'm entirely right on the inside."

"There are things we can try. Perhaps you could get into therapy. I know some of your children go. And we can make sure we set up check-ins for each other. Maybe, when you need a break to sort yourself out, you can just give a code word."

"You pull all of that out of your back pocket?"

"Yes. You could say I'm pretty motivated for this to work out."

Monty held her. His body was so warm, and she could smell his aftershave ever so faintly. She wanted to melt into him, so neither of them had to feel alone anymore. That they didn't have to be scared of the emotions that churned within them.

"Jeanette..."

His husky murmur of her name had her looking upwards, and she met his eyes.

"What are you thinking, Monty?"

"That I've wanted to kiss you for months."

"Then why don't you?"

"Because I'm scared."

Poor Montgomery. She hated to see him struggle, but she also knew that he was sorting things out that were so incredibly important. She couldn't rush him, and she didn't want to. She just wanted to be there with him so he didn't have to navigate it alone.

"That's okay. We don't have to rush anything. I'm happy just being beside you."

He closed his eyes, and one of those tears dribbled out. "I'm so tired of being scared," he murmured, and then his face was descending towards hers.

Oh *goodness.*

His lips pressed to hers, gentle at first, a breath of a kiss. But as the moments passed, his hold on her tightened and his kiss grew more confident. Bold, brave, and full of a passion that she hadn't known he had pent up inside of him.

As for Jeanette, she felt like her feet were stuck to the ground while the whole world spun around her in a tempest. But that storm didn't matter, because all that mattered was Monty.

Eventually, they broke apart, and Jeanette buried her face into his chest.

"Thank you," she whispered, voice sounding rough even to herself.

"For what?" At least he sounded similarly affected.

"For being brave."

He was quiet a long moment, then squeezed her tighter.

"There's a lot I'm willing to do for you, Jeanette Edalira. The least I could do is be a little brave for you."

She pressed her face more firmly against his chest. There, she felt safe, wanted, and valued. It was a whole new chapter in their lives, and although she was apprehensive, she couldn't help but hope that it was going to be better than ever.

18

Papa

Time continued its relentless march on, and somehow, Papa found himself busier than ever. All of his children were spreading out more, doing their own thing, including Charlie going full time at the rodeo. Clara was dating Mr. Westbrook, Cass was dating Mick, and Charity and Alejandro were officially engaged. It wasn't that chores were left undone or that the ranch was abandoned, but suddenly Papa found himself pulled into four times as many social engagements, celebrations and things that forced him outside of the ranch.

And for the most part, he didn't mind, even if it was quite exhausting. Which was probably because he had Jeanette beside him, always encouraging him to be a better person than he sometimes wanted to be.

It wasn't easy, and sometimes they went weeks without

seeing each other if Papa was having a bad stint, but it was working for them. They talked on the phone at least every other day and texted a few times a day. Sometimes it was as simple as a hello or goodnight, but every time he saw her name on his phone, it made his heart glow.

He still struggled with feelings of guilt, but he had gone to a therapist and was working with them on that. His promise to Mama helped, as he knew it was what she wanted, but there was still something deep down inside of him that muttered he should be alone for the rest of his life, because being happy again meant he never really loved her. Even if intellectually he knew that wasn't correct, it was a pretty convincing voice.

But Jeanette seemed to understand. She told him about her husband, who'd died suddenly. One moment she was married, and the next she was widowed. Papa couldn't even imagine that. He'd had time to come to terms with losing his wife. He'd tried to cram as many memories, trips, and bucket list activities that they could in before she was too ill to get out of bed. Sure, he had to watch a sickness eat away at her far too quickly, but at least he'd had almost a year. Jeanette had had a single phone call where she was asked to come identify her husband's body.

And that was it.

But somehow, despite the sorrowful topic, discussing such things with Jeanette helped him. He didn't believe for a second that she hadn't loved her husband with all of her heart. And if he could understand her moving on, her not wanting to be alone, why couldn't he allow that same grace for himself?

Easier said than done, he supposed. But still, it helped.

Papa was having one of his good days when he called Jeanette. They were over halfway through the summer, and they hadn't had a nice, casual dinner on the ranch since the school year.

"Hello, Monty. Something exciting happening?"

"No, but that's why I'm calling. I was wondering if you wanted to come over for dinner? I got some venison from my brother up in Montana. It'd be nice to have someone to cook it up for."

"Venison? Sign me up! What time do you want me to come by?"

"Any time after noon. I want to wrap up my chores and weeding before I get started."

"You sure? I wouldn't mind helping you in the garden."

"It's too hot in the afternoons now, but if you're feeling it, we can always try in the evening. We can have more of a late lunch/early dinner instead of the usual time."

"That works for me. I just ate breakfast an hour ago. I might have slept in until nine today, so I'm behind on my usual routine."

"It's summer. Isn't this the time you're supposed to catch up on all your missing sleep from the school year?"

"I'm not sure that's how it works, but I'll text you before I head out."

"Perfect! I'll see you later, Jeanette."

With that sorted, Papa went about his chores. They were in the wild part of the year where the garden was truly insane, and he did end up filling his cart twice between the beans, zucchini, and tomatoes. He was going to need to do another preserving session on the weekend, but hopefully he could rope Clara into it. Maybe even Savannah. She'd expressed an interest in wanting to learn how to make salsa and pickled okra.

But that would have to wait, because he had plenty of work to do.

Thankfully Clara was still on top of checking in with the chickens and milking the goats, but he did like to visit with both of them. Keeping their animals well socialized was key to having smoother interactions with them and keeping ahead of any injuries or sicknesses that might pop up.

By the time he made it to the kitchen after a cool shower, it was indeed just noon, and he poured himself some blackcap-honey iced tea before starting in with the venison.

Normally he'd go for a delicious, slow-cooked roast that really helped the gamey meat break down, but roasts weren't really summer fare. Instead, he chose to do it with some cast irons on the stove.

Chopping the onions, garlic and carrots came first, as he wanted to give the venison every extra minute he could to soak in its marinade. He'd prepped it the previous morning, a combination of salt, pepper, a little bit of lemon juice, olive oil, red wine vinegar and a couple of other things in a container that he'd lovingly dropped the venison steaks into. It was one of the easier recipes, next to venison tacos, which involved lugging the slow cooker out of the pantry.

He'd just finished putting everything onto the stove when Jeanette texted that she was on her way; she just had to make a quick stop at the grocery store. She was definitely going to get there before he had the vegetables caramelized. He wanted to get them to almost perfect before adding the steaks. The key with venison was to heat them to just about 125 degrees, since they cooked even after being removed from the heat, and then let them rest for ten minutes. He'd made plenty of accidental venison briquettes when he was younger.

It wasn't long before the kitchen began to smell delicious, and Papa felt that particular sense of satisfaction that came from making something delicious for someone he cared very much for. Just Jeanette, and him. He would have made some extra for the kids, but venison really was best fresh and none of them were going to be back at any sort of reasonable time for dinner.

"Hullo! Hope you don't mind. I let myself in."

Papa looked to the entryway of the kitchen to see Jeanette there, dressed in a simple summer dress. She looked so pretty, loose strands of peppered hair falling from her bun, and he immediately stopped what he was doing to cross the room and kiss her.

He was never going to get tired of kissing Jeanette. Every time was a new experience, reminding him of all he could have and all that he'd given up for so long.

Something he'd discussed with his therapist was the idea that he'd been punishing himself. Denying himself affection, love, romance or even being close to anyone his age, had been his penalty to himself for not being able to save Mama in the end.

He wasn't sure if he entirely bought the idea, but it made a strange sort of sense in the back of his head. It was easy for him to believe, in his grief, that he didn't deserve anything good. That he'd used it all up in the first half of his life and that was it.

But when he held Jeanette, he *wanted* to deserve the nicer things. He wanted to love, hold, and cherish.

It was just sometimes an uphill battle.

At least she understood, and that made everything so much easier.

"Goodness, that was a welcome and a half," she said, grinning. "And I have to say, it smells *amazing* in here."

"Glad you like it. I haven't cooked venison in a while. Probably last winter?"

"Well, I'm honored that you invited me for the event. I always love what you cook me."

"I'm just glad you never mind that I always cook."

She shrugged. "Usually, if I don't cook, I don't eat, so I always feel particularly pampered when you treat me." She sent him a grin that never failed to make his face heat. "Besides, I like how contented and prideful you get any time someone loves a meal you make."

"What? I do not get *prideful,*" Papa objected, giving her the stink eye. But she just laughed and batted her eyelashes impishly like she did every so often.

"Sure you don't."

"Hey, it's not too late for me to ruin these."

"Yes, it is. You would never purposefully ruin food."

"Alright. Fair enough." That was one thing that was true of almost all the Millers. Despite their wealthy status, Montgomery's father had always drilled into him never to purposefully waste. Accidents happened, and it was important to roll with them when they did, but it was another thing entirely to willingly contribute to needless waste.

"Need me to do anything?"

"Just wash your hands and grab yourself a drink. I'm about to take the steaks off to rest."

"Rest?"

"You ever grill before? Some meats need to be taken off and sit for a bit to reabsorb their juices."

"That almost sounds fake, but I suppose I don't grill many expensive cuts of meat."

Papa didn't say it out loud, but that just made him more

resolved to cook for Jeanette. Maybe their every-other-week dinners weren't quite enough. Maybe he could pull a Clara and drop meals off to her. It was a thought. Although it would certainly be more difficult once the school year came up.

Then again… he had enough time in the day. Would it be so hard to drop off a nice lunch to her at school? She'd mentioned that she actually liked the cafeteria food and was friends with several of the lunch ladies, but if there was one thing that he learned about Jeanette, it was that she was so used to providing for herself, to only having herself to rely on and that was it, that even just having a mediocre primary school meal was a blessing.

It was certainly something to think about.

"You okay there? You drifted off on me."

"Oh, just thinking," Papa answered, jerking back to life. It seemed all of the Millers struggled a little with occasionally slipping deep into their own thoughts. But it wasn't like Papa didn't have a whole lot to think about. "We've got about five more minutes on this rest."

"I'm feeling a little adventurous, so I hope you don't mind that I grabbed a wine that looked interesting from your rack."

"Oh! Good idea!" They were a gift from his brother's wife, something that she had fermented herself with the help of a couple of her daughters-in-law. No one in the family was overly interested in alcohol, but it was lovely for holidays and special occasions. Papa was more of a draft brew man himself, but he was always happy to try a treat that was made with love and caring. "I'm sure my sister-in-law would love to hear what we think of it."

"Wait, your family made this?"

He nodded. "Not as a business, or anything. Just a fun hobby and way to use fruits that might otherwise go bad. I think she's working on a honey mead this year."

"That's amazing. Your family is just so interesting."

"That's one way to put it."

He grabbed them some wine glasses then opened the bottle, pouring them both a glass. Once that was all settled, the venison was fully rested and it was finally time to eat.

"Perfect timing. My stomach was just really starting to throw a hissy fit."

"We wouldn't want that," he teased, giving her a wink while sliding her plate over to her. Maybe it seemed informal to eat at the kitchen island, but Papa liked that. Sure, he loved having an official, romantic dinner at the fancy table in the dining room. But being casual and relaxed was nice too.

"This. Is. *Amazing*," she said after her first bite, eyes closing and her head tilting back a little. Papa always loved how unabashedly she enjoyed things, never trying to hide her appreciation or appear demure. Life was far too short to pretend to be too cool to be excited.

"Glad you like it."

"Man, I definitely have to sneak around here more often if this is what I get."

"We don't have venison on hand all of the time, but you're more than welcome to it whenever we do."

"You are a blessing, but at the same time, you are utterly ruining me. How am I supposed to go back to frozen lasagnas after this?"

Papa froze with his fork halfway up to his mouth, the onions, carrots, and meat dripping slightly down onto his plate. "Frozen lasagna?"

But Jeanette just burst out into laughter. "You should see

your face right now! I- I-" She dissolved into more cackles, and it was truly impressive how long she went on before she was able to gather herself, wiping at the corners of her eyes. "Look, it's filling. I can use it for dinner the next day. Plus it's cheap and doesn't take much prep work. I realize you and Clara would probably have a heart attack at not lovingly laying each noodle, but it works for me."

Papa didn't answer, instead just narrowing his eyes at her and finishing his forkful. Jeanette watched him a moment, before realization crossed her face.

"You're plotting."

He shrugged.

"You're planning on making me one from scratch to ruin frozen lasagna for me, aren't you?" she accused playfully, pointing her fork at him. "Knowing that I can't resist your delicious food whenever you offer."

"What a dastardly plan," he managed to say flatly before breaking into chuckles himself.

"I would fight you on that, but I'm actually pretty excited to see what your lasagna tastes like."

"Italian isn't my strongest suit, but I'd like to think I make a good one."

"I'm for it whenever you are."

"I'll keep that in mind."

The conversation lulled as they returned their attention to their food, and they fell right back into their natural cadence. Naturally, that made the meal stretch out, and it wasn't until after three that they finally wrapped up.

"Shall we go weed?" Jeanette asked, grinning broadly.

"Let's shoot for after four, when it finally cools down somewhat. I'll clean up here if you want to sit in the living room."

"Nah, let me help you and then we can sit together."

"Together, yeah. That'd be nice."

LIKE USUAL, time went quickly, and dark fell while he and Jeanette were still weeding and pruning outside. But with mosquitos coming out in force, they retreated to the porch with some sorbet, lemonade and citronella candles.

"The ranch really is beautiful at night," Jeanette murmured. "I mean, it's beautiful all the time, but I don't get to see it this late that often."

"That's true. Normally you're at home and in bed by now."

"Well, not *in* bed, but getting ready for bed, yes." She yawned. "I should probably clear out now."

"Probably..." He must have not been very convincing because she chuckled.

"You know, I could always crash on your couch. I've sat on that thing. I know it's comfy."

"We have two guest rooms," Papa answered idly, trying not to be offended at the thought of the woman he was courting having to sleep in his living room.

"You have two guest rooms and yet I've been rushing away from here every night for months?"

"I just assumed you preferred your own bed."

"During the week, yeah, but I wouldn't mind sticking around and being able to help with morning chores tomorrow. That is, if you want me here. I don't mean to overstep any boundaries."

"No, no, you're more than welcome to, if you want."

"I do. That sounds like it'd be a lovely time." She let out a long yawn. "Goodness, I woke up late, but I'm still exhausted. Do you think you could show me that guest room now?"

"Sure, I can do that."

He showed her the guest room and the guest bathroom, made sure she had everything she needed, but as she went into her normal night routine, Papa found that he wasn't quite tired enough yet. He needed a good cup of calming tea and some more time rocking on the porch.

Heading downstairs, he brewed himself some blueberry chamomile tea, poured it into the teddy bear mug that Jeanette had bought him, then went outside.

He wasn't out there for very long before he saw a tall figure approaching. It was vaguely familiar in the dark, and yet he was still surprised when it was Charlie who entered into the soft lights of their front porch.

"Hey there, son," he said, trying to figure out if he'd forgotten that he was supposed to be home. As far as Papa knew, his one son was still supposed to be in his trailer at the rodeo. "You missed dinner." He didn't say it to be rude, of course, but just to let Charlie know that there wasn't a fresh meal inside for him, so he'd have to cook for himself or make do with leftovers.

"I had a lot on my mind."

Huh. Papa had known Charlie for over twenty years, watched him go from a colicky infant with an opinion, to a charming young man with many opinions, so he could tell when his son was off.

And he was most definitely off.

"You alright?"

A lot of emotions crossed Charlie's face all at once, and Papa sat up, realizing that something very important was happening, even if he had no idea what it was.

That was the interesting thing about children growing up. As their parent, he'd gone from their biggest confidant to... well, maybe in their top five. And that was the natural progression of life as they branched out, built relationships and walked their own paths, but sometimes it did hit Papa a certain way.

"I'm on my way there," he answered before drawing in a deep breath. "But, uh, Papa, I..."

Montgomery wasn't used to seeing his son struggle with his words. Charlie was perhaps the most gregarious of all of them, full of charm and flirtatious charisma that often left Papa wondering why his son was perpetually single.

"Yes, son?"

"There's something I've been needing to tell you for a long time. Would you take a walk with me?"

"Of course, son," Papa answered, putting his mug to the side. Maybe there was a reason he hadn't quite been tired enough to go to bed yet. "Whatever you need."

Charlie nodded, walking off, and Papa followed him. His son didn't say anything for a long, long time, and after about twenty minutes or so, he began to wonder if they were going to speak at all.

But then Charlie did start talking, and one terrible sentence after another, Papa learned the horrible trauma his only son had gone through while at college.

And he was horrified.

He did his best not to show his anger. But, as much as he wanted to rage, as much as he wanted to drive to that college with a flock of lawyers, he recognized that wasn't what his son needed.

So he listened, offered comfort, and did his best to be present with his darling child. After quite a while, they ended up on the porch again, Charlie choking back tears.

Papa couldn't hold himself back. He drew his son up in a tight hug, holding him with all the comfort he had in his body. "It's okay, son. It's okay. You're not in this alone. We're all in this with you."

"I was so sure that you'd think I wasn't a man," Charlie whispered before his voice cracked and sobs began to peel out of him, one right after the other.

Papa's heart was aching, squeezing so tightly in his chest that it was hard to breathe, but he never let go of his son. "No, Charlie. Never. What she did has no effect on your masculinity. You're one of the best young men I know. Period."

"...how many young men are you acquainted with?"

At least Charlie still had a little bit of his snark. That left Papa with plenty of hope. "Shush, you."

But Charlie didn't shush, thankfully. He cried. He talked more. He got out a lot of things that Papa got the feeling he'd been holding back for years. And while that thought was so incredibly painful, Montgomery was happy that his son was trusting him now.

He couldn't say how long they were out there, holding each other, but eventually, Charlie seemed to have cried and talked himself out. He dismissed himself to bed, and Papa was sure that he was going to pass out as soon as he hit his mattress.

But Montgomery didn't go inside right away. Instead he paced, absorbing everything he'd just learned. It was a lot. It was heartbreaking. It was enraging. But he was glad it wasn't a burden his son was dealing with alone now.

He didn't deserve that. Nobody did.

When Papa eventually did go in as well, he was too crackling with energy and shock to go to sleep. He was ready to heat up his tea and try again, when a familiar figure greeted him in the kitchen.

"Hey there," Jeanette said softly.

"Hey there. I thought you were going to sleep?"

"I got washed up, but I heard crying, so I thought I'd just check in on you and make sure you're alright."

"You didn't have to stay up so late. I know it's pretty important to you to keep your schedule."

"It's alright. It seemed like you maybe needed not to be alone."

He could have argued with her, but what was the point when she was right? Instead, he crossed over to her and pulled her into a hug. But unlike with Charlie, how he was the one offering comfort, how he was the strong one who had to provide a haven for his struggling son, he was able to sag into Jeanette.

And she just held him, gently patting his back. She let him cling to her until he felt less overwhelmed, less like he wanted to fight the sky itself.

When their eyes met, he was drawn into them, plunging into the emotional depth that she always seemed to have. Slowly, gently, he bent down to place a quick kiss on her lips.

Like every time, it caught him up in a sweep of emotions. For a moment he deepened it, but then those negative feelings came swirling back in, so he took a step away.

"Sorry," he murmured, feeling suddenly very, very exhausted. "I guess I still need more time."

"That's alright," Jeanette said, standing on tiptoe to kiss his cheek. "You can have all the time you need. Just know you're not in this alone. I'm right here whenever you need me."

19

───────

*M*ore time passed, and Jeanette found herself becoming more and more a part of the family. It was never her set goal, but it was an undeniable truth that brought her plenty of peace. Once a week she had dinner with them at the house, and occasionally she went grocery shopping with Charity, Clara or even Savannah. She learned how the ranch ran and how to take care of the animals, and all of the Millers showed up at least once to help with the school play, sports events, Battle of the Books, or whatever else Jeanette got wrapped up in.

And even more of a blessing, she felt closer to Papa than ever before. Sure, it wasn't exactly smooth sailing sometimes, but she experienced all of the family's highs and lows right alongside him. She still wasn't sure what happened with his son, but whatever it was, she knew that it was serious and traumatic. She also met Cici around the same time, who popped up behind the kitchen counter the morning after Jeanette had spent the night, and certainly had left an impression. She was on her very last year of schooling before she got her master's degree, and Jeanette couldn't help but be impressed.

She even went to a family reunion with him up in Montana and goodness, if *that* wasn't an experience.

Jeanette had always been dazzled by how handsome Monty was, and she'd noticed that his children were all handsome folks, but no one had prepared her for just how strong those Miller genes were all throughout their family line.

Seriously. Jeanette didn't think she'd ever been around so many tall, strapping men with strong jaws and intense gazes. It was like stumbling onto the middle of a Hollywood set, except with less makeup and more beautiful women of various sizes.

Perhaps that was the most surprising to her. Although Jeanette had been of average size most of her life, she'd seen plenty how people treated fat people, and women in general. Seeing the Millers dating slender, curvy, and plus-sized women with unabashed respect made her feel less self-conscious about Papa being so far out of her league. Because, at least from what she'd observed, all of the Millers were completely, totally and irrevocably in love with their partners.

Also, Papa's sister-in-law could *cook*. Jeanette thought that Monty and Clara were good, but his sister-in-law in Montana was able to cook a truly massive amount of delicious food in all different styles with impeccable timing.

It was amazing. Better than Jeanette could have ever imagined, and as a librarian, she liked to think that she had a pretty good imagination. And with every day she felt a little safer, a little more secure in the wild rollercoaster that was realizing her affection for Monty.

But that trepidation began to seep in again when they approached the one-year mark of their dating but also kind-of-not dating. Jeanette's nerves told her that the experiment was over, that Monty would realize they could never progress further and that he didn't want to. But another part of her told her that they'd become so entrenched in each other's lives that there was no way he'd just want to kick her to the curb.

Or... so she hoped.

However, those worries were at least somewhat appeased when he called her up and asked her to dinner at his place to celebrate.

He wouldn't have used the word celebrate if he wanted to break up. Right? There was no way he'd ever be that sadistic.

So she dressed up, putting on a nice pair of slacks and a blouse she liked, then popped over at his place as the sun was setting. She walked in, expecting the hustle and bustle of dinner with the Millers, only to see Clara sitting by herself on the couch, watching an old movie.

"Hello there, Miss Edalira," she said, pausing the movie. "How have you been? I haven't seen you in a while."

"That's because you've been busy yourself."

"Isn't that true! Between making rodeo costumes, helping Nathan, and sewing everything for Charity's wedding, I have been kind of a recluse."

"Well, I'm glad—"

Jeanette was interrupted by a shrill ring and Clara jolted. "I'm sorry, hold that thought! It's Nathan's ringtone."

Clara answered, and the conversation seemed quite urgent. Jeanette tried not to eavesdrop, but it was difficult when she was in the same room. Quickly, she surmised that Clara wasn't going to stick around.

"I'm so sorry," she said as soon as she hung up. "I hate to run in the middle of a conversation, but Nathan found a poor fox that's been caught in a hunter's trap and we need to get it out. It's a swift fox, and he's pretty sure she has kits somewhere."

"Goodness, by all means, go save the day. It sounds like she needs it."

"Thanks for understanding. Give Papa my love." With that, she hurried off, grabbing a couple of things before racing off the porch. It was only a few minutes later that Papa descended the stairs, looking confused when he saw Jeanette standing in the living room but not his daughter.

"Clara had to go. Fox emergency."

He chuckled. "That girl is always off saving something or other."

"Gee, I wonder where she gets it from?"

"Please, I wish I had half of her animal husbandry skills. Ain't never been a critter that she couldn't bond with." He finished descending the stairs and looked to their truly large television. "Oh hey, I like this movie. You ever seen it?"

"I'm not entirely sure, actually. I've always been more of a book reader."

"Do you want to start it over from the beginning? Clara won't mind, and we've got a good while until dinner's ready."

"Sure, I'd like that."

They sat down on the Miller's truly luxurious couch together, Jeanette curling into Montgomery's side, their hands finding each others. He started the video over and it was an old black and white feature. Jeanette was pretty sure she'd seen it once, long ago, but she couldn't remember the plot at all so it was pretty much like watching it for the first time.

About an hour in or so, during a lull in the movie, Monty let out a thoughtful hum.

"Penny for your thoughts?" she questioned.

"Huh? Oh, I was just recalling what Clara told me about how Nathan wooed her."

"Oh?"

"They watched her favorite old films and he paid enough attention to pick up on what the song in her favorite scene was, and then he played it for her and asked her to dance."

"Wow." Jeanette whistled. "That is pretty romantic."

"Yeah, it was. And when she told me that, that's when I decided to trust her about the fellow."

"Is he not particularly trustworthy?" Although she knew the stereotype was for fathers to be overprotective of their daughters and weirdly obsessed with their child's love life, Monty didn't really fall into that trope. He loved his children—he was protective of them absolutely—but he seemed to generally trust their judgment.

"He was very rude when she first started out with him. A real Grumpy Gus. She even quit helping him for a while."

"That sounds like quite the story."

"It is. If she ever gets a free moment, you should have her tell you sometime."

"I'll try to catch her one of these days."

The conversation petered out and the romantic music started to swell. Jeanette leaned her head back against Monty's shoulder, relaxed and content.

It was his low, rumble of a voice that stirred her a few minutes later. "Would you like to dance?"

Jeanette sat up, looking him over to see if he was teasing, but no. He was as sincere as ever.

"You want to dance with me?"

"Yeah, I'd like that a whole lot."

A little, self-conscious voice inside of her hissed that she didn't know how to dance and she'd make an utter fool of herself. But Jeanette had let herself lose so much in life by listening to that voice, so she promptly stood up. "Let's dance then."

Montgomery stood as well, taking her hand in his and his other arm sliding around her middle. She could feel the corded muscles of his arm even through her clothes, and it sent security flowing through her. She was safe in Monty's arms. Safe and treasured in a way she never thought was possible since she'd become a widow.

They swayed together to the music, taking small steps. Even when the music faded, they didn't stop, her cheek resting against his chest and his chin on top of her head.

It was so beautiful and tender, perfect in every way. Jeanette felt tears prick at the corners of her eyes, happiness flowing through her so thick and wonderful that the small voice had no choice but to run and hide. Hopefully it would stay away. Jeanette was very tired of losing out on things because she'd listened to it for so long.

"I would say that I'd like to stay like this forever," Monty said. "But I don't." Jeanette grew concerned for a moment before he continued. "Because I want to wake up and see you in the next day. I want to build plans with you. I'm looking forward to all of the amazing future we can build together."

"You want to build a future together?" Jeanette whispered,

tears rolling in earnest now. But Montgomery just raised his hand and gently wiped the tears away.

"I do. I know I still make mistakes and experience pitfalls, but I don't have any doubt anymore. I don't want to listen to the fear."

"I want a future with you too, Montgomery. More than anything. I understand that sometimes you still get scared. I know you're still working on things with your therapist. But I'll be here. You're stuck with me."

"I wouldn't have it any other way."

20

———

Papa

The whole entire world was just Jeanette in his arms.

Papa hadn't planned on saying any of the things he said, but holding Jeanette, her head against his chest, made him realize that he didn't want to ever be without her.

Because he didn't. The very thought made him shudder. He loved how she drew him out of the house. He loved how she helped him find excitement in the little things again. He loved gardening with her and that she was just excited about weeding as she was about reading a good book.

He loved her smile. Her laugh. The gentle way she worked with children.

He loved *her*.

It was the first time he'd allowed himself to actually think the word. Instead of guilt, something bold and brilliant built in his chest, shining like its own little star.

He *loved* her.

He loved Jeanette Edalira and that was okay.

They danced together for a long while, until the movie finished and the menu began to play on a loop. But it wasn't until the timer dinged in the kitchen that they broke apart.

Jeanette sat quietly at the kitchen island while he prepped their dinner, and Papa didn't have many words either. But that was okay. They'd said everything they needed to say for the moment and that was enough.

They held hands as they dug into their food, which certainly required some creative fork and knife choreography, but they made do. Papa found himself grinning across the island from her several times, and she grinned right back.

He wanted to kiss her again, but he was pretty sure that should wait until after they'd eaten. Nobody, even people on cloud nine, wanted to kiss and miss out on an excellent meal. But he could do that later. Or whenever he wanted.

The truth was, Papa wanted to kiss her most of the time. Whenever she laughed at one of Clara's terrible puns. Whenever she sternly scolded a weed for being particularly difficult to pull. When she tucked her hair behind her ear or groaned in satisfaction when she ate something he'd cooked. The list went on and on. But he stopped himself more often than not because kissing her made it hard to deny just how strong his feelings were for her, and his strong feelings had always made him feel like he was betraying Mama.

But not anymore. He'd let his fear rule him and used it as an excuse for far too long. He was wasting so much time when he knew more than most just how precious time was. He knew better than to take her for granted, than to waste almost a year being too scared to listen to his heart.

And besides, he'd made a promise to Mama, long ago. He told her he wouldn't let himself wallow. Over a decade later, he was going to finally keep that promise.

"It's hard for me to believe this is real," Jeanette whispered as their meal began to wind down.

"I understand," he answered back, throat squeezing. "But it is. I promise you that, Jeanette."

"I..." She trailed off, just like she always did when she was thinking particularly hard. It was amusing when it happened whenever she was trying to instruct him in helping her at school, or with her planning out how to best tackle their garden tasks for the day, but it was much less entertaining when it came to matters of their future. Of their feelings. "I need to say something, Monty, and I'm afraid that it's going to upset you."

Uh-oh.

The cloud beneath his feet thinned ever so slightly, but Papa steeled himself for it. He'd put Jeanette through so much that the least he could do was listen to whatever it was she needed to say. Even if it was that he'd missed his window and she didn't want to be with someone as wishy-washy as him. Or that she wanted to stay in their nebulous, not-quite-a-relationship relationship.

"Go ahead."

"Alright. Well, I, uh, I... I..." She stopped again, shook her head and took a deep breath. Meanwhile, Papa felt like he couldn't even breathe. "I'm in love with you, Monty. Fully. I have been for a long time. And I've been okay with what you've been comfortable giving me, but I want to make sure we're both on the same page right now.

"Because I was content, but you talking about the future, you saying you want to build something with me, makes me want so much *more*. And I need to know if you'll be able to give me more, or if I need to..." She almost seemed to wilt as she thought of how to phrase her words. "...manage my expectations."

Papa put down his knife and fork. This wasn't a sentence that he wanted to utter while also waving around cutlery.

"I love you too."

"You... you what?"

"I love you, Jeanette. And I'm sorry that it took me so long to say it. But I'd love the chance to make it up to you."

"*Monty.*" Suddenly Jeanette was up off her feet and rounding the island. She practically threw herself at Papa, but he stood and accepted her hug. If he were younger, he might have picked her up and whirled her around, but he had a feeling that wouldn't be good for either of them.

"Jeanette," he murmured before crashing his lips to hers.

It was a kiss, alright, full of so much desire, want and feeling that Papa had been holding back for far too long. He held her like he wanted to meld them into one, and she clung to him like she wanted that too.

He was breathing hard when she broke away from him, staring up at him like he was the center of the whole world. But when she looked at him like that, when she returned his kiss like she was just as starving for him as he was for her, he felt like he was indeed the center of it all.

And for once, that didn't terrify him out of his mind.

"Are you sure?" Jeanette whispered, her voice ragged. "You don't have to rush this. If you're not ready, that's okay."

"No, I'm ready," Papa answered resolutely. "I want to go into tomorrow being completely open, honest and brave. I love you,

Jeanette, and I don't want to be scared of that anymore. It's not worth it."

"You're not just saying that because you think it's what I want to hear?"

"No, not at all. I'm just glad to know that's what you wanted to hear in the first place. I want to court you, Jeanette, with no half measures. I can see you in the rest of my life."

"Me too, Monty," she said, kissing him again. "Me too."

EPILOGUE: PAPA

"Are you ready, Papa?"

Montgomery Miller looked over to his daughter, who looked resplendent in her white dress. Her hair was done up in a mass of curls that framed her lovely, strong features perfectly.

"Is a father ever ready for his little girl's big day?"

"*Papa*," Charity said, playfully swatting at his arm. "I've already been married once."

"Doesn't matter. You're still my daughter about to join herself to a man she's very, very much in love with."

"I really am," she whispered, squeezing her eyes shut. "Papa, you're gonna make me *cry*."

"That's alright. Clara said she purposefully chose waterproof makeup, remember?"

"You're the only father I know who would pay attention to that."

"Well, it was important."

She laughed, leaning in to plant a dramatic kiss on his cheek.

"Thank you, Papa, for everything. I'm so lucky that, out of all the men in the world, I was born to you."

Goodness, that just wasn't fair. Papa felt his own eyes start to tear up and he had to take a deep breath. "I'm so proud of you, Charity. You may be my little girl, but you've grown up into a beautiful and brilliant woman."

She opened her mouth in a gasp, and a tear did manage to escape her meticulously made-up eyes. Whatever she was going to say, however, was cut off by a very familiar melody playing over the sound system.

The wedding march.

"That's my cue," Charity whispered, looking up at him with watery eyes.

"Shall we?" Papa asked, offering her his arm.

"Let's."

Arm in arm, they walked into the large event hall of her wedding. Although they'd already gone through the whole thing in the rehearsal, he was still struck by the beautiful scene.

Alejandro stood at the end of the room in a dapper suit with Savannah beside him as his best man. It was unorthodox, sure, but Papa couldn't imagine anyone else who could stand in her spot.

On the other side stood all of Charity's siblings, each of them dressed in their wedding colors, with Clara and Cici already bawling. It was hard not to get messy almost immediately, but Papa managed to restrain himself to gentle tears. He could let himself go later, when there weren't several official photographers capturing every moment.

They reached the end of the walkway too soon and they faced each other once more. Papa wanted to say so much, tell

Charity of all the ways she'd blessed his life, but she already knew.

So instead, he leaned in and kissed her cheek through her veil, then helped guide her to stand across from the man she was marrying.

His eyes never leaving her, Papa went to his seat where Jeanette was already waiting, dabbing at her eyes with a tissue.

"I'm always a wreck at weddings," she whispered, voice already breathy and squeaky.

"Me too," Papa admitted.

The couple said their vows, which they'd written themselves, and Papa was taken back to when he'd held Mama's hands and made his own promises. It seemed like an entirely different life-time, and yet it was all a part of the extensive tapestry that made up his life. Tragedy and blessings all woven together in patterns that seemed like chaos when they happened, but once he was able to step back and look at it, a beautiful picture formed.

As for Jeanette, she was quietly sobbing beside him, occasionally blowing her nose. Her cheeks were red, her eyes were watery, and she never looked so beautiful.

He really was so lucky.

A cheer sounded from the crowd and he realized the newly-weds were kissing. He clapped as well and was more than happy to throw the flower petals that had been handed out while the couple walked back down the aisle.

Everything got hectic after that, with Papa and Jeanette being whisked off to some wedding photos, while most of the crowd went to the reception where there was a live band and a full table of appetizers so they wouldn't be bored or hungry while waiting for the wedding party.

Papa wanted to take every moment and savor it, to burn it

into his mind so he didn't forget a single thing, but so much was happening at once that it was hard to keep track. Charity was crying, then Clara was, then he was, then Charlie was cracking a joke. Daisy stopped by with water for everyone, then Charity and Alejandro were kissing while Savannah did cartwheels. Then there were the photographer's directions, one right after the other, trying to be efficient but also give everyone all the time they needed to enjoy the experience.

By the time they were heading to the reception, Papa felt like he'd gone through a whirlwind. He wasn't cranky or worried about it, however. Just breathlessly excited at the future his eldest had ahead of her.

And she wasn't the only one. As the reception started and the bridal party split up to sit with their significant others, Papa wasn't blind to the sparks flying. There was Cass and Mick, him loading up a plate for her while she sat at the table, her trusty walker beside her. He wouldn't be surprised if the two were engaged before summer hit.

Mr. Westbrook was even present, trying to look like he was having a good time, even though Papa didn't miss how his eyes would occasionally shuttle around the room like he was waiting for a threat. But then his fervid gaze would land on Clara and it was like all the storm clouds settled all at once. Nathan had some health scares, sure, but he'd proven he was a good man and truly cared for Papa's little girl.

Charlie and Daisy were already snickering together, looking at something on her phone. He had no doubt that they would be cutting up a rug as soon as the dance floor was open to everyone. Those two had the same sort of electric energy and extroverted tendencies.

Speaking of dances...

"Thank you, everyone, for coming today to this joyous union. Now that everyone knows where their seats are and some of you are even getting food, we wanted to open the floor to Charity and Montgomery Miller, in the father and bride dance."

Papa stood, walking to the bride and groom's table, offering his hand to Charity. She took it, and together, they walked to the dance floor. After a few beats, the music began to play, and Papa took his little, yet eldest girl into his arms.

It was a slow, gentle song, but Papa had taken his practice seriously. They'd practiced every day for the past month, and he was grateful for that, as it helped him be in the moment rather than worrying about his choreography.

"I love you, Charity. So much."

"I know, Papa. And I love you too."

They didn't say anything else, but what else needed to be said? Charity rested her head on his shoulder and let him guide her through the steps. It was lovely, and Papa had every bit of faith that it would go better than her last marriage.

The song ended all too soon. Papa wasn't quite ready to let go, and yet he knew that he had to. It was part of his duty. To protect Charity, sure. To raise her. To teach her. But also to let her go when it was time.

And it was time.

Their family was expanding, their bounty overflowing, and he couldn't be happier for her. But he also couldn't help but wonder where had the years all gone. It felt like she'd just graduated high school less than a few years ago. And yet that had been more than a decade earlier.

Life was funny that way.

He gave his daughter yet another kiss on the cheek once she

reached her seat, then returned to his own. Jeanette was misty-eyed again, sipping at her water before clearing her throat.

"Told you I'd be a wreck," she murmured, cheeks colored pink.

"I know, and I don't mind," Papa replied. Not for the first time, he found himself admiring how unabashedly Jeanette felt whatever she felt. She didn't try to be stoic or too cool for it. She was genuine in all of her reactions.

"And now, before we open the floor to everyone, we want to invite the bride and groom to share their first dance with all of you."

"Oh, I'm gonna lose it," Jeanette quietly wailed beside him. "Do you have any tissues? I'm out."

Papa wordlessly handed the extra travel pack he'd slid into his vest pocket, but his eyes were entirely on his daughter and Alejandro as they took to the floor.

Goodness, they were so in love.

Papa's heart swelled. Both with happiness at his daughter's blessings, but also with pride that he'd done right by her. He'd made mistakes, of course, but in the end, he'd given her all the tools she needed to end up with a wonderful future ahead of her.

The two of them held each other, love shining in their eyes for the whole room to see, practically floating across the floor to their romantic song. Papa had seen many livelier or funny dances in his life, but that wasn't for Charity or Alejandro. No, they needed something serious, where they could just hold each other and forget the rest of the outside world. It was their first dance together as husband and wife, something that they'd only get to do once.

But hopefully, they'd always remember that they could dance together whenever they wanted to.

There was hardly a dry eye in the room when they finished. And the DJ drew in a breath like he was about to invite everyone onto the dance floor like he'd said earlier, when Savannah ran up to him and whispered in his ear.

There was a murmur from a few people, no doubt curious what was going on, but Papa could tell from the grin on Charity's face and sparkle in Alejandro's eye that they knew what was up.

"Apologies, folks, apparently I missed a very important dance on our itinerary. Might I introduce you to the Miller-Lumis family!"

At that Savannah ran onto the floor, grabbing her father and her new mother's hand, and a funkier, more contemporary beat began to play.

"Oh my goodness!" Jeanette said, putting her tissues down. "This is just... oh, it's so lovely, Monty. It really is. Savannah is practically shining!"

And she was. The little girl he'd met a little more than three years earlier was growing into a fine young woman. Thankfully, even with her launch into teenagerhood, she still hadn't lost her youthful joy. It was probably why she and Jeanette got along so well.

The crowd was feeling the dance as well, clapping along and cheering. Papa couldn't wait to see the photos that came out of it. And given that he'd made sure they hired three photographers, there would be plenty of pictures to choose from.

"Thank you, friends and family! Let's give one more round of applause for the happy family! Nothing like laughter to have y'all sticking together like glue!"

There were more cheers and claps as the family made their way to the bridal table, and then the DJ was speaking again.

"Now, it's finally time for all you ladies and gentlemen who want to cut up a rug or just burn off some of the delicious food you've already eaten. Seriously, who catered this event, because the spread is the best I've ever seen?"

"I did!" came Aunt Annie's voice from across the room, causing another ripple of laughter.

"Well, you and me can have a talk later, ma'am. I'm dying to get some of your recipes. As for everyone else, feel free to join the dance floor at your leisure. I'll be playing from a list of favorites chosen by the wedding party with a few other of my most requested hits peppered in. If you have a request yourself, feel free to submit it by scanning the QR code I have on the front table here."

That seemed like an awfully complicated way to request a song, but Papa guessed it was better than dozens of wedding guests lining up beside his booth to no doubt request the same four songs. Besides, he had other things to worry about besides the slow creep of technology.

Turning to Jeannette, he cleared his throat. "Would you like to dance?"

"Oh?" She looked at him with that cute expression she had whenever she was particularly surprised. "Are you sure?"

"Yeah, I am."

Papa knew that he struggled with being decisive when it came to matters of the heart. He knew that he wavered and waffled and otherwise let the negative influence him far too much. But one thing he was absolutely sure of was that he wanted to dance with the woman he was in love with.

"Then I'd like that too."

Grinning, Papa extended his hand. Jeanette took it, her cheeks pinkening for a different reason, and followed him out to the dance floor.

There, she let him hold her again, her face resting on his chest once more. They drifted across the floor, letting the music carry them off into their own fantasy world of just him and her and their love.

It astounded him sometimes, the depth of feeling he had for Jeanette. Made his heart ache and swell at the same time. She'd been so patient with him, never rushing him. As long as he communicated with her, she always understood.

And the more unabashedly he sat in his emotions, in his truth, the less terrifying it was.

He'd been looking at it wrong for so long. Jeanette wasn't a surprise in his life that he had to bargain for to deserve. She was a gift. A wonderful, amazing woman who he'd been lucky enough to meet.

"I love you," he whispered, the sheer truth of it almost enough to make him cry again. Because he did love her. He loved her so much that it was hard to put into words. The way he loved her was something new, something different unto itself.

"I love you too, Monty," she whispered back, her head tilted up and her eyes sparkling. He knew an invitation for a kiss when he saw it and dipped his head down to gently press his lips to hers.

It was sweet, it was soft, but he treasured it along with all the other kisses. He would never get tired of it, never take a single one for granted.

But however long they were going to be in each other's life,

Papa was going to march forward with his head held high and eyes open to every experience they were given.

Together, just like they were supposed to be.

EPILOGUE: JEANETTE

"Five golden rings!!!!!"

"Come on," Charlie groaned between chuckles. "Are we really going to go through all bajillion verses?"

Everyone else kept on singing, but Jeanette couldn't help leaning towards the young man. "What's the matter, Charlie, not enough of the Christmas spirit?"

"Oh, I've got plenty of Christmas spirit, but I'm not exactly an enthusiast about any song with twelve verses."

"Fair enough. Want to go make some cocoa with me in the kitchen while they finish up?"

"You know, that's a brilliant idea."

Charlie followed her to the kitchen and put some milk on to boil. Jeanette couldn't help but think back to her very first time spending a winter's night at the Millers, and she'd offered to help Monty make hot chocolate. She'd expected him to pull out the same powder packets she was used to, only to realize he was making it from scratch. Boiled milk, cream, sugar, cocoa powder and all.

It had been so interesting, watching such a lengthy process for something that she'd thought was rather instantaneous. But there was a certain loveliness to it. A time to slow down and enjoy the process of making something delicious with love and care.

"Wow, you're getting right at home here in the kitchen, aren't you?"

Jeanette grinned, stirring the sugar in dutifully, making sure it fully melted into the liquid. "Don't worry. I'm not secretly vying for Clara or Monty's place."

"Nah, but you sure do add to it."

He said it absently while he was reaching up for mugs that were too high up out of Jeanette's reach, but her mind basically screeched to a stop. That was really what he thought? Now that made her feel good.

That was something she would never get over with the Millers. They doled out compliments as matters of fact and seemed to be always ready to tell their loved ones just how much they improved their lives.

It wasn't that Jeanette didn't have a supportive family. She'd thought her parents were lovely when they were alive, but she didn't remember them being nearly as warm as the Millers were.

"Could you grab the marshmallows for me as well?" Jeanette asked, hoping to give herself another moment to recover from how his caring comment had sideswiped her.

It had been quite a journey since meeting Montgomery Miller, and she couldn't be happier with where they were. She spent most of her weekends at the ranch, and during the summer, one of the guest rooms was basically hers. It had become more of a home than her own small place, always full of life, love, and everything she'd been missing for so long.

She loved seeing Savannah continue to grow. She loved doting on the chickens with Clara. And she loved the absolute mayhem some of the goats got into and was vastly interested in the family's stewardship of the land.

So hearing that she added to it, that she somehow made it better, said as a matter of course by Charlie… well, it touched her heart quite deeply.

"I think this is ready," she said once he returned to her with the bag. At least the Millers didn't make those from scratch. Jeanette wasn't sure what she'd think of that.

"We're gonna have to make a few trips for this. We almost didn't have enough mugs."

"We do have quite a crowd here, don't we?" Jeanette chuckled, looking over her shoulder into the living room. There was Monty, of course, and all the Miller kids including Cici, but there was also Alejandro, Savannah, Mick, Nathan, Daisy, Baz, Baz's family, and a few others. For anyone else it'd be a whole party they couldn't accommodate, but the Miller's understated mansion had plenty of room.

"It's nice." A strange look crossed the young man's face. Jeanette spent the least amount of time with him compared to the rest of his siblings, but he seemed to have been going through some serious personal development in the past couple of years. Jeanette still wasn't informed of everything that had happened, but she was happy that he seemed to be progressing with healing whatever details that had been haunting him.

"You know, after Mama died, we spent years with just us and only us here. It was kind of like our own personal tomb. Our relatives would come sometimes, or invite us up, but that was it."

Jeanette had known that, but it was so sad to hear it out loud. The Millers were unbelievably wealthy, sure, but they'd gone through so much it didn't always seem fair. Jeanette was more than happy to slowly witness them finding love, branching out, and making friendships so they weren't isolated in their own little world.

And she was even happier to be a part of that.

"I'm glad you're all no longer alone."

"Me too, Miss Edalira. Me too."

And then he beamed at her, reminding him so much of Monty. He really was his father's child.

Together, the two of them started marching the cocoa out to the main sitting room, to a very positive reaction. It was so natural, being with the whole clan, and despite the fact that she hadn't known a single one of them for longer than three years. They truly were so much more than she ever thought she could have, and she loved each of them dearly.

They were her family, no doubt about it. A family that she'd thought was so far out of her future that it was hard not to look at them and resist breaking into tears.

"Is it present time?" Savannah asked, rolling across the floor. Thankfully her father stopped her before she kicked anything over. The poor girl was still getting used to all the inches that she'd grown and had a tendency to cause plenty of unintentional mayhem when her limbs went flailing.

"Not yet, *mija*. Drink your cocoa."

"Oh, I don't see why we have to make her wait," Jeanette said. "We can get to opening them."

Because there was quite the pile. It was Jeanette's second full Christmas with the Millers, so she'd gotten over her shock at their truly massive pile of gifts the year previous. Even still, it was truly impressive, with the boxes and bags stacked in artful piles as tall as the tree.

If it weren't for the sheer number of people present, Jeanette might have been concerned. But she knew that the Millers made sure every one of their Christmas guests had at least three personalized presents, and she thought that was very generous of them.

...it also made her nervous about her own gifts, but she didn't think she would ever get over that.

Because what was a school librarian supposed to get people who had everything? If they wanted something, they could just purchase it. But after talking with Mick and Daisy, she'd learned that the best gifts for the Millers were things that couldn't be bought. Handmade things, things based on memories together. Incredibly personalized, one-of-a-kind things that could never be found in a shop. So, while Jeanette wasn't a seamstress like Clara, or a preserving master like Monty, she hoped that she'd hit the spot with her presents.

"Awwww yeah! Present time!"

It was a long, exhausting, but joy-filled process of handing out every box one by one. With the sheer number of gifts, a stranger might think it was a free-for-all all, but no. The Millers liked to hand things out one by one so they could watch everyone's reactions. If there was a card attached, they read the full card. It made the whole process seem far more down-to-earth, with them not taking a single present for granted and making sure every single one was given proper gratitude.

As for herself, Jeanette cleaned up. Logically, she knew that the Millers were beyond rich, but their generosity still shocked her so many times. Charity and Cass got her a new laptop after learning she didn't have one to take between her home and work.

Clara gave her a handmade riding dress, which Jeanette almost cried over too. She'd never shed so many happy tears as she had in the past few years of her life, and she couldn't help but wonder if she was turning into a softy.

But how could she not be affected? The riding dress was because Jeanette had expressed interest in learning how to ride a horse, and Charlie had promised to teach her once spring rolled around. It was a completely unsubtle endorsement of her efforts, and the fact that Clara spent so much time and effort on making an outfit for the endeavor. Well... it was a lot. Wonderful, but a lot.

Thankfully, she recovered and was able to move onto a spa package in the city from Charlie and a pair of thick, hardy riding boots from Cici. Jeanette thanked all of them profusely, giving each of them hugs every single time.

They loved her gifts as well, with Clara adoring the interesting fabric Jeanette had managed to find while at a flea market a state over during a daytrip with Cici. Savannah loved her weighted hula hoops and almost immediately went into the entryway to try it without knocking anything over. Charlie liked the driftwood art she'd purchased directly from a native creator. While none of them were showstoppers, each of them seemed touched by the effort she'd gone through to get them something truly original.

"Wait, Papa Miller, where's your gift for your girlfriend?"

Even as she grew, Savannah still had a knack for blurting out things that she probably shouldn't have. But Jeanette couldn't help but agree with her. She'd gotten so much that she couldn't ask for anything more, but at the same time, she couldn't help but wonder why her partner hadn't gotten her anything. He certainly seemed to love the book of different pressed flowers arranged into artful scenes.

"I'll go last," he said, face impassive.

That was strange.

It was nearly another hour before everyone had exhausted all of the present pile, and the room was a mess of trash bags filled with wrapping and tissue paper, gifts and cards. It was a lovely mess to look at, that was for sure, but Jeanette was antsy.

Goodness, she felt like a young kid again, getting all antsy over a present.

"Alright, suit up everyone," Montgomery Miller said.

"Pardon?" Charlie asked from where he'd leaned back on one of the couches, his arm around Daisy who was already wearing the thick, fluffy onesie that Clara had made her. Jeanette didn't quite understand why a fully grown woman wanted a onesie, but Daisy was clearly thrilled so that was all that mattered.

"We're going outside. If you don't want to come, you don't have to." His face was completely stoic as he spoke, which only made Jeanette that much more intrigued. "But you're gonna want to come."

It took another good while for everyone to get appropriately dressed for outside. Although New Mexico winters weren't harsh in any shape, they still required a few layers and definitely shoes, not overly fluffy house slippers.

By the time everyone was finally bundled up, Jeanette was beyond antsy and almost right on to impatient. But Monty was as impassive as he'd been since the whole thing started, giving no clue as he led them across the property.

Jeanette had been hanging out on the ranch enough to know

the way to their small barn, however, and her mind quickly began to wonder what he could have stowed there for her. She hoped he hadn't bought her a new car. She liked her old beater and had no desire for a new one, but for some reason, that seemed to be the gift that everyone expected her rich boyfriend to get her. No fewer than three of her coworkers had asked her if he was getting her one.

"Ready?" Monty asked, standing in front of the door.

"More than you know," she answered, shifting from foot to foot.

Finally, he grinned, and opened the door, letting her in. The whole crew entered, with Papa leading them to the farthest end of the barn where the birthing and nursing pens were. But, since it was winter, the space wasn't usually occupied.

Except that it was.

A plaintive bleat sounded, and Jeanette hurried forward to see two goat kids standing there with blue ribbons around their necks. They looked old enough to be fully weaned and away from their mother, but they still had all the somewhat manic energy that baby goats always had.

"What are these?" Jeanette whispered, not daring to hope. Sure, she'd pretty much fallen in love with the goats and all of their chaos, but that didn't mean that Monty had gone out and bought her a couple.

"I mean, I thought you've spent enough time on the ranch to know what baby goats are."

"You're hilarious," Jeanette retorted. "But these are... these aren't mine, are they?"

"They are," Monty said, the corner of his eyes wrinkling as he grinned. "Yours to name and care for whenever you're here, and we'll babysit them when you're not. When they're older, you can milk them, and whatever they produce will be yours to do whatever you please, and if you want to breed them, we'll teach you how."

"Oh my goodness," Jeanette breathed, going right into the pen. The goats trotted right up to her, bleating and sniffing around for treats, no doubt. "They're mine? They're really mine?"

"If you want them," Monty said, grinning so softly at her. "I wanted you to have something of your very own here, because you're just as much a part of this family as anyone else."

"Monty, I... I..." Jeanette's words failed her and she picked one of them up, the kid mouthing at her nose. The little goat's breath was terrible, but she didn't care. "Oh, I'm gonna spoil the two of you rotten, just you wait. You're gonna be my fat, happy goats."

She couldn't believe it! She hadn't so much as had a pet in twenty years, and yet she had two little wee things. She knew how seriously all of the Millers took their animal husbandry, so the fact that they trusted her with two young lives was... well, it was amazing.

The other one gave a weak little headbutt to her shin, and Jeanette had to laugh, hauling her up too. She had an armful of baby goats and she couldn't imagine a better Christmas.

Until she turned back around to everyone else and saw Monty kneeling behind her.

It took all of her self-control to set the kids down, her hands shaking and the world getting a little swimmy around her.

Was she dreaming? It felt like she was dreaming.

"Monty?" she squeaked, knowing her voice was high and reedy but not caring. "What are you doing?"

But he just grinned at her, expression warm and eyes misty.

"Jeanette, you are a wonderful, amazing, driven and caring woman. You have been so patient with me, and you have brought so much joy to my home."

He couldn't be. He *couldn't* be!

"I've been living half a life for so long that I thought that was all I needed. But you swept in and proved to me how wrong I was. You're so incredibly brave, Jeanette. You haven't had the easiest life dealt to you, and yet you kept persevering all on your own. I never would have survived in your situation."

He thought all of that of her? Her head was spinning. She knew what was happening, and yet it seemed so impossible.

"And I am so inspired by you. You make me a better person than I ever thought I could be. You make me look forward to tomorrow and believe that there's more to be done than I ever thought possible.

"So Jeanette, it's with all of my heart that I ask you to marry me. I don't want to live another day without you."

"Oh, Monty, yes, *yes!* Absolutely yes!" She was crying outright now, and her hands were shaking so much she was surprised that he was able to get the ring on her finger. But once he did, he stood, and she launched herself into his arms as best her older body could.

"I love you! I love you so much, Monty. I'm never letting you go."

She could feel some of his own tears dripping down onto her scalp, and he squeezed her tightly just the way she liked. "Me either. You're stuck with me now."

"I couldn't imagine anyone else I'd rather be stuck with."

They kissed, they hugged, and everyone gathered around them, crying, congratulating them, and otherwise sharing in their joy. And there was so much joy to be shared in the future, because Jeanette knew for certain, no matter what happened, that she never had to be alone again.

It was never too late for a happily ever after, and Jeanette was certain she'd found hers.

Hello reader! If you've been reading my Miller stories for a while, I'm sorry to say this is the last full Miller book, though I did write a "Where are they now?," book. I'll tell you more about that in a moment, but if this is the only Miller Family series you've read, I have two more Miller Family series where this came from. Brothers of Miller Ranch and Miller Brothers of Texas, and you'll want to read those before you read the Miller Wrap-up Story.

If you have read all of those books, then it's time for you to read the Miller Wrap-up Story. It gives you a peek at where everyone is in their lives. Every single Miller couple gets two chapters, one for the man and one for the woman, as is my usual way of doing things. You can find it on each Miller series page on my website, Natalie Dean Books. Here's the link: nataliedean books.com

MILLER
FAMILY
Wrap-up
Story
NATALIE DEAN

MILLER
FAMILY
Wrap-up
Story
NATALIE DEAN

ABOUT THE AUTHOR

Born and raised in a small coastal town in the south, I was raised to treasure family and love the Lord. I'm a dedicated homeschooling mom who loves to travel and spend time with my growing-up-too-fast son.

When I'm not busy writing or running my business, you can find me cleaning house, cooking dinner, feeding our three rescue cats, trying to make learning fun and coaxing my son to pick up his toys. On less busy days, you may also find me paddling down a spring run in Florida, hiking a mountain trail in Georgia (on the rare vacation to the mountains), or enjoying a book.

If you love Natalie Dean books, you can be notified of new releases by signing up to my newsletter at nataliedeanauthor.com, where you will also receive two free short stories for signing up. Just click on the "Free Books" tab at the top and you'll be on your way!

Also, as previously mentioned, I've opened my own online bookstore and I'd love your support! As of June 2024, I'm selling my ebooks at Natalie Dean Books. By late summer or fall 2024, I should have audiobooks, regular paperbacks, large print paperbacks, dyslexic print paperbacks and signed paperbacks all available. At the request of my loyal readers, I'll also be adding merchandise, such as glasses, cups, magnets and more. So come check out my small mom-owned author business at nataliedeanbooks.com.

You can also scan the QR code below to be taken to the home page of Natalie Dean Books.

facebook.com/nataliedeanromance

www.ingramcontent.com/pod-product-compliance
Lightning Source LLC
Chambersburg PA
CBHW031559310726
48974CB00003B/736

Also by Quick Solutions

Quick Solutions Group

Maestría en Seducción: *Ciencia y Arte para Relaciones Auténticas*
Emprende Online: *Tu Guía Definitiva para Crear Negocios Exitosos*
en la Era Digital
Estrategias de Marketing para Pequeñas y Medianas Empresas
El Camino del Coach:
Cómo Convertirte en un Líder Transformacional
El Arte de la Viralización en Redes Sociales
Neuroventas: *La Ciencia de Conectar y Vender*

Hexágono

El Hexágono del Cambio

Hexágono del Progreso
Los Hexágonos: Mas allá del Liderazgo

Standalone

Cómo Volverme
Millonario

Deja De Ser Flojo
¿Estás Donde Quieres Estar?
Lo Peor en esta Vida es Malgastar los
Talentos
No Hay Peor Negocio Que El Que No Se
Hace
Todo Tiene Solución Menos la Muerte

Copyright © 2024 Quick Solutions Group

Todos los derechos reservados.

ISBN:

Diseño de Portada: Quick Solutions

Madre Primeriza: De la Panza a la Vida

Guía Completa para una Maternidad Feliz

QUICK SOLUTIONS GROUP

Colaboración: Marami

Quick Solutions Group (Escuela de Soluciones) *es un colectivo de profesionales dedicados a ofrecer orientación práctica y accesible para todo tipo de público. Compuesto por expertos en diversas áreas, este grupo se especializa en la creación de libros que abordan una amplia gama de temas, desde el desarrollo personal y profesional hasta la resolución de problemas cotidianos.*

Con un enfoque claro y directo, Quick Solutions Group se destaca por su capacidad de simplificar conceptos complejos, haciéndolos comprensibles para cualquier lector, sin importar su nivel de conocimiento previo. Su misión es empoderar a las personas mediante la educación, proporcionándoles herramientas útiles y aplicables para enfrentar los desafíos de la vida moderna.

La diversidad de temas tratados por Quick Solutions Group refleja la amplitud de la experiencia de sus miembros, quienes aportan sus conocimientos y vivencias para crear contenidos enriquecedores y de alta calidad. A través de sus publicaciones, este grupo busca no solo informar, sino también inspirar a sus lectores a tomar acción y mejorar sus vidas en todos los aspectos.

Quick Solutions Group *es, en esencia, una escuela de soluciones prácticas que se adapta a las necesidades de su audiencia, ofreciendo recursos valiosos que promueven el crecimiento personal y colectivo. Su compromiso con la excelencia y la utilidad de sus obras ha consolidado su reputación como un referente en el campo de la orientación y el desarrollo integral.*

Tu Primer Viaje a la Maternidad: Guía Completa Desde el Embarazo Hasta los Primeros Años

La Historia de Madre Primeriza

Este libro surgió de un profundo deseo de acompañar y guiar a las futuras mamás en el extraordinario viaje hacia la maternidad. Todo comenzó en una cálida tarde de verano, cuando un grupo de madres experimentadas se reunió en un pequeño café, compartiendo historias y consejos sobre sus propias experiencias como madres primerizas. Entre risas, lágrimas y tazas de café, se dieron cuenta de la necesidad de un recurso que combinara información práctica con apoyo emocional, algo que ellas mismas hubieran querido tener durante sus embarazos.

El proyecto tomó vida cuando una de las madres, una escritora apasionada, decidió compilar todas esas conversaciones y conocimientos en un libro. Se inspiró en las historias conmovedoras y las lecciones aprendidas, decidida a crear una guía que no solo proporcionara datos médicos y consejos prácticos, sino que también ofreciera un abrazo cálido y comprensivo a cada mujer que lo leyera.

Cada capítulo del libro está impregnado de amor y sabiduría, escrito con la intención de hacer sentir a las futuras madres que no están solas en su viaje. Desde los primeros latidos del corazón del bebé hasta sus primeros pasos, el libro ofrece orientación detallada, consejos basados en la evidencia y reflexiones sobre la maravillosa experiencia de la maternidad. Además, enfatiza la importancia de confiar en los propios instintos y celebrar cada pequeño logro.

Este manual fue creado no solo para informar, sino para inspirar y consolar. Se diseñó para ser un compañero constante, proporcionando apoyo en cada momento de alegría y desafío. La autora, junto con su equipo de colaboradoras, se aseguró de que cada página reflejara el amor y la dedicación que sienten hacia todas las futuras mamás, formando una comunidad de apoyo y solidaridad.

Así, "Madre Primeriza: De la Panza a la Vida" nació del deseo de transformar el viaje de la maternidad en una experiencia llena de amor, confianza y alegría, ofreciendo a cada madre la guía y el apoyo necesarios para navegar esta hermosa etapa de la vida con seguridad y felicidad.

Prólogo:

Querida futura mamá,

Es un honor y un privilegio acompañarte en este viaje extraordinario que es la maternidad. En estas páginas encontrarás no solo información valiosa y consejos prácticos, sino también un cálido abrazo de apoyo en cada paso del camino.

Convertirse en madre primeriza es un momento lleno de emociones, expectativas y preguntas. Este manual ha sido cuidadosamente diseñado para brindarte la orientación que necesitas, desde los primeros latidos del corazón de tu bebé hasta sus primeros pasos y más allá.

Cada página está impregnada de amor, experiencia compartida y sabiduría, con el objetivo de inspirarte, consolarte y guiarte en este hermoso viaje de la maternidad. Recuerda, cada mamá es única y cada niño es un regalo especial, y juntas formamos una comunidad de amor y apoyo.

Prepárate para abrazar la maravillosa experiencia de la maternidad. ¡Estamos aquí para ti, en cada momento, en cada alegría y en cada desafío!

Con cariño,

El equipo de "De la Panza a la Vida: Tu Guía Completa para una Maternidad Feliz"

¿Qué puedo aprender de este libro?

¿Qué tipo de consejos y orientación puedo encontrar en este manual?

En "De la Panza a la Vida: Tu Guía Completa para una Maternidad Feliz", encontrarás una variedad de consejos y orientación para ayudarte en tu viaje como madre primeriza. Algunos temas que se abordan en el manual incluyen:

1. Cuidados desde el inicio: Se destaca la importancia de cuidar tanto de ti misma durante el embarazo como del recién nacido después del parto, incluyendo pautas sobre la dieta, el ejercicio, la salud emocional y la lactancia materna.

2. Celebración de cada etapa: Se enfatiza la importancia de celebrar cada etapa del embarazo y los logros de tu bebé, desde los primeros latidos del corazón hasta sus primeros pasos, fomentando así un vínculo especial entre madre e hijo.

3. Confianza en tus instintos: Se alienta a confiar en ti misma como madre, reconociendo que tus instintos y amor serán tus guías más fuertes en este viaje único y asombroso.

4. Preparación para el parto: Se brindan consejos sobre cómo prepararte física y emocionalmente para el parto, así como la importancia de aceptar la ayuda de amigos y familiares durante este proceso.

5. Reflexiones sobre la maternidad: Se comparten reflexiones sobre el poder del amor maternal, el crecimiento mutuo entre madre e hijo, la celebración de logros y la

preparación para el futuro, destacando la importancia de cada momento invertido en la crianza de tu hijo.

Estos son solo algunos ejemplos de la orientación y consejos que encontrarás en este manual, diseñado para ser tu compañero confiable en el maravilloso viaje de la maternidad.

¿Cómo puedo utilizar esta guía para criar a mi hijo desde su nacimiento hasta la preadolescencia?

Para utilizar "De la Panza a la Vida: Tu Guía Completa para una Maternidad Feliz" en la crianza de tu hijo desde su nacimiento hasta la preadolescencia, puedes seguir estos consejos:

1. Establece una base sólida: Utiliza la información y consejos proporcionados en el manual para establecer una base sólida desde el inicio, centrándote en la importancia de los cuidados desde el embarazo y los primeros años de vida.

2. Celebra cada etapa: Aprovecha las reflexiones sobre la celebración de logros y la importancia de cada momento en la crianza de tu hijo para disfrutar y valorar cada etapa de su crecimiento.

3. Confía en tus instintos: Recuerda la importancia de confiar en tus instintos como madre, ya que serán una guía invaluable en la crianza de tu hijo a lo largo de los años.

4. Prepara a tu hijo para el futuro: Utiliza el manual para obtener orientación sobre cómo preparar a tu hijo para

enfrentar el mundo, brindándole no solo conocimientos académicos, sino también valores, empatía y resiliencia.

5. Busca apoyo y comunidad: Aprovecha los recursos y consejos sobre la importancia de conectarte con otros padres, buscar grupos de apoyo y compartir experiencias, ya que la crianza de un hijo es un esfuerzo colectivo.

Al utilizar esta guía como tu compañero confiable, podrás cultivar el amor, la paciencia y la confianza necesarios para criar a tu hijo desde su nacimiento hasta la preadolescencia, brindándole un ambiente amoroso y de apoyo para su crecimiento y desarrollo.

¿Qué recursos y herramientas se proporcionan para ayudarme a ser la mejor madre posible?

En "De la Panza a la Vida: Tu Guía Completa para una Maternidad Feliz", se proporcionan una variedad de recursos y herramientas para ayudarte a ser la mejor madre posible. Algunos de estos recursos incluyen:

1. Consejos basados en la evidencia: El manual ofrece consejos prácticos basados en la evidencia científica y en la experiencia compartida por otras madres, brindándote información confiable y actualizada para guiar tus decisiones en la crianza de tu hijo.

2. Experiencias compartidas: A través de las experiencias compartidas por otras madres, podrás sentirte acompañada y comprender que no estás sola en este viaje, lo que puede brindarte consuelo y apoyo emocional.

3. Orientación de expertos: Además de las experiencias de otras madres, el manual también incluye la orientación de expertos en el cuidado infantil, lo que te proporciona información especializada y consejos profesionales para abordar diversas situaciones en la crianza de tu hijo.

4. Reflexiones y consejos sobre la maternidad: Las reflexiones sobre el amor maternal, el crecimiento mutuo entre madre e hijo, la celebración de logros y la confianza en tus instintos te brindarán inspiración y guía para ser la mejor madre posible a lo largo de los años.

Al utilizar estos recursos y herramientas proporcionados en el manual, podrás cultivar el amor, la paciencia y la confianza necesarios para criar a tu hijo de manera amorosa y efectiva, creando un ambiente propicio para su desarrollo y bienestar

Querida futura Mamá,

¡Felicidades por tomar el primer paso hacia una maternidad llena de amor y cuidado! Este manual ha sido creado especialmente para ti, una madre primeriza llena de emociones y ansias de dar lo mejor a tu pequeño tesoro desde el inicio hasta sus primeros diez años de vida.

La maternidad es un viaje extraordinario, lleno de descubrimientos, alegrías y desafíos que te transformarán de una manera única. Este manual está diseñado para ser tu compañero confiable, proporcionándote orientación práctica, información valiosa y, sobre todo, el apoyo que necesitas para criar a tu hijo desde su nacimiento hasta la preadolescencia.

En cada página encontrarás consejos basados en la evidencia, experiencias compartidas por otras madres, y la orientación de expertos en el cuidado infantil. Desde los primeros momentos de la gestación hasta los primeros pasos de tu hijo, estamos aquí para guiarte y acompañarte en esta emocionante travesía.

Recuerda, cada mamá es única y cada niño es un regalo especial. Este manual te brindará herramientas para cultivar el amor, la paciencia y la confianza que necesitas para ser la mejor madre posible. Estamos emocionados de ser parte de tu viaje y esperamos que encuentres inspiración, consuelo y alegría en cada página.

Prepárate para abrazar la maravillosa experiencia de la maternidad. ¡Estamos aquí para apoyarte en cada paso del camino!

INDICE

Capítulo 1

Descubriendo la Maternidad

El inicio de una aventura única y transformadora

El proceso de convertirse en madre marca uno de los cambios más profundos en la vida de una mujer. No solo implica una transformación física, sino también emocional, psicológica y, en muchos casos, espiritual. Este capítulo explora las primeras etapas de la maternidad, desde el momento en que una mujer descubre su embarazo, hasta el manejo de las emociones y los cambios físicos que experimenta. A través de la ciencia, la experiencia y el sentido común, te acompañaremos en esta travesía inicial para entender mejor lo que significa estar en el camino hacia la maternidad.

El Comienzo de una Nueva Vida

El descubrimiento de un embarazo puede desencadenar una compleja mezcla de emociones, convirtiendo este momento en una experiencia profundamente transformadora. Para algunas mujeres, la noticia se recibe con una inmensa alegría y anticipación, mientras que otras pueden experimentar temor, dudas o incluso incredulidad. Estas respuestas emocionales varían significativamente entre mujeres, y todas ellas son válidas. Aunque el embarazo es un proceso biológico común en la experiencia humana, es único para cada mujer y está profundamente influenciado por factores personales, sociales y psicológicos. De acuerdo con estudios sobre la adaptación emocional al embarazo, la forma en que las mujeres perciben y manejan estas emociones iniciales puede influir en su bienestar durante todo el proceso gestacional (Cohen et al., 2018).

Emociones durante las primeras semanas

Las primeras semanas de embarazo traen consigo importantes cambios hormonales que no solo afectan el cuerpo de la mujer, sino también su estado emocional. A medida que el cuerpo se adapta al embarazo, los niveles de hormonas como el estrógeno y la progesterona aumentan rápidamente. El estrógeno, por ejemplo, puede aumentar hasta 100 veces durante el embarazo, mientras que la progesterona también crece exponencialmente para apoyar el desarrollo del bebé y preparar el útero (American Pregnancy Association, 2015). Estos cambios hormonales no solo preparan el cuerpo para el embarazo, sino que también impactan en el cerebro y en el estado emocional de la madre.

Este aumento hormonal puede generar síntomas físicos comunes como fatiga, náuseas matutinas y sensibilidad en los senos, que a menudo se intensifican durante el primer trimestre. Sin embargo, lo que es menos evidente para muchos es cómo estos cambios afectan el bienestar emocional. Las investigaciones en endocrinología y neurociencia han demostrado que las fluctuaciones hormonales durante el embarazo influyen en los neurotransmisores que regulan el estado de ánimo, como la serotonina y la dopamina, lo que puede explicar las alteraciones emocionales que muchas mujeres experimentan en esta etapa (Nolen-Hoeksema, 2012).

Los cambios repentinos de humor, la irritabilidad, la ansiedad o incluso la euforia son respuestas emocionales comunes durante las primeras semanas de gestación. Algunas mujeres pueden sentirse desconectadas o abrumadas por el proceso, mientras que otras experimentan una profunda conexión con el desarrollo del bebé. Según estudios realizados por el *American Psychological Association* (2019), las mujeres que experimentan altos niveles de ansiedad durante el primer trimestre también pueden presentar mayores niveles de fatiga, lo que subraya la interacción entre los cambios físicos y emocionales durante el embarazo.

Aceptando los cambios físicos y emocionales

La clave para sobrellevar los cambios del embarazo con una actitud positiva es aceptar que tanto los cambios físicos como los emocionales son parte natural del proceso. Sentir incomodidad o incertidumbre ante lo desconocido es completamente normal. La educación sobre el proceso de gestación y sus etapas puede ser una herramienta poderosa para aliviar muchas preocupaciones comunes. La comprensión de cómo el cuerpo se adapta para nutrir al bebé y proteger su desarrollo puede ayudar a la mujer a desarrollar una mayor apreciación por los cambios que experimenta.

Aceptar estos cambios implica también practicar la autocompasión, un concepto psicológico que se ha demostrado como eficaz en la reducción de la ansiedad y el estrés en diversas etapas de la vida, incluido el embarazo (Neff, 2003). La autocompasión implica ser amable contigo misma en lugar de criticarte por tus emociones o las dificultades que enfrentas. Esta actitud no solo mejora el bienestar emocional, sino que también puede tener un impacto positivo en la salud física. Un estudio de la *Maternal and Child Health Journal* (2018) encontró que las mujeres que practicaban la autocompasión durante el embarazo reportaron menores niveles de ansiedad y síntomas depresivos, y una mayor satisfacción con sus experiencias prenatales.

Practicar la gratitud también puede ser una herramienta útil para manejar los cambios emocionales y físicos. Las investigaciones sugieren que las mujeres embarazadas que practican gratitud diaria tienen una mayor resiliencia emocional y son capaces de afrontar mejor los desafíos del embarazo (Wood et al., 2010). Incorporar actividades que promuevan el bienestar mental, como la meditación, la respiración profunda o el yoga prenatal, puede proporcionar un alivio adicional de la tensión física y emocional. Estas prácticas no solo ayudan a reducir el estrés, sino que también preparan el cuerpo para el parto. El yoga prenatal, por ejemplo, no solo fortalece los músculos necesarios para el parto, sino que también enseña técnicas de respiración y relajación que pueden ser útiles durante el trabajo de parto (Field, 2012).

Consejos prácticos para la adaptación emocional

Mantén un diario de embarazo: Una de las formas más efectivas de manejar las emociones durante el embarazo es registrar tus pensamientos, sentimientos y experiencias diarias en un diario. Esto no solo te permitirá seguir de cerca tu evolución emocional y física, sino también identificar patrones y estrategias que te ayuden a gestionar los desafíos que puedan surgir. Escribir sobre tus emociones puede proporcionar una válvula de escape para el estrés y ayudarte a reflexionar sobre los cambios que estás experimentando.

Los estudios han demostrado que escribir sobre las emociones puede mejorar el bienestar emocional y disminuir los síntomas de ansiedad y depresión (Pennebaker, 1997). En el contexto del embarazo, el diario puede servir como una herramienta para monitorear las emociones, lo que puede ser especialmente útil si experimentas cambios de humor frecuentes o ansiedad. Además, registrar las experiencias del embarazo te permite crear un registro que podrás compartir con tu hijo en el futuro, lo que añade un valor sentimental al proceso.

Involucra a tu red de apoyo: Compartir tus emociones y experiencias con tu pareja, amigos o familiares cercanos también es fundamental. Estudios han demostrado que el apoyo emocional durante el embarazo tiene un impacto directo en la percepción del bienestar, reduciendo el riesgo de desarrollar problemas de salud mental como la depresión posparto (Collins et al., 2011). Expresar tus sentimientos abiertamente y aceptar el apoyo de los demás puede ayudarte a sentirte más conectada y comprendida, aliviando el estrés de manera significativa.

En conclusión, aceptar los cambios emocionales y físicos durante el embarazo requiere una actitud de apertura, autocompasión y, sobre todo, conocimiento. Estar informada sobre lo que ocurre en tu cuerpo y tu mente no solo te empodera, sino que también facilita un mayor bienestar a lo largo del proceso gestacional.

A medida que la noticia de una nueva vida comienza a asentarse en tu corazón, surgen emociones intensas y, a veces, contradictorias. La alegría y la emoción son palpables, pero también puede haber miedo, incertidumbre o ansiedad. No te preocupes, es completamente normal. Este viaje está lleno de altibajos emocionales que te transformarán de maneras que aún no puedes imaginar. En el siguiente apartado, nos adentraremos en lo que sucede dentro de ti, no solo físicamente, sino en tu mundo emocional. Porque el embarazo no solo se vive en el cuerpo, sino también en el alma.

El impacto emocional del embarazo

El embarazo es una etapa marcada por una amplia gama de emociones intensas. Enfrentar la realidad de traer una nueva vida al mundo puede ser tanto una fuente de inmensa alegría como de incertidumbre y miedo. Es común que las emociones fluctúen entre el entusiasmo por la llegada del bebé y la ansiedad sobre los desafíos del parto y la maternidad. Estos sentimientos no solo varían entre una mujer y otra, sino también dentro de la misma mujer a lo largo de su embarazo. Lo que una madre siente en el primer trimestre puede diferir considerablemente de sus emociones en el tercer trimestre, a medida que el parto se acerca. Entender y aceptar estas emociones, y aprender a gestionarlas, es esencial para navegar el embarazo de una manera más tranquila y equilibrada.

La ciencia detrás de las emociones en el embarazo

Desde una perspectiva biológica, las emociones durante el embarazo están profundamente ligadas a los cambios hormonales que se producen para sustentar el desarrollo del bebé. Los estudios en endocrinología muestran que el aumento de hormonas, como el estrógeno, la progesterona y la oxitocina, influyen no solo en los cambios físicos, sino también en las emociones. Estos cambios hormonales tienen un impacto directo en los neurotransmisores que regulan el estado de ánimo, como la serotonina y la dopamina, lo que puede explicar la inestabilidad emocional que muchas mujeres experimentan durante el embarazo (Glynn et al., 2018).

Las fluctuaciones hormonales son solo una parte de la ecuación. Las expectativas sociales y personales también juegan un papel crucial en el bienestar emocional de la madre. Muchas mujeres experimentan una presión interna y externa para ser "madres perfectas", lo que puede generar estrés y ansiedad. Según un estudio publicado en la revista *Perinatal Mental Health* (Field, 2017), las mujeres que tienen expectativas rígidas o perfeccionistas sobre la maternidad tienen más probabilidades de experimentar emociones negativas durante el embarazo, como la ansiedad o la depresión prenatal. Estos factores psicológicos y sociales interactúan con los cambios hormonales, creando una experiencia emocional multifacética que puede ser difícil de gestionar.

El impacto de estas emociones no se limita a la madre. Numerosos estudios sugieren que el bienestar emocional de la madre durante el embarazo tiene efectos directos sobre el desarrollo del bebé. El campo de la psicología perinatal ha investigado cómo el estrés y la ansiedad durante el embarazo pueden influir en la salud física y mental del bebé, tanto a corto como a largo plazo. Por ejemplo, investigaciones han demostrado que niveles elevados de cortisol, la hormona del estrés, en la madre pueden afectar el desarrollo del cerebro del bebé, predisponiéndolo a problemas emocionales y cognitivos más adelante en la vida (Monk et al., 2016). Por lo tanto, gestionar las emociones durante el embarazo no solo es esencial para la madre, sino también para el bienestar del bebé.

Estrategias para manejar las emociones mixtas

Dado el complejo entrelazamiento de factores hormonales, psicológicos y sociales, es fundamental que las mujeres embarazadas adopten estrategias para gestionar sus emociones de manera efectiva. A continuación, se presentan algunas de las estrategias respaldadas por investigaciones científicas para ayudar a las madres a transitar esta etapa con mayor serenidad:

1. Reconocer las emociones

El primer paso para manejar las emociones durante el embarazo es aprender a reconocerlas y aceptarlas sin juzgarlas. Es completamente normal sentirse abrumada, ansiosa o incluso tener días en los que el miedo parece sobrepasar la emoción. Estas emociones no significan que una mujer sea inadecuada para la maternidad, ni reflejan debilidad. En lugar de reprimir o ignorar las emociones, es importante darles espacio y reconocerlas como una parte natural del proceso. La *Terapia de Aceptación y Compromiso* (ACT, por sus siglas en inglés) es una estrategia psicológica que se centra en aceptar los pensamientos y emociones tal como son, sin intentar cambiarlos ni juzgarlos, lo que puede ser útil para las madres que se sienten abrumadas por la intensidad emocional del embarazo (Hayes et al., 2011).

Reconocer las emociones también implica identificar sus posibles desencadenantes. A veces, una emoción intensa puede estar vinculada a una preocupación particular, como el miedo al parto o la incertidumbre sobre el futuro. Al entender el origen de la emoción, es más fácil encontrar formas constructivas de lidiar con ella.

2. Técnicas de relajación

El estrés prolongado y la ansiedad no gestionada durante el embarazo pueden tener efectos adversos tanto para la madre como para el bebé. Incorporar técnicas de relajación diarias puede ayudar a reducir el estrés y crear una mayor sensación de calma y bienestar. Investigaciones han demostrado que prácticas como la respiración profunda, la meditación y el mindfulness tienen un impacto positivo en la reducción de los niveles de cortisol y en la mejora del estado de ánimo (Shorey et al., 2016).

Respiración profunda: Esta técnica, que implica inhalaciones largas y profundas seguidas de exhalaciones controladas, puede activar el sistema nervioso parasimpático, lo que ayuda a reducir el ritmo cardíaco y a inducir una sensación de relajación. Las mujeres embarazadas pueden practicar la respiración profunda en momentos de ansiedad o antes de acostarse para mejorar la calidad del sueño.

Meditación y mindfulness: La meditación guiada o el mindfulness pueden ser herramientas poderosas para manejar el estrés emocional del embarazo. Estas prácticas ayudan a las personas a centrarse en el momento presente, lo que puede reducir los pensamientos ansiosos sobre el futuro o los arrepentimientos del pasado. Estudios han mostrado que las mujeres embarazadas que practican mindfulness experimentan menores niveles de ansiedad y tienen una mayor capacidad para afrontar las dificultades emocionales del embarazo (Duncan et al., 2017).

Yoga prenatal: El yoga prenatal combina movimientos suaves con ejercicios de respiración, ayudando a las mujeres embarazadas a relajarse mientras mejoran su flexibilidad y fuerza física para el parto. Un estudio realizado por Field (2012) encontró que las mujeres que practicaban yoga prenatal experimentaban menos síntomas de ansiedad y depresión, y reportaban una mayor sensación de bienestar general.

3. Red de apoyo

Una de las herramientas más importantes para gestionar las emociones durante el embarazo es contar con una red de apoyo sólida. Los estudios han demostrado que el apoyo social puede actuar como un amortiguador del estrés, mejorando significativamente el bienestar emocional durante el embarazo (Collins et al., 2011). Ya sea a través de amigos, familiares o profesionales de la salud mental, tener personas con quienes compartir las preocupaciones y las alegrías del embarazo puede marcar una gran diferencia en cómo se transita esta etapa.

Apoyo de la pareja: El embarazo puede ser una experiencia compartida con la pareja, y el apoyo emocional de ésta es crucial para el bienestar de la madre. Las investigaciones sugieren que una comunicación abierta y efectiva con la pareja sobre las emociones y preocupaciones del embarazo puede fortalecer la relación y reducir los niveles de ansiedad de la madre (Cowan et al., 2011). La pareja puede jugar un papel fundamental en ofrecer seguridad y ayuda práctica, especialmente durante los momentos de mayor estrés.

Profesionales de la salud mental: Si las emociones se vuelven abrumadoras o comienzan a interferir con la vida diaria, buscar el apoyo de un profesional de salud mental es un paso crucial. La terapia cognitivo-conductual (TCC), por ejemplo, ha demostrado ser eficaz en el tratamiento de la ansiedad y la depresión durante el embarazo, al proporcionar a las mujeres herramientas para manejar sus pensamientos y emociones de manera más efectiva (Sockol et al., 2011).

Grupos de apoyo para madres: Unirse a grupos de apoyo para madres embarazadas o nuevas madres también puede proporcionar un valioso sentido de comunidad. Estos grupos ofrecen un espacio seguro para compartir experiencias, discutir preocupaciones comunes y recibir apoyo emocional de personas que están viviendo experiencias similares.

A lo largo de estos meses, tus emociones habrán fluctuado como una montaña rusa, desde los momentos más dulces hasta los más desafiantes. Cada sentimiento tiene un propósito, y aunque a veces puedan parecer abrumadores, cada uno de ellos te está preparando para la increíble tarea que tienes por delante. Llegamos al final de este capítulo, pero no al final de tu viaje emocional. Esto es solo el principio. Ahora, hagamos una pausa para reflexionar y dar sentido a lo vivido hasta ahora, preparándonos para lo que vendrá.

Conclusión del Capítulo

La maternidad es un proceso que comienza mucho antes del parto, en el momento en que una mujer acepta los profundos cambios que el embarazo trae consigo. No se trata solo de prepararse para la llegada de un bebé, sino de una transformación personal que abarca el cuerpo, la mente y el corazón. Desde el instante en que una mujer sabe que está embarazada, inicia un viaje de autodescubrimiento. Cada etapa del embarazo, desde los primeros síntomas hasta los últimos momentos antes del nacimiento, es una oportunidad para conocerse mejor, para entender las nuevas emociones y para reconocer la increíble capacidad del cuerpo para crear y nutrir una vida.

Los cambios físicos son obvios: el crecimiento del vientre, las hormonas que fluctúan, el cansancio, las náuseas y tantas otras transformaciones que pueden ser desconcertantes. Sin embargo, estos cambios físicos son solo una parte del proceso. El embarazo también lleva consigo una montaña rusa emocional, llena de momentos de alegría, dudas, temores y anticipación. Es normal sentir una mezcla de emociones, a veces incluso contradictorias. ¿Estoy preparada? ¿Seré una buena madre? ¿Cómo cambiará mi vida? Estas preguntas son universales y forman parte del viaje de convertirse en madre. Aceptar estas emociones, sin juzgarse a una misma, es el primer paso hacia una maternidad plena.

Prepararse para ser madre va más allá de leer libros o asistir a clases de preparación para el parto. Se trata de cultivar una relación profunda con una misma. Escuchar las propias necesidades, entender los propios límites y encontrar formas de nutrir el cuerpo y el alma es esencial. El autocuidado en esta etapa no es un lujo, sino una necesidad. Cuidar del propio bienestar no solo beneficiará a la madre, sino que también prepara el terreno para ofrecer lo mejor de sí misma al bebé que está por venir. Es aprender a reconocer que no se puede dar lo que no se tiene, y que para cuidar a otro ser humano, primero hay que cuidarse a una misma.

Además, es fundamental comprender que no se está sola en este camino. Aceptar el apoyo de seres queridos, profesionales de la salud, grupos de apoyo y otras madres que han pasado por experiencias similares puede marcar una gran diferencia. La maternidad no es una travesía que deba recorrerse en soledad. Al contrario, rodearse de una red de apoyo sólida permite aliviar el peso emocional que a veces acompaña este viaje y proporciona el espacio para compartir experiencias, miedos y alegrías.

En última instancia, los desafíos emocionales y físicos que acompañan al embarazo son parte integral del proceso. Son inevitables, pero no son insuperables. Con el conocimiento adecuado, una mentalidad de autocuidado y un sistema de apoyo sólido, cada madre tiene el poder de transformar estos desafíos en oportunidades de crecimiento personal y fortaleza interior. Abordar cada etapa con paciencia, compasión y amor propio es clave para vivir una maternidad más plena, saludable y consciente. Este es solo el comienzo de una aventura de por vida, donde el crecimiento no solo será para el bebé, sino también para la madre, quien descubrirá nuevas facetas de sí misma a lo largo de este extraordinario viaje.

Al llegar al final de este recorrido inicial, no puedo evitar sentir la necesidad de ofrecerte un consejo sincero, desde mi corazón. Todo lo que estás experimentando es una parte esencial de la maternidad, incluso los momentos difíciles. Así que, aquí va: sé amable contigo misma. La perfección no es lo que te hará una gran madre, sino el amor, la paciencia y la capacidad de seguir adelante a pesar de las dificultades. Quiero que sigas leyendo con esa confianza en ti misma, sabiendo que cada paso que das es el correcto para ti y tu bebé.

> **Consejo del autor:** El embarazo es un momento de conexión profunda entre mente, cuerpo y espíritu. Aprovecha esta etapa para conocerte más, ser compasiva contigo misma y estar presente en cada momento. Si te encuentras lidiando con emociones difíciles, recuerda que no estás sola: busca el apoyo de seres queridos o de profesionales cuando lo necesites.

Ahora que hemos hablado sobre la importancia de ser compasiva contigo misma, quiero proponerte un pequeño ejercicio reflexivo. Este no es solo un momento de lectura, sino también de conexión profunda contigo misma. Este ejercicio te permitirá tomar un respiro, centrarte y hacer una introspección sobre cómo te sientes realmente en este viaje. ¿Estás lista para mirar hacia adentro y darte un espacio de honestidad y autocuidado? Tomémonos un momento para explorar tus pensamientos y emociones más allá de las palabras.

<table>
<tr><td>Ejercicio reflexivo</td></tr>
<tr><td>Tómate unos minutos cada día para reflexionar sobre tu experiencia en el embarazo. Hazte las siguientes preguntas:</td></tr>
<tr><td>1. ¿Qué emociones predominan en mi día a día?</td></tr>
<tr><td>2. ¿Qué me preocupa más sobre el embarazo y la maternidad?</td></tr>
<tr><td>3. ¿Cómo puedo cuidar mejor de mi bienestar emocional en esta etapa?</td></tr>
<tr><td>Escribe tus respuestas en un cuaderno y observa cómo evolucionan con el tiempo. A veces, simplemente poner nuestros pensamientos en palabras puede ayudarnos a entender mejor lo que estamos experimentando.</td></tr>
</table>

Después de tomarte ese momento para reflexionar, te invito a volver a lo práctico. Ser consciente de tus emociones es crucial, pero también lo es cuidar de tu cuerpo. Mantener una rutina saludable durante el embarazo no tiene por qué ser complicado, pero puede marcar una gran diferencia en cómo te sientes día a día. A continuación, quiero compartir contigo algunos consejos sencillos que te ayudarán a tener una experiencia más placentera y saludable en este hermoso camino. ¡Pequeños ajustes pueden traer grandes resultados!

Tips y trucos para una experiencia más saludable

1. **Alimentación equilibrada**: Mantén una dieta rica en frutas, verduras y proteínas magras. Los nutrientes son esenciales para el desarrollo del bebé y para tu bienestar.

2. **Descanso adecuado**: Escucha a tu cuerpo y descansa cuando lo necesites. El sueño es crucial para la regeneración celular y el equilibrio hormonal.

3. **Ejercicio moderado**: Actividades como caminar, nadar o yoga prenatal pueden ayudarte a mantenerte activa y a mejorar tu estado de ánimo.

4. **Hidratación constante**: Bebe suficiente agua para mantenerte hidratada y ayudar a tu cuerpo a manejar los cambios hormonales y físicos.

Ahora que tienes algunas herramientas prácticas para hacer más llevadero este camino, es momento de equiparte con aún más información. El conocimiento es poder, y quiero asegurarme de que tengas acceso a los mejores recursos disponibles para que sigas avanzando con confianza. A continuación, te ofrezco una lista de recursos adicionales, desde lecturas inspiradoras hasta contactos con profesionales, para que sepas dónde acudir si necesitas más apoyo o información. ¡Recuerda que no estás sola en este viaje!

Recursos adicionales

- **Libros recomendados**:
    - *Qué se puede esperar cuando se está esperando* de Heidi Murkoff.

- o *La maternidad y el encuentro con la propia sombra* de Laura Gutman.

- **Aplicaciones útiles**:

  - o "Ovia Pregnancy Tracker"

  - o "BabyCenter Pregnancy App"

- **Centros de apoyo psicológico**:

  - o Psicólogos especializados en salud perinatal y psicología del embarazo.

Después de ese primer momento en el que una nueva vida empieza a crecer dentro de ti, un viaje emocional y físico se despliega frente a tus ojos. El asombro y la emoción te llenan al descubrir la maternidad, pero ahora es cuando la verdadera preparación comienza. Aquí es donde empiezas a descubrir que, además de dar vida, también estás llamada a cuidarte, a amarte y a proteger a ese ser que crece en ti. Entramos ahora en un capítulo que no solo hablará de los cuidados del bebé, sino también de la importancia de cuidarte a ti misma, porque solo desde tu bienestar podrás brindar lo mejor. ¿Estás lista para este nuevo paso?

*"La maternidad tiene un efecto humanizante. Todo se reduce a lo esencial." – **Meryl Streep***

Capítulo 2

Cuidando de Ti y de Tu Bebé

Balance entre el Autocuidado y la Dedicación a tu Pequeño

El embarazo es una etapa de gran cambio físico y emocional, y cuidarte a ti misma es fundamental para garantizar el bienestar tanto tuyo como el de tu bebé. Este capítulo te guiará en dos aspectos cruciales del cuidado prenatal: la nutrición adecuada y la importancia del ejercicio y la salud emocional. Ambos son pilares esenciales para un embarazo saludable, y abordarlos con conocimiento te permitirá sentirte más empoderada y preparada.

Nutrición Durante el Embarazo

Durante el embarazo, el cuerpo de la mujer experimenta cambios significativos que requieren un mayor aporte de nutrientes para apoyar tanto su propio bienestar como el desarrollo del bebé. Una nutrición adecuada no solo facilita un embarazo más cómodo, sino que también reduce el riesgo de complicaciones como la preeclampsia, la anemia, el bajo peso al nacer o el parto prematuro. La alimentación equilibrada durante esta etapa es un pilar fundamental para asegurar que tanto la madre como el bebé reciban los nutrientes esenciales para su salud y desarrollo.

Alimentos esenciales

Durante el embarazo, es crucial incorporar en la dieta una variedad de alimentos ricos en nutrientes. Estos son algunos de los más importantes:

1. Ácido fólico

El ácido fólico es una de las vitaminas más importantes durante las primeras semanas de embarazo, ya que juega un papel vital en la prevención de defectos en el tubo neural del bebé, como la espina bífida y la anencefalia. El tubo neural se forma durante las primeras semanas del embarazo, a menudo antes de que muchas mujeres sepan que están embarazadas, lo que subraya la importancia de empezar a consumir ácido fólico incluso antes de concebir.

La Organización Mundial de la Salud (OMS) recomienda una ingesta diaria de al menos 400 microgramos de ácido fólico durante los primeros tres meses del embarazo, y preferiblemente desde antes de la concepción. Los alimentos ricos en ácido fólico incluyen verduras de hoja verde como espinacas, brócoli y espárragos, así como frutas cítricas, nueces, legumbres y suplementos prenatales específicos. En muchos países, los cereales y otros alimentos están fortificados con ácido fólico para asegurar una ingesta adecuada (OMS, 2020).

2. Hierro

El embarazo aumenta la demanda de hierro debido a la expansión del volumen sanguíneo de la madre, que requiere más hemoglobina para transportar oxígeno al bebé en desarrollo. La deficiencia de hierro puede provocar anemia, una condición común en mujeres embarazadas que puede causar fatiga extrema, mareos y aumentar el riesgo de parto prematuro o bajo peso al nacer. La ingesta diaria recomendada de hierro para mujeres embarazadas es de 27-30 mg, según la American Pregnancy Association.

Las fuentes más ricas de hierro incluyen la carne roja magra, el pollo, los mariscos, así como opciones vegetarianas como las legumbres, los frijoles, las espinacas y los cereales fortificados. Sin embargo, el hierro de origen vegetal se absorbe con menos eficiencia que el de origen animal, por lo que es recomendable acompañar estos alimentos con una fuente de vitamina C, como las naranjas, los tomates o los pimientos, para mejorar su absorción (De-Regil et al., 2017). Por otro lado, es aconsejable evitar consumir grandes cantidades de café o té junto con comidas ricas en hierro, ya que estos pueden inhibir su absorción.

3. Proteínas

Las proteínas son esenciales para la formación de los tejidos del bebé, el desarrollo de los órganos y la construcción de estructuras como la piel, los músculos y el cerebro. A lo largo del embarazo, el requerimiento de proteínas aumenta aproximadamente en un 25%, por lo que se recomienda consumir entre 75 y 100 gramos de proteínas al día.

Fuentes de proteínas de alta calidad incluyen las carnes magras, como el pollo y el pavo, el pescado (especialmente aquellos bajos en mercurio, como el salmón y el bacalao), los huevos, los productos lácteos como el yogur y el queso, las legumbres, las nueces y las semillas. Las proteínas vegetales, como las de los frijoles y las lentejas, también son excelentes opciones, y su combinación con cereales integrales puede proporcionar un perfil de aminoácidos completo. De hecho, un estudio publicado por el *American Journal of Clinical Nutrition* (2018) destacó que las dietas ricas en proteínas tanto de origen animal como vegetal pueden apoyar un crecimiento fetal adecuado.

4. Calcio

El calcio es otro mineral esencial durante el embarazo, ya que contribuye al desarrollo de los huesos y dientes del bebé. Además, el calcio es necesario para que el sistema nervioso, los músculos y el corazón del bebé funcionen correctamente. Si la madre no obtiene suficiente calcio a través de su dieta, su cuerpo lo tomará de los huesos para asegurar las necesidades del bebé, lo que puede comprometer su propia salud ósea a largo plazo.

La ingesta recomendada de calcio durante el embarazo es de 1000 mg diarios. Las fuentes alimentarias más ricas en calcio incluyen los productos lácteos como la leche, el yogur y el queso, así como las verduras de hoja verde como la col rizada y el brócoli, las almendras y los pescados con espinas suaves como las sardinas. Además, algunas bebidas vegetales y cereales están fortificados con calcio, lo que los convierte en una buena opción para quienes siguen dietas vegetarianas o veganas (Kovacs & Kronenberg, 2019).

5. Omega-3

Los ácidos grasos omega-3, en particular el DHA (ácido docosahexaenoico), desempeñan un papel crucial en el desarrollo cerebral y visual del bebé. Durante el tercer trimestre del embarazo, el cerebro del bebé se desarrolla rápidamente, y el DHA es fundamental para la formación de las membranas celulares del cerebro y los ojos. Estudios han demostrado que una ingesta adecuada de omega-3 durante el embarazo puede mejorar el desarrollo cognitivo del bebé y reducir el riesgo de parto prematuro (Coletta et al., 2010).

Las mejores fuentes de DHA son los pescados grasos como el salmón, las sardinas, el arenque y la caballa, aunque también se puede obtener de alimentos fortificados como los huevos o la leche enriquecida con omega-3, así como a través de suplementos de aceite de pescado. Para quienes no consumen pescado, las nueces, las semillas de chía y las semillas de lino ofrecen una fuente vegetal de ALA (ácido alfa-linolénico), que el cuerpo puede convertir parcialmente en DHA y EPA (aunque la conversión es limitada).

Consejos para una alimentación equilibrada

Mantener una dieta equilibrada durante el embarazo no significa solo consumir los nutrientes clave mencionados anteriormente, sino también asegurar que tu ingesta diaria esté alineada con las necesidades energéticas y nutricionales específicas de cada trimestre. A continuación, se ofrecen algunos consejos prácticos para garantizar una nutrición óptima:

1. Planifica tus comidas

Tomarse el tiempo para planificar comidas nutritivas es una excelente manera de asegurarse de que se están obteniendo todos los nutrientes necesarios. La planificación de comidas no solo reduce el estrés de decidir qué comer cada día, sino que también te ayuda a incluir una variedad de alimentos ricos en nutrientes, como frutas, verduras, proteínas magras y granos integrales. Intenta incorporar alimentos de diferentes colores y grupos alimenticios para asegurarte de que estás obteniendo una amplia gama de vitaminas y minerales.

2. Controla las porciones

Contrario a la creencia popular, no es necesario "comer por dos" durante el embarazo. De hecho, las necesidades calóricas adicionales son relativamente modestas y varían según el trimestre. Durante el primer trimestre, la ingesta calórica no necesita aumentar significativamente. En el segundo trimestre, se recomienda un incremento de aproximadamente 300 calorías adicionales por día, y en el tercer trimestre, este aumento puede llegar a entre 400 y 500 calorías adicionales diarias, dependiendo del nivel de actividad y el metabolismo individual (American College of Obstetricians and Gynecologists, 2020).

Es importante optar por alimentos ricos en nutrientes en lugar de calorías vacías, ya que los requerimientos nutricionales durante el embarazo son más altos. Elegir alimentos densos en nutrientes, como frutas, verduras, nueces, proteínas magras y cereales integrales, garantizará que obtengas las calorías adicionales de una fuente saludable.

3. Hidratación adecuada

La hidratación es esencial durante el embarazo, ya que el cuerpo requiere más líquidos para mantener el aumento de volumen sanguíneo, apoyar la formación del líquido amniótico y ayudar en la digestión. La recomendación general es consumir al menos 8 vasos de agua al día, aunque las necesidades pueden variar según el clima, el nivel de actividad y las necesidades individuales.

Además del agua, las infusiones de hierbas sin cafeína, los caldos y las frutas con alto contenido de agua, como las sandías o las naranjas, también pueden contribuir a mantener una hidratación adecuada. Evita las bebidas azucaradas y limita el consumo de cafeína, que en exceso puede aumentar el riesgo de deshidratación y complicaciones en el embarazo (Chen et al., 2016).

Consejo práctico: Además de las comidas principales, incorpora snacks saludables como nueces, frutas frescas o yogur natural. Estos snacks te ayudarán a mantener tus niveles de energía estables a lo largo del día y a proporcionar nutrientes clave en momentos en que las náuseas o el hambre repentina puedan aparecer.

Mientras nutres a tu bebé con los alimentos que mejorarán su desarrollo, también estás sembrando la base para tu propia energía y bienestar. Pero la nutrición es solo una parte del rompecabezas. Ahora es el momento de hablar de algo igualmente importante: el movimiento y el bienestar emocional. Durante el embarazo, cuidar de tu mente y tu cuerpo va de la mano. A medida que vamos descubriendo cómo el ejercicio y las prácticas de bienestar pueden elevar tu estado emocional, recuerda que cada acción que tomas en favor de ti misma impacta positivamente en esa vida que llevas dentro. Vamos a explorar cómo el bienestar físico se conecta con tu paz interior.

Ejercicio y Bienestar Emocional

El ejercicio regular durante el embarazo es seguro y altamente beneficioso, tanto para la madre como para el bebé. Mantener una rutina de actividad física moderada no solo mejora la salud cardiovascular y ayuda a mantener un peso saludable, sino que también reduce el riesgo de complicaciones como la diabetes gestacional y la hipertensión. Además de los beneficios físicos, el ejercicio tiene un impacto positivo en el bienestar emocional, ayudando a aliviar el estrés, la ansiedad y mejorando el estado de ánimo. Las mujeres que realizan actividad física durante el embarazo también suelen tener una mejor calidad del sueño y una recuperación posparto más rápida.

La importancia del ejercicio moderado

El ejercicio durante el embarazo debe ser de intensidad moderada y estar adaptado a las capacidades individuales de cada mujer. La actividad física excesiva o de alta intensidad no es recomendable, ya que podría sobrecargar el cuerpo. Sin embargo, mantener el cuerpo en movimiento de manera segura y controlada no solo prepara a la mujer para el esfuerzo físico del parto, sino que también tiene un impacto significativo en la salud emocional.

A continuación, se describen algunas formas de ejercicio recomendadas durante el embarazo:

1. Caminatas

Caminar es una de las formas más seguras y accesibles de ejercicio durante el embarazo. Es una actividad de bajo impacto que puede ser realizada casi en cualquier lugar y no requiere equipo especial. Caminar a un ritmo moderado durante 30 minutos al día contribuye a mejorar la circulación, aumentar los niveles de energía y reducir el riesgo de hinchazón en las extremidades, una queja común en mujeres embarazadas debido a la retención de líquidos y los cambios hormonales.

Un estudio publicado en *The Journal of Maternal-Fetal & Neonatal Medicine* (2015) encontró que las mujeres embarazadas que caminan regularmente experimentan menos molestias musculares y articulares y reportan niveles más bajos de ansiedad. Además, caminar puede ser un excelente momento para la reflexión personal o para pasar tiempo al aire libre, lo que también contribuye a mejorar el bienestar emocional.

2. Yoga prenatal

El yoga prenatal es una excelente opción para las mujeres que desean mantener su flexibilidad y tonificar el cuerpo de una manera suave. Las posturas de yoga prenatal están diseñadas para adaptarse a las necesidades y limitaciones del embarazo, lo que permite a las mujeres estirar y fortalecer sus músculos sin sobrecargar las articulaciones. Además, el yoga prenatal es conocido por mejorar la postura y aliviar la tensión muscular, especialmente en la espalda, donde muchas mujeres embarazadas tienden a acumular tensión debido al aumento de peso y al desplazamiento del centro de gravedad.

Una ventaja adicional del yoga prenatal es que incorpora ejercicios de respiración profunda y relajación, que no solo son útiles durante el embarazo, sino que también preparan a las mujeres para el trabajo de parto. Según un estudio realizado por Field (2012), las mujeres que practican yoga prenatal experimentan menos estrés y ansiedad, y reportan mejoras significativas en la calidad del sueño. El yoga también puede ayudar a reducir la presión arterial, promover una mejor digestión y aliviar las molestias comunes del embarazo, como los calambres en las piernas y el dolor de ciática.

3. Nadar

La natación es otra forma de ejercicio muy recomendada durante el embarazo, ya que ofrece un entorno de bajo impacto que alivia la presión sobre las articulaciones y la espalda. Estar en el agua brinda una sensación de ligereza que puede ser particularmente agradable para las mujeres en las etapas avanzadas del embarazo, cuando el aumento de peso y el tamaño del vientre pueden causar incomodidad. Además de mejorar la resistencia cardiovascular, la natación tonifica los músculos y mejora la circulación, lo que ayuda a reducir la hinchazón y las venas varicosas.

Según un estudio publicado en el *International Journal of Aquatic Research and Education* (2016), la natación durante el embarazo también tiene efectos positivos en el estado de ánimo de las mujeres, ayudándolas a combatir la fatiga y el estrés. El agua también actúa como un masaje natural para el cuerpo, lo que puede reducir la tensión muscular.

4. Ejercicios de fortalecimiento

El fortalecimiento de los músculos centrales y el suelo pélvico es esencial durante el embarazo. Los ejercicios de Kegel, por ejemplo, ayudan a fortalecer el suelo pélvico, lo que puede prevenir la incontinencia urinaria, un problema común durante el embarazo y el posparto. Además, un suelo pélvico fuerte puede facilitar el parto y acelerar la recuperación posparto.

El fortalecimiento de la musculatura abdominal y de la espalda también es importante para mantener una buena postura y reducir el dolor lumbar, que es una queja frecuente en las mujeres embarazadas. Ejercicios sencillos de fortalecimiento con bandas de resistencia, pesas ligeras o el propio peso corporal pueden ser seguros y efectivos para este propósito. Un estudio en la *Journal of Orthopaedic & Sports Physical Therapy* (2014) destacó que los ejercicios de fortalecimiento durante el embarazo contribuyen a reducir el riesgo de lesiones musculares y mejoran el equilibrio, lo que es particularmente importante a medida que el vientre crece.

Salud mental durante el embarazo

El embarazo no solo trae consigo cambios físicos, sino también emocionales. Los cambios hormonales, el estrés asociado a la llegada del bebé y la incertidumbre sobre el futuro pueden afectar significativamente el bienestar mental de la mujer. Por ello, es fundamental cuidar la salud mental tanto como la física durante esta etapa. Estrategias para el manejo del estrés y el bienestar emocional no solo benefician a la madre, sino que también tienen efectos positivos en el bebé. Las investigaciones en psicología perinatal sugieren que los niveles elevados de estrés y ansiedad en la madre pueden estar asociados con complicaciones durante el embarazo y afectar el desarrollo del bebé (Monk et al., 2016).

Aquí te presentamos algunas estrategias efectivas para mantener el bienestar emocional durante el embarazo:

1. Prácticas de mindfulness y meditación

El mindfulness y la meditación son técnicas poderosas para reducir el estrés y la ansiedad. El mindfulness, en particular, implica prestar atención plena al momento presente, aceptando las emociones y sensaciones tal como son, sin juzgarlas. Esta práctica ha demostrado ser eficaz para reducir los niveles de cortisol, la hormona del estrés, y promover una mayor sensación de calma y control emocional.

Según un estudio realizado por Duncan et al. (2017), las mujeres embarazadas que practicaban meditación mindfulness experimentaron menos síntomas de ansiedad y depresión y fueron más capaces de gestionar las preocupaciones relacionadas con el embarazo. Además, la meditación puede mejorar la calidad del sueño, reducir la tensión muscular y preparar la mente para el parto. Invertir al menos 10-15 minutos al día en la práctica de la meditación o la respiración consciente puede ser extremadamente beneficioso para mantener una buena salud mental.

2. Red de apoyo emocional

El embarazo puede ser una etapa emocionalmente compleja, y tener una red de apoyo sólida puede marcar una gran diferencia. La comunicación abierta con la pareja, amigos y familiares es fundamental para compartir las emociones y preocupaciones que surgen durante el embarazo. El apoyo emocional, además de proporcionar alivio, puede fortalecer los lazos familiares y ayudar a construir un ambiente de seguridad y estabilidad para el bebé que está por llegar.

Estudios han demostrado que las mujeres que cuentan con un sistema de apoyo fuerte experimentan niveles más bajos de ansiedad y depresión, y se adaptan mejor a los cambios físicos y emocionales del embarazo (Collins et al., 2011). Participar en grupos de apoyo para madres embarazadas o nuevas madres también es útil, ya que ofrece la oportunidad de compartir experiencias y recibir consejos de personas que están pasando por situaciones similares.

3. Terapia o consejería

En algunos casos, las emociones durante el embarazo pueden volverse abrumadoras. Si las preocupaciones, los cambios de humor o el estrés afectan el día a día o interfieren con el bienestar general, es importante buscar ayuda profesional. La terapia cognitivo-conductual (TCC), por ejemplo, ha demostrado ser eficaz en el manejo de la ansiedad y la depresión durante el embarazo, proporcionando herramientas prácticas para manejar los pensamientos negativos y las emociones intensas (Sockol et al., 2011).

Un profesional de la salud mental especializado en salud perinatal puede ofrecer apoyo en la gestión de las emociones y ayudar a las mujeres a desarrollar estrategias para enfrentar los desafíos emocionales del embarazo de manera más saludable. Además, la terapia no solo beneficia a la madre, sino que también puede tener efectos positivos en el bienestar del bebé al reducir los niveles de estrés en el ambiente prenatal.

Consejo práctico: Si en algún momento te sientes estresada o abrumada, dedica al menos 10 minutos al día a realizar ejercicios de respiración profunda o a practicar una meditación guiada. Estos breves momentos de relajación pueden ayudarte a reducir la tensión, mejorar tu concentración y reenfocar tus pensamientos, preparándote para enfrentar los desafíos del embarazo con una mayor sensación de calma y claridad.

Ya sea una caminata tranquila o una sesión de estiramientos suaves, cada momento de actividad física es una oportunidad para reconectar contigo misma. A lo largo de este capítulo, hemos tocado los pilares que sostienen tu bienestar integral: alimentación, ejercicio y emociones. Ahora, es momento de detenernos y tomar conciencia de lo que has aprendido. Este es el momento de pausar, respirar profundo y celebrar los pasos que estás tomando para cuidar de ti y de tu bebé. En la conclusión del capítulo, vamos a reflexionar sobre todo lo que hemos recorrido hasta ahora y cómo estos pequeños cambios pueden hacer una gran diferencia.

Conclusión del Capítulo

Cuidar de ti misma durante el embarazo es, sin duda, la mejor manera de garantizar no solo un embarazo saludable, sino también una experiencia más positiva y plena en esta etapa transformadora de tu vida. En este periodo, tu cuerpo trabaja incansablemente para nutrir y proteger a la vida que crece dentro de ti, por lo que es fundamental retribuirle dándole lo que necesita para funcionar de la mejor manera posible. Esto comienza con la alimentación: nutrir tu cuerpo con alimentos esenciales no solo asegura que tú tengas la energía necesaria para afrontar los desafíos diarios del embarazo, sino que también proporciona los nutrientes vitales que tu bebé necesita para desarrollarse de manera óptima. Cada bocado saludable es un acto de amor hacia ti misma y hacia tu bebé.

Mantenerte activa también juega un papel crucial. El ejercicio moderado, adaptado a tus circunstancias, no solo ayuda a mantenerte en forma física, sino que también contribuye significativamente a tu bienestar mental. La actividad física durante el embarazo puede mejorar tu estado de ánimo, reducir el estrés y la ansiedad, y preparar tu cuerpo para el parto. Además, mantenerte activa puede aliviar molestias comunes del embarazo, como el dolor de espalda y la hinchazón, y mejorar la calidad de tu sueño. Pero más allá de los beneficios físicos, la sensación de mantenerte conectada con tu cuerpo durante este proceso de cambio te ayudará a sentirte más empoderada y en control de tu experiencia.

Sin embargo, cuidar de ti misma no se limita solo al cuerpo físico. Tu salud emocional es igualmente importante, si no más. El embarazo es un periodo de intensas emociones, y a menudo puede ser abrumador. Es normal experimentar una montaña rusa emocional, que va desde la alegría y la excitación hasta la preocupación y el miedo. Por ello, es esencial que prestes atención a tu bienestar mental y emocional. Tomarte tiempo para relajarte, para conectar con lo que sientes y para buscar apoyo cuando lo necesites es parte integral de un embarazo saludable. Ya sea a través de la meditación, el yoga, o simplemente pasar tiempo en un ambiente tranquilo, encontrar maneras de calmar tu mente y centrarte emocionalmente te preparará mejor para la maternidad.

Un punto clave a recordar es que el bienestar de la madre está profundamente entrelazado con el bienestar del bebé. Cuando tú te cuidas, cuando te alimentas de manera adecuada, te mantienes activa y cuidas de tu salud emocional, le estás dando a tu bebé el mejor comienzo posible. La conexión entre tu cuerpo y el de tu bebé es tan íntima que todo lo que haces por tu salud también lo haces por la de él. Tu cuerpo es el primer hogar de tu hijo, y cuando lo tratas con amor y cuidado, estás creando el ambiente perfecto para que tu bebé crezca y se desarrolle en las mejores condiciones posibles.

Finalmente, el autocuidado durante el embarazo también establece una base sólida para lo que vendrá después: la maternidad. La llegada de tu bebé será un momento lleno de cambios y desafíos, y cuanto mejor preparada estés física y emocionalmente, más fácil será adaptarte a esta nueva etapa. Cultivar el hábito de cuidarte a ti misma desde el embarazo te ayudará a mantener el equilibrio y a seguir priorizando tu bienestar una vez que te conviertas en madre. Porque al final del día, una madre saludable y equilibrada es la mejor madre que un bebé puede tener. Al cuidar de ti misma, estás invirtiendo en el bienestar de ambos.

Al cerrar este capítulo, quiero dejarte con una reflexión personal. El embarazo es un momento en el que a menudo sientes que el mundo espera que lo hagas todo bien, pero aquí va mi consejo: deja espacio para la imperfección. La clave no es ser perfecta, sino ser presente. Disfruta de los momentos de calma, no te castigues en los días difíciles, y sigue adelante con la certeza de que lo que estás haciendo es suficiente. En la próxima sección, me gustaría invitarte a hacer un ejercicio sencillo pero profundo para conectar aún más contigo misma. ¿Te animas?

Consejo del autor: Recuerda que el embarazo no es un proceso perfecto. Habrá días en los que te sientas increíble y otros en los que las molestias sean abrumadoras. Lo más importante es escuchar a tu cuerpo, nutrirlo adecuadamente y mantenerte activa dentro de tus posibilidades. Cada pequeño esfuerzo que hagas en el cuidado de ti misma repercutirá positivamente en la salud de tu bebé.

Después de compartirte este consejo, te propongo un ejercicio que te permitirá ir un poco más allá en tu introspección. Ahora que hemos hablado sobre la importancia de mantener un equilibrio entre la mente y el cuerpo, quiero que te tomes unos minutos para escuchar lo que tu cuerpo y tus emociones te están diciendo. Este ejercicio reflexivo te ayudará a tomar conciencia de cómo te sientes en este preciso momento. Vamos a dar un paso atrás del ruido cotidiano y mirar hacia adentro con amor y paciencia.

Ejercicio reflexivo
Escribe una lista de tres acciones diarias que puedas incorporar a tu rutina para mejorar tu bienestar físico y emocional durante el embarazo. Reflexiona sobre cómo puedes integrar una alimentación equilibrada, el ejercicio y técnicas de relajación en tu vida diaria. Pregúntate:
• ¿Cómo me siento física y emocionalmente hoy?
• ¿Qué puedo hacer para nutrir mejor mi cuerpo y mente?

Con una nueva claridad y conexión contigo misma, volvemos a lo práctico. La reflexión es un paso poderoso, pero también necesitas herramientas tangibles para hacer más fácil y saludable tu día a día. Por eso, en la próxima sección, te comparto algunos tips y trucos sencillos que puedes aplicar hoy mismo para mejorar tu bienestar durante el embarazo. Estos consejos te ayudarán a sentirte más ligera, más energética y, sobre todo, más en sintonía con las necesidades de tu cuerpo. ¡Pequeños cambios que pueden tener un gran impacto!

Tips y trucos

1. **Prepara comidas con anticipación**: Cocinar grandes cantidades de alimentos nutritivos los fines de semana puede facilitar la preparación de comidas durante la semana.

2. **Descanso activo**: Si sientes fatiga, prueba a realizar estiramientos suaves o dar un paseo corto. Esto puede ayudarte a sentirte más enérgica sin agotarte.

3. **Evita saltarte comidas**: Aunque las náuseas matutinas pueden ser un reto, comer pequeñas porciones de alimentos blandos y fáciles de digerir puede mantener tus niveles de energía estables.

4. **Consulta siempre a tu médico**: Antes de comenzar cualquier programa de ejercicio, asegúrate de consultarlo con tu obstetra o médico de cabecera.

Ya tienes algunos trucos bajo la manga para enfrentar este maravilloso viaje, pero sé que a veces puede surgir la necesidad de más información o de buscar el apoyo de expertos. Es por eso que ahora quiero presentarte una lista de recursos adicionales que pueden serte de gran ayuda. Aquí encontrarás lecturas recomendadas, enlaces a sitios confiables y contactos de profesionales que estarán allí para apoyarte cuando lo necesites. Al final del día, estar informada y rodeada de apoyo es uno de los regalos más grandes que puedes darte a ti misma y a tu bebé. ¡Estás en el camino correcto!

Recursos adicionales

- **Libros recomendados**:

  o *Embarazo y nutrición* de Sarah Brewer.

  o *Yoga para el embarazo* de Francoise Barbira Freedman.

- **Aplicaciones útiles**:

  o "MyFitnessPal" (para seguimiento de nutrientes).

  o "Down Dog Prenatal Yoga" (para rutinas de yoga).

- **Guías en línea**:

  o Organización Mundial de la Salud (OMS) – Recomendaciones sobre nutrición y actividad física durante el embarazo.

A medida que avanzas en este recorrido, el lazo con tu bebé se vuelve más fuerte, más profundo. Pero hay un momento que se acerca con rapidez, el cual cambiará tu vida por completo: el parto. Es natural sentir emociones encontradas, desde una inmensa expectativa hasta un pequeño nudo en el estómago de incertidumbre. No estás sola en esto. Al prepararte para el nacimiento, estarás también preparándote emocional y mentalmente para uno de los momentos más poderosos de la vida. Respiramos profundo, juntas, mientras te acompañamos en cada paso de esta preparación. El gran día está más cerca de lo que imaginas.

*"El cuerpo humano es la mejor obra de arte." – **Jess C. Scott***

Capítulo 3

Preparación para el Parto

Preparándote mental, emocional y físicamente para el gran día

El momento del parto es uno de los más esperados y, al mismo tiempo, más desconocidos para muchas futuras madres. Aunque cada experiencia de parto es única, preparar y planificar este evento crucial puede reducir el estrés, proporcionar claridad y aumentar tu sensación de control sobre el proceso. Este capítulo explora los aspectos más importantes para prepararte, desde la creación de un plan de parto personalizado hasta qué esperar durante el trabajo de parto, abordando también las opciones de manejo del dolor.

Creando tu Plan de Parto

Un plan de parto es una herramienta valiosa que permite a la madre expresar sus deseos y preferencias sobre cómo le gustaría que se desarrollara el nacimiento de su bebé. Aunque es importante recordar que el parto puede ser impredecible y no todo saldrá exactamente como se planea, tener un plan te ayuda a sentirte más preparada y en control de las decisiones clave durante el proceso. Este documento también proporciona una guía clara para el personal médico y las personas que te acompañarán, garantizando que todos estén alineados con tus preferencias y necesidades. Además, tener un plan de parto bien estructurado puede reducir la ansiedad, ya que te permitirá visualizar los diferentes escenarios que podrían presentarse y cómo abordarlos.

Tipos de parto

Conocer los diferentes tipos de parto disponibles es esencial para que puedas elegir el que más se ajuste a tus deseos y necesidades. Las siguientes son algunas de las opciones más comunes:

1. Parto vaginal

El parto vaginal es el tipo más común y natural de nacimiento. Durante el parto vaginal, el bebé pasa por el canal de parto para nacer. Este proceso puede durar varias horas, especialmente en madres primerizas, pero generalmente es el más seguro para la madre y el bebé en embarazos de bajo riesgo.

En un parto vaginal, algunas intervenciones médicas pueden ser necesarias para aliviar el dolor o acelerar el proceso si es preciso. La anestesia epidural es una de las formas más comunes de alivio del dolor durante el parto vaginal. Se administra en la zona lumbar para bloquear las sensaciones en la parte inferior del cuerpo, proporcionando un alivio significativo del dolor sin perder la capacidad de participar activamente en el parto. Sin embargo, también existen alternativas sin medicación, como las técnicas de respiración y relajación, que pueden ser utilizadas por mujeres que desean un parto natural. La episiotomía, una incisión quirúrgica en el perineo para facilitar la salida del bebé, es otra intervención que puede ser necesaria en ciertos casos, aunque las recomendaciones actuales sugieren limitar su uso a situaciones estrictamente necesarias (American College of Obstetricians and Gynecologists, 2018).

2. Parto por cesárea

El parto por cesárea es un procedimiento quirúrgico en el que el bebé se extrae a través de una incisión en el abdomen y el útero de la madre. Puede ser programado de antemano o realizarse de manera urgente si surgen complicaciones durante el trabajo de parto. Las razones comunes para una cesárea programada incluyen la posición de nalgas del bebé, placenta previa (cuando la placenta bloquea el canal de parto) o un embarazo múltiple. En algunos casos, la cesárea puede ser preferida para evitar riesgos que el parto vaginal podría representar para la madre o el bebé.

Aunque la cesárea es una cirugía segura y común, requiere un tiempo de recuperación más largo que el parto vaginal, y puede haber riesgos quirúrgicos como infecciones o complicaciones postoperatorias (National Institute for Health and Care Excellence, 2021). Las mujeres que planean una cesárea o creen que podrían necesitar una deben incluir sus preferencias en su plan de parto, como la administración de anestesia y el contacto piel con piel inmediato con el bebé, si es posible.

3. Parto inducido

El parto inducido ocurre cuando el proceso de trabajo de parto no comienza por sí solo y se utilizan intervenciones médicas para iniciarlo. Las razones para inducir el parto incluyen complicaciones como preeclampsia, embarazo prolongado (más de 41 semanas), o si hay problemas con el crecimiento del bebé. Los métodos de inducción incluyen la administración de oxitocina, un medicamento que estimula las contracciones uterinas, o la ruptura artificial de las membranas (romper aguas).

El proceso de inducción puede hacer que el trabajo de parto progrese más rápido que el parto natural, lo que puede aumentar la intensidad de las contracciones y el dolor. Por ello, muchas mujeres que son inducidas optan por algún tipo de alivio del dolor, como la epidural, aunque el manejo del dolor puede variar según la mujer. La inducción debe ser cuidadosamente monitoreada por el equipo médico para asegurar que tanto la madre como el bebé estén seguros durante el proceso (NICE, 2021).

4. Parto en casa o en centros de parto

Algunas mujeres optan por dar a luz en un entorno más íntimo, como en casa o en un centro de partos, en lugar de un hospital. Estos tipos de parto son recomendados únicamente para embarazos de bajo riesgo y suelen estar asistidos por parteras profesionales que están capacitadas para manejar complicaciones menores y derivar a la madre a un hospital si es necesario.

El parto en casa o en un centro de partos puede proporcionar una experiencia más natural y relajada, donde la madre tiene mayor control sobre el entorno. Muchas mujeres que eligen esta opción desean evitar intervenciones médicas a menos que sean absolutamente necesarias. En este tipo de partos, es común utilizar métodos alternativos de alivio del dolor, como el agua caliente (parto en agua), la acupuntura o los masajes. Las investigaciones sugieren que para las mujeres con embarazos de bajo riesgo, el parto planificado en casa o en un centro de partos puede ser tan seguro como el parto hospitalario (de Jonge et al., 2013).

Cómo crear un plan de parto personalizado

A la hora de redactar un plan de parto, es importante considerar todas las posibles situaciones que podrían surgir y cómo te gustaría manejarlas. El plan de parto no solo debe reflejar tus deseos, sino también ser flexible para adaptarse a cambios inesperados. Aquí hay algunas áreas clave que podrías considerar:

1. Preferencias sobre el manejo del dolor

Una de las decisiones más importantes en tu plan de parto es cómo te gustaría manejar el dolor durante el proceso. Algunas mujeres prefieren un enfoque sin medicación, utilizando técnicas de relajación como la respiración profunda, la hipnosis o los masajes para aliviar el dolor. Otras prefieren opciones médicas como la epidural o los analgésicos intravenosos.

Es importante tener en cuenta que, aunque puedes tener una preferencia clara antes del parto, la situación puede cambiar a medida que avanza el trabajo de parto. Muchas mujeres que planean un parto natural deciden usar alguna forma de alivio del dolor cuando las contracciones se vuelven más intensas de lo esperado. Tu plan de parto debe reflejar tus preferencias iniciales, pero también permitirte la flexibilidad para cambiar de opinión si lo consideras necesario durante el proceso.

2. Intervenciones médicas

Determinar tus preferencias sobre las intervenciones médicas es otro aspecto importante. Algunas intervenciones comunes incluyen el uso de oxitocina para acelerar el parto, la ruptura artificial de las membranas o la episiotomía. Algunas mujeres prefieren limitar el uso de intervenciones a menos que sean estrictamente necesarias, mientras que otras se sienten más cómodas con un enfoque más intervencionista.

También es útil incluir en tu plan cómo te sentirías respecto a posibles cesáreas de emergencia u otras intervenciones si el parto no progresa como esperabas. Si estás considerando un parto por cesárea programado, también puedes detallar tus preferencias sobre aspectos como el uso de anestesia, la música en la sala de operaciones o el contacto piel con piel con el bebé inmediatamente después del nacimiento.

3. Entorno del parto

El ambiente en el que te gustaría dar a luz es un aspecto importante para muchas mujeres. Puedes especificar detalles como el tipo de iluminación que prefieres (luz tenue o luz natural), si te gustaría escuchar música relajante, o si prefieres un ambiente más tranquilo y privado. También puedes incluir quiénes te gustaría que estuvieran presentes en la sala de parto, ya sea tu pareja, una doula, familiares o amigos cercanos.

El entorno puede tener un gran impacto en cómo te sientes durante el parto. Algunas mujeres se relajan mejor en un ambiente tranquilo y poco iluminado, mientras que otras prefieren un entorno más estimulante con la presencia de seres queridos. Asegúrate de discutir estos aspectos con tu equipo médico para que tus deseos sean respetados tanto como sea posible.

4. Cuidados para el recién nacido

Tu plan de parto también puede incluir tus preferencias sobre los cuidados inmediatos que te gustaría que recibiera tu bebé. Por ejemplo, muchas madres optan por el contacto piel con piel inmediato después del nacimiento, lo que tiene numerosos beneficios para la vinculación emocional y la regulación de la temperatura corporal del bebé. También puedes detallar tus deseos sobre la lactancia materna, especificando si deseas amamantar tan pronto como sea posible.

Otros aspectos que podrías considerar incluyen la administración de vitamina K o vacunas al bebé poco después del nacimiento, así como tus preferencias respecto al pinzamiento tardío del cordón umbilical, una práctica que ha demostrado tener beneficios para el bebé al permitir un mayor flujo de sangre desde la placenta (McDonald et al., 2013).

5. Flexibilidad

Aunque es importante ser clara con tus deseos, también es fundamental ser flexible. El parto puede desarrollarse de maneras imprevistas, y tu seguridad y la de tu bebé siempre serán la prioridad. Estar abierta a cambios en el plan, como la necesidad de intervenciones médicas que no habías anticipado, puede ayudarte a evitar frustraciones y a mantener la calma si las cosas no salen como esperabas.

Asegúrate de discutir tu plan de parto con tu obstetra o partera, ya que ellos pueden ofrecerte recomendaciones y ajustes basados en tu situación médica particular.

Has dedicado tiempo a imaginar cómo quieres que sea ese momento tan esperado: el nacimiento de tu bebé. Tu plan de parto es una expresión de tus deseos y necesidades, un mapa para guiarte en medio de lo desconocido. Pero, aunque hayas pensado en cada detalle, es importante saber que el trabajo de parto puede tener sorpresas. Y es aquí donde nos detenemos un momento, porque estar preparada no solo significa tener un plan, sino también saber qué esperar y cómo responder a lo que pueda suceder. Así que, mientras tu plan está listo, acompáñame a descubrir los posibles escenarios que el trabajo de parto podría traer consigo.

Qué Esperar Durante el Trabajo de Parto

El trabajo de parto es un proceso fisiológico complejo y extraordinario por el cual el cuerpo de la mujer se prepara para el nacimiento de su bebé. Cada experiencia de parto es única, pero conocer las señales de su inicio y las etapas que lo componen puede ayudarte a sentirte más preparada y confiada. Comprender qué esperar y cómo manejar las diversas fases del trabajo de parto, desde las primeras contracciones hasta el nacimiento, te permitirá afrontar esta experiencia de manera más consciente y controlada.

Señales de que el trabajo de parto ha comenzado

Existen varios signos que indican que el trabajo de parto está comenzando, y reconocerlos puede ayudarte a saber cuándo es el momento de dirigirte al hospital o centro de parto, o cuándo prepararte para las siguientes etapas del proceso.

1. Contracciones regulares

Las contracciones son una señal clara de que el trabajo de parto está comenzando. A diferencia de las contracciones de Braxton Hicks, que son irregulares y tienden a desaparecer con el descanso, las contracciones verdaderas son rítmicas, regulares y aumentan en frecuencia, intensidad y duración con el tiempo. Durante una contracción, el útero se contrae, lo que provoca una sensación de presión en el abdomen o la parte baja de la espalda. Estas contracciones ayudan a dilatar el cuello del útero y empujar al bebé hacia el canal de parto.

Un estudio publicado por Zhang et al. (2010) demostró que, en promedio, las contracciones verdaderas comienzan a intervalos de 10 a 20 minutos, pero progresan rápidamente hasta ocurrir cada 5 minutos o menos, con una duración de entre 60 y 90 segundos cada una. La frecuencia y la regularidad son las características clave que distinguen a las contracciones de parto de las contracciones falsas. Además, estas no desaparecen con el descanso ni cambian de intensidad al cambiar de posición.

2. Pérdida del tapón mucoso

El tapón mucoso es una barrera protectora que se forma en el cuello del útero durante el embarazo para evitar que bacterias y otros patógenos ingresen al útero. A medida que el cuello del útero comienza a dilatarse y afinarse (lo que se conoce como borramiento), el tapón mucoso puede desprenderse y ser expulsado, lo que indica que el cuerpo está preparándose para el parto. La pérdida del tapón mucoso puede ocurrir como un flujo mucoso espeso, transparente o teñido de sangre. Aunque su expulsión no significa que el parto sea inminente, puede suceder horas o días antes de que el trabajo de parto activo comience.

Un estudio en la *Journal of Obstetrics and Gynaecology Research* (2015) señaló que el desprendimiento del tapón mucoso suele acompañar a otros signos del parto temprano, pero no siempre es un indicador fiable de la progresión inmediata hacia el parto activo. Sin embargo, es importante prestar atención a este signo, ya que indica que el cuello del útero está cambiando.

3. Rotura de bolsa

La rotura de la bolsa amniótica, también conocida como "romper aguas", es cuando el saco amniótico que rodea al bebé se rompe, lo que provoca la salida del líquido amniótico. Este suceso puede presentarse como un chorro repentino de líquido o un goteo continuo. Aunque algunas mujeres rompen aguas antes de que comiencen las contracciones, otras pueden experimentar esta ruptura durante las fases avanzadas del trabajo de parto.

Si las aguas se rompen antes de que comiencen las contracciones, es crucial contactar a tu médico o partera, ya que la rotura prolongada de la bolsa amniótica puede aumentar el riesgo de infección. Según las recomendaciones del *American College of Obstetricians and Gynecologists* (2017), la mayoría de las mujeres deben dirigirse al hospital o centro de parto poco después de la rotura de la bolsa, incluso si no han comenzado las contracciones, para monitorear al bebé y evitar posibles complicaciones.

4. Dolor en la parte baja de la espalda

Algunas mujeres experimentan un dolor agudo en la parte baja de la espalda al inicio del trabajo de parto, lo que se conoce como "dolor de espalda del parto". Este tipo de dolor ocurre cuando el bebé está en una posición posterior (mirando hacia la columna vertebral de la madre) y presiona los nervios en la espalda baja durante las contracciones. A diferencia del dolor abdominal que es más común durante las contracciones, el dolor de espalda puede ser más continuo y difícil de aliviar.

El dolor de espalda del parto no es inusual y puede requerir diferentes enfoques para su manejo, como masajes, compresas calientes o cambios en la posición para facilitar que el bebé se mueva hacia una posición más favorable para el parto.

Cuando ir al hospital o centro de Parto

Saber cuándo dirigirse al hospital o centro de parto es una de las decisiones más importantes durante el trabajo de parto. Aunque cada embarazo es diferente y las recomendaciones pueden variar según las circunstancias individuales, aquí hay algunas pautas generales:

- **Contracciones regulares**: Debes ir al hospital cuando las contracciones duren entre 60 y 90 segundos, ocurran cada 5 minutos, y se mantengan regulares durante al menos una hora. Esta es una señal de que estás entrando en el trabajo de parto activo, especialmente si es tu primer bebé. Para las madres que ya han tenido hijos, el intervalo entre las contracciones puede ser más corto antes de llegar al trabajo de parto activo.

- **Rotura de aguas**: Si rompes aguas, ya sea en forma de un chorro o un goteo constante, es importante ir al hospital, incluso si no has comenzado con las contracciones. La rotura del saco amniótico aumenta el riesgo de infección, por lo que es esencial que el equipo médico te evalúe.

- **Sangrado vaginal intenso o emergencia**: Cualquier signo de sangrado vaginal anormal o intenso, mareos, dificultad para respirar o dolor severo no relacionado con las contracciones, debe ser evaluado inmediatamente en un entorno médico. Estos signos podrían indicar una emergencia obstétrica.

Manejo del dolor durante el parto

El dolor es una parte natural del proceso de parto, pero existen diversas opciones para su manejo, desde técnicas naturales hasta métodos médicos. Familiarizarte con las opciones disponibles te permitirá tomar decisiones más informadas y adaptar tu plan de parto según tus necesidades y deseos.

1. Métodos naturales

Muchas mujeres optan por manejar el dolor del parto sin medicación, utilizando técnicas de alivio natural que les permiten mantener el control y la movilidad durante el trabajo de parto. Algunas de las técnicas más comunes incluyen:

- **Respiración profunda y controlada**: La respiración controlada, a menudo enseñada en clases prenatales, puede ayudar a relajar el cuerpo y reducir la percepción del dolor. Al enfocar la respiración, las mujeres pueden mantenerse más calmadas y reducir la tensión durante las contracciones.

- **Uso de pelota de parto**: Sentarse en una pelota de parto (pelota suiza) permite a las mujeres balancearse suavemente, lo que puede ayudar a aliviar la presión sobre la pelvis y la espalda. También ayuda a facilitar el movimiento del bebé hacia el canal de parto.

- **Hidroterapia**: Sumergirse en una tina de agua caliente o una ducha tibia puede aliviar el dolor muscular y proporcionar una sensación de flotación que reduce la presión sobre las articulaciones. Varios estudios han mostrado que la hidroterapia reduce la percepción del dolor y mejora la sensación de bienestar durante el trabajo de parto (Cluett et al., 2018).

- **Masajes y acupresión**: Aplicar presión en puntos específicos del cuerpo, como las caderas o la parte baja de la espalda, puede ayudar a aliviar el dolor. Los masajes proporcionados por la pareja o una doula también pueden ser efectivos para reducir la tensión muscular.

2. Anestesia epidural

La epidural es una opción común para el alivio del dolor durante el parto. Este anestésico se administra a través de una aguja colocada en la parte baja de la espalda y bloquea las señales de dolor desde el abdomen hacia abajo. Proporciona un alivio significativo del dolor sin sedar a la madre, lo que permite que esté despierta y alerta durante el parto.

Sin embargo, la epidural puede limitar la movilidad de la madre, ya que bloquea la sensación en la parte inferior del cuerpo, y en algunos casos, puede ralentizar el progreso del parto. También puede aumentar el riesgo de intervenciones como la oxitocina o el uso de fórceps (Anim-Somuah et al., 2018). Es importante discutir estos posibles efectos secundarios con el equipo médico para tomar una decisión informada.

3. Analgesia intravenosa

Otra opción para manejar el dolor es la analgesia intravenosa, que consiste en la administración de medicamentos para el dolor a través de una vía intravenosa. Estos medicamentos, como el fentanilo, pueden reducir la percepción del dolor sin bloquearlo por completo, y tienen un efecto menos duradero que la epidural. Aunque ofrecen alivio temporal, pueden tener efectos secundarios como somnolencia o náuseas, y pueden cruzar la placenta, afectando al bebé.

4. Otros métodos farmacológicos

En algunas situaciones, se pueden utilizar anestésicos locales para aliviar el dolor en áreas específicas, como el perineo, si se necesita una episiotomía o reparación de desgarros después del parto. También puede considerarse la sedación ligera en casos de parto prolongado o situaciones médicas específicas.

Consejo práctico: Familiarízate con las diversas opciones de manejo del dolor, tanto naturales como médicas, y mantén una mentalidad flexible. El trabajo de parto puede desarrollarse de manera diferente a lo planeado, y tener una mente abierta te ayudará a adaptarte mejor a las circunstancias.

A medida que te adentras en la comprensión de lo que puede ocurrir durante el trabajo de parto, es natural que surjan preguntas, dudas e incluso algunos miedos. Pero recuerda: la preparación es poder, y ahora que tienes una visión más clara de lo que puedes esperar, estarás más equipada para enfrentar ese día con confianza y calma. Llegamos al final de este capítulo, donde resumiremos lo esencial y te dejaremos con una sensación de seguridad sobre el emocionante camino que tienes por delante. No se trata de controlar cada detalle, sino de estar abierta y lista para lo que venga.

Conclusión del Capítulo

La preparación para el parto es un paso crucial en el camino hacia la maternidad. Es un proceso que no solo te ayudará a sentirte más segura y empoderada, sino que también te permitirá abordar el parto con una mayor sensación de control y serenidad. Aunque el parto es, sin duda, un evento físico intenso, la preparación mental y emocional es igualmente importante. Informarte, conocer tus opciones y visualizar el nacimiento de tu bebé de una manera positiva puede transformar esta experiencia en algo menos intimidante y más gratificante. Sentirte preparada te permitirá enfrentar cada contracción, cada decisión, con la confianza de que tienes las herramientas necesarias para tomar las mejores decisiones para ti y tu bebé.

Uno de los aspectos más importantes de esta preparación es la creación de un plan de parto. Este documento no es solo una lista de deseos, sino una forma de comunicar tus preferencias de manera clara y efectiva a tu equipo médico. Al detallar cómo te gustaría que se desarrollara tu parto, desde las intervenciones médicas hasta las técnicas de manejo del dolor, estás garantizando que tu voz sea escuchada en un momento en el que podrías sentirte vulnerable. Si bien el parto puede no seguir siempre el plan al pie de la letra, el simple hecho de haber tomado el tiempo para reflexionar sobre tus opciones y expresar tus deseos te ayudará a sentirte más empoderada. Este plan también fomenta una mejor comunicación con los profesionales que estarán a tu lado durante el parto, creando un entorno de confianza y respeto mutuo.

Conocer las señales del trabajo de parto es otro componente esencial de la preparación. Saber identificar cuándo comienza el proceso y qué esperar en cada etapa puede aliviar gran parte de la incertidumbre y ansiedad que muchas madres experimentan. Entender las fases del parto, cómo cambia tu cuerpo y qué hacer en cada momento te permitirá responder de manera más tranquila y consciente cuando llegue el día. Estar informada sobre las señales tempranas, como las contracciones regulares, la rotura de la bolsa amniótica o los cambios en el cuello uterino, te permitirá tomar acción de manera oportuna y evitará que el miedo o la confusión te superen.

Asimismo, es importante estar familiarizada con las diferentes opciones de manejo del dolor. El dolor del parto es una realidad, pero cada mujer tiene la capacidad de elegir cómo manejarlo. Desde opciones naturales, como la respiración controlada, las posturas y el uso de agua tibia, hasta intervenciones médicas como la epidural, tener conocimiento de estas alternativas te permitirá tomar decisiones informadas en el momento adecuado. No hay una respuesta correcta o incorrecta: lo más importante es que sientas que tienes el poder de elegir lo que mejor funcione para ti en ese momento. Prepararte de antemano te permitirá sentirte más tranquila y segura de que, cuando llegue el momento, sabrás qué camino tomar.

Aunque el parto es, por naturaleza, impredecible, estar bien informada y preparada puede marcar una gran diferencia en tu experiencia. Saber que cuentas con las herramientas, la información y el apoyo necesario te ayudará a enfrentar cualquier cambio o imprevisto con mayor resiliencia y calma. El parto puede presentar desafíos, pero también es una oportunidad única para descubrir tu fuerza interior y conectar profundamente con tu cuerpo y tu bebé.

Finalmente, es fundamental recordar que, aunque el plan y la preparación son importantes, también es esencial mantener una mentalidad flexible. El parto no siempre sigue un guion, y estar abierta a adaptarte a lo que sea necesario es una muestra de fortaleza, no de debilidad. En última instancia, lo más importante es el bienestar tuyo y el de tu bebé. Aceptar que el proceso puede tomar giros inesperados, pero confiar en que estás preparada para manejar lo que venga, hará que este evento tan significativo sea menos intimidante y mucho más empoderador.

Mientras cierras este capítulo en tu mente, me gustaría ofrecerte una pequeña reflexión personal. El parto es un momento poderoso y, aunque puedas planear y anticipar, te invito a dejar espacio para la flexibilidad. A veces, los planes pueden cambiar, y está bien. Confía en tu cuerpo, en tu equipo médico y, sobre todo, en tu instinto. Mi consejo: no te aferres al plan como algo rígido, sino como una guía que te ayudará a sentirte más segura, pero que también puede adaptarse. La clave está en fluir con el momento, en lugar de luchar contra él.

> **Consejo del autor:** El parto es un proceso natural y poderoso. Escucha a tu cuerpo y mantente flexible. No temas pedir ayuda, ya sea para aliviar el dolor o para tomar decisiones durante el trabajo de parto. Recuerda que cada parto es único, y lo más importante es que tú y tu bebé estén seguros.

Para complementar este consejo, quiero invitarte a un ejercicio que te ayudará a conectar con la flexibilidad mental y emocional. Tomarte unos minutos para reflexionar sobre cómo te sientes ante lo desconocido y cómo puedes hacer las paces con la posibilidad de que los planes cambien te dará fortaleza para el día del parto. Este ejercicio reflexivo te ayudará a cultivar una mentalidad de aceptación y serenidad, herramientas fundamentales para cualquier escenario que se presente. Es un momento solo para ti, para respirar y dejar ir las expectativas rígidas.

Ejercicio reflexivo

Reflexiona sobre tus expectativas y miedos en relación al parto. Tómate unos minutos para escribir una carta a ti misma respondiendo a estas preguntas:

- ¿Qué es lo que más me emociona del parto?

- ¿Qué me preocupa o me causa miedo?

- ¿Qué apoyo necesito de mi pareja, familia o equipo médico?

Guardar esta carta te ayudará a conectar con tus emociones y expectativas, y te permitirá aclarar qué tipo de experiencia de parto deseas.

Después de haberte tomado ese tiempo para conectar con tu lado más intuitivo y relajado, volvemos a lo práctico. El trabajo de parto puede ser impredecible, pero hay pequeños trucos y tips que pueden hacer que te sientas más cómoda y en control. En la siguiente sección, te compartiré algunas sugerencias simples que pueden ayudarte a sobrellevar el parto con mayor confianza y tranquilidad. Porque estar preparada también significa tener a mano esas pequeñas cosas que pueden marcar la diferencia cuando llegue el momento. ¡Vamos a por esos tips prácticos!

Tips y trucos

1. **Empaca con anticipación**: Prepara una bolsa para el hospital o centro de parto con al menos un mes de antelación. Incluye ropa cómoda, artículos de aseo personal, documentación médica, y cualquier objeto que te ayude a relajarte (como música o aceites esenciales).

2. **Prueba las técnicas de respiración**: Practica técnicas de respiración y relajación antes del parto. Respirar lenta y profundamente durante las contracciones puede ayudarte a manejar el dolor y mantener la calma.

3. **Habla con tu médico**: Si tienes preguntas sobre algún procedimiento o intervención, no dudes en plantearlas. Tener claridad sobre lo que podría suceder en el parto reducirá el estrés y te permitirá tomar decisiones informadas.

4. **Mantente activa**: Si las condiciones lo permiten, intenta caminar o moverte durante las primeras fases del trabajo de parto. El movimiento puede acelerar el proceso y reducir el dolor.

Ahora que tienes algunos trucos bajo la manga para enfrentar el gran día, es posible que quieras profundizar más o tener más apoyo a tu disposición. Por eso, quiero compartir contigo algunos recursos adicionales que podrían serte útiles en esta etapa. Desde artículos y lecturas recomendadas, hasta enlaces a comunidades y profesionales que pueden brindarte apoyo adicional, todo lo que necesitas para sentirte más informada y acompañada está a tu alcance. ¡Porque estar rodeada de información y apoyo es el mejor regalo que puedes darte antes del nacimiento!

Recursos adicionales

- **Libros recomendados**:

  - *Parto seguro y natural* de Ina May Gaskin.

  - *El gran libro del embarazo* de Silvia de Béjar.

- **Clases prenatales**: Investiga si tu hospital o centro de salud ofrece clases prenatales para prepararte para el parto y aprender técnicas de manejo del dolor.

- **Aplicaciones útiles**:

  o "Full Term – Labor Contraction Timer" (para medir la duración e intensidad de las contracciones).

  o "GentleBirth" (para prácticas de mindfulness y relajación durante el embarazo y el parto).

Y luego llega ese instante, ese momento que recordarás para siempre. El día en que finalmente conocerás a quien has estado esperando con tanto amor. El nacimiento trae consigo una oleada de emociones, de esas que no se pueden describir con palabras sencillas. La alegría, la sorpresa, el miedo... todo se mezcla en una experiencia única. Pero no estás sola en esto, porque ahora te guiaremos paso a paso en los cuidados iniciales de tu bebé, desde ese primer llanto que te llenará de alivio hasta el primer contacto piel con piel, donde ambos comenzarán a conocerse de una manera tan íntima como maravillosa.

*"El nacimiento es el acto más profundo de la creatividad humana." – **Mary Ruckdeschel***

Capítulo 4

El Nacimiento y los Primeros Cuidados

El momento más esperado: cómo enfrentar los primeros días con confianza

El nacimiento de tu bebé es un momento lleno de emoción y, para muchas, también de incertidumbre. Los primeros días, tanto para la madre como para el recién nacido, implican un ajuste importante a nivel físico, emocional y práctico. Este capítulo está diseñado para brindarte una guía clara sobre el posparto inmediato y los cuidados esenciales que tu bebé necesitará durante sus primeros días de vida. Con el apoyo de la ciencia y la experiencia de otras madres, te ayudaremos a comprender mejor este período de adaptación, para que puedas enfrentarlo con mayor seguridad y confianza.

El Posparto Inmediato

El posparto, o puerperio, es el período que sigue al nacimiento del bebé y suele durar alrededor de seis semanas. Durante este tiempo, el cuerpo de la madre comienza a recuperarse de los cambios físicos y hormonales experimentados durante el embarazo y el parto. A nivel emocional, también es una etapa de transición que puede estar acompañada de una variedad de sensaciones intensas. Es fundamental comprender qué esperar en estos primeros días y semanas para facilitar una recuperación saludable, tanto física como emocionalmente.

Qué esperar después del parto

El posparto inmediato implica varios cambios físicos y emocionales. A continuación, se detallan algunos de los aspectos más comunes que las madres experimentan en esta etapa:

1. Cambios físicos

Después del parto, el cuerpo inicia un proceso de recuperación natural que incluye la involución uterina, es decir, la reducción gradual del tamaño del útero a su estado previo al embarazo. Este proceso se produce mediante contracciones denominadas *entuertos*, que pueden sentirse como cólicos menstruales. Estas contracciones son más notorias en mujeres que ya han tenido hijos, y suelen intensificarse durante la lactancia, ya que la hormona oxitocina, que estimula la producción de leche, también provoca la contracción del útero. Según estudios, la oxitocina juega un papel fundamental en la recuperación uterina y en la prevención de hemorragias postparto (Buckley, 2015).

Otro cambio físico importante es la aparición de los *loquios*, que es el sangrado vaginal que ocurre mientras el útero se cura y expulsa los restos de tejido de la placenta.

Este flujo puede durar entre cuatro y seis semanas, pasando de un color rojo intenso a rosa y finalmente blanco o amarillento a medida que disminuye. Es normal que el flujo sea más abundante los primeros días, pero si aumenta bruscamente o presenta un olor fuerte y desagradable, es necesario consultar a un médico, ya que puede ser signo de infección (American College of Obstetricians and Gynecologists, 2021).

2. Dolor y molestias

Si tuviste una cesárea o una episiotomía, es probable que experimentes dolor en el área de la incisión o desgarro. En el caso de una cesárea, la recuperación puede tomar más tiempo, ya que implica una intervención quirúrgica mayor. La recuperación física incluye cuidados específicos para la herida, así como evitar esfuerzos excesivos para permitir una cicatrización adecuada. Es fundamental seguir las recomendaciones médicas sobre el uso de analgésicos y reposo.

En las mujeres que tuvieron un parto vaginal, es común sentir molestias en el perineo, especialmente si hubo desgarros o episiotomía. Para aliviar el dolor, se pueden aplicar compresas frías en la zona, tomar baños de asiento o utilizar medicamentos antiinflamatorios, siempre bajo la indicación médica.

3. Cambios hormonales

Uno de los cambios más marcados durante el posparto inmediato es la abrupta disminución de las hormonas del embarazo, como el estrógeno y la progesterona. Este descenso hormonal puede afectar significativamente el estado de ánimo de la madre. Aproximadamente un 70-80% de las mujeres experimentan el *baby blues*, una condición temporal caracterizada por episodios de llanto, irritabilidad, ansiedad y fatiga. El baby blues suele durar entre dos y tres semanas y está vinculado a los cambios hormonales y al ajuste emocional que implica la llegada del bebé (Bobo et al., 2014).

Sin embargo, si estos síntomas persisten o se agravan, es posible que la madre esté experimentando depresión posparto, una condición que afecta entre el 10% y el 15% de las mujeres. La depresión posparto puede incluir síntomas como tristeza profunda, dificultad para vincularse con el bebé, pérdida de interés en actividades diarias, fatiga extrema y pensamientos negativos. Este trastorno requiere tratamiento y apoyo profesional para garantizar el bienestar de la madre y del bebé (O'Hara & McCabe, 2013).

4. Lactancia

La lactancia es otro desafío común en el posparto inmediato. Los primeros días después del nacimiento son cruciales para establecer la lactancia. Durante estos días, el cuerpo de la madre produce *calostro*, una leche espesa y rica en nutrientes que contiene anticuerpos esenciales para proteger al recién nacido de infecciones. Después de unos días, el calostro se convierte en leche madura, lo que puede provocar congestión mamaria, una sensación de hinchazón y dolor en los senos debido a la acumulación de leche.

Para aliviar esta incomodidad, se recomienda amamantar frecuentemente al bebé, aplicar compresas frías después de las tomas o utilizar un extractor de leche si es necesario. La lactancia no siempre es fácil al principio, y muchas mujeres enfrentan problemas como el dolor en los pezones o la dificultad para que el bebé se agarre correctamente. Buscar el apoyo de una consultora de lactancia o de grupos de apoyo puede ser muy útil durante esta etapa (American Academy of Pediatrics, 2019).

Manejo de las emociones

El posparto inmediato no solo implica la recuperación física, sino también un proceso de ajuste emocional significativo. La llegada de un bebé representa un cambio profundo en la vida de una madre y su familia, lo que puede generar una mezcla de emociones. El agotamiento físico, la falta de sueño y las nuevas responsabilidades pueden contribuir a que las emociones sean intensas y, a veces, abrumadoras. Aquí te presentamos algunas estrategias para manejar estas emociones de manera saludable:

1. Apoyo emocional

El apoyo social juega un papel crucial en la adaptación emocional posparto. Hablar con la pareja, familiares cercanos o amigos de confianza sobre las preocupaciones, emociones y desafíos puede ser de gran ayuda para reducir el estrés y la ansiedad. También es importante permitir que otros te ayuden con las responsabilidades diarias, como el cuidado del bebé, las tareas domésticas o la preparación de comidas, para que puedas descansar y recuperarte físicamente.

Además, los grupos de apoyo para madres pueden proporcionar un espacio para compartir experiencias y recibir consejo de otras mujeres que están pasando por la misma etapa. Estudios han demostrado que el apoyo social durante el posparto está asociado con una mejor salud mental y menor riesgo de depresión posparto (Leahy-Warren et al., 2012).

2. Tiempo para ti

Es fácil para las madres primerizas concentrarse por completo en el cuidado del bebé y olvidarse de sus propias necesidades. Sin embargo, es esencial que también reserves tiempo para ti misma. Un paseo corto, una ducha tranquila o simplemente unos minutos de descanso pueden hacer una gran diferencia en tu bienestar emocional. Según la *American Psychological Association* (2020), dedicar tiempo a actividades que promuevan el autocuidado, aunque sean breves, puede mejorar el estado de ánimo y reducir la sensación de agotamiento.

Pedir ayuda no debe ser visto como una señal de debilidad, sino como una necesidad para garantizar tu bienestar y el de tu bebé. La recuperación posparto requiere tiempo y apoyo, y cuanto más cuides de ti misma, mejor podrás cuidar de tu bebé.

Consejo práctico: Acepta la ayuda de tus seres queridos para las tareas diarias, como cocinar, limpiar o cuidar al bebé. Esto te permitirá disponer de tiempo para descansar, relajarte y concentrarte en tu propia recuperación.

Has dado a luz, y aunque parece que la montaña más alta ya quedó atrás, un nuevo y hermoso desafío comienza: el posparto inmediato. Este es un tiempo de recuperación, tanto física como emocional. Las primeras horas después del parto son cruciales para ti y para tu bebé. Es un momento lleno de emociones intensas, donde empiezas a descubrir lo que significa ser mamá. Pero, mientras te das ese respiro tan necesario, tu pequeño también está adaptándose a su nueva vida fuera del útero. Aquí es donde tu instinto entra en juego: el cuidado de tu recién nacido. A medida que tu cuerpo descansa y se recupera, tu corazón estará listo para guiarte en cada paso de este nuevo rol. Ahora, adentrémonos en lo que necesitas saber para cuidar de ese pequeño ser que depende completamente de ti.

Cuidado del Recién Nacido

Los primeros días con un recién nacido son una etapa de inmenso aprendizaje y descubrimiento. Cada bebé es único, y adaptarse a sus necesidades básicas, como la alimentación, el sueño, el cambio de pañales y el contacto piel con piel, es esencial para establecer una rutina saludable. Aunque el proceso puede parecer abrumador al principio, abordar estas primeras semanas con una actitud tranquila y flexible te permitirá adaptarte mejor a las demandas de tu bebé y crear un vínculo profundo con él.

Alimentación

La alimentación es una de las primeras y más importantes necesidades de un recién nacido. Dado que el estómago de un bebé al nacer es extremadamente pequeño, necesitará alimentarse con frecuencia para obtener los nutrientes necesarios para su crecimiento y desarrollo. Durante las primeras semanas, la alimentación a demanda es clave para garantizar que el bebé esté bien nutrido y para estimular la producción de leche en caso de lactancia materna.

1. Lactancia materna

La leche materna es considerada el alimento ideal para un recién nacido. No solo contiene todos los nutrientes esenciales, sino que también está llena de anticuerpos que ayudan a proteger al bebé de infecciones y enfermedades. La Organización Mundial de la Salud (OMS) recomienda la lactancia materna exclusiva durante los primeros seis meses de vida, promoviendo así un desarrollo óptimo y una salud robusta (OMS, 2020).

- **Frecuencia de las tomas**: Los recién nacidos suelen alimentarse entre 8 y 12 veces al día. Esto se debe a que la leche materna se digiere rápidamente y el bebé necesita alimentarse con frecuencia para satisfacer sus necesidades nutricionales. La clave es alimentar al bebé "a demanda", lo que significa ofrecerle el pecho cada vez que muestre señales de hambre. Entre las señales tempranas de hambre se incluyen chuparse las manos, hacer movimientos de succión y girar la cabeza buscando el pecho (reflejo de búsqueda).

Estudios sugieren que la lactancia a demanda, más allá de garantizar una alimentación adecuada, fortalece el vínculo emocional entre la madre y el bebé, y facilita el establecimiento de la producción de leche a largo plazo (Brown, 2016).

2. Lactancia artificial

En algunos casos, los padres optan o necesitan recurrir a la lactancia con fórmula. Si decides alimentar a tu bebé con fórmula, es importante seguir cuidadosamente las recomendaciones del pediatra y las instrucciones del fabricante para asegurarte de que el bebé esté recibiendo la cantidad correcta de nutrientes.

La lactancia artificial requiere una mayor planificación en cuanto a la preparación y limpieza de los biberones. Es fundamental mantener los utensilios bien higienizados para evitar la introducción de bacterias que puedan afectar la salud del bebé. Las tomas de fórmula suelen ser menos frecuentes que las de la leche materna, ya que la fórmula tarda más en digerirse (Renfrew et al., 2012).

Sueño

El sueño de un recién nacido es muy distinto al de los adultos. Durante las primeras semanas, los bebés duermen entre 16 y 18 horas al día, pero este sueño está dividido en pequeños periodos de dos a tres horas. Este patrón de sueño fragmentado puede ser un desafío para los padres, pero es completamente normal y necesario para el desarrollo del cerebro del bebé.

1. Ciclo de sueño del recién nacido

A lo largo del día y la noche, el sueño del bebé estará dividido en ciclos de sueño profundo y ligero, alternando entre ambas fases con frecuencia. Durante el sueño ligero, los recién nacidos pueden moverse, hacer sonidos o incluso abrir brevemente los ojos. Este tipo de sueño es fundamental para el desarrollo cerebral, ya que es cuando el cerebro procesa la información y consolida los aprendizajes.

Es importante recordar que los ciclos de sueño del bebé cambiarán a medida que crezca. Según un estudio publicado en *Pediatrics* (2015), los patrones de sueño de los bebés se van estabilizando gradualmente en los primeros seis meses, con ciclos de sueño más largos y menos despertares nocturnos.

2. Seguridad al dormir

La seguridad durante el sueño es un aspecto crucial para los recién nacidos. La Academia Americana de Pediatría (AAP) recomienda que los bebés duerman boca arriba, sobre una superficie firme y sin almohadas, mantas pesadas, peluches o cualquier otro objeto que pueda aumentar el riesgo de asfixia o síndrome de muerte súbita del lactante (SIDS). Se recomienda compartir la habitación con el bebé durante los primeros seis meses, pero no la misma cama, para reducir el riesgo de SIDS (AAP, 2016).

Mantener el entorno de sueño libre de riesgos y asegurarse de que el bebé esté en una posición segura cada vez que se duerme son medidas clave para garantizar su seguridad.

Cambio de pañales

Durante los primeros días, tu bebé necesitará cambiarse el pañal con frecuencia. El sistema digestivo de un recién nacido se está adaptando, y el número de pañales que utiliza a diario puede ser alto. Al principio, las heces del bebé estarán compuestas de *meconio*, una sustancia espesa, negra o verde oscura, que es completamente normal. A medida que se establezca la lactancia materna o artificial, las heces cambiarán a un color más claro y una consistencia más suave.

1. Frecuencia

Los recién nacidos pueden necesitar entre 8 y 12 cambios de pañal al día, especialmente en las primeras semanas. Es importante limpiar suavemente el área genital del bebé en cada cambio de pañal para evitar la irritación y la dermatitis del pañal. El uso de productos suaves y específicos para la piel del bebé, como toallitas sin fragancia y cremas barrera, puede ayudar a prevenir problemas de la piel.

2. Cuidado del cordón umbilical

El cordón umbilical del bebé se seca y se cae generalmente entre 1 y 3 semanas después del nacimiento. Durante este tiempo, es esencial mantener la zona limpia y seca para prevenir infecciones. Se recomienda limpiar el área alrededor del cordón con agua tibia y evitar cubrirlo con el pañal, doblándolo hacia abajo para dejar el cordón expuesto al aire. Si notas enrojecimiento, hinchazón o secreción en la zona del cordón, es importante consultar al pediatra, ya que podría ser un signo de infección (Mancini & Jones, 2020).

Contacto piel con piel

El contacto piel con piel es una de las prácticas más recomendadas en el cuidado del recién nacido, especialmente en los primeros días y semanas de vida. Este contacto directo entre el bebé y la madre (o el padre) no solo fortalece el vínculo emocional, sino que también tiene múltiples beneficios físicos y psicológicos tanto para el bebé como para la madre.

El contacto piel con piel ayuda a regular la temperatura corporal del bebé, estabilizar su frecuencia cardíaca y respiratoria, y reducir los niveles de cortisol (la hormona del estrés). Además, esta práctica estimula la producción de leche materna y facilita el establecimiento de la lactancia (Moore et al., 2016).

Se recomienda iniciar el contacto piel con piel lo antes posible, preferiblemente en la primera hora después del nacimiento, y continuar realizándolo con frecuencia durante las primeras semanas. Esta cercanía física también contribuye a calmar al bebé, proporcionándole una sensación de seguridad y bienestar.

Consejo práctico: Es normal sentirse abrumada al principio por las múltiples necesidades del recién nacido. Con el tiempo, aprenderás a reconocer las señales de tu bebé y a responder de manera más eficiente a sus demandas, desarrollando un sentido de confianza en tus capacidades como madre. Recuerda que el cuidado del bebé es un proceso de aprendizaje continuo, y está bien pedir apoyo cuando lo necesites.

A lo largo de este primer encuentro con tu bebé, habrás aprendido que el cuidado no es solo un conjunto de acciones, sino una forma de amar profundamente. Desde los primeros pañales hasta ese contacto piel con piel, cada pequeño gesto fortalece el vínculo entre ambos. Cuidar de un recién nacido es un acto de entrega total, pero también de aprendizaje constante. Al concluir este capítulo, quiero que te lleves la tranquilidad de que cada día será una oportunidad para conocer mejor a tu bebé y a ti misma en este nuevo papel. Ahora, respiremos juntas y celebremos todo lo que ya has logrado en este corto, pero transformador, tiempo.

Conclusión del Capítulo

El nacimiento de tu bebé marca el comienzo de una nueva y transformadora etapa en tu vida, una experiencia que no solo cambia tu cuerpo, sino también tu mundo emocional y mental. Desde el momento en que sostienes a tu bebé por primera vez, una oleada de emociones puede invadirte: desde el amor más puro hasta la incertidumbre y el agotamiento. Estos primeros días, llenos de asombro, pueden ser tan gratificantes como desafiantes, y es fundamental recordar que es normal sentirse abrumada mientras te adaptas a esta nueva realidad. El cuerpo, la mente y el corazón pasan por una fase de ajuste, y prepararte para lo que viene en el posparto puede ayudarte a navegar estos primeros días con mayor serenidad.

El posparto, a menudo llamado el "cuarto trimestre", es una etapa de recuperación tanto física como emocional. Tu cuerpo ha pasado por un esfuerzo increíble durante el parto y necesita tiempo y cuidado para sanar. Es importante que te des permiso para tomarte las cosas con calma y no apresurarte en volver a la "normalidad" de inmediato. El descanso, la buena alimentación y la hidratación son claves para una recuperación saludable. Asimismo, muchas mujeres experimentan cambios emocionales durante este periodo. El "baby blues", una montaña rusa de emociones, es común en los primeros días después del parto debido a los cambios hormonales. Sentirse cansada, sensible o incluso abrumada no es raro. Sin embargo, si estas emociones se prolongan o se intensifican, es importante buscar apoyo, ya que la depresión posparto puede necesitar atención profesional. Cuidar de ti misma es tan crucial como cuidar de tu bebé en estos primeros días.

A la par de tu recuperación, los primeros días de vida de tu bebé son un periodo de adaptación tanto para ti como para tu pequeño. Saber qué esperar, desde los cambios en los patrones de sueño y alimentación hasta cómo interpretar los llantos y las señales de tu recién nacido, te dará mayor confianza. Cada bebé es diferente, pero comprender los aspectos básicos del cuidado del recién nacido —como el agarre correcto durante la lactancia, la frecuencia de las tomas, y la higiene adecuada— te permitirá sentirte más preparada para abordar las demandas diarias. La paciencia es esencial, ya que estos primeros días pueden sentirse caóticos e impredecibles. Tu bebé también está aprendiendo a vivir fuera del útero, y ambos necesitarán tiempo para establecer un ritmo que funcione para ustedes.

Este periodo, aunque agotador, está lleno de oportunidades para crear una conexión profunda con tu bebé. El contacto piel con piel, el tiempo de calidad y simplemente observar y responder a las necesidades de tu pequeño son esenciales para construir ese vínculo especial. Aunque es normal sentir que no lo sabes todo de inmediato, confía en que con el tiempo aprenderás a leer las señales de tu bebé y a responder de manera instintiva. La maternidad es un proceso de aprendizaje continuo, y cada pequeño logro, como un buen agarre en la lactancia o una tranquila siesta del bebé, es una victoria que debe celebrarse.

Es importante recordar que no tienes que enfrentar este periodo sola. El apoyo es fundamental para sobrellevar los primeros días después del nacimiento. Rodearte de personas que te ayuden, ya sea tu pareja, familia o amigos, puede marcar una gran diferencia. Acepta la ayuda que te ofrezcan, ya sea para cuidar del bebé, preparar una comida o simplemente brindarte compañía. También es recomendable mantener una comunicación abierta con tu equipo médico y no dudar en buscar consejo o aclarar dudas sobre la recuperación posparto o el cuidado del bebé. No hay preguntas "tontas" en esta etapa; la información y el apoyo son tus aliados.

Con el tiempo, tanto tú como tu bebé encontrarán un ritmo que funcione. Los días iniciales pueden parecer un torbellino, pero poco a poco, a medida que te recuperas y conoces mejor a tu bebé, las cosas comenzarán a sentirse más manejables. Acepta que la maternidad no se trata de hacerlo todo a la perfección, sino de aprender y adaptarse cada día. La clave está en la paciencia y en ser amable contigo misma durante este proceso de ajuste. Con el tiempo, tu confianza crecerá, y tú y tu bebé desarrollarán una rutina que funcione para ambos, creando una base sólida para los meses y años que vendrán.

En resumen, el nacimiento y los primeros días de vida de tu bebé son una experiencia profundamente transformadora, tanto para tu cuerpo como para tu mente. Aceptar que este es un periodo de ajuste y permitirte el tiempo para sanar y aprender te ayudará a enfrentar esta etapa con mayor calma y confianza. Con paciencia, apoyo y amor, tú y tu bebé encontrarán su propio ritmo, uno que se adaptará a las necesidades y personalidades de ambos, marcando el comienzo de una hermosa nueva etapa en tu vida.

Mientras reflexionas sobre este primer capítulo lleno de emociones y nuevos aprendizajes, quiero compartir un consejo que quizás te ayude a navegar estos días de cambio. El posparto es un proceso tan único como lo es cada madre. Si bien es importante cuidar de tu bebé, nunca olvides que tú también necesitas cuidados. Mi consejo: sé paciente contigo misma. Permítete sentir, descansar y pedir ayuda cuando lo necesites. Ser madre es un trabajo inmenso, pero no tienes que hacerlo todo sola. En la siguiente sección, te propongo un ejercicio que te ayudará a procesar y abrazar esta nueva etapa con más calma y confianza.

> **Consejo del autor:** Recuerda que no existe una manera "correcta" de ser madre. Confía en tus instintos y escucha las necesidades de tu cuerpo y de tu bebé. El posparto es una etapa de adaptación tanto para ti como para tu pequeño, y es normal que los primeros días estén llenos de aprendizajes. Mantén la calma y pide ayuda cuando la necesites.

Con ese consejo en mente, ahora te invito a sumergirte en un ejercicio reflexivo. Sabemos que el posparto puede ser abrumador, con tantas emociones y responsabilidades girando alrededor. Este ejercicio te brindará un espacio para escuchar lo que realmente sientes en tu interior, para ponerle palabras a esas emociones que quizá no has tenido tiempo de procesar. Es una oportunidad de reconectar contigo misma, en medio de esta nueva rutina que estás construyendo. Así que, toma una pausa, respira profundamente y permítete este momento de introspección.

Ejercicio reflexivo
Dedica unos minutos a reflexionar sobre tus primeras semanas con tu bebé. Anota tus pensamientos sobre:
• ¿Qué es lo que más te emociona de conocer a tu bebé?
• ¿Qué aspectos del posparto te generan más incertidumbre?
• ¿Qué apoyo crees que necesitarás en las primeras semanas?
Escribir estas reflexiones puede ayudarte a aclarar tus expectativas y prepararte emocionalmente para esta nueva etapa.

Después de haber conectado contigo misma a un nivel más profundo, es hora de volver a lo práctico. Sabemos que el día a día con un recién nacido puede estar lleno de incertidumbres, pero con algunos trucos sencillos, puedes hacer que todo fluya con más suavidad. En la próxima sección, te compartiré tips útiles que te ayudarán a manejar los pequeños retos cotidianos. Desde trucos para dormir mejor hasta consejos para organizar tu tiempo, estas sugerencias te darán un poco de alivio y te permitirán disfrutar más de este hermoso pero desafiante periodo. ¡A por esos tips!

Tips y trucos

1. **Descansa cuando puedas**: Duerme cuando tu bebé duerma, incluso si es durante el día. El descanso es esencial para tu recuperación posparto.

2. **Cuidado del pecho**: Si amamantas, aplica compresas frías para aliviar la congestión mamaria o usa cremas para pezones agrietados.

3. **Organiza tu entorno**: Ten a mano los artículos esenciales para el bebé (pañales, toallitas, ropa) en un lugar accesible para evitar tener que buscar cosas cuando estés cansada.

4. **Mantén expectativas realistas**: La vida con un recién nacido puede ser impredecible. Acepta que habrá días más difíciles que otros y no te exijas demasiado.

Ya tienes algunos consejos para hacer más llevadero el cuidado de tu bebé y el tuyo propio, pero hay momentos en que un poco más de información o apoyo extra es justo lo que necesitas. Por eso, quiero ofrecerte una lista de recursos adicionales que te serán de gran utilidad. Ya sea que busques guías más detalladas, apoyo de profesionales o comunidades de otras mamás que están pasando por lo mismo que tú, aquí encontrarás herramientas que te ayudarán a sentirte más segura y acompañada. ¡Porque en este viaje no estás sola, y siempre hay manos dispuestas a apoyarte!

Recursos adicionales

- **Libros recomendados**:

  - *El bebé es un mamífero* de Michel Odent.

  - *Crianza con apego* de William Sears.

- **Aplicaciones útiles**:

  - "The Wonder Weeks" (para seguir el desarrollo del bebé).

  - "Baby Tracker" (para registrar alimentación, sueño y cambios de pañal).

- **Grupos de apoyo**: Investiga si hay grupos de apoyo locales para madres primerizas o comunidades en línea donde puedas compartir tus experiencias y recibir consejos.

El primer encuentro ha sido mágico, pero ahora comienza una etapa llena de aprendizaje y paciencia. La alimentación de tu bebé es uno de los aspectos más importantes de su desarrollo, y para ti, un proceso de conexión profunda. Ya sea que elijas lactancia materna o alguna otra opción, cada momento de alimentación será un acto de amor, de dedicación y, a veces, de desafío. Las dudas y preocupaciones son normales, pero en este capítulo te brindaremos las herramientas y el apoyo que necesitas para sentirte segura y confiada en cada decisión que tomes. Recuerda, en cada biberón o toma de pecho, estás dándole mucho más que alimento: le estás brindando tu calor, tu consuelo y todo tu amor.

*"El nacimiento de un hijo es la experiencia más transformadora que una persona puede tener." – **M. J. Rose***

Capítulo 5

Lactancia y Alimentación

Nutriendo a tu bebé con amor y seguridad: tu guía esencial

La alimentación del recién nacido es uno de los aspectos más importantes y discutidos de los primeros meses de vida. Elegir la mejor forma de alimentar a tu bebé, ya sea a través de la lactancia materna, la fórmula infantil o una combinación de ambas, es una decisión que influye no solo en el desarrollo físico del bebé, sino también en el bienestar emocional de la madre. Este capítulo está diseñado para brindarte información basada en la evidencia científica, para que puedas tomar una decisión informada y ajustada a tus circunstancias personales.

Beneficios de la Lactancia Materna

La lactancia materna es reconocida por organismos de salud globales como la Organización Mundial de la Salud (OMS) y la Academia Americana de Pediatría (AAP) como la forma más adecuada y beneficiosa de alimentar a los recién nacidos. La OMS recomienda la lactancia materna exclusiva durante los primeros seis meses de vida y su continuación, junto con la introducción de alimentos complementarios, hasta los dos años o más, dependiendo de los deseos de la madre y el bebé (OMS, 2020). Este enfoque no solo asegura que el bebé reciba los nutrientes esenciales para su crecimiento, sino que también proporciona una variedad de beneficios para su salud física, emocional y cognitiva, así como para la madre.

Ventajas para el bebé

1. Nutrientes ideales

La leche materna contiene una mezcla perfecta de nutrientes, adaptada a las necesidades específicas del bebé en cada etapa de su desarrollo. A lo largo del tiempo, la composición de la leche materna cambia para ajustarse a los requerimientos del bebé. Por ejemplo, en los primeros días, el calostro, una sustancia rica en anticuerpos y nutrientes esenciales, proporciona al bebé una defensa inmunológica crucial. Luego, la leche madura continúa ofreciendo proteínas, grasas saludables, vitaminas y minerales en la proporción ideal. Además, la leche materna es más fácil de digerir que la fórmula, lo que ayuda a prevenir problemas digestivos como el estreñimiento.

La *American Academy of Pediatrics* (2019) ha subrayado que la leche materna es el estándar biológico de referencia en la nutrición infantil, ya que no solo cubre las necesidades nutricionales del bebé, sino que también contiene factores bioactivos que promueven el desarrollo óptimo del sistema inmunológico, digestivo y neurológico.

2. Fortalecimiento del sistema inmunológico

Una de las mayores ventajas de la leche materna es su capacidad para fortalecer el sistema inmunológico del bebé. Está cargada de anticuerpos, especialmente IgA secretora, que protegen al bebé contra infecciones, como diarreas, infecciones respiratorias y otitis media (Victora et al., 2016). Los bebés amamantados tienen menos probabilidades de sufrir infecciones recurrentes en los primeros meses de vida en comparación con aquellos alimentados con fórmula. Además, los estudios muestran que los bebés amamantados tienen menos riesgo de desarrollar enfermedades crónicas más adelante en la vida, como asma, diabetes tipo 1, enfermedades alérgicas y obesidad infantil.

El acto de amamantar también estimula el desarrollo del microbioma intestinal del bebé, lo que refuerza aún más su inmunidad y promueve una salud digestiva óptima. La leche materna fomenta la colonización de bacterias beneficiosas, lo que tiene efectos duraderos en la protección contra enfermedades.

3. Desarrollo cognitivo

La lactancia materna está vinculada a un mejor desarrollo cognitivo a lo largo de la infancia y la adolescencia. Numerosos estudios han encontrado que los bebés amamantados tienden a obtener mejores puntajes en pruebas de inteligencia y tienen mejores resultados académicos en comparación con los niños alimentados con fórmula (Horta et al., 2015). Estos beneficios se atribuyen a los ácidos grasos poliinsaturados de cadena larga (DHA y ARA) presentes en la leche materna, los cuales son esenciales para el desarrollo del cerebro y la retina del bebé.

El *Lancet Breastfeeding Series* (2016) también destaca que el mayor tiempo de lactancia materna se asocia con mejoras en las habilidades cognitivas a largo plazo, lo que respalda el vínculo entre la nutrición temprana y el desarrollo neurológico.

4. Vínculo emocional

El contacto físico cercano durante la lactancia promueve un fuerte vínculo emocional entre la madre y el bebé. Este vínculo, conocido como apego seguro, es fundamental para el desarrollo emocional del bebé y su capacidad para establecer relaciones sociales en el futuro. La proximidad física, el contacto piel con piel y el contacto visual durante la lactancia generan una conexión especial que proporciona al bebé una sensación de seguridad y confianza.

El apego temprano también está relacionado con la producción de oxitocina, la hormona del amor, tanto en la madre como en el bebé. La oxitocina no solo facilita la lactancia al estimular la producción de leche, sino que también reduce el estrés y la ansiedad en ambos, creando un ambiente emocionalmente saludable y de apoyo.

Ventajas para la madre

1. Recuperación posparto

Amamantar no solo beneficia al bebé, sino que también tiene efectos positivos en la recuperación física de la madre después del parto. Durante la lactancia, el cuerpo libera oxitocina, una hormona que estimula las contracciones uterinas. Estas contracciones ayudan al útero a reducirse más rápidamente a su tamaño previo al embarazo y a expulsar los restos del parto, lo que disminuye el riesgo de hemorragias posparto (Buckley, 2015). Además, la lactancia materna promueve la pérdida de peso posparto al consumir calorías adicionales para la producción de leche.

El *National Institutes of Health* (2021) también señala que las mujeres que amamantan suelen experimentar una menor duración del sangrado posparto en comparación con aquellas que no lo hacen, debido a la rápida involución uterina promovida por la lactancia.

2. Reducción de riesgos a largo plazo

La lactancia materna también está asociada con beneficios a largo plazo para la salud de la madre. Numerosos estudios han demostrado que las mujeres que amamantan tienen un menor riesgo de desarrollar ciertos tipos de cáncer, incluidos el cáncer de mama y el cáncer de ovarios. Un análisis de Chowdhury et al. (2015) indicó que las mujeres que amamantaron durante más tiempo tenían una reducción significativa en el riesgo de cáncer de mama. Este efecto protector se atribuye a la supresión de los niveles hormonales que pueden promover el crecimiento de células cancerígenas.

Además, la lactancia materna está vinculada con una menor incidencia de enfermedades cardiovasculares y diabetes tipo 2. Amamantar ayuda a mejorar la sensibilidad a la insulina y reduce los niveles de grasa corporal, lo que protege a la madre contra la obesidad y otros factores de riesgo metabólicos.

3. Beneficios emocionales

La lactancia también puede tener un impacto positivo en la salud mental de la madre. La producción de oxitocina durante la lactancia no solo fomenta el apego con el bebé, sino que también actúa como un modulador natural del estado de ánimo, ayudando a reducir el estrés y la ansiedad en la madre. Estos beneficios emocionales pueden desempeñar un papel clave en la prevención de la depresión posparto, una condición que afecta a muchas mujeres en las semanas o meses después del nacimiento.

La lactancia materna también puede generar un sentimiento de logro y empoderamiento, ya que proporciona a la madre una forma directa de nutrir y proteger a su bebé. Este sentimiento de conexión y bienestar emocional puede ser crucial para fortalecer la autoestima de la madre durante los primeros meses de la maternidad.

Técnicas para una lactancia exitosa

El éxito en la lactancia materna depende en gran medida de un buen agarre del bebé y de una postura adecuada, además de contar con apoyo y recursos para resolver problemas que puedan surgir. Aquí te ofrecemos algunas técnicas que pueden ayudarte a establecer una lactancia exitosa desde el principio:

1. Posicionamiento adecuado

Un agarre y posicionamiento correctos son fundamentales para evitar el dolor en los pezones y asegurar una extracción eficiente de la leche. Asegúrate de que el bebé tome una buena porción de la areola, no solo el pezón, para reducir el riesgo de grietas o irritación en los pezones. Existen varias posiciones que puedes probar para amamantar, como la posición de cuna, en la que el bebé está apoyado en tus brazos; la posición de balón de rugby, que coloca al bebé de lado y debajo del brazo; y la posición acostada de lado, que puede ser útil para las tomas nocturnas.

Es recomendable buscar asesoría con un especialista en lactancia si se experimentan dificultades en el agarre o dolor persistente. Un buen posicionamiento no solo asegura que el bebé obtenga suficiente leche, sino que también previene problemas como la congestión mamaria y la mastitis (Riordan & Wambach, 2016).

2. Frecuencia de las tomas

Alimentar al bebé a demanda es una de las claves para establecer una lactancia exitosa. Durante las primeras semanas, el bebé necesitará alimentarse entre 8 y 12 veces al día. La lactancia a demanda asegura que el bebé obtenga la cantidad adecuada de leche y también estimula la producción de leche en la madre. Además, alimentarlo cuando muestra signos tempranos de hambre, como mover la cabeza hacia los lados, chuparse las manos o abrir la boca, puede ayudar a prevenir el llanto excesivo, que suele ser una señal tardía de hambre.

3. Cuidados del pecho

Es común que las madres experimenten molestias en los pezones o congestión mamaria durante las primeras semanas de lactancia. Para aliviar el dolor, se recomienda aplicar cremas específicas para pezones a base de lanolina o utilizar compresas frías para reducir la inflamación en los senos. Además, es importante asegurarse de que el bebé vacíe completamente un seno antes de cambiar al otro, ya que esto ayuda a prevenir la congestión y a mantener un suministro de leche equilibrado.

Si las molestias persisten o empeoran, es aconsejable consultar a un especialista en lactancia para recibir orientación y resolver posibles problemas de agarre o posicionamiento.

4. Apoyo profesional

Muchas madres encuentran la lactancia desafiante al principio, especialmente si es su primera vez. No dudes en buscar apoyo profesional si tienes dificultades con la lactancia. Un consultor de lactancia certificado puede proporcionarte asesoría personalizada y ayudarte a superar los obstáculos comunes. También es útil unirse a grupos de apoyo locales o en línea para compartir experiencias y obtener consejos prácticos de otras madres.

El apoyo temprano y constante es fundamental para asegurar que la lactancia sea exitosa y gratificante, tanto para la madre como para el bebé (WHO, 2020).

Consejo práctico: La lactancia materna puede ser un proceso desafiante al principio, especialmente si eres madre primeriza. Sé paciente contigo misma y con tu bebé. Recuerda que es normal que ambos necesiten tiempo para adaptarse, y no dudes en buscar ayuda si es necesario.

La lactancia materna es un regalo increíble que fortalece el vínculo entre madre e hijo y ofrece innumerables beneficios, tanto nutricionales como emocionales. Cada toma es una conexión íntima, un acto de amor que nutre a tu bebé y, al mismo tiempo, te llena de una sensación única de plenitud. Sin embargo, sabemos que la lactancia no siempre es posible o la opción más adecuada para todas las madres. A veces, por razones físicas, emocionales o prácticas, hay que buscar otras formas de alimentar a tu bebé, y eso está bien. En la siguiente sección, exploraremos las alternativas a la lactancia materna, recordándote que lo más importante siempre será el bienestar de ambos, sin importar el camino que elijas.

Alternativas a la Lactancia Materna

Si bien la lactancia materna es ampliamente recomendada como la mejor forma de alimentar a los recién nacidos, no siempre es posible o deseable para todas las madres. En estos casos, la fórmula infantil es una alternativa segura y nutritiva que proporciona los nutrientes necesarios para el crecimiento y desarrollo del bebé. Gracias a los avances en la ciencia de la nutrición infantil, las fórmulas han sido formuladas para imitar, en la medida de lo posible, la composición de la leche materna, aunque no pueden reproducir completamente sus propiedades inmunológicas y protectoras.

Fórmula infantil

Las fórmulas infantiles están diseñadas para cubrir las necesidades nutricionales de los bebés cuando la lactancia materna no es viable. Estas fórmulas contienen una mezcla balanceada de proteínas, carbohidratos, grasas, vitaminas y minerales, y están reguladas para garantizar su seguridad y adecuación nutricional. Aunque no proporcionan los anticuerpos que se encuentran en la leche materna, las fórmulas actuales han avanzado significativamente para ofrecer una opción viable y saludable.

1. Ventajas de la fórmula infantil

Aunque la leche materna es única en sus propiedades, la fórmula infantil ofrece varios beneficios prácticos que pueden ser importantes para algunas familias:

- **Flexibilidad**: La alimentación con fórmula permite que otros miembros de la familia, como el padre, abuelos o cuidadores, participen en la alimentación del bebé. Esto no solo facilita el descanso y la recuperación de la madre, sino que también permite que otros miembros del hogar se involucren en la alimentación y el cuidado del bebé. Esto es especialmente útil para madres que regresan al trabajo temprano o que necesitan compartir las responsabilidades de alimentación.

- **Mayor control sobre las tomas**: La fórmula permite medir con precisión la cantidad de leche que consume el bebé en cada toma. Esto puede ser tranquilizador para los padres que desean asegurarse de que el bebé esté recibiendo la cantidad adecuada de alimento. Según la *Academia Americana de Pediatría* (2019), una ventaja importante de la fórmula es que la cantidad exacta que el bebé consume puede ser monitoreada, lo que ayuda a los padres a identificar posibles problemas con la alimentación más fácilmente.

- **Menos restricciones dietéticas para la madre**: Las madres que optan por la alimentación con fórmula no necesitan preocuparse por cómo su dieta o consumo de medicamentos pueden afectar la leche materna. Aunque las restricciones dietéticas durante la lactancia suelen ser mínimas, algunas madres prefieren la libertad que ofrece la fórmula en este sentido.

2. Tipos de fórmula

No todas las fórmulas infantiles son iguales, y existen diferentes tipos diseñados para satisfacer necesidades específicas. Es importante elegir la fórmula más adecuada para el bebé según sus necesidades de salud y bajo la guía del pediatra.

- **Fórmulas a base de leche de vaca**: Estas son las fórmulas más comunes y están diseñadas para ser lo más parecidas posible a la leche materna en términos de composición nutricional. La mayoría de los bebés sanos pueden consumir este tipo de fórmula, que contiene proteínas de la leche de vaca que han sido modificadas para facilitar la digestión del bebé. Estas fórmulas también contienen carbohidratos como la lactosa y grasas esenciales para el desarrollo cerebral y el crecimiento del bebé.

- **Fórmulas sin lactosa**: Estas fórmulas están diseñadas para bebés que tienen intolerancia a la lactosa, el azúcar presente en la leche. Aunque la intolerancia a la lactosa es rara en los bebés, algunos pueden tener dificultades para digerirla, lo que puede provocar síntomas como diarrea, gases o malestar estomacal. Las fórmulas sin lactosa sustituyen este carbohidrato por otros, como la glucosa, para facilitar la digestión (Vandenplas et al., 2015).

- **Fórmulas a base de soja**: Estas son una alternativa para los bebés con alergias a las proteínas de la leche de vaca o para familias que prefieren una opción no derivada de productos animales. Las fórmulas de soja contienen proteínas de soya modificadas y están enriquecidas con nutrientes esenciales. Sin embargo, no son recomendadas para todos los bebés, ya que algunos estudios han sugerido que las fórmulas de soja podrían no ser adecuadas en ciertos casos, especialmente para bebés prematuros o con problemas específicos de salud (Vandenplas et al., 2015).

3. Cómo preparar la fórmula correctamente

Es esencial seguir buenas prácticas de higiene y preparación para garantizar que la fórmula infantil sea segura y esté libre de contaminantes. Aquí hay algunas pautas fundamentales:

- **Seguir las instrucciones del fabricante**: Cada fórmula viene con instrucciones específicas de preparación que deben seguirse al pie de la letra. Esto incluye la cantidad de agua que debe mezclarse con el polvo o el concentrado. Agregar demasiada o muy poca agua puede alterar el equilibrio nutricional de la fórmula y afectar la salud del bebé.

- **Usar agua segura**: Si vives en una zona donde el agua del grifo no es segura o no estás segura de su calidad, es recomendable usar agua hervida o agua embotellada específicamente para la preparación de alimentos infantiles. El uso de agua no tratada puede aumentar el riesgo de infecciones o enfermedades en el bebé.

- **Higiene adecuada**: Lávate siempre las manos antes de preparar los biberones y asegúrate de que los biberones y las tetinas estén bien esterilizados. Los biberones sucios o mal lavados pueden albergar bacterias que podrían ser peligrosas para el bebé. La *Academia Americana de Pediatría* (2019) recomienda esterilizar los biberones y las tetinas antes del primer uso y luego lavarlos con agua caliente y jabón entre las tomas.

- **No reutilizar la fórmula sobrante**: Cualquier fórmula que quede sin consumir después de una toma debe desecharse. La fórmula preparada puede desarrollar bacterias si se deja a temperatura ambiente durante más de una hora, lo que podría provocar enfermedades gastrointestinales en el bebé.

Cómo tomar la mejor decisión

Decidir entre la lactancia materna y la alimentación con fórmula es un proceso profundamente personal. Hay muchos factores que pueden influir en esta decisión, desde las condiciones de salud de la madre o el bebé hasta las necesidades prácticas y las preferencias familiares. Es esencial que las madres sientan que tienen el apoyo y la información necesarios para tomar la decisión que mejor se adapte a sus circunstancias.

- **Salud de la madre**: Algunas madres pueden tener condiciones médicas que dificultan o impiden la lactancia materna, como infecciones que pueden transmitirse a través de la leche o el uso de medicamentos que son incompatibles con la lactancia. En estos casos, la fórmula infantil puede ser la mejor opción para garantizar la seguridad tanto de la madre como del bebé.

- **Regreso al trabajo**: Muchas madres eligen la fórmula o una combinación de lactancia y fórmula para poder adaptarse a las demandas laborales. Si bien es posible extraer leche materna y almacenarla, algunas madres encuentran que la fórmula ofrece una mayor flexibilidad cuando vuelven al trabajo.

- **Preferencias individuales**: Algunas madres pueden simplemente no sentirse cómodas con la lactancia materna o prefieren la fórmula por razones personales. Lo importante es que cada madre pueda tomar una decisión informada y sin presión externa. La *American Psychological Association* (2020) enfatiza que la elección de alimentación debe ser la que mejor se ajuste a las necesidades físicas y emocionales de la madre y el bebé.

Independientemente de la opción que se elija, es fundamental que las madres reciban apoyo y comprensión, ya que tanto la lactancia materna como la fórmula infantil pueden proporcionar una nutrición adecuada para el crecimiento y desarrollo del bebé.

Consejo práctico: La decisión sobre cómo alimentar a tu bebé no debe estar influenciada por presiones externas o comparaciones con otras madres. Cada familia es única, y lo que funciona mejor para ti y tu bebé es lo que importa. No dudes en buscar el apoyo de profesionales de la salud o de grupos de apoyo si necesitas ayuda para tomar esta decisión o si deseas combinar ambas formas de alimentación.

Ya sea que decidas optar por la lactancia materna o una alternativa, la decisión que tomes será la mejor para ti y para tu bebé. Al final del día, lo esencial es que ambos estén sanos, felices y conectados. Lo que has aprendido aquí te brinda el poder de decidir con confianza, sabiendo que cada opción tiene sus beneficios. Con esto en mente, cerramos este capítulo, reafirmando que el amor y el cuidado que ofreces en cada toma, sin importar la forma, es lo que realmente importa. Ahora, tomemos un momento para reflexionar sobre lo que significa alimentar desde el corazón.

Conclusión del Capítulo

La alimentación del recién nacido es, sin duda, uno de los pilares fundamentales para su crecimiento, desarrollo y bienestar. Desde el momento en que tu bebé llega al mundo, su nutrición se convierte en una de tus principales preocupaciones. Es a través de la alimentación que no solo se le proporcionan los nutrientes esenciales para crecer, sino que también se fortalece el vínculo entre madre e hijo, especialmente durante la lactancia. La leche materna es reconocida como el alimento óptimo para los recién nacidos, ya que contiene una mezcla única de anticuerpos, enzimas y nutrientes que no solo satisfacen las necesidades nutricionales del bebé, sino que también refuerzan su sistema inmunológico. Además, la lactancia tiene beneficios emocionales tanto para el bebé como para la madre, creando un espacio de conexión y cercanía inigualable.

Sin embargo, la lactancia materna, aunque ideal en muchos casos, no siempre es posible o no siempre es la opción elegida, y es importante normalizar estas situaciones. Las madres pueden enfrentar diversos desafíos en el camino de la lactancia, como problemas de agarre, producción insuficiente de leche, o condiciones médicas que dificultan el proceso. En otras ocasiones, simplemente puede no ser la opción más adecuada para la madre o la familia debido a circunstancias personales o laborales. Aquí es donde la fórmula infantil se convierte en una alternativa segura, nutritiva y perfectamente válida para alimentar al bebé. La fórmula moderna está diseñada para imitar los nutrientes esenciales que la leche materna proporciona, asegurando que el bebé reciba lo que necesita para desarrollarse de manera saludable.

Lo esencial en este tema es que cada madre y cada familia puedan tomar la decisión que mejor se adapte a sus circunstancias particulares. No existe una solución única que funcione para todas las familias. Lo que es crucial es que la madre se sienta apoyada e informada en su decisión, ya sea continuar con la lactancia materna, recurrir a la fórmula o incluso combinar ambas opciones. La salud y el bienestar tanto de la madre como del bebé deben ser siempre la prioridad principal en este proceso. Una madre bien informada y que se siente segura en su elección tendrá un mayor bienestar emocional, lo cual, a su vez, influye positivamente en el cuidado y la conexión con su bebé.

Es importante recordar que la lactancia y la alimentación en general no deben ser una fuente de presión o culpa para las madres. A menudo, la sociedad crea expectativas muy altas sobre cómo debería ser la experiencia de alimentar a un bebé, pero cada madre tiene una realidad diferente. Si bien la lactancia materna es la recomendación más común debido a sus beneficios, no todas las madres pueden o desean seguir ese camino, y eso está bien. Lo más importante es que el bebé esté alimentado y sano, y que la madre esté tranquila y apoyada en su decisión. Ya sea a través de la lactancia materna, la fórmula o una combinación de ambas, lo más relevante es que el bebé reciba el amor, el cuidado y la atención que necesita.

Además, el proceso de alimentación, independientemente del método elegido, es una oportunidad para fortalecer el vínculo afectivo con el bebé. El tiempo que se pasa alimentándolo, ya sea amamantando o dando el biberón, es un momento de conexión, en el que el bebé se siente seguro, amado y protegido. Estos momentos de intimidad son igual de valiosos y esenciales para su desarrollo emocional, sin importar si el alimento proviene del pecho o de una botella. Lo que realmente importa es la calidad del tiempo que pasas con tu bebé, el contacto visual, las caricias, el tono de tu voz y la cercanía física que lo hacen sentir amado y protegido.

Por último, la flexibilidad y la capacidad de adaptarse a las necesidades cambiantes son clave en esta etapa. Los primeros meses con un recién nacido están llenos de ajustes, tanto para el bebé como para los padres, y la alimentación es solo una parte de este proceso. Es importante mantenerse abierta a las posibilidades y confiar en que, al final, encontrarás el equilibrio que funcione mejor para ti y tu bebé. Ya sea a través de la lactancia materna, la fórmula infantil o una combinación de ambas, lo fundamental es que ambos estén sanos y felices.

En resumen, la alimentación del recién nacido es una de las decisiones más importantes que tomarás como madre, pero no tiene que ser una fuente de estrés. La clave es informarse, escuchar tu instinto y tomar la decisión que mejor se ajuste a las necesidades de tu familia. Ya sea que elijas la lactancia materna, la fórmula o ambas, lo más importante es que la salud y el bienestar tanto del bebé como de la madre siempre sean la prioridad. Con el apoyo adecuado y una decisión bien fundamentada, esta etapa será una oportunidad para construir una conexión fuerte y saludable con tu bebé, independientemente del método de alimentación que elijas.

Al concluir esta reflexión sobre la alimentación de tu bebé, quiero dejarte con un consejo muy personal: no te castigues por las decisiones que tomes. La maternidad está llena de caminos y cada uno tiene sus retos y recompensas. Mi consejo es que sigas lo que te haga sentir más tranquila y en paz. Confía en ti, en tus instintos, y recuerda que no hay una única manera correcta de hacer las cosas. Ser madre es un acto de amor constante, y ese amor es lo que define cada una de tus decisiones.

Consejo del autor: No te presiones a ti misma para cumplir con estándares externos en relación a la lactancia. Escucha a tu cuerpo y a tu bebé, y busca apoyo cuando lo necesites. La maternidad no es una experiencia lineal y perfecta; cada madre y bebé tienen su propio ritmo. Lo importante es que ambos estén saludables y felices.

Después de recibir este consejo, te invito a hacer una pausa y sumergirte en un ejercicio reflexivo que te ayudará a conectar con tus emociones y pensamientos. Alimentar a tu bebé, ya sea mediante lactancia o fórmula, es una de las experiencias más profundas que vivirás, y cada madre siente y experimenta este proceso de manera única. Este ejercicio te permitirá escuchar tus propias necesidades y emociones, para que encuentres la serenidad en las decisiones que tomes, libres de juicio o presión externa. Vamos a tomarnos unos minutos para mirar hacia adentro.

<table>
<tr><td>

Ejercicio reflexivo

</td></tr>
<tr><td>

Reflexiona sobre tus expectativas en relación a la lactancia o la alimentación con fórmula. Responde las siguientes preguntas:

</td></tr>
<tr><td>

- ¿Qué es lo que más te emociona o te preocupa sobre la lactancia?

</td></tr>
<tr><td>

- ¿Cómo te sientes con respecto a la fórmula infantil como opción?

</td></tr>
<tr><td>

- ¿Qué tipo de apoyo necesitarás para alcanzar tus objetivos de alimentación?

</td></tr>
<tr><td>

Escribir estas respuestas puede ayudarte a aclarar tus pensamientos y a identificar el tipo de apoyo que necesitarás en el proceso.

</td></tr>
</table>

Después de haber reflexionado, es momento de pasar a lo práctico. Cada etapa de la maternidad trae consigo pequeños desafíos, y la alimentación no es la excepción. En la siguiente sección, te compartiré algunos tips y trucos que te ayudarán a hacer este proceso más fácil, ya sea que amamantes o alimentes con fórmula. Estos consejos te permitirán gestionar mejor tu tiempo, reducir el estrés y disfrutar más de esos momentos de conexión con tu bebé. Recuerda, lo importante es que ambos estén tranquilos y bien cuidados.

Tips y trucos

1. **Busca apoyo temprano**: Si tienes dificultades con la lactancia, no esperes para pedir ayuda. Consultar con un especialista en lactancia o un grupo de apoyo puede resolver problemas comunes rápidamente.

2. **Asegúrate de descansar**: La alimentación, ya sea por lactancia o fórmula, puede ser demandante, especialmente al principio. No dudes en pedir ayuda a tu pareja o familiares para que puedas descansar.

3. **Crea un espacio cómodo**: Si estás amamantando, organiza un lugar cómodo en tu hogar donde puedas relajarte mientras alimentas a tu bebé. Tener agua a mano y una almohada para lactancia puede hacer que el proceso sea más placentero.

4. **Hidratación**: Mantente bien hidratada, especialmente si estás amamantando, ya que la producción de leche requiere un aumento en el consumo de líquidos.

Ya tienes algunos trucos prácticos en tu arsenal, pero es normal que a veces necesites más información o apoyo adicional. Por eso, en la siguiente sección te ofrezco una lista de recursos adicionales, desde artículos sobre técnicas de alimentación hasta comunidades de apoyo para mamás. Tener a tu disposición información confiable y una red de personas que te entiendan puede marcar una gran diferencia en cómo te sientes en este camino. No olvides que, aunque eres increíblemente fuerte, siempre es válido buscar ayuda y apoyo cuando lo necesites. ¡Vamos a explorar los recursos que están aquí para ti!

Recursos adicionales

- **Libros recomendados**:
  - *Un regalo para toda la vida* de Carlos González.
  - *El arte femenino de amamantar* de La Liga de la Leche Internacional.

- **Aplicaciones útiles**:
  - "LactApp" (para seguimiento y consejos sobre lactancia).
  - "Baby Tracker" (para registrar tomas de leche, cambios de pañal y sueño).

- **Grupos de apoyo**:
  - *La Liga de la Leche Internacional*: Organización dedicada a brindar apoyo y recursos sobre la lactancia materna.
  - Grupos locales de apoyo a la lactancia, donde puedes conectarte con otras madres que atraviesan situaciones similares.

Al cuidar de tu bebé, es fácil olvidar que tú también necesitas cuidados. Ser madre es un trabajo inigualable, pero también puede ser agotador, tanto física como emocionalmente. No te sientas culpable por sentirte desbordada o por necesitar un respiro. Ahora más que nunca, tu salud mental es vital para ti y para tu pequeño. Este es un recordatorio amoroso de que eres humana y mereces el mismo amor y atención que estás dando. En el siguiente capítulo, exploraremos cómo cuidar de tu mente y de tus emociones, porque una mamá feliz es el mejor regalo que puedes darle a tu bebé.

"La lactancia no es sólo cuestión de nutrición, es también un acto de amor." – **Carlos González**

Capítulo 6

Cuidando de tu Salud Mental

Ser madre sin perderte a ti misma: claves para mantener el equilibrio emocional

La llegada de un bebé trae consigo una mezcla de emociones intensas, desde la alegría y el amor hasta el agotamiento y la incertidumbre. Adaptarse a la nueva vida de madre implica muchos cambios, no solo físicos, sino también emocionales y psicológicos. En este capítulo, exploraremos cómo cuidar de tu salud mental durante esta etapa crucial, con especial atención a la adaptación a la vida de mamá y la importancia de identificar y manejar la depresión posparto. Cuidarte a ti misma es clave para cuidar bien a tu bebé, por lo que es esencial poner atención a tu bienestar emocional.

Adaptación a la Vida de Mamá

La transición hacia la maternidad es una de las experiencias más profundas y transformadoras que puede vivir una mujer. De un momento a otro, tus prioridades cambian por completo, y gran parte de tu energía y atención se dirigen hacia el cuidado de tu bebé. Esta etapa puede ser tanto gratificante como desafiante, ya que muchas madres se encuentran lidiando con una nueva identidad mientras buscan mantener su bienestar personal. Encontrar un equilibrio entre las exigencias del cuidado del bebé y el tiempo para ti misma es fundamental no solo para tu salud física, sino también para tu salud mental y emocional.

El desafío del equilibrio

La maternidad es una responsabilidad que, especialmente en los primeros meses, parece absorber toda tu atención y energía. Con frecuencia, las madres se enfrentan a expectativas elevadas, tanto autoimpuestas como externas, sobre lo que significa ser una "buena madre". Estas expectativas pueden generar sentimientos de frustración o agotamiento, particularmente si sientes que no cumples con tus propias normas o con las que la sociedad impone. Reconocer y aceptar que la maternidad es un proceso de aprendizaje continuo puede aliviar parte de esa presión.

1. Autoexpectativas realistas

Las expectativas poco realistas son una fuente común de estrés para muchas madres. La idea de ser una "supermamá", capaz de manejar todas las responsabilidades sin dificultad, es un mito que puede llevar al agotamiento y a sentimientos de inadecuación. Es normal cometer errores, sentirse abrumada o tener días difíciles. La maternidad es una experiencia que evoluciona constantemente, y no existe una forma perfecta de abordarla.

Estudios han mostrado que las madres que establecen expectativas más realistas para sí mismas y aceptan que no necesitan tener el control de todo tienden a tener mejor bienestar emocional y a experimentar menos síntomas de depresión y ansiedad (Beck, 2001). Parte de este proceso implica ser amable contigo misma y aceptar que los desafíos forman parte del crecimiento como madre.

2. Tiempo para ti

El autocuidado no es un lujo, es una necesidad. A menudo, las madres se sienten culpables por dedicar tiempo a sí mismas, pensando que están restando atención a su bebé. Sin embargo, es fundamental que encuentres momentos para hacer actividades que disfrutes o que te ayuden a relajarte. Tomarte pequeños descansos puede tener un impacto significativo en tu bienestar emocional. Ya sea leer, dar un paseo, meditar o simplemente descansar, estas actividades son esenciales para recargar energías y evitar el agotamiento.

Un estudio sobre salud materna encontró que las madres que se reservan tiempo para actividades de autocuidado informan menos estrés y una mayor satisfacción en su rol como madres (Pritchard et al., 2014). Estos momentos no solo te permiten reconectar contigo misma, sino que también te preparan para estar más presente y disponible emocionalmente para tu bebé.

3. Cuidar tu cuerpo

El ejercicio físico es una herramienta poderosa para mejorar tanto la salud física como mental. Aunque es fácil relegar la actividad física cuando estás ocupada cuidando de un bebé, hacer ejercicio suave puede tener enormes beneficios. Actividades como caminar, practicar yoga o hacer ejercicios de estiramiento no solo te ayudan a mantenerte en forma, sino que también liberan endorfinas, los químicos del cerebro que mejoran el estado de ánimo y combaten la fatiga (Dunn et al., 2005).

Además del ejercicio, una alimentación equilibrada es esencial para mantener tus niveles de energía. El posparto puede ser una etapa física y emocionalmente agotadora, y asegurarte de que estás nutriendo tu cuerpo adecuadamente puede marcar una gran diferencia. Una dieta rica en proteínas, frutas, verduras y grasas saludables te ayudará a recuperar fuerzas y a manejar mejor el estrés diario. Estudios en nutrición posparto indican que las madres que siguen una dieta equilibrada tienen menos riesgo de experimentar síntomas depresivos y se sienten más energizadas (Bodnar et al., 2009).

4. Red de apoyo

El apoyo social es un factor crucial para mantener un equilibrio saludable en la maternidad. Las madres a menudo pueden sentir la necesidad de manejar todas las responsabilidades por sí solas, pero pedir ayuda es no solo válido, sino esencial para evitar el agotamiento. Ya sea tu pareja, familiares, amigos o grupos de apoyo para madres, compartir tus experiencias, preocupaciones y desafíos te puede proporcionar un gran alivio.

Los estudios muestran que las madres con un sistema de apoyo fuerte tienen menos probabilidades de experimentar depresión posparto y mayor satisfacción en su rol maternal (Leahy-Warren et al., 2012). Además, delegar algunas de las tareas del hogar o del cuidado del bebé a otros miembros de la familia puede darte el tiempo necesario para descansar o dedicarte a ti misma.

Estrategias para el autocuidado

El autocuidado no siempre requiere de grandes inversiones de tiempo o energía. Implementar pequeñas estrategias en tu día a día puede ayudarte a mantener el equilibrio y reducir el estrés.

1. Establece límites

Uno de los primeros pasos hacia un autocuidado efectivo es aprender a establecer límites. No es necesario aceptar todas las invitaciones o asumir todas las responsabilidades. Aprende a decir "no" cuando te sientas sobrecargada o necesites tiempo para ti. Establecer límites saludables con tus seres queridos y con tus actividades diarias te permitirá reservar energía y tiempo para lo que realmente importa.

Investigaciones sobre el bienestar materno subrayan la importancia de establecer límites para evitar el agotamiento emocional. Las madres que establecen límites claros tienen más probabilidades de mantener su salud mental a lo largo del tiempo (Giallo et al., 2013).

2. División de responsabilidades

Si tienes pareja, es importante que ambos compartan las responsabilidades del cuidado del bebé y las tareas del hogar. El trabajo en equipo es esencial para garantizar que ambos puedan descansar y mantener un equilibrio saludable. Las madres que asumen todas las responsabilidades corren un mayor riesgo de experimentar fatiga crónica, lo que a su vez puede afectar su salud física y mental.

Un estudio publicado en *Family Relations* (2018) encontró que las parejas que compartían de manera equitativa las tareas del hogar y el cuidado del bebé reportaban mayor satisfacción en su relación y menos estrés general. La división de responsabilidades no solo mejora el bienestar de la madre, sino también fortalece la relación con la pareja, creando un entorno más equilibrado y cooperativo.

3. Prácticas de relajación

Técnicas como la meditación, el mindfulness y la respiración profunda pueden ser de gran ayuda para reducir el estrés diario de la maternidad. Estas prácticas permiten a las madres encontrar momentos de calma en medio de las demandas cotidianas, ayudándolas a relajarse y reenfocarse. La meditación y el mindfulness, en particular, han demostrado ser eficaces en la reducción del estrés y la ansiedad, incluso en situaciones de alta demanda (Duncan et al., 2017).

El mindfulness, que consiste en centrarse en el momento presente sin juzgarlo, puede ayudar a reducir el "ruido mental" y a aceptar las emociones y pensamientos tal como son. Incluso dedicar solo unos minutos al día a estas prácticas puede tener un impacto positivo en tu bienestar emocional y ayudarte a manejar el estrés.

Consejo práctico: El autocuidado no debe ser visto como un lujo, sino como una parte esencial de la maternidad. Al cuidar de ti misma, también estás cuidando de tu bebé. Aunque al principio pueda parecer difícil encontrar tiempo para ti en medio de las nuevas demandas, pequeños momentos de autocuidado, como una breve caminata, leer un capítulo de un libro o simplemente sentarte a disfrutar de una taza de té, pueden marcar una gran diferencia en tu bienestar general. Recuerda que una madre más feliz y equilibrada puede ofrecer un mejor cuidado a su bebé.

La llegada de un bebé transforma todo tu mundo. Aprender a adaptarte a la vida como mamá es un viaje lleno de momentos de amor profundo, pero también de desafíos inesperados. Estás descubriendo una nueva versión de ti misma: más fuerte, más capaz, pero también, a veces, más vulnerable. Y aunque la maternidad trae consigo una alegría inmensa, es normal que algunos días no se sientan como imaginabas. Para muchas mujeres, esa adaptación puede venir acompañada de una tristeza inexplicable, una nube que parece opacar la luz. Es importante que hablemos de la depresión posparto, un tema que suele ser ignorado pero que afecta a muchas madres. Aquí, no estás sola. Vamos a entender más sobre este tema para que, si es tu caso, puedas enfrentarlo con valentía y el apoyo adecuado.

Depresión Posparto

El período posparto es una etapa de intensos cambios físicos y emocionales. Si bien el nacimiento de un bebé trae alegría y nuevas experiencias, también puede desencadenar dificultades de salud mental. Muchas madres experimentan lo que se conoce como *baby blues*, una respuesta emocional leve y transitoria que dura aproximadamente dos semanas después del parto. Sin embargo, cuando los sentimientos de tristeza, ansiedad o desesperanza persisten o empeoran, puede tratarse de una condición más grave conocida como *depresión posparto*. Esta es una forma de depresión clínica que requiere atención y tratamiento profesional para garantizar el bienestar de la madre y su capacidad para cuidar de su bebé.

Reconocer los síntomas

La depresión posparto afecta aproximadamente a 1 de cada 7 mujeres, lo que la convierte en una condición relativamente común (O'Hara & Wisner, 2014). Los síntomas pueden variar en intensidad y manifestarse de manera diferente en cada mujer, pero suelen incluir una combinación de factores emocionales, físicos y cognitivos. Distinguir estos síntomas y actuar rápidamente es clave para una intervención eficaz.

1. Tristeza persistente

Una de las señales más claras de depresión posparto es la presencia de una tristeza constante que no desaparece. Esta tristeza puede ir acompañada de sentimientos de desesperanza, vacío o llanto frecuente sin una razón aparente. Mientras que el *baby blues* puede implicar episodios de tristeza leves que desaparecen rápidamente, la depresión posparto involucra emociones más profundas y duraderas.

El *Manual Diagnóstico y Estadístico de los Trastornos Mentales* (DSM-5) clasifica la depresión posparto como un subtipo de trastorno depresivo mayor, destacando que este estado emocional puede durar semanas o incluso meses sin tratamiento (American Psychiatric Association, 2013).

2. Irritabilidad y ansiedad

Es común que las madres con depresión posparto experimenten irritabilidad extrema o ansiedad, a menudo sin una causa clara. Pueden tener cambios de humor bruscos o sentirse abrumadas por una sensación persistente de miedo o preocupación. La ansiedad puede manifestarse en pensamientos intrusivos sobre la salud del bebé o la capacidad de la madre para cuidarlo, lo que puede interferir con las actividades diarias.

Un estudio realizado por Wenzel et al. (2005) demostró que la ansiedad es uno de los componentes más frecuentes en la depresión posparto, afectando la capacidad de la madre para relajarse y disfrutar de su nuevo rol.

3. Cansancio extremo

Aunque es normal sentir fatiga tras el nacimiento de un bebé, la depresión posparto puede hacer que este cansancio sea abrumador, independientemente de la cantidad de descanso que la madre logre obtener. Esta fatiga extrema puede afectar la capacidad de realizar tareas cotidianas, incluyendo el cuidado del bebé y el mantenimiento de la rutina familiar. En algunos casos, las madres pueden sentirse tan agotadas que les resulta difícil levantarse de la cama o cumplir con sus responsabilidades.

4. Falta de interés

Uno de los síntomas más preocupantes de la depresión posparto es la pérdida de interés en actividades que antes eran placenteras, incluyendo el vínculo con el bebé. Algunas madres pueden sentir una desconexión emocional con su bebé o tener dificultades para disfrutar de los momentos que, en teoría, deberían ser gratificantes. Esta falta de interés también puede extenderse a otras áreas de la vida, como relaciones personales o pasatiempos que solían ser significativos.

Investigaciones sugieren que la desconexión emocional entre madre e hijo en los primeros meses de vida puede afectar el desarrollo emocional y social del niño, lo que subraya la importancia de abordar estos sentimientos lo antes posible (Murray et al., 2010).

5. Sentimientos de culpa o inutilidad

Las madres que sufren de depresión posparto a menudo experimentan un sentimiento abrumador de culpa, creyendo que no están cumpliendo adecuadamente con su rol como madres. Pueden tener pensamientos negativos sobre su capacidad para cuidar del bebé o sentir que están fallando en su nuevo rol. Estos sentimientos de inutilidad pueden hacer que se aíslen de sus seres queridos y teman pedir ayuda.

Este patrón de pensamiento autocrítico está estrechamente relacionado con la baja autoestima, lo que puede empeorar la situación si no se aborda a tiempo (Beck, 2001).

6. Cambios en el apetito y el sueño

La depresión posparto también puede manifestarse a través de alteraciones en los patrones de sueño y alimentación. Algunas madres pueden tener dificultades para dormir, incluso cuando el bebé está durmiendo, mientras que otras pueden sentir la necesidad de dormir constantemente. Del mismo modo, pueden experimentar una pérdida significativa de apetito o comer en exceso como una forma de enfrentar el estrés emocional.

Las alteraciones del sueño y el apetito son criterios clave para diagnosticar la depresión clínica en cualquier etapa de la vida, y su presencia en el posparto debe ser tomada en serio (American Psychiatric Association, 2013).

Cómo pedir ayuda

Es importante que cualquier madre que sienta que puede estar experimentando depresión posparto busque ayuda lo antes posible. Esta condición no es un reflejo de debilidad o fracaso, sino un problema médico que requiere tratamiento. La intervención temprana es fundamental para garantizar una recuperación rápida y para proteger tanto a la madre como al bebé.

1. Habla con tu médico

El primer paso es consultar a un médico de confianza, ya sea un obstetra, pediatra o médico de cabecera. Los profesionales de la salud están capacitados para evaluar los síntomas de la depresión posparto y pueden referirte a un especialista en salud mental si es necesario. En algunos casos, el tratamiento puede incluir asesoramiento psicológico, terapia o medicación.

Es fundamental ser abierta y honesta acerca de tus emociones con tu médico, ya que esto permitirá una evaluación más precisa y un tratamiento adecuado.

2. Apoyo emocional

Hablar con tu pareja, amigos o familiares cercanos sobre cómo te sientes puede ser un alivio importante. Compartir tus emociones evita que te sientas aislada y te permite recibir el apoyo necesario. La familia y los amigos pueden ayudarte con las tareas cotidianas o simplemente ofrecerte compañía, lo que puede marcar una gran diferencia en tu bienestar.

Un estudio realizado por Leahy-Warren et al. (2012) destaca que el apoyo emocional es un factor clave en la recuperación de las madres con depresión posparto, ya que les ayuda a sentirse más conectadas y comprendidas.

3. Terapia y tratamiento

La terapia cognitivo-conductual (TCC) ha demostrado ser particularmente eficaz en el tratamiento de la depresión posparto. Esta forma de terapia ayuda a las madres a identificar y modificar patrones de pensamiento negativos, sustituyéndolos por formas más positivas y realistas de pensar (Sockol et al., 2011). La TCC puede ser complementada con otros enfoques, como la terapia interpersonal, que se enfoca en mejorar las relaciones y las habilidades de comunicación de la madre.

En algunos casos, los médicos pueden recomendar el uso de antidepresivos. Muchas de las opciones actuales son seguras para las madres que están amamantando, aunque la decisión de utilizar medicación debe tomarse en conjunto con un profesional de la salud que pueda evaluar los beneficios y riesgos.

4. Grupos de apoyo

Unirse a un grupo de apoyo puede proporcionar una gran sensación de alivio y conexión. Los grupos de apoyo para madres con depresión posparto permiten compartir experiencias, obtener consejos y recibir apoyo emocional de otras personas que están pasando por situaciones similares. Estos grupos pueden ser presenciales o en línea y son una excelente herramienta para sentirse comprendida y acompañada durante la recuperación.

Recursos disponibles

Existen numerosas organizaciones y recursos dedicados a apoyar a las madres que enfrentan la depresión posparto. Estos recursos incluyen líneas de ayuda, asesoramiento en línea, grupos de apoyo locales y materiales educativos que pueden guiarte hacia el tratamiento adecuado. Algunos de los recursos recomendados incluyen:

- **Postpartum Support International (PSI)**: Ofrece una red de apoyo mundial con recursos y grupos de apoyo en varios idiomas.

- **March of Dimes**: Proporciona información y recursos sobre salud materna y posparto, incluyendo la depresión posparto.

- **National Suicide Prevention Lifeline**: Proporciona asistencia inmediata para madres que se sienten emocionalmente abrumadas o tienen pensamientos negativos.

Consejo práctico: Si en algún momento te sientes abrumada por tus emociones o pensamientos, no dudes en buscar ayuda. La depresión posparto es una condición tratable, y con el apoyo adecuado, puedes recuperar tu bienestar emocional y fortalecer tu relación con tu bebé.

Reconocer que la depresión posparto es una posibilidad no te hace débil, al contrario, te hace consciente de las realidades de la maternidad. Hablar de ello es el primer paso hacia la sanación. Ya sea que lo estés viviendo o conozcas a alguien que lo esté, recordar que buscar ayuda no es solo válido, sino necesario, es esencial para tu bienestar. A medida que concluyes este capítulo, quiero que te lleves un mensaje claro: tu salud emocional es tan importante como la de tu bebé. Juntas, podemos construir un camino hacia una maternidad más plena y consciente. Ahora, tomemos un respiro y reflexionemos sobre lo aprendido hasta aquí.

Conclusión del Capítulo

Cuidar de tu salud mental es tan crucial como cuidar de tu bebé, especialmente en los primeros meses de maternidad, cuando todo parece nuevo, abrumador y a veces agotador. Ser madre es una experiencia increíble, pero también puede venir acompañada de desafíos emocionales que no siempre son fáciles de manejar. Las demandas físicas y psicológicas que la maternidad implica pueden afectar tu bienestar emocional si no prestas atención a tus propias necesidades. Por eso, es fundamental que te des permiso para cuidar de tu salud mental de la misma manera en que te preocupas por la salud de tu bebé. Solo cuando tú estés bien podrás ofrecerle a tu hijo lo mejor de ti.

La maternidad, aunque llena de momentos de alegría, también puede ser agotadora y estresante. Las expectativas sociales, la falta de sueño, la nueva responsabilidad constante y el cambio en las rutinas diarias pueden generar un nivel de cansancio emocional que a veces es difícil de expresar. Por eso, encontrar el equilibrio entre cuidar a tu bebé y cuidarte a ti misma es esencial para tu bienestar a largo plazo. Esto no significa que debes hacerlo todo sola ni que debas alcanzar un ideal de perfección. Al contrario, parte de ese equilibrio radica en reconocer cuándo necesitas un descanso, cuándo es el momento de pedir ayuda y, lo más importante, en aceptar que está bien hacerlo. Ser madre no significa tener que ser infalible; es completamente normal tener momentos de duda, agotamiento o vulnerabilidad.

Pedir ayuda no es una señal de debilidad, sino de fortaleza y sabiduría. Ya sea el apoyo de tu pareja, familiares, amigos o incluso de un profesional de la salud mental, contar con una red de apoyo sólida puede marcar una gran diferencia en tu experiencia como madre. Hablar de lo que sientes, compartir tus preocupaciones y expresar tus emociones con personas de confianza te ayudará a liberar tensiones y a poner en perspectiva los desafíos. Además, si sientes que las emociones negativas persisten o se intensifican, como la ansiedad o la depresión, buscar ayuda profesional es fundamental. Las condiciones de salud mental relacionadas con la maternidad, como la depresión posparto, son comunes y tratables, y recibir tratamiento puede ser un acto liberador que te permitirá disfrutar más plenamente de tu nueva vida como madre.

Adaptarse a la vida de mamá es un proceso que toma tiempo. Cada mujer lo vive de manera diferente y no existe un "camino correcto" o un cronograma fijo que seguir. Algunas madres se sienten cómodas rápidamente con los cambios que la maternidad trae, mientras que otras pueden tardar más en ajustarse. Ambas experiencias son válidas y normales. Lo importante es que te permitas vivir este proceso de adaptación a tu propio ritmo, sin compararte con los demás o presionarte para cumplir con expectativas externas. Acepta que habrá días más difíciles que otros, y que es completamente normal tener altibajos emocionales mientras te acostumbras a esta nueva etapa. La clave está en no ser demasiado dura contigo misma y en entender que no tienes que tenerlo todo bajo control todo el tiempo.

Priorizar tu salud emocional no es un acto egoísta, sino una inversión en tu bienestar y en el bienestar de tu familia. Cuando cuidas de tu salud mental, te permites estar más presente, paciente y receptiva con tu bebé, lo cual mejora tanto tu experiencia de maternidad como el ambiente en el que tu hijo crece. Establecer pequeños hábitos de autocuidado en tu día a día puede ser muy beneficioso. Ya sea dedicar unos minutos a respirar profundamente, hacer una pausa para disfrutar de un café en silencio, o simplemente darte un tiempo para descansar mientras alguien más cuida del bebé, estos momentos pueden tener un gran impacto en tu estado emocional. Reconocer que tu bienestar es importante te ayudará a ser una madre más plena y satisfecha.

Finalmente, recuerda que la maternidad es una etapa llena de aprendizajes y desafíos, pero también de momentos de inmensa felicidad. Darte permiso para disfrutar de esta nueva vida sin la carga de la perfección hará que esta experiencia sea mucho más gratificante. Al priorizar tu salud mental y aprender a equilibrar las demandas diarias con el autocuidado, podrás enfrentar los desafíos con mayor serenidad y disfrutar más plenamente de los pequeños momentos de alegría que la maternidad trae consigo.

En resumen, cuidar de tu salud mental no solo es esencial para tu bienestar personal, sino también para el bienestar de tu bebé y tu familia. La maternidad es un proceso de adaptación que cada mujer vive de manera diferente, y es fundamental que encuentres el equilibrio que funcione para ti. Al pedir ayuda, aceptar tus emociones y priorizar tu bienestar emocional, estarás creando una base sólida para vivir esta etapa con más tranquilidad, satisfacción y, sobre todo, con la capacidad de disfrutar plenamente del hermoso viaje de ser madre.

Después de explorar los retos emocionales que pueden surgir en el posparto, quiero ofrecerte un consejo desde el corazón: no te exijas perfección. La sociedad a veces nos pinta una imagen de la maternidad como si debiera ser un constante estado de felicidad, pero la realidad es que es una mezcla de emociones. Mi consejo es que seas amable contigo misma. Habrá días en los que no te sientas al 100%, y eso está bien. El simple hecho de estar aquí, haciendo lo mejor que puedes, es suficiente. No estás sola en este camino, y siempre hay una red lista para sostenerte cuando lo necesites.

> **Consejo del autor:** Ser madre no significa que tengas que sacrificar tu bienestar emocional. El cuidado personal no es un lujo, es una necesidad. Si en algún momento sientes que estás perdiendo el control o que tus emociones te abruman, da el primer paso: pide ayuda. No estás sola en esta experiencia, y con el apoyo adecuado, puedes superar cualquier desafío.

Con ese consejo en mente, te invito a tomarte un momento para hacer un ejercicio reflexivo. La maternidad no es solo un viaje externo, también es un proceso de transformación interior. Este ejercicio te ayudará a conectar con tus emociones y pensamientos, a reconocer las alegrías y los desafíos que has enfrentado, y a darte permiso para sentir. Es un momento para ti, para mirarte con compasión y darte el espacio de ser, sin expectativas ni juicios. Vamos a sumergirnos en este ejercicio que te permitirá escuchar lo que tu corazón necesita.

<table>
<tr><td>

Ejercicio reflexivo
</td></tr>
<tr><td>

Dedica unos minutos a reflexionar sobre tus emociones en esta etapa de tu vida. Anota tus respuestas a las siguientes preguntas:
</td></tr>
<tr><td>

- ¿Qué es lo que más disfruto de la maternidad hasta ahora?
</td></tr>
<tr><td>

- ¿Qué aspectos me generan más ansiedad o preocupación?
</td></tr>
<tr><td>

- ¿Qué acciones puedo tomar para cuidar mejor de mi salud mental?
</td></tr>
<tr><td>

Escribir estas reflexiones puede ayudarte a identificar áreas en las que necesitas apoyo y a crear un plan de autocuidado.
</td></tr>
</table>

Después de haber reflexionado sobre tus emociones y cómo te sientes en este nuevo rol, es hora de pasar a lo práctico. La maternidad trae consigo desafíos diarios, pero hay formas de hacerlos más manejables. En la siguiente sección, te compartiré algunos tips y trucos para ayudarte a navegar el día a día de una manera más ligera. Desde cómo organizarte mejor hasta pequeños momentos de autocuidado que puedes integrar en tu rutina, estos consejos están diseñados para darte un respiro y recordarte que, aunque las cosas puedan ser caóticas a veces, hay formas sencillas de aligerar la carga.

Tips y trucos

1. **Organiza tu día**: Planifica tu día de manera flexible, priorizando el descanso y el autocuidado, aunque sean solo 10 o 15 minutos.

2. **Acepta ayuda**: Si alguien se ofrece a ayudarte con el bebé o las tareas del hogar, acéptalo. El apoyo de otros te permitirá descansar y recuperar energías.

3. **Toma aire fresco**: Salir a caminar al aire libre, aunque sea por unos minutos, puede mejorar tu estado de ánimo y brindarte una sensación de claridad mental.

4. **No te compares**: Cada experiencia de maternidad es diferente. Evita compararte con otras madres, ya que esto puede aumentar tu ansiedad. En lugar de eso, céntrate en lo que es mejor para ti y tu bebé.

Ya tienes algunas herramientas prácticas a tu disposición, pero quiero recordarte que no estás sola en este camino. En la siguiente sección, encontrarás una lista de recursos adicionales que pueden ser de gran ayuda. Ya sea que busques apoyo profesional, lecturas inspiradoras o comunidades de otras madres que comparten tus experiencias, estos recursos te ofrecerán la compañía y la orientación que podrías necesitar. La maternidad es más llevadera cuando tienes una red de apoyo, y aquí tienes opciones para fortalecerla aún más. ¡Vamos a descubrir juntos lo que está disponible para ti!

Recursos adicionales

- **Libros recomendados**:

  - *Cuando ser mamá nos cuesta* de Laura Gutman.

  - *Maternidad y salud mental* de Maureen Boyle.

- **Grupos y organizaciones**:

  - *Postpartum Support International* (PSI): Ofrece apoyo a madres con depresión posparto a través de líneas de ayuda y grupos en línea.

  - *La Liga de la Leche Internacional*: Además de brindar apoyo en la lactancia, ofrece recursos sobre salud mental posparto.

- **Aplicaciones útiles**:

  - "Headspace" (para prácticas de mindfulness y meditación).

  - "Panda" (una aplicación que conecta a las madres con apoyo emocional y orientación).

Tu bebé ya está aquí, y aunque cada día trae nuevos desafíos, también trae nuevas alegrías. El primer año de vida es un torbellino de descubrimientos, para ambos. Tú aprendes a ser mamá, a conocer a tu pequeño, mientras él descubre el mundo a través de ti. Será un viaje lleno de primeras veces: la primera sonrisa, el primer balbuceo, el primer gateo. Y aunque a veces puede parecer abrumador, la recompensa de verlo crecer y desarrollarse a su propio ritmo hará que cada noche sin dormir, cada preocupación, valga la pena. Vamos juntas, explorando este primer año con amor y paciencia.

"El acto más valiente que una mujer puede hacer es cuidar de su salud mental mientras cría a sus hijos." –
Kate Winslet

De la Panza a la Vida

Capítulo 7

El Primer Año del Bebé

Los doce meses de descubrimiento y crecimiento: una guía mes a mes

El primer año de vida de un bebé está lleno de descubrimientos y aprendizajes tanto para él como para sus padres. Durante este tiempo, el desarrollo del recién nacido avanza rápidamente, con una serie de hitos importantes que marcan su crecimiento físico, emocional y cognitivo. Además, la creación de rutinas adecuadas para el sueño, la alimentación y el juego no solo ayuda al bebé a sentirse seguro y cómodo, sino que también contribuye al bienestar y la tranquilidad de los padres. Este capítulo explora las etapas clave del desarrollo del bebé durante su primer año y te ofrece consejos sobre cómo establecer rutinas saludables y efectivas.

El Desarrollo del Recién Nacido

El primer año de vida de un bebé es un periodo de crecimiento acelerado y descubrimiento continuo. A lo largo de estos meses, el bebé experimentará una serie de hitos fundamentales que señalan su progreso físico, cognitivo, emocional y social. Cada bebé sigue su propio ritmo de desarrollo, y aunque existen puntos de referencia comunes, es normal que algunos niños alcancen ciertos hitos antes o después que otros. Entender estas etapas de desarrollo ayuda a los padres a reconocer el progreso de su bebé y a proporcionarle el estímulo y el apoyo adecuado en cada fase.

Primeras etapas de desarrollo: hitos importantes

A continuación, se describen algunos de los hitos más importantes que los bebés alcanzan durante su primer año. Estos hitos son indicadores clave de su desarrollo, pero es importante recordar que cada bebé es único y puede desarrollarse a un ritmo ligeramente diferente.

1. Primeras semanas (0-2 meses)

En las primeras semanas de vida, el bebé se adapta al mundo fuera del útero y comienza a desarrollar sus habilidades sensoriales y motoras básicas.

- **Visión y enfoque**: Durante las primeras semanas, la visión del bebé es limitada. Solo puede ver claramente objetos a una distancia corta, como el rostro de su madre cuando lo amamanta. A medida que pasan los días, el bebé comienza a enfocar mejor los objetos cercanos y empieza a reconocer patrones y caras familiares. La investigación muestra que los recién nacidos tienen una preferencia innata por los rostros humanos, lo que les ayuda a establecer vínculos emocionales con sus cuidadores (Maurer & Lewis, 2001).

- **Sonrisas reflexivas**: Las primeras sonrisas que se observan en un bebé son generalmente reflejas y no voluntarias. Sin embargo, alrededor de las seis semanas, los bebés empiezan a sonreír de forma intencionada, respondiendo a la interacción social y al entorno, lo que marca uno de los primeros signos de desarrollo emocional y social.

- **Movimientos corporales**: Al principio, los movimientos de los brazos y piernas del bebé son descoordinados y poco controlados, debido a que su sistema nervioso aún está en desarrollo. Sin embargo, en las primeras semanas, comienza a ganar un mayor control sobre sus extremidades, y pronto sus movimientos reflejan una intención más clara, como intentar agarrar objetos.

2. De 3 a 4 meses

Durante esta etapa, el bebé empieza a interactuar de manera más activa con su entorno, demostrando avances significativos en su desarrollo físico y social.

- **Sonrisa social**: A los 3 meses, la sonrisa del bebé se convierte en una respuesta más clara a las interacciones sociales. Sonreirá intencionadamente en respuesta a las voces y caras familiares, mostrando su creciente capacidad para relacionarse con su entorno social.

- **Sostener la cabeza**: Uno de los principales logros físicos de esta etapa es la capacidad de sostener la cabeza. Alrededor de los 4 meses, el bebé puede levantar y mantener la cabeza erguida cuando está boca abajo, un avance importante que precede al desarrollo del control motor necesario para gatear y sentarse.

- **Exploración oral**: En este momento, los bebés comienzan a explorar el mundo llevándose las manos y objetos a la boca. Esto no solo les permite conocer texturas y formas, sino que también es una manera de calmarse a sí mismos. La exploración oral es esencial para el desarrollo sensorial y la motricidad.

3. De 5 a 6 meses

A medida que el bebé crece, sus habilidades motoras y sensoriales se desarrollan rápidamente, permitiéndole una mayor interacción con su entorno.

- **Girar sobre sí mismo**: A partir de los 5 meses, muchos bebés comienzan a girar del estómago a la espalda y viceversa, un signo de que están ganando fuerza en sus músculos centrales y mayor control motor. Este hito es un precursor del gateo y el movimiento independiente.

- **Sentarse con apoyo**: A los 6 meses, muchos bebés ya pueden sentarse con apoyo, lo que les permite interactuar con su entorno desde una nueva perspectiva. Algunos incluso intentan sentarse solos, un signo clave de su creciente independencia física.

- **Reconocer voces**: Los bebés de esta edad son capaces de reconocer y responder al sonido de voces familiares, especialmente la de sus padres. Esta habilidad es una manifestación temprana de la capacidad auditiva y lingüística del bebé, ya que está comenzando a asociar los sonidos con las personas y los objetos de su entorno.

4. De 7 a 9 meses

Entre los 7 y 9 meses, el bebé comienza a experimentar con el movimiento independiente y el lenguaje, lo que marca un avance crucial en su desarrollo cognitivo y físico.

- **Gateo**: Muchos bebés comienzan a gatear durante este período, aunque algunos pueden optar por arrastrarse o desplazarse de otras formas. El gateo es importante no solo para el desarrollo motor, sino también para el fortalecimiento de la coordinación mano-ojo. Algunos bebés pueden saltarse el gateo y comenzar a caminar directamente, lo que también es normal.

- **Palabras simples**: En esta etapa, los bebés comienzan a balbucear sonidos como "mamá" o "papá", aunque aún no los usen con un significado claro. Este balbuceo es un precursor del desarrollo del lenguaje, y los estudios muestran que los bebés que tienen más oportunidades de interactuar verbalmente con sus cuidadores tienden a desarrollar habilidades lingüísticas más rápidamente (Kuhl, 2004).

- **Desarrollo de la motricidad fina**: El bebé comienza a utilizar los dedos para agarrar objetos pequeños, como trozos de comida o juguetes. Este hito es fundamental para el desarrollo de la coordinación mano-ojo y el control motor fino, habilidades que serán esenciales más adelante para tareas como alimentarse o manipular objetos con precisión.

5. De 10 a 12 meses

A medida que el bebé se acerca a su primer cumpleaños, muchos alcanzan hitos importantes en su desarrollo físico y emocional que marcan el inicio de una nueva etapa de independencia.

- **Primeros pasos**: Aunque algunos bebés pueden comenzar a caminar antes de los 12 meses, otros pueden tardar un poco más. Los primeros pasos son un hito emocionante que refleja el desarrollo muscular y el equilibrio. Incluso si el bebé no camina por sí solo, es probable que intente ponerse de pie o caminar con apoyo.

- **Imitación**: Alrededor de los 12 meses, los bebés comienzan a imitar gestos y acciones de los adultos, como aplaudir o saludar con la mano. Este comportamiento de imitación es una señal de que están desarrollando habilidades sociales y de observación, lo que les ayuda a aprender del entorno.

- **Desarrollo emocional**: Hacia el final del primer año, los bebés ya han formado un vínculo claro con sus cuidadores principales y pueden experimentar ansiedad por separación cuando sus padres no están cerca. Este apego emocional es un componente clave del desarrollo social, ya que demuestra la capacidad del bebé para formar relaciones afectivas profundas.

Importancia de la estimulación en el desarrollo del bebé

El desarrollo del bebé en su primer año está profundamente influenciado por el entorno y las interacciones que tiene con sus cuidadores. La estimulación adecuada puede ayudar a potenciar sus habilidades cognitivas, emocionales y motoras. A continuación, algunas estrategias respaldadas por la investigación para estimular el desarrollo del bebé:

- **Juegos interactivos**: Los juegos que involucran el contacto visual, el sonido y el movimiento, como las canciones infantiles o los juegos de esconder y buscar, ayudan a desarrollar las habilidades sociales y cognitivas del bebé (Tamis-LeMonda et al., 2004).

- **Lectura temprana**: Aunque un bebé no entiende las palabras, la lectura en voz alta le expone al ritmo y la melodía del lenguaje, lo que puede acelerar el desarrollo del habla y el vocabulario.

- **Exploración sensorial**: Proporcionar juguetes con diferentes texturas, formas y sonidos ayuda a estimular el desarrollo sensorial y la curiosidad natural del bebé.

Ver cómo tu bebé crece día a día es uno de los mayores regalos de la maternidad. Cada pequeño avance, desde sus primeras miradas curiosas hasta los movimientos de sus diminutas manos, es un recordatorio de la vida que florece ante tus ojos. El desarrollo de tu recién nacido es un proceso lleno de pequeños pero poderosos hitos. Sin embargo, este crecimiento no ocurre de forma aislada: es en la consistencia de los cuidados diarios donde tu bebé encuentra el soporte que necesita. Ahora, vamos a adentrarnos en las rutinas y cuidados diarios, esas pequeñas acciones que hacen una gran diferencia en su bienestar y desarrollo.

Rutinas y Cuidados Diarios

Las rutinas son fundamentales en el bienestar y desarrollo del bebé. Un entorno predecible ayuda al bebé a sentirse seguro, lo que facilita el establecimiento de hábitos saludables. A lo largo del primer año de vida, las necesidades del bebé cambian drásticamente, especialmente en áreas clave como el sueño, la alimentación y el juego. Crear rutinas en estas áreas no solo beneficia al bebé, sino que también permite a los padres organizar mejor su tiempo y energía.

Rutinas de sueño

El sueño es un aspecto esencial para el desarrollo saludable del bebé, ya que durante el descanso el cerebro procesa nuevas experiencias y consolida la memoria, al tiempo que el cuerpo crece y se recupera. Los patrones de sueño de un bebé varían significativamente en su primer año, y es fundamental adaptar las rutinas de descanso a sus necesidades cambiantes.

1. Sueño del recién nacido

Los recién nacidos suelen dormir entre 16 y 18 horas al día, pero su sueño está fragmentado en intervalos de 2 a 4 horas debido a la necesidad de alimentarse con frecuencia. Este patrón de sueño es normal y responde al rápido crecimiento y desarrollo del cerebro en esta etapa. Es importante tener en cuenta que los ciclos de sueño de los recién nacidos son más cortos que los de los adultos, alternando rápidamente entre sueño ligero y profundo.

Un estudio del *American Academy of Sleep Medicine* (2016) sugiere que el sueño ininterrumpido durante la noche empieza a estabilizarse alrededor de los 3 a 4 meses, momento en que algunos bebés pueden empezar a dormir por períodos más largos, especialmente si han desarrollado una rutina de sueño consistente. Sin embargo, cada bebé es diferente, y algunos pueden tardar más en lograr estos períodos de descanso más prolongados.

2. Crear una rutina de sueño

Establecer una rutina consistente para la hora de dormir puede ayudar al bebé a asociar ciertas actividades con el sueño, lo que facilita que se duerma de manera más rápida y tranquila. La rutina de sueño puede incluir actividades calmantes, como un baño tibio, leerle un cuento o cantarle una canción suave, actividades que le envían señales de que es hora de descansar. Según la investigación, las rutinas estructuradas antes de dormir pueden mejorar tanto la calidad del sueño del bebé como su estado de ánimo durante el día (Mindell et al., 2015).

Otro aspecto clave es la consistencia. Tratar de acostar al bebé a la misma hora cada noche, en un ambiente tranquilo y oscuro, puede ayudar a regular su reloj biológico y promover un patrón de sueño saludable.

3. Rutinas de siesta

Las siestas diurnas son igualmente importantes para el desarrollo del bebé. Durante los primeros meses, los bebés pueden necesitar entre 3 y 4 siestas al día. A medida que crecen, este número se reduce gradualmente, pero las siestas siguen siendo necesarias hasta los 18 meses o incluso más. Las siestas ayudan a consolidar el aprendizaje y permiten al bebé reponer energía para mantenerse activo y receptivo durante las horas de vigilia.

La cantidad y duración de las siestas variará según el bebé, pero establecer un horario regular puede facilitar la transición a la siesta y garantizar que el bebé esté descansado a lo largo del día. Los estudios indican que los bebés que mantienen rutinas regulares de siesta suelen tener menos problemas de comportamiento y muestran mejores habilidades de regulación emocional (Scher et al., 2005).

Alimentación

El primer año de vida es un periodo de grandes cambios en cuanto a la alimentación del bebé. Durante los primeros seis meses, la lactancia materna o la fórmula proporcionan toda la nutrición que el bebé necesita. Después de los seis meses, se introducen los alimentos sólidos, lo que representa una nueva etapa tanto para el bebé como para los padres.

1. Lactancia o fórmula

La lactancia materna es ampliamente recomendada por organizaciones de salud globales como la *Organización Mundial de la Salud* (OMS) y la *Academia Americana de Pediatría* (AAP) como el alimento ideal para los bebés durante los primeros seis meses de vida. La leche materna proporciona todos los nutrientes necesarios para el crecimiento, junto con anticuerpos que fortalecen el sistema inmunológico del bebé (Victora et al., 2016).

Para aquellas madres que optan por la fórmula infantil, esta también es una opción segura y nutritiva. La fórmula está diseñada para imitar la composición de la leche materna y proporcionar los nutrientes esenciales que el bebé necesita. En ambos casos, es fundamental seguir las indicaciones del pediatra sobre la cantidad y frecuencia de las tomas, que variará a medida que el bebé crezca.

2. Introducción de sólidos

Alrededor de los seis meses, los bebés están listos para comenzar con la introducción de alimentos sólidos, ya que en este momento suelen desarrollar las habilidades motoras necesarias para tragar sólidos y mostrar interés en la comida. La introducción de sólidos debe comenzar con alimentos blandos y fáciles de digerir, como puré de verduras, frutas o cereales fortificados con hierro, que son cruciales para el desarrollo cognitivo y físico del bebé.

Se recomienda introducir un alimento nuevo a la vez y esperar entre tres y cinco días antes de probar otro, para poder identificar posibles alergias o intolerancias. Investigaciones han demostrado que la exposición temprana a una variedad de alimentos puede ayudar a prevenir problemas alimenticios más adelante, fomentando la aceptación de nuevos sabores y texturas (Birch et al., 2007).

3. Desarrollo de hábitos alimenticios saludables

El primer año de vida es una oportunidad clave para establecer hábitos alimenticios saludables. Introducir una variedad de alimentos nutritivos y permitir al bebé experimentar diferentes texturas y sabores fomenta una alimentación equilibrada. También es importante permitir que el bebé aprenda a autorregularse, lo que significa que el bebé debe comer según su propio ritmo y señales de hambre y saciedad, en lugar de seguir horarios estrictos.

Además, involucrar al bebé en el proceso de alimentación, como permitirle comer con las manos, ayuda a desarrollar habilidades motoras finas y promueve una relación positiva con la comida.

Juego y estimulación

El juego es esencial para el desarrollo integral del bebé, ya que, a través del juego, los bebés no solo exploran su entorno, sino que también desarrollan habilidades motoras, cognitivas y sociales. Cada etapa del primer año ofrece diferentes oportunidades de juego y estimulación que son cruciales para el crecimiento del bebé.

1. Estimulación sensorial

Durante los primeros meses, el juego se centra en la estimulación de los sentidos. Los bebés son naturalmente curiosos sobre el mundo que los rodea y, en esta etapa, su capacidad para ver, oír y tocar está en pleno desarrollo. Hablarle, cantarle y mostrarle objetos de diferentes colores y texturas son formas de estimular su percepción visual, auditiva y táctil. Estudios en desarrollo infantil han demostrado que la estimulación temprana y repetida de los sentidos contribuye al crecimiento cerebral y al desarrollo cognitivo (Bergen et al., 2010).

2. Juego físico

A medida que el bebé crece y comienza a moverse, el juego físico adquiere mayor importancia. El gateo, el rodar o los intentos de ponerse de pie son actividades que ayudan a fortalecer los músculos y a mejorar la coordinación motora. Proporcionar un entorno seguro y espacioso para que el bebé se mueva libremente es crucial para fomentar el desarrollo de habilidades motoras gruesas, que son la base de otras habilidades físicas, como caminar y correr.

El tiempo de juego en el suelo y la exploración física también ayudan a desarrollar la conciencia espacial del bebé, mientras que el uso de juguetes apropiados para su edad puede estimular la coordinación mano-ojo y las habilidades de resolución de problemas (Adolph & Tamis-LeMonda, 2014).

3. Juegos de imitación

Entre los 9 y 12 meses, los bebés disfrutan de juegos que involucran la imitación de gestos y acciones de los adultos, como aplaudir, saludar con la mano o decir adiós. Estos juegos no solo fomentan el desarrollo de habilidades motoras finas, sino que también son fundamentales para el aprendizaje social y emocional. Al imitar las acciones de los adultos, los bebés están desarrollando su capacidad para interpretar y replicar el comportamiento social, lo que contribuye a su comprensión de las interacciones humanas y las normas sociales.

Consejo práctico: Aunque las actividades estructuradas pueden ser útiles, no es necesario llenar el día del bebé con ellas. El juego libre y el tiempo de calidad con los padres son igualmente importantes para su desarrollo emocional y cognitivo.

Cada día con tu bebé está lleno de rituales, desde las suaves caricias mientras lo alimentas hasta el momento en que se queda dormido en tus brazos. Estos cuidados diarios son mucho más que simples tareas: son la base de su seguridad y tu oportunidad de conectar con él a un nivel profundo. A medida que llegamos al final de este capítulo, hemos cubierto lo esencial sobre el desarrollo y las rutinas que ayudan a tu pequeño a sentirse amado y seguro. Pero esto es solo el comienzo. Recuerda que, aunque cada día pueda parecer una repetición, estás construyendo un vínculo que durará toda la vida.

Conclusión del capítulo

El primer año de vida de tu bebé es, sin duda, uno de los periodos más transformadores que experimentarás como madre. Es un tiempo lleno de descubrimientos, emociones y momentos únicos que marcan el inicio de una profunda conexión entre tú y tu hijo. Cada día trae consigo algo nuevo: desde la primera sonrisa y el balbuceo, hasta los primeros intentos de gatear o caminar. Estos hitos en su desarrollo físico y emocional no solo son motivo de celebración, sino que también te permiten ver de cerca cómo tu bebé comienza a descubrir el mundo y a desarrollarse de manera increíblemente rápida. Este primer año es un viaje de aprendizaje, tanto para tu bebé como para ti, y aunque puede estar lleno de desafíos, también está repleto de momentos de alegría y asombro.

Una de las formas más efectivas de crear una experiencia más tranquila y estructurada tanto para ti como para tu bebé es estableciendo rutinas saludables. Crear una estructura diaria que incluya tiempos consistentes para el sueño, la alimentación y el juego puede ser un salvavidas durante este primer año. Las rutinas no solo brindan a tu bebé un sentido de seguridad y previsibilidad, lo cual es fundamental para su bienestar emocional, sino que también te ayudan a manejar mejor las demandas diarias de la maternidad. El sueño, por ejemplo, es crucial para el desarrollo del cerebro de tu bebé y para tu propia salud mental. Establecer buenos hábitos de sueño desde el principio ayudará a que ambos puedan descansar mejor, lo cual es vital en esta etapa donde el agotamiento puede ser común.

Del mismo modo, las rutinas de alimentación y juego son esenciales para su desarrollo físico y cognitivo. La alimentación no solo es una necesidad básica, sino un momento de conexión íntima que fortalece el vínculo entre tú y tu bebé. Ya sea a través de la lactancia o el biberón, cada toma es una oportunidad para ofrecerle no solo nutrición, sino también consuelo y cercanía. A medida que introduces alimentos sólidos, este proceso también se convierte en una experiencia de descubrimiento para tu bebé, que empezará a explorar nuevos sabores y texturas. Además, el tiempo de juego es fundamental no solo para su entretenimiento, sino para fomentar su curiosidad, su coordinación y su desarrollo mental. Jugar con tu bebé no solo le enseña habilidades motoras y cognitivas, sino que también fortalece la relación afectiva entre ambos.

Sin embargo, es importante recordar que cada bebé es único, y su desarrollo puede variar significativamente.

Aunque los hitos del desarrollo, como sentarse, gatear o hablar, son importantes, no debes preocuparte demasiado si tu bebé no sigue el "calendario" perfecto que a veces se presenta en los libros o en las consultas médicas. Cada bebé tiene su propio ritmo, y lo más importante es que esté progresando de manera constante, feliz y saludable. La comparación con otros niños puede generar estrés innecesario, pero lo que realmente importa es que tu bebé esté explorando su entorno, desarrollando sus habilidades y mostrando curiosidad por el mundo que lo rodea. Los hitos del desarrollo son una guía, no una regla rígida.

Durante este primer año, también es esencial que te des espacio para adaptarte a tu nuevo rol de madre. No es raro sentirse abrumada a veces, especialmente cuando intentas equilibrar todas las responsabilidades y expectativas que vienen con la maternidad. Sin embargo, recuerda que este es un proceso de aprendizaje constante para ti también. Al igual que tu bebé está aprendiendo a vivir en el mundo, tú estás aprendiendo a ser madre, y ambas experiencias están llenas de desafíos y momentos gratificantes. No tengas miedo de buscar apoyo cuando lo necesites, ya sea de tu pareja, familia, amigos o profesionales. La maternidad no es un camino que debas recorrer sola, y recibir ayuda puede hacer que la experiencia sea más enriquecedora y menos agotadora.

El primer año de vida de tu bebé es también un tiempo para construir recuerdos y disfrutar de los pequeños momentos. La primera risa, el primer abrazo, o ver cómo tu bebé empieza a reconocer tu voz y tu rostro son momentos que quedarán grabados en tu memoria. Aunque puede ser un año lleno de incertidumbres y nuevos desafíos, también está lleno de oportunidades para crecer juntos y para formar un vínculo inquebrantable. Es importante que te tomes el tiempo para disfrutar de estos momentos, sin presionarte por hacerlo todo "perfecto". La perfección no es el objetivo; lo que importa es el amor, el cuidado y la conexión que construyes con tu bebé.

En resumen, el primer año de vida de tu bebé es una etapa increíblemente rica en aprendizajes, tanto para él como para ti. Crear rutinas saludables para el sueño, la alimentación y el juego no solo beneficiará a tu bebé al proporcionarle seguridad y estabilidad, sino que también te ayudará a sentirte más organizada y tranquila en tu rol de madre. Recuerda que cada bebé se desarrolla a su propio ritmo, y lo importante es que esté progresando de manera constante y feliz. Al permitirte disfrutar de este proceso sin las presiones de la perfección, estarás creando una base sólida para el crecimiento y bienestar de tu bebé, mientras construyes una maternidad más plena y satisfactoria para ti misma.

A lo largo de estos primeros días con tu bebé, es posible que te hayas enfrentado a momentos de incertidumbre, preguntándote si lo estás haciendo bien. Mi consejo es simple: confía en ti misma. No hay un manual perfecto para ser madre, pero cada día que pasas cuidando a tu bebé es un paso hacia adelante. La perfección no es el objetivo; el amor, la paciencia y la dedicación lo son. Permítete aprender a lo largo del camino, porque, al final, lo que más recordará tu bebé es cómo lo hiciste sentir. Ahora, vamos a tomarnos un momento para reflexionar sobre todo lo que has aprendido y experimentado hasta aquí.

Consejo del autor: Disfruta cada etapa del crecimiento de tu bebé, ya que estos momentos pasan rápidamente. No te apresures en hacer que alcance ciertos hitos; cada bebé tiene su propio ritmo de desarrollo. Lo más importante es que tanto tú como tu bebé se sientan seguros y conectados mientras exploran el mundo juntos.

Con el consejo de confiar en tu propio instinto en mente, quiero proponerte un ejercicio que te ayudará a conectar aún más con tu rol como madre. Este ejercicio reflexivo es una oportunidad para pausar y mirar hacia adentro, para darte cuenta de lo lejos que has llegado y reconocer tus emociones en este proceso. Es un espacio para abrazar tus logros y también tus desafíos, sin juzgarte, solo observándote con amor. A través de este ejercicio, te invito a recordar que la maternidad es un viaje que vives a tu propio ritmo, y que cada paso, por pequeño que parezca, es valioso.

<table>
<tr><td>

Ejercicio reflexivo

</td></tr>
<tr><td>

Tómate unos minutos para reflexionar sobre el primer año de vida de tu bebé. Pregúntate:

</td></tr>
<tr><td>

- ¿Qué hitos ha alcanzado mi bebé recientemente que me han sorprendido o emocionado?

</td></tr>
<tr><td>

- ¿Qué aspectos de las rutinas diarias funcionan bien para nosotros?

</td></tr>
<tr><td>

- ¿Qué ajustes puedo hacer para mejorar nuestras rutinas o reducir el estrés?

</td></tr>
<tr><td>

Escribir estas respuestas puede ayudarte a identificar áreas que pueden necesitar más atención y a celebrar los logros de tu bebé.

</td></tr>
</table>

Después de haber conectado contigo misma a través de la reflexión, es hora de pasar a lo práctico. Sabemos que el día a día con un recién nacido puede ser abrumador, pero con algunos tips y trucos, todo puede volverse un poco más sencillo. A continuación, te compartiré sugerencias que harán que las rutinas diarias, como el baño, la alimentación y el sueño, sean más manejables y placenteras tanto para ti como para tu bebé. Estos pequeños consejos te permitirán disfrutar más de los momentos cotidianos, quitando un poco de estrés y trayendo más armonía a tu hogar.

Tips y trucos

1. **Sigue los signos de tu bebé**: Si bien las rutinas son útiles, es importante ser flexible y seguir las señales de tu bebé. Si parece cansado antes de la hora de la siesta, intenta adelantarla.

2. **Fomenta la independencia**: A medida que tu bebé crece, fomenta pequeñas actividades que promuevan su independencia, como dejar que se alimente solo con las manos.

3. **Haz del juego un momento de aprendizaje**: Aprovecha los momentos de juego para estimular el desarrollo cognitivo de tu bebé, hablándole y explicándole lo que estás haciendo.

4. **Sé paciente contigo misma**: No todas las rutinas funcionarán a la perfección desde el principio. Sé paciente y ajusta según sea necesario.

Con algunos trucos útiles bajo la manga, estás mejor preparada para enfrentar esos pequeños desafíos diarios. Sin embargo, siempre es bueno saber que hay más apoyo disponible si lo necesitas. En la siguiente sección, te proporcionaré recursos adicionales que te serán de gran ayuda en esta nueva etapa. Desde lecturas recomendadas hasta grupos de apoyo y plataformas online, estos recursos te brindarán información valiosa y compañía en esos momentos en los que necesitas una mano amiga o un consejo experto. ¡Vamos a explorar estas opciones que están aquí para ti!

Recursos adicionales

- **Libros recomendados**:

  - *El concepto del continuum* de Jean Liedloff.

  - *El desarrollo del bebé y el niño* de T. Berry Brazelton.

- **Aplicaciones útiles**:

  - "The Wonder Weeks" (para seguir los hitos del desarrollo).

  - "BabySparks" (con actividades de estimulación para el bebé).

- **Webs recomendadas**:

  - *Healthy Children* (AAP) para información sobre el desarrollo del bebé.

  - *La Liga de la Leche Internacional* para consultas sobre alimentación y lactancia.

A lo largo de este viaje, habrás recibido consejos, opiniones y advertencias de todas partes. Sin embargo, hay algo dentro de ti que sabe más que nadie: tu instinto. Es esa voz suave pero firme que te susurra qué es lo mejor para tu bebé, y en este capítulo vamos a recordarte la importancia de confiar en ella. Porque, aunque haya muchos caminos a seguir, solo tú conoces a tu hijo como nadie más lo hará. Es hora de reconectar con esa sabiduría interna, la que te guiará en cada paso, te fortalecerá en los momentos de duda y te hará sentir poderosa.

"Los bebés son como pequeños soles que, de una manera mágica, traen calidez, felicidad y luz a nuestras vidas." –
Kartini Diapari-Oengider

Capítulo 8

Confía en tus Instintos

La sabiduría interior de una madre: aprendiendo a escuchar tu voz

La maternidad es una experiencia profundamente personal y transformadora. A lo largo de este viaje, los consejos y recomendaciones abundan, desde expertos en salud hasta amigos y familiares. Sin embargo, en medio de todas esas voces, es importante recordar que el instinto maternal es una herramienta poderosa e innata que te guiará en la toma de decisiones más adecuadas para ti y tu bebé. Este capítulo se centra en cómo cultivar y confiar en tu intuición como madre, reconociendo que no existe un enfoque único para la crianza y que cada experiencia es única.

El Poder del Instinto Maternal

El instinto maternal es una fuerza poderosa que guía a las madres en la toma de decisiones sobre el bienestar de sus hijos. Más allá de los consejos de expertos o manuales de crianza, este instinto se basa en una conexión natural y profunda que las madres desarrollan con sus bebés. Aunque en la sociedad actual se ofrece una gran cantidad de información sobre cómo criar a los hijos, es fundamental que las madres aprendan a confiar en sí mismas y en su capacidad innata para comprender y satisfacer las necesidades de sus bebés.

La ciencia ha demostrado que el cerebro de la madre experimenta una serie de cambios neuroquímicos tras el parto, lo que mejora su capacidad para interpretar y responder a las señales del bebé. Estos cambios biológicos subyacen en lo que comúnmente conocemos como "instinto maternal". Es una forma intuitiva de respuesta que, aunque no siempre es consciente, está respaldada por transformaciones profundas en el cerebro que preparan a la madre para la crianza (Swain et al., 2007).

Mientras el mundo te ofrece un sinfín de guías y consejos sobre la crianza, hay algo en ti que va más allá de lo aprendido: esa conexión profunda e innata que tienes con tu bebé. Ese instinto maternal, tan antiguo como la vida misma, se convierte en tu brújula en medio de la vastedad de información que te rodea. Sin embargo, aprender a confiar en esa brújula, a darle valor frente a las voces externas, es un proceso que lleva tiempo y que se va fortaleciendo con cada día de experiencia como madre. Es aquí donde tu confianza personal se convierte en el cimiento de todas las decisiones que tomes. Vamos a explorar cómo puedes fortalecer esa confianza para que cada paso en tu camino como madre sea seguro y lleno de amor.

Cómo Confiar en Ti Misma y en Tus Decisiones

La confianza en el instinto maternal es clave para navegar la experiencia de la maternidad con seguridad. Aprender a escuchar tu voz interior y combinar ese conocimiento con información externa es un proceso que se perfecciona con el tiempo.

1. Escucha tu voz interior

Una de las formas más efectivas de tomar decisiones como madre es confiar en lo que tu instinto te dice. Si sientes que algo no está bien con tu bebé, o si intuyes que debes hacer ajustes en su rutina o en su cuidado, es fundamental que te escuches a ti misma. Esta capacidad de reconocer lo que es mejor para tu bebé, sin necesidad de guías estrictas, está respaldada por estudios que sugieren que la intuición materna es una combinación de experiencia, conocimiento y una empatía profunda hacia el bebé (Hoffman et al., 2016).

El instinto maternal no es infalible, pero es una herramienta extremadamente valiosa que te permite ajustar las respuestas en tiempo real. Las madres suelen ser expertas en captar las pequeñas señales que indican que algo no está bien, como cambios sutiles en el comportamiento o la alimentación del bebé. Esta habilidad innata es una guía que merece ser valorada y seguida.

2. Reconoce tu conocimiento

Desde el momento en que nace tu bebé, tú eres quien pasa la mayor parte del tiempo con él. A través de esta cercanía diaria, desarrollas un conocimiento profundo de sus comportamientos, expresiones y necesidades. Este conocimiento no es algo que se pueda aprender en un manual, ya que surge de la interacción constante y del amor incondicional que le brindas.

La observación diaria te permite identificar rápidamente lo que funciona y lo que no en la crianza de tu bebé. Esta experiencia práctica te convierte en la persona más capacitada para tomar decisiones sobre su cuidado. Reconocer que tienes una comprensión única y valiosa de tu bebé te ayudará a confiar más en ti misma. Un estudio de Saxe et al. (2017) encontró que las madres son excepcionalmente hábiles para reconocer las señales emocionales de sus bebés, lo que les permite actuar de manera efectiva para calmar o estimular a sus hijos según sea necesario.

3. Sé flexible y abierta a aprender

Aunque el instinto maternal es una herramienta poderosa, también es importante recordar que la maternidad es un proceso continuo de aprendizaje. A medida que tu bebé crece, sus necesidades cambian, y es probable que lo que funcionó en un momento ya no sea efectivo en el siguiente. Ser flexible y estar dispuesta a ajustar tu enfoque es clave para adaptarte a las nuevas etapas del desarrollo de tu hijo.

La combinación del instinto con la disposición a aprender es lo que permite a las madres evolucionar en su rol. Según investigaciones, las madres que mantienen una mente abierta y flexible son más capaces de adaptarse a los desafíos de la crianza y de encontrar soluciones creativas cuando surgen problemas (Bornstein et al., 2011). Este enfoque te permitirá mantener un equilibrio entre confiar en tu instinto y aceptar que siempre hay nuevas formas de mejorar la experiencia de crianza.

4. Supera la presión externa

Una de las mayores barreras para confiar en los propios instintos como madre es la presión social. Las opiniones y consejos de amigos, familiares e incluso de las redes sociales pueden ser abrumadores y a menudo te hacen dudar de tus decisiones. Aunque estos consejos suelen ser bienintencionados, pueden generar inseguridad si sientes que no estás cumpliendo con las expectativas externas.

Es importante recordar que cada madre y cada bebé son únicos, y lo que funciona para otros puede no ser lo mejor para ti y tu hijo. Las decisiones sobre la crianza no son de "talla única". En lugar de sucumbir a las comparaciones, es esencial enfocarte en lo que sientes que es mejor para tu familia. Un estudio realizado por Davis et al. (2015) encontró que las madres que confían en su capacidad para tomar decisiones, en lugar de depender exclusivamente de las opiniones externas, experimentan menos estrés y tienen una mayor satisfacción en su rol de madres.

A medida que te sumerges en el día a día con tu bebé, te darás cuenta de que las respuestas correctas no siempre están en los libros ni en los consejos de los demás. Tu intuición se convierte en una aliada silenciosa, guiándote con pequeñas señales que solo tú puedes percibir. Sin embargo, confiar en ese instinto no significa que debas rechazar el aprendizaje; de hecho, este proceso de combinar lo que sientes con lo que aprendes es lo que te permite crecer como madre. Y mientras sigues explorando este equilibrio, es reconfortante saber que no solo se trata de una "corazonada", sino que también está respaldada por la ciencia. A continuación, descubriremos los fundamentos neurobiológicos que explican cómo tu cerebro se adapta y refuerza ese instinto maternal.

La Ciencia Detrás del Instinto Maternal

El instinto maternal no es solo una creencia cultural; tiene una base neurobiológica sólida. Durante el embarazo y después del parto, el cerebro de la madre se "reorganiza" en áreas clave que involucran la empatía, la toma de decisiones y la vigilancia, lo que mejora su capacidad para percibir y responder a las necesidades del bebé (Kim et al., 2010). Esta reconfiguración cerebral refuerza la capacidad de la madre para estar atenta a las señales emocionales y físicas del bebé, lo que le permite responder de manera intuitiva y eficaz.

Es fascinante pensar que, mientras tú cambias emocionalmente, tu cerebro también se transforma para sintonizarse con las necesidades de tu bebé. Estos cambios no son meramente anecdóticos, sino que están profundamente arraigados en la biología del cuerpo. La ciencia nos muestra cómo tu cerebro se reorganiza, cómo ciertos procesos neuroquímicos se activan para mejorar tu capacidad de proteger y cuidar a tu hijo. Desde la oxitocina hasta la activación de áreas clave del cerebro, cada parte de ti está diseñada para crear ese lazo especial con tu bebé. Vamos a adentrarnos en los detalles de estos cambios y entender cómo funcionan en tu día a día.

Cambios Neuroquímicos

Uno de los cambios más importantes que ocurren en el cerebro materno es el aumento de la producción de oxitocina, una hormona que juega un papel crucial en la formación del vínculo madre-hijo. La oxitocina no solo facilita el parto y la lactancia, sino que también promueve sentimientos de amor, confianza y conexión con el bebé. Este "cóctel neuroquímico" fortalece el instinto maternal, permitiendo que las madres sientan un impulso natural de cuidar y proteger a sus hijos (Swain et al., 2007).

Los estudios de neuroimagen han demostrado que cuando las madres interactúan con sus bebés, se activan áreas específicas del cerebro relacionadas con la empatía y la recompensa, lo que refuerza el comportamiento maternal y motiva a las madres a responder de manera protectora y afectuosa (Kim et al., 2010). Estos cambios biológicos son una de las razones por las cuales muchas madres pueden tomar decisiones rápidas y acertadas basadas en su instinto.

Los cambios hormonales, como la liberación de oxitocina, no solo facilitan la lactancia y el apego, sino que también fortalecen esa sensación de saber, de comprender lo que tu bebé necesita sin que te lo diga. Pero más allá de los aspectos neuroquímicos, hay algo más profundo que ocurre: esa capacidad intuitiva que tienes como madre. A veces es difícil explicar por qué sabes lo que está ocurriendo, pero ese conocimiento interno, esa "certeza inexplicable", es lo que llamamos intuición. Y aunque pueda parecer subjetiva, esta intuición está respaldada por años de evolución y biología. A continuación, veremos cómo esta intuición no solo es válida, sino esencial en tu rol como madre.

La Intuición Como Guía Válida

La intuición materna, que a menudo se manifiesta como un "sentimiento visceral" o una certeza inexplicable sobre lo que necesita el bebé, está respaldada por una combinación de factores biológicos y psicológicos. Según estudios en el campo de la psicología evolutiva, la intuición en los padres, especialmente en las madres, es una forma de "toma de decisiones rápida" que se basa en la experiencia acumulada, las señales del bebé y los cambios hormonales que afectan el comportamiento (Hoffman et al., 2016). Esta intuición, aunque a veces difícil de explicar, es una herramienta confiable en la crianza y no debe ser subestimada.

El instinto maternal es una fuerza silenciosa pero poderosa. No necesitas libros, ni consejos constantes para saber lo que es mejor para tu bebé; hay algo en lo profundo de ti que simplemente lo sabe. Cada vez que respondes a su llanto, lo consuelas con tus abrazos o intuyes lo que necesita antes de que pueda decírtelo, ese instinto está actuando. A medida que confías más en él, descubrirás que es tu guía más fiel en este viaje de la maternidad. Ahora, mientras cerramos este capítulo, quiero invitarte a reflexionar sobre la grandeza de ese poder interno que habita en ti. Confía en ti, en esa voz que siempre te orienta con amor.

Conclusión del Capítulo

La maternidad es, sin duda, una experiencia profundamente personal, única y absolutamente irrepetible. Cada madre vive su propio recorrido, marcado por las particularidades de su historia, sus circunstancias y la relación única que construye con su hijo. A lo largo de este camino, es natural que recibas una avalancha de consejos, opiniones y recomendaciones de familiares, amigos, profesionales e incluso de fuentes externas como libros o redes sociales. Aunque toda esta información puede ser valiosa, es fundamental que, en medio de todo ese ruido, aprendas a escuchar y a confiar en ti misma. Tú conoces a tu bebé mejor que nadie, y tu instinto maternal es una guía poderosa que te ayudará a tomar decisiones acertadas para su crianza y bienestar.

A medida que te sumerges en la maternidad, descubrirás que tu intuición comienza a desarrollarse y fortalecerse con el tiempo. Es ese conocimiento profundo, casi innato, que se despierta cuando observas las necesidades de tu bebé y aprendes a interpretarlas de manera única. Esa conexión especial entre madre e hijo te permite tomar decisiones que resuenan contigo y con lo que consideras mejor para tu familia. No siempre será fácil, y habrá momentos en los que dudarás o te sentirás insegura, pero es precisamente en esos momentos cuando confiar en tu instinto puede marcar la diferencia. La maternidad no se trata de seguir un manual estricto o una serie de reglas inquebrantables; se trata de adaptarte, aprender sobre la marcha y confiar en la sabiduría que ya tienes dentro de ti.

Cada madre y cada bebé son diferentes, por lo que no existe un "camino correcto" universal para la maternidad. Lo que funciona para una familia puede no ser adecuado para otra, y eso está perfectamente bien. La comparación constante con los demás, o con las ideas preconcebidas sobre cómo "debería" ser la maternidad, puede generar frustración y dudas. Por eso, es fundamental que te permitas crear tu propio camino, basado en las necesidades y características únicas de tu bebé y en tu propia manera de ser madre. El éxito en la maternidad no se mide por cuán bien sigas un conjunto de normas externas, sino por la capacidad de conectar emocionalmente con tu hijo y responder de manera amorosa y consciente a lo que él necesita.

Confiar en ti misma también implica aceptar que cometerás errores, y eso es completamente normal. La maternidad no es un proceso lineal ni perfecto, y cada día trae consigo nuevos desafíos y oportunidades de aprendizaje. Habrá días en los que sentirás que has hecho todo bien y otros en los que te preguntarás si estás tomando las decisiones correctas. Lo importante es que te permitas aprender de cada experiencia y sigas adelante con la certeza de que siempre estás haciendo lo mejor que puedes con las herramientas que tienes en ese momento. La flexibilidad, la paciencia y el amor propio son tan importantes como el amor que le das a tu hijo.

A lo largo del tiempo, verás cómo tu capacidad para adaptarte y confiar en tu instinto se convertirá en una de las mayores fortalezas en tu viaje de maternidad. Los primeros meses y años de vida de tu hijo estarán llenos de momentos de incertidumbre, pero también de momentos de claridad en los que sentirás que, pese a los desafíos, estás encontrando el equilibrio. Con el tiempo, te sorprenderás de la sabiduría interna que has acumulado, no solo sobre tu bebé, sino también sobre ti misma. La maternidad no solo es una experiencia de crianza, sino también de autodescubrimiento, y confiar en tu instinto es parte integral de ese proceso.

Recuerda que, si bien es útil estar informada y abierta a recibir consejos, la decisión final siempre debe estar alineada con lo que sientes que es mejor para ti y tu hijo. Tu instinto, alimentado por el amor profundo que tienes por tu bebé, es una herramienta poderosa. No lo subestimes. Aunque pueda ser tentador seguir las recomendaciones de otros, nunca pierdas de vista la voz interior que te guía y que te recuerda que tú eres la experta en tu propio hijo. Nadie conoce mejor que tú sus particularidades, sus ritmos y sus necesidades, y confiar en tu capacidad para interpretarlas es clave para criar a tu hijo de la mejor manera posible.

En conclusión, la maternidad es una experiencia que se vive de manera única e irrepetible. No existe un "camino correcto" para ser madre, porque cada madre y cada bebé tienen sus propias necesidades y desafíos. Confiar en ti misma, en tu capacidad para aprender, adaptarte y tomar decisiones basadas en tu instinto es lo que te permitirá navegar este viaje con mayor confianza y tranquilidad. Tu instinto es una herramienta valiosa, y al escucharla, estarás creando un entorno amoroso, seguro y auténtico para tu hijo, mientras disfrutas de la experiencia de ser madre en tus propios términos.

Al llegar al final de este capítulo, me gustaría compartir un consejo que me ha ayudado a lo largo del camino. El mundo está lleno de consejos bien intencionados, pero nadie conoce a tu bebé mejor que tú. Escuchar a los demás es importante, pero escuchar tu propio corazón lo es aún más. Mi consejo es sencillo: sigue ese instinto que te dice qué es lo correcto, porque es una sabiduría que va más allá de la lógica. Serás sorprendida por cómo esa intuición te guiará en cada paso. No tengas miedo de seguirla, incluso cuando los demás te sugieran caminos distintos.

Consejo del autor: No te sientas presionada a ser la madre "perfecta". La perfección en la crianza no existe. Lo que sí existe es el amor incondicional, la paciencia y la intuición que te guiarán en este proceso. Permítete cometer errores, aprender de ellos y confiar en tu capacidad para tomar las decisiones adecuadas para tu bebé. No olvides que tu instinto, combinado con el amor, es la brújula más precisa que tienes como madre.

Con este consejo en mente, ahora quiero invitarte a hacer una pausa para un ejercicio reflexivo. Este es un momento solo para ti, para desconectar del ruido exterior y escuchar lo que tu corazón tiene que decir. Pregúntate: ¿cuándo fue la última vez que confié plenamente en mi instinto? ¿Qué decisiones tomé guiada por mi intuición? Al reflexionar sobre estas preguntas, estarás fortaleciendo tu conexión contigo misma y con ese poder interno que te ayuda a ser la mejor madre para tu bebé. Vamos a dedicar unos minutos a esta introspección, recordando que el instinto es tu mejor aliado.

Ejercicio reflexivo
Reflexiona sobre las decisiones que has tomado recientemente en la crianza de tu bebé. Pregúntate:
• ¿En qué momentos he confiado en mi instinto y qué resultado he obtenido?
• ¿Cuándo he sentido presión externa para hacer las cosas de manera diferente?
• ¿Cómo puedo fortalecer mi confianza en mis propias decisiones?
Escribir estas reflexiones te permitirá identificar patrones y situaciones en las que tu intuición ha sido clave y te ayudará a reforzar tu confianza para el futuro.

Después de este momento de conexión interior, volvamos al presente con algunos consejos prácticos que te ayudarán en tu día a día. Aunque el instinto maternal es una guía poderosa, siempre es útil tener a mano algunos trucos para facilitar las rutinas cotidianas. En la siguiente sección, te compartiré tips que te permitirán hacer frente a los desafíos más comunes de manera más eficiente, mientras sigues confiando en tu intuición. A veces, solo necesitas un par de ajustes prácticos para sentirte más en control y disfrutar aún más de los pequeños momentos con tu bebé.

Tips y trucos

1. **Desconecta de la sobreinformación**: Si te sientes abrumada por la cantidad de información contradictoria que encuentras, permite un descanso. Tomarte un tiempo para escuchar solo a tu bebé y a ti misma puede aclarar tus pensamientos.

2. **Crea una red de apoyo respetuosa**: Rodéate de personas que te apoyen y respeten tus decisiones. Busca aquellos amigos o familiares que te brinden apoyo sin juzgar tus elecciones.

3. **Confía en los pequeños logros**: A medida que tu bebé crezca, habrá momentos pequeños y grandes en los que verás el impacto positivo de tus decisiones. Usa estos logros como recordatorios de que tu instinto está alineado con lo que tu bebé necesita.

4. **Permítete la duda**: No es necesario tener todas las respuestas de inmediato. Permítete dudar y aprender sobre la marcha. Ser madre no significa tener todas las respuestas, sino estar dispuesta a descubrirlas a medida que surgen las situaciones.

Ahora que tienes algunos consejos útiles que puedes aplicar de inmediato, quiero recordarte que siempre hay más apoyo disponible si lo necesitas. En la próxima sección, encontrarás recursos adicionales que te brindarán aún más herramientas para navegar la maternidad con confianza. Desde lecturas inspiradoras hasta grupos de apoyo donde otras mamás comparten sus experiencias, estos recursos están aquí para asegurarse de que nunca te sientas sola en este viaje. ¡Vamos a explorar estas opciones que te permitirán seguir confiando en ti misma mientras descubres nuevas formas de crecer como mamá!

Recursos adicionales

- **Libros recomendados**:

  - *El cerebro de la madre* de Katherine Ellison: Este libro explora cómo el cerebro de una mujer cambia con la maternidad y cómo estos cambios favorecen el instinto maternal.

  - *Crianza respetuosa* de Rosa Jové: Ofrece consejos prácticos sobre cómo guiar la crianza desde una perspectiva empática y basada en la intuición.

- **Webs y comunidades**:

  - *Maternidad consciente*: Espacio en línea que promueve la confianza en la intuición maternal y el autocuidado.

  - *La Liga de la Leche Internacional*: Además de apoyo a la lactancia, ofrecen recursos que ayudan a las madres a conectarse con su instinto.

- **Aplicaciones útiles**:

  - "Peanut": Una red social para madres que facilita la conexión entre mujeres que comparten experiencias y ofrecen apoyo respetuoso.

  - "The Wonder Weeks": Aplicación que ayuda a las madres a entender las fases de desarrollo de su bebé, lo que puede reforzar la confianza en cómo responder a sus necesidades.

El tiempo pasa en un abrir y cerrar de ojos, y antes de que te des cuenta, tu bebé empieza a tomar sus primeros pasos hacia la independencia. Es un proceso natural, lleno de pequeños logros y grandes emociones, tanto para ti como para él. De repente, te das cuenta de que ya no necesita tanto de tus brazos como antes, y aunque puede ser difícil soltar, también es una oportunidad hermosa para verlo crecer y convertirse en su propia personita. No estás perdiendo a tu bebé, estás ganando un niño fuerte, valiente y curioso. Vamos a explorar este proceso con amor y paciencia.

*"El instinto es la brújula natural que guía a una madre, no hay un mapa que seguir, pero siempre encontrarás el camino." – **Harriet Lerner***

Capítulo 9

Los Primeros Pasos Hacia la Independencia

Fomentando la confianza y autonomía de tu bebé desde el inicio

A medida que tu bebé pasa de ser un infante a un niño pequeño, comienza a descubrir el mundo con mayor independencia y curiosidad. Durante esta etapa, que abarca aproximadamente desde el primer hasta el tercer año de vida, se producen desarrollos cruciales en sus habilidades cognitivas, emocionales y motoras. Al mismo tiempo, como padres, es común enfrentarse a nuevos desafíos en la crianza, incluyendo el manejo de los berrinches y la implementación de estrategias de disciplina. Este capítulo te proporcionará herramientas y consejos para estimular el desarrollo de tu hijo, al mismo tiempo que fomentas una crianza basada en el amor y la comprensión.

Desarrollo del bebé de 1 a 3 años

El período comprendido entre el primer y el tercer año de vida es una etapa crucial de avances significativos en el desarrollo físico, cognitivo y emocional del niño. En estos años, los niños pasan de ser bebés dependientes a pequeños exploradores llenos de energía, curiosidad y un creciente sentido de independencia. Durante este tiempo, el juego y la estimulación temprana desempeñan un papel fundamental en el desarrollo de habilidades que prepararán al niño para futuros aprendizajes. Proporcionar un entorno enriquecedor y creativo es clave para apoyar su crecimiento integral.

Habilidades motoras y cognitivas

A medida que los niños pequeños crecen, sus habilidades motoras y cognitivas se desarrollan a gran velocidad. Estas habilidades permiten que los niños interactúen con el mundo de manera más compleja y les proporcionan las herramientas necesarias para enfrentarse a nuevos desafíos.

1. Desarrollo motor grueso

Uno de los hitos más notables en el desarrollo infantil es el aprendizaje de la marcha. Alrededor del primer año de vida, la mayoría de los niños comienzan a caminar, lo que marca un avance significativo en su autonomía y su capacidad para explorar el entorno. Este desarrollo motor grueso continúa progresando entre los 18 meses y los 3 años, cuando los niños comienzan a correr, saltar, subir y bajar escaleras y lanzar pelotas.

Proporcionarles un entorno seguro donde puedan moverse libremente es esencial para fomentar este desarrollo. Espacios como parques o áreas de juego al aire libre les permiten mejorar su equilibrio y coordinación mientras exploran su entorno físico. Investigaciones sobre desarrollo motor infantil muestran que los niños que tienen acceso regular a oportunidades de juego activo desarrollan una mejor coordinación y habilidades motoras más avanzadas en comparación con aquellos que no cuentan con estas oportunidades (Piek et al., 2006).

2. Desarrollo motor fino

El desarrollo de las habilidades motoras finas también es fundamental en esta etapa. Estas habilidades involucran movimientos más pequeños y precisos, como agarrar objetos pequeños, manipular juguetes y herramientas, o coordinar las manos y los ojos para completar tareas más complejas. Durante este período, los niños aprenden a dibujar formas simples, a apilar bloques para hacer torres y a usar cubiertos básicos.

Estas actividades no solo promueven el control físico, sino que también ayudan a mejorar la concentración, la planificación y la resolución de problemas. Los juegos que implican el uso de los dedos, como pintar con los dedos o manipular piezas pequeñas, fortalecen la coordinación mano-ojo y preparan a los niños para futuros aprendizajes, como escribir o cortar con tijeras (Suggate et al., 2017).

3. Desarrollo del lenguaje

El crecimiento del vocabulario y las habilidades de comunicación durante los primeros tres años es impresionante. Alrededor de los 18 meses, los niños comienzan a pronunciar palabras sueltas, y para los 2-3 años, la mayoría ya puede formar frases cortas de dos o tres palabras. La interacción verbal constante con el niño, a través de conversaciones, lectura de cuentos y canciones, es crucial para el desarrollo del lenguaje.

La exposición al lenguaje en estas primeras etapas tiene un impacto directo en el desarrollo cognitivo a largo plazo. Estudios sugieren que los niños que son expuestos a un mayor número de palabras y conversaciones en sus primeros tres años tienden a tener un vocabulario más amplio y mejores habilidades de comprensión verbal en la infancia y la adolescencia (Hart & Risley, 2003). Esto subraya la importancia de que los padres y cuidadores hablen regularmente con sus hijos, incluso desde una edad temprana, para fomentar el desarrollo lingüístico.

4. Desarrollo cognitivo

Los niños pequeños son naturalmente curiosos y utilizan el juego como una herramienta para explorar el mundo y resolver problemas. Juegos de construcción, rompecabezas simples y actividades creativas, como la pintura o el dibujo, les permiten comprender conceptos básicos como la causa y el efecto, las relaciones espaciales y la secuencia. Estas actividades también estimulan su imaginación y les permiten expresar sus emociones y pensamientos a través del juego simbólico.

El juego simbólico, en el que los niños imitan acciones y roles de los adultos, como cocinar o cuidar a un muñeco, es un signo importante del desarrollo cognitivo y emocional. Según Piaget, el juego simbólico permite a los niños construir su comprensión del mundo al experimentar roles sociales y procesos que observan en los adultos (Piaget, 1952). Además, este tipo de juego promueve la creatividad y la capacidad de resolución de problemas, habilidades que serán esenciales en su desarrollo posterior.

Estimulación temprana a través del juego

El juego es la principal forma de aprendizaje para los niños pequeños. No solo es un medio de entretenimiento, sino una actividad crucial para el desarrollo de sus habilidades cognitivas, motoras y emocionales. Los niños necesitan tiempo y espacio para jugar, explorar y experimentar el mundo que los rodea. Además, el juego interactivo con los padres y otros niños es una excelente forma de promover el desarrollo social y la empatía.

Juegos físicos

Actividades físicas como correr, saltar y jugar en el parque son fundamentales para el desarrollo motor grueso. A medida que los niños pequeños ganan confianza en sus habilidades físicas, necesitan oportunidades para practicar y perfeccionar esas habilidades. Juguetes como triciclos, juguetes de empuje o arrastre, y actividades en el parque infantil ayudan a mejorar su equilibrio y coordinación.

Según estudios sobre desarrollo infantil, la actividad física regular no solo mejora las habilidades motoras, sino que también contribuye al desarrollo cognitivo, ya que el movimiento está estrechamente relacionado con la exploración y el aprendizaje (Diamond, 2000). Por lo tanto, es importante que los niños pequeños tengan oportunidades diarias para moverse libremente y participar en juegos activos.

Juegos creativos

Los juegos creativos permiten a los niños explorar su imaginación y desarrollar habilidades motoras finas. Proporcionarles materiales simples, como bloques de construcción, arcilla o lápices de colores, les permite expresar su creatividad y desarrollar su capacidad para resolver problemas de manera independiente. Además, estas actividades les ayudan a desarrollar su sentido de logro y confianza en sí mismos.

El juego con materiales abiertos, como bloques o arcilla, fomenta la creatividad porque no tiene un objetivo predeterminado. En lugar de seguir instrucciones específicas, los niños pueden experimentar, construir y crear libremente, lo que también promueve el pensamiento crítico y la resolución de problemas (Whitebread et al., 2012).

Juegos de imitación

A partir de los 2 años, los niños comienzan a participar en juegos de imitación, en los que reproducen acciones y roles que ven en los adultos, como hacer de "mamá" o "papá", "médico" o "cocinero". Este tipo de juego no solo fomenta el desarrollo de habilidades sociales y emocionales, sino que también les permite comprender mejor el mundo que los rodea. A través de la imitación, los niños experimentan con diferentes roles y situaciones, lo que fortalece su capacidad para relacionarse con los demás y les proporciona una mayor sensación de control sobre su entorno.

El juego simbólico también está vinculado al desarrollo del lenguaje, ya que los niños practican el uso de palabras y frases mientras imitan conversaciones y acciones que ven en los adultos. Esto les ayuda a reforzar el vocabulario y a desarrollar habilidades comunicativas más avanzadas (Hughes, 2010).

El crecimiento de tu bebé entre los 1 y 3 años es como ver una flor abrirse lentamente: cada día trae nuevas palabras, gestos y descubrimientos. En esta etapa, tu pequeño se está afirmando en el mundo, aprendiendo no solo a caminar y hablar, sino también a expresar sus emociones de maneras más complejas. Y con ese crecimiento viene uno de los desafíos más temidos: los berrinches. Es natural que el desarrollo emocional de tu bebé traiga consigo frustraciones que se manifiestan en momentos de descontrol. Pero no temas, porque estos episodios no son un reflejo de fracaso, sino una oportunidad para practicar la crianza con amor y paciencia. Vamos a explorar cómo puedes abordar estos momentos difíciles con una perspectiva de cariño y enseñanza.

Manejo de los Berrinches y la Crianza con Amor

Durante el período de 1 a 3 años, los niños pequeños experimentan un rápido desarrollo emocional y cognitivo. Este es un momento en el que están aprendiendo a ser más independientes y a expresar sus deseos y necesidades de manera más directa. Sin embargo, su capacidad para regular sus emociones y comunicarse de manera efectiva aún está en desarrollo. Como resultado, es común que los niños en esta etapa experimenten frustración cuando no pueden obtener lo que desean de inmediato, lo que puede llevar a episodios de berrinches o rabietas. Estos comportamientos son normales y esperados durante este período del desarrollo infantil.

El manejo de los berrinches de manera constructiva es una oportunidad para enseñar a los niños habilidades emocionales fundamentales. La clave está en utilizar la disciplina positiva, un enfoque que fomenta el respeto mutuo y guía el comportamiento a través de la empatía y la comprensión. Esto permite que los niños desarrollen la capacidad de regular sus emociones y tomar mejores decisiones a medida que crecen.

¿Por qué ocurren los Berrinches?

Los berrinches son una respuesta natural a la frustración, ya que los niños pequeños no han desarrollado completamente las habilidades verbales y emocionales para expresar sus sentimientos de manera más adecuada. Durante los primeros años de vida, el cerebro del niño todavía está en proceso de maduración, especialmente las áreas responsables del autocontrol y la regulación emocional, como el córtex prefrontal. Dado que esta parte del cerebro sigue en desarrollo, los niños pequeños tienden a reaccionar impulsivamente cuando se sienten abrumados o frustrados.

Existen varios factores que pueden desencadenar berrinches. Entre los más comunes están el cansancio, el hambre, los cambios en la rutina diaria, la incapacidad de comunicar lo que desean o simplemente el hecho de no poder realizar una actividad que quieren. Los niños pequeños también pueden experimentar berrinches cuando se enfrentan a límites o reglas que no comprenden completamente, lo que les genera una sensación de impotencia.

Investigaciones sobre el desarrollo emocional infantil han demostrado que los berrinches son una parte natural del proceso de aprendizaje emocional. Aunque estos episodios pueden ser estresantes para los padres, también son una oportunidad para enseñar al niño a manejar sus emociones y a desarrollar estrategias más efectivas para expresarse (Thompson, 2006).

Estrategias para manejar los Berrinches

El manejo de los berrinches requiere paciencia, consistencia y un enfoque comprensivo. Las siguientes estrategias basadas en la disciplina positiva pueden ayudar a gestionar estos episodios de manera eficaz, enseñando al niño habilidades emocionales clave.

1. Mantén la calma

Cuando un niño tiene un berrinche, es fácil que los padres también se sientan frustrados o irritados. Sin embargo, es crucial que los adultos mantengan la calma, ya que los niños pequeños aprenden observando las reacciones de sus cuidadores. Si un padre responde con calma y control, el niño puede aprender a regular sus emociones de manera similar. Esto se debe a que los niños suelen imitar los comportamientos emocionales que ven en los adultos.

La investigación sobre la regulación emocional muestra que los niños que son expuestos a un entorno calmado y controlado durante los momentos de estrés desarrollan mejores habilidades de autocontrol a largo plazo (Morris et al., 2007). Mantener la calma también permite a los padres pensar con claridad y responder de manera más efectiva a la situación.

2. Valida sus emociones

Aunque no siempre puedas cumplir los deseos de tu hijo, es importante que reconozcas y valides sus sentimientos. Decir cosas como "Sé que estás molesto porque no podemos ir al parque ahora" o "Entiendo que te sientas frustrado porque no puedes tener ese juguete" ayuda a que el niño se sienta comprendido. Esto no significa que estés cediendo a sus demandas, sino que estás enseñándole a identificar y expresar sus emociones de manera saludable.

La validación emocional fomenta el desarrollo de la inteligencia emocional, un factor clave en la capacidad de los niños para manejar sus emociones y relacionarse con los demás. Estudios han demostrado que cuando los padres validan las emociones de sus hijos, estos son más propensos a desarrollar habilidades efectivas de regulación emocional y a experimentar menos problemas de comportamiento (Gottman et al., 1997).

3. Redirige la atención

Una técnica efectiva para manejar los berrinches es redirigir la atención del niño hacia otra actividad. Los niños pequeños tienen una capacidad limitada para mantener su atención en una sola cosa durante mucho tiempo, por lo que ofrecerles una alternativa interesante puede ayudar a desactivar la situación. Proponer un juego, ofrecerles un objeto nuevo o sugerir que realicen una actividad que disfrutan puede ser suficiente para calmar un berrinche incipiente.

Este enfoque no solo ayuda a reducir el estrés tanto para el niño como para el adulto, sino que también enseña al niño a cambiar su enfoque hacia algo positivo, una habilidad que es útil para lidiar con la frustración en el futuro.

4. Establece límites claros y consistentes

Los niños pequeños necesitan estructura y límites para sentirse seguros y comprender qué se espera de ellos. Establecer límites claros y consistentes ayuda a prevenir algunos berrinches, ya que los niños empiezan a entender qué comportamientos son aceptables y cuáles no. Sin embargo, es fundamental que estos límites se establezcan con amor y respeto, de modo que el niño sepa que, aunque su comportamiento tiene consecuencias, siempre será tratado con cariño.

La consistencia en la aplicación de límites también es importante. Si un comportamiento tiene una consecuencia un día, pero no la siguiente, el niño puede sentirse confundido, lo que puede aumentar la frecuencia de los berrinches. Los estudios sugieren que los niños criados en entornos con límites claros y consistentes tienen menos problemas de comportamiento y muestran un mejor ajuste emocional en general (Baumrind, 1996).

5. Sé consistente

La coherencia en las respuestas ante los berrinches es crucial para que el niño entienda las reglas y los límites. Si los padres responden de manera inconsistente, el niño puede tener dificultades para prever las consecuencias de sus acciones, lo que puede aumentar su frustración y provocar más berrinches.

La consistencia también refuerza la confianza del niño en su entorno y en sus cuidadores, lo que le proporciona una mayor sensación de seguridad y previsibilidad. Esta seguridad emocional es fundamental para el desarrollo de una autoimagen saludable y un comportamiento adecuado a largo plazo.

Disciplina positiva

La disciplina positiva es un enfoque que se centra en enseñar habilidades y comportamientos a través de la empatía, el respeto y la comprensión, en lugar de recurrir a castigos severos o autoritarios. Esta forma de crianza tiene como objetivo guiar al niño en su aprendizaje, proporcionándole herramientas para que pueda tomar mejores decisiones en el futuro. En lugar de centrarse en lo que el niño hizo mal, la disciplina positiva se enfoca en lo que puede aprender de la situación y cómo puede actuar de manera más constructiva.

1. Ofrece opciones

Cuando los niños pequeños sienten que tienen algún control sobre su entorno, es menos probable que se sientan frustrados y, por tanto, disminuye la posibilidad de un berrinche. Ofrecer opciones dentro de los límites que has establecido les da a los niños una sensación de autonomía. Por ejemplo, en lugar de dar una orden directa como "Ponte los zapatos ahora", puedes decir: "¿Quieres ponerte los zapatos rojos o los azules?".

Este enfoque les enseña a tomar decisiones, a asumir responsabilidades y a seguir instrucciones, mientras les permite sentir que tienen cierto control sobre la situación. Según un estudio de Grolnick et al. (1997), ofrecer elecciones dentro de un marco de límites claros promueve el sentido de autonomía en los niños, lo que a su vez mejora su bienestar emocional y reduce el comportamiento desafiante.

2. Enseña mediante el ejemplo

Los niños aprenden observando a los adultos a su alrededor, especialmente a sus padres. Si manejas tus frustraciones y situaciones difíciles con calma y respeto, tu hijo aprenderá a imitar ese comportamiento. Modelar conductas apropiadas es una de las formas más efectivas de enseñar. Las investigaciones indican que los niños tienden a emular las reacciones emocionales y comportamientos de sus padres, lo que refuerza la importancia de ser un ejemplo positivo en la forma de gestionar el estrés y las emociones (Bandura, 1977).

3. Refuerza el buen comportamiento

Es importante no solo corregir el mal comportamiento, sino también reforzar el buen comportamiento. Asegúrate de elogiar y agradecer a tu hijo cuando haga algo bien, ya sea que guarde sus juguetes o que se exprese de manera calmada. El refuerzo positivo ayuda a que los niños asocien comportamientos específicos con resultados agradables, lo que aumenta la probabilidad de que repitan esas acciones en el futuro.

Pequeños elogios como "Me gusta cómo has esperado tu turno" o "Gracias por ayudarme a recoger los juguetes" pueden tener un gran impacto en la autoestima del niño y fomentar un comportamiento cooperativo y respetuoso (Schwartz et al., 2014).

Lidiar con los berrinches puede ser agotador, pero cada momento de frustración es también una lección, tanto para tu hijo como para ti. A través del amor, la calma y la consistencia, puedes guiarlo hacia el entendimiento de sus emociones, enseñándole que está bien sentir frustración, pero que también hay maneras más saludables de expresarla. A medida que llegamos al final de este capítulo, quiero que te lleves una sensación de confianza: estos desafíos son parte del desarrollo natural, y cada berrinche que enfrentes con amor está ayudando a formar a un ser humano más empático y resiliente. Ahora, tomemos un momento para reflexionar sobre el increíble trabajo que haces cada día.

Conclusión del Capítulo

El desarrollo de los niños entre 1 y 3 años es un periodo fascinante, lleno de cambios rápidos y momentos transformadores. Durante estos años, los pequeños pasan de ser bebés dependientes a convertirse en niños curiosos y activos que desean explorar todo a su alrededor. Cada día trae consigo nuevos descubrimientos, y es a través del juego, la exploración y las interacciones diarias que los niños comienzan a comprender el mundo que los rodea. Sus sentidos están siempre en acción, y con cada objeto que tocan, cada palabra que escuchan y cada nueva experiencia, están construyendo las bases de su aprendizaje futuro. Este período es una oportunidad única para nutrir su crecimiento y su desarrollo de manera integral, ya que cada interacción cuenta en el proceso de formación de su personalidad y habilidades.

Uno de los cambios más notables en esta etapa es el desarrollo del lenguaje. Los niños comienzan a ampliar su vocabulario rápidamente, y aunque en los primeros meses las palabras puedan parecer incompletas o limitadas, pronto se transforman en frases que expresan ideas y sentimientos. Este desarrollo del lenguaje no solo es fascinante de observar, sino que también les permite empezar a comunicarse de manera más efectiva con quienes los rodean. Tu papel como madre o padre en este proceso es clave, ya que, a través de la conversación diaria, la lectura de libros, y el simple hecho de escuchar y responder a sus intentos de comunicación, ayudas a fortalecer sus habilidades lingüísticas. Recuerda que no solo están aprendiendo a hablar, sino también a entender el poder de las palabras, a expresar sus necesidades y emociones, y a formar sus primeras conexiones sociales.

El desarrollo físico también avanza a pasos agigantados durante estos años. Las habilidades motoras finas y gruesas se desarrollan rápidamente: desde aprender a caminar con mayor seguridad y coordinación hasta dominar el uso de las manos para tareas más complejas, como armar bloques, comer por sí solos o dibujar. Este proceso de aprendizaje motriz a menudo ocurre a través del juego y la exploración libre, que es una parte fundamental del crecimiento. Como padres, proporcionar un entorno seguro pero estimulante, lleno de oportunidades para moverse y explorar, les dará a los niños la confianza que necesitan para seguir desarrollando sus habilidades físicas. Jugar al aire libre, ofrecer juguetes educativos y participar en actividades que fomenten el movimiento no solo ayuda a su desarrollo físico, sino que también estimula su imaginación y creatividad.

A la par de estos avances, también comienzan a emerger los desafíos emocionales propios de esta etapa, y los berrinches son una expresión común de las emociones abrumadoras que los niños aún están aprendiendo a manejar. Es importante recordar que estos momentos no son solo episodios difíciles de atravesar, sino valiosas oportunidades para enseñarles a gestionar sus emociones y a comprender los límites. Los niños pequeños aún no tienen las herramientas necesarias para regular sus emociones, por lo que dependen de sus cuidadores para guiarlos en este proceso. Fomentar un ambiente de calma y comprensión durante un berrinche, en lugar de reaccionar con frustración, puede ayudar a que el niño comience a entender cómo manejar mejor sus sentimientos con el tiempo.

Este es también el momento en el que los padres pueden empezar a establecer límites claros y consistentes, no como un castigo, sino como una forma de enseñarles que ciertas acciones tienen consecuencias. La crianza basada en la disciplina positiva se enfoca en guiar a los niños con amor, paciencia y firmeza, ayudándolos a entender el concepto de los límites de una manera respetuosa y constructiva. Enseñar con el ejemplo, mostrando calma y autocontrol, y ofreciendo explicaciones claras y apropiadas para su edad, les proporciona una base emocional segura. Al hacerlo, no solo los ayudas a navegar las frustraciones y desafíos propios de la edad, sino que también fortaleces el vínculo afectivo entre ustedes.

El amor y la disciplina positiva son fundamentales en este proceso, y cuando se combinan, no solo guían el desarrollo del niño, sino que también construyen una relación sólida y de confianza entre padres e hijos. Los niños necesitan sentir que están seguros y amados, pero también necesitan estructura para aprender a interactuar con el mundo de manera saludable. Una crianza basada en el respeto mutuo les enseña a gestionar sus emociones y comportamientos, lo cual es crucial para su desarrollo emocional a largo plazo. A través de estas interacciones, el niño no solo aprende a obedecer reglas, sino también a entender el "por qué" detrás de las mismas, desarrollando empatía y responsabilidad.

En última instancia, los años de 1 a 3 son un tiempo de inmenso crecimiento tanto para el niño como para los padres. Cada pequeño avance, cada desafío y cada momento compartido es una oportunidad para fortalecer los lazos afectivos y fomentar el desarrollo saludable. Si bien esta etapa puede estar llena de cambios rápidos y momentos de prueba, también es un periodo lleno de alegrías y satisfacciones, donde los pequeños logros se celebran con entusiasmo. Al enfocarte en fomentar un ambiente de amor, apoyo y disciplina positiva, estarás guiando a tu hijo no solo en su desarrollo físico y emocional, sino también en la creación de una relación duradera basada en la confianza y el cariño.

En resumen, los primeros años de vida son una época emocionante y transformadora para los niños, en la que cada día trae consigo nuevas habilidades y desafíos. A través del juego, la exploración y las interacciones diarias, los niños desarrollan su lenguaje, mejoran sus habilidades motoras y aprenden a gestionar sus emociones. Fomentar una crianza basada en el amor y la disciplina positiva no solo ayuda a guiar su desarrollo, sino que también fortalece el vínculo entre padres e hijos, estableciendo las bases para un crecimiento emocional saludable a largo plazo.

Al finalizar este capítulo, me gustaría ofrecerte un consejo que podría iluminar tu camino en estos años tan importantes: ten paciencia contigo misma. No se espera que lo sepas todo ni que manejes cada situación con perfección. Mi consejo es simple: en cada desafío, recuerda que eres la persona ideal para acompañar a tu hijo en su viaje. Estás aprendiendo junto a él, y eso es lo que realmente importa. Así que, cuando las cosas se pongan difíciles, respira profundo, recuérdate a ti misma que estás haciendo lo mejor que puedes, y sigue adelante con amor y compasión hacia ti y hacia tu pequeño.

Consejo del autor: No subestimes el poder del juego y la conexión emocional durante esta etapa. Mientras tu hijo explora su independencia, también necesita sentir tu presencia constante y tu apoyo. En los momentos difíciles, como los berrinches, recuerda que tu respuesta paciente y amorosa es una lección valiosa que le ayudará a aprender cómo manejar sus propias emociones en el futuro.

Con el consejo de ser paciente contigo misma, quiero invitarte a un ejercicio reflexivo. Este es un espacio para pausar y conectar con tus emociones, reconocer tus logros y aceptar que los desafíos también forman parte del aprendizaje. Piensa en un momento reciente en el que enfrentaste un berrinche o una situación difícil con tu hijo. ¿Cómo te sentiste? ¿Qué hiciste bien? ¿Qué podrías haber hecho diferente? Este ejercicio te permitirá ver que, aunque no siempre parezca evidente, estás creciendo y aprendiendo cada día. Vamos a dedicar unos minutos a esta introspección, recordando que la crianza es un proceso en constante evolución.

Ejercicio reflexivo
Reflexiona sobre cómo manejas los desafíos emocionales de tu hijo, como los berrinches. Pregúntate:
• ¿Cómo suelo reaccionar cuando mi hijo tiene un berrinche?
• ¿Hay alguna estrategia de disciplina positiva que me gustaría implementar más?
• ¿De qué manera puedo equilibrar la firmeza con el cariño en la crianza de mi hijo?
Escribir estas reflexiones te ayudará a identificar áreas de mejora y a reforzar las estrategias que ya funcionan bien.

Después de reflexionar sobre esos momentos desafiantes, es hora de pasar a lo práctico. Sabemos que criar a un niño pequeño puede ser abrumador, pero hay estrategias simples que pueden ayudarte a manejar las rutinas diarias y las emociones intensas de manera más tranquila. En la siguiente sección, te compartiré algunos tips y trucos que pueden hacer la crianza un poco más ligera, desde técnicas para manejar berrinches hasta formas de fomentar la independencia y la cooperación en tu pequeño. Con estas sugerencias, tendrás herramientas que te permitirán abordar cada día con más confianza.

Tips y trucos

1. **Anticipa los desencadenantes**: Identifica los momentos en los que tu hijo es más propenso a tener berrinches (como cuando está cansado o tiene hambre) y ajusta las actividades para prevenirlos.

2. **Establece rutinas consistentes**: Los niños pequeños prosperan con rutinas predecibles. Crear horarios regulares para las comidas, siestas y actividades puede reducir su ansiedad y frustración.

3. **Fomenta la independencia**: Permitir que tu hijo realice pequeñas tareas por sí mismo, como vestirse o guardar juguetes, puede fortalecer su sentido de autonomía y reducir los episodios de frustración.

4. **Mantén la calma**: Cuando surja un berrinche, respira profundo y recuerda que es parte del proceso de aprendizaje emocional de tu hijo. Mantener la calma es clave para ayudarlo a autorregularse.

Con estos tips y trucos prácticos a tu disposición, ya cuentas con varias herramientas para enfrentar los altibajos de la crianza. Sin embargo, siempre es útil tener más apoyo a tu alcance. Por eso, en la siguiente sección te presento una serie de recursos adicionales. Desde lecturas recomendadas sobre el desarrollo infantil hasta comunidades online de padres que están pasando por las mismas etapas, estos recursos te brindarán más perspectivas y apoyo para que nunca te sientas sola en este viaje. ¡Vamos a descubrir todo lo que tienes a tu disposición para seguir creciendo junto a tu hijo!

Recursos adicionales

- **Libros recomendados**:

  - *Cómo hablar para que los niños escuchen y cómo escuchar para que los niños hablen* de Adele Faber y Elaine Mazlish.

  - *Disciplina sin lágrimas* de Daniel J. Siegel y Tina Payne Bryson.

- **Aplicaciones útiles**:

  - "Kinedu": Proporciona actividades de desarrollo infantil basadas en la edad del niño.

  - "BabySparks": Ofrece miles de actividades para el desarrollo cognitivo, emocional y físico de los niños pequeños.

- **Grupos de apoyo y webs**:

  - *Positive Parenting Solutions*: Ofrece cursos y recursos sobre crianza positiva.

  - *American Academy of Pediatrics*: Proporciona información confiable sobre el desarrollo infantil y el manejo de comportamientos.

Ser madre puede parecer una travesía solitaria a veces, pero la verdad es que no tienes que hacerlo sola. Tener una red de apoyo sólida puede marcar la diferencia en esos días en los que todo parece demasiado. Desde amigas, familia, hasta otros padres que están viviendo lo mismo que tú, esa red te dará la fuerza y el consuelo que necesitas para seguir adelante. Vamos a adentrarnos en cómo puedes crear y fortalecer esos lazos, y cómo, al cuidar de ti misma y aceptar ayuda, también le das a tu hijo el regalo de una mamá más fuerte y feliz.

"A través del juego, los niños aprenden a resolver problemas, a hacer amigos y a descubrir su mundo. El juego es el trabajo de la infancia." – **Fred Rogers**

Capítulo 10

Creando una Red de Apoyo

Nunca sola: cómo construir un círculo de apoyo para ti y tu bebé

La maternidad es una experiencia profunda y transformadora, pero también puede ser abrumadora en algunos momentos. Aunque el instinto maternal y la intuición son herramientas poderosas, nadie debe transitar este camino solo. Contar con una red de apoyo sólida, tanto en el ámbito familiar como social, es esencial para el bienestar emocional y mental de la madre, así como para el desarrollo saludable del bebé. En este capítulo, exploraremos la importancia de pedir ayuda y cómo construir una comunidad de apoyo que te sostenga en los momentos de desafío, además de recursos útiles para conectarte con otras madres y obtener el respaldo que necesitas.

La Importancia de Pedir Ayuda

Uno de los desafíos más comunes que enfrentan las madres en la actualidad es la creencia errónea de que deben asumir todas las responsabilidades por sí mismas. La figura de la "supermamá", capaz de manejar todas las tareas del hogar y la crianza sin apoyo, es un mito que, en lugar de empoderar, puede tener efectos negativos. En la sociedad moderna, esta expectativa, aunque idealizada, no solo es poco realista, sino que puede llevar a problemas graves como la fatiga, el aislamiento y el agotamiento emocional. Pedir ayuda no es una señal de debilidad, sino una estrategia clave para promover el bienestar tanto de la madre como del niño.

Los beneficios de pedir ayuda

El apoyo social es fundamental para la salud física y mental de las madres. Construir una red de apoyo puede ser una de las decisiones más importantes para mantener una crianza equilibrada y saludable. Pedir ayuda permite a las madres compartir las responsabilidades del cuidado del bebé, lo que puede aliviar el estrés y promover un ambiente más positivo en el hogar.

1. Mejor salud mental

Pedir ayuda, ya sea a la pareja, familiares o amigos, tiene un impacto significativo en la salud mental. Delegar responsabilidades permite a las madres disponer de tiempo para descansar y cuidarse a sí mismas. La falta de apoyo, por el contrario, puede llevar a un agotamiento emocional que afecta negativamente la capacidad de la madre para cuidar de su bebé.

Numerosos estudios han demostrado que las madres que cuentan con una red de apoyo emocional y práctico tienen menos probabilidades de experimentar síntomas de depresión posparto. Por ejemplo, un estudio realizado por Leahy-Warren et al. (2012) mostró que las madres que participan en redes de apoyo estructuradas experimentan menores niveles de ansiedad y una mayor sensación de competencia en su rol de madres, lo que reduce significativamente el riesgo de depresión.

2. Crianza compartida

Compartir la crianza no solo alivia la carga sobre la madre, sino que también enriquece la experiencia del cuidado infantil para toda la familia. Cuando la pareja, los abuelos u otros miembros de la familia participan activamente en las tareas diarias del bebé —como cambiar pañales, alimentar o bañar—, se fortalece el vínculo entre ellos y el niño. Además, la madre puede disfrutar de más tiempo para descansar o dedicar tiempo a otras actividades que le aporten bienestar.

El concepto de crianza compartida no se limita a la pareja. Los abuelos y otros familiares pueden proporcionar un apoyo valioso que no solo reduce el estrés, sino que también fomenta el desarrollo social del bebé al interactuar con diferentes figuras de apego. La investigación ha mostrado que los bebés que crecen en un entorno con múltiples cuidadores estables tienden a desarrollar vínculos afectivos más seguros y una mayor confianza en sus relaciones sociales (Bowlby, 1969).

3. Perspectivas y experiencia

A menudo, las madres primerizas se sienten abrumadas por la cantidad de decisiones que deben tomar diariamente. Pedir ayuda a personas con más experiencia, como los abuelos o amigos cercanos que ya han pasado por la maternidad, puede proporcionar una valiosa fuente de consejos prácticos. Estas personas pueden ofrecer soluciones a problemas cotidianos, como el sueño del bebé, la alimentación o el manejo de los cambios de comportamiento, que quizás no hayas considerado.

Además, buscar el apoyo de profesionales también puede ser de gran ayuda. Las asesoras en lactancia, los pediatras, o los terapeutas infantiles pueden ofrecer recomendaciones específicas basadas en investigaciones científicas y en la experiencia clínica. Esta orientación experta puede ayudar a resolver problemas que, si se dejan sin abordar, pueden afectar tanto al bebé como a la madre.

4. Construcción de comunidad

Uno de los mayores beneficios de pedir ayuda es la oportunidad de construir una comunidad de apoyo alrededor de ti y de tu hijo. Criar a un niño no debería ser un viaje solitario. Al rodearte de personas que te apoyen emocional y prácticamente, estás creando un entorno más enriquecedor y positivo para tu familia. Esta red de apoyo no solo alivia el estrés, sino que también beneficia al niño, que crece rodeado de un círculo de amor y cuidado.

La construcción de una comunidad de apoyo tiene implicaciones a largo plazo. Los niños que crecen en entornos con redes sociales fuertes tienden a desarrollar mejores habilidades sociales y emocionales. La presencia de varias figuras de apego y el hecho de interactuar con diferentes personas permite al niño aprender a confiar y a relacionarse con los demás desde una edad temprana, lo que sienta una base sólida para su desarrollo futuro (Collins & Laursen, 2004).

Cómo construir una comunidad de apoyo

Crear una red de apoyo puede parecer un desafío al principio, especialmente si no tienes familiares cercanos o amigos disponibles para ayudar de manera inmediata. Sin embargo, hay pasos prácticos que puedes seguir para construir una comunidad sólida y de confianza.

1. Involucra a tu pareja

La paternidad es una responsabilidad compartida, y es importante involucrar a tu pareja desde el principio. Dividir las responsabilidades del cuidado del bebé no solo alivia la carga sobre la madre, sino que también fortalece el vínculo entre ambos. Un estudio de Cabrera et al. (2000) encontró que los padres que participan activamente en el cuidado de sus hijos desde el principio desarrollan relaciones más cercanas con sus hijos y una mayor satisfacción en su rol de padres.

Al compartir tareas como cambiar pañales, alimentar o bañar al bebé, la pareja no solo contribuye al bienestar del niño, sino que también se fortalece como equipo. La comunicación abierta y el trabajo en conjunto son esenciales para mantener una crianza equilibrada y positiva.

2. Comunícate abiertamente con familiares y amigos

En muchos casos, los amigos y familiares desean ayudar, pero no saben cómo o cuándo ofrecer su apoyo. Hablar abiertamente sobre tus necesidades puede facilitar que te brinden la ayuda que necesitas. Pide ayuda específica, como cuidar al bebé mientras tomas una siesta, o ayudar con las tareas del hogar, como preparar la comida o hacer las compras.

La investigación ha demostrado que las madres que se sienten cómodas al solicitar apoyo a su red social tienen una mejor salud mental y menos probabilidades de experimentar estrés crónico. Un estudio de Feldman et al. (2004) sugiere que las redes de apoyo familiares, cuando están disponibles y son accesibles, juegan un papel crucial en la prevención de la fatiga materna.

3. Considera el apoyo profesional

En algunos casos, puede ser útil buscar apoyo profesional. Las asesoras en lactancia, las niñeras por horas o incluso los terapeutas pueden proporcionar asistencia especializada que marca una gran diferencia en tu bienestar diario. No debes sentirte culpable por buscar ayuda externa, ya que la asistencia profesional puede permitirte concentrarte mejor en tu bebé y en ti misma.

Los profesionales también pueden ofrecer herramientas y estrategias para enfrentar los desafíos de la maternidad. Por ejemplo, una terapeuta puede ayudarte a desarrollar habilidades para manejar el estrés o la ansiedad, mientras que una asesora en lactancia puede brindarte orientación sobre la alimentación del bebé. Estos recursos pueden ser invaluables, especialmente durante los momentos más difíciles.

4. Rodéate de otras madres

Conectarte con otras madres que están atravesando experiencias similares puede proporcionarte una fuente de apoyo emocional importante. Unirte a grupos de apoyo, tanto locales como en línea, te permite compartir consejos, experiencias y emociones en un entorno comprensivo. Las madres que se apoyan entre sí a menudo se sienten menos aisladas y más empoderadas para enfrentar los desafíos de la maternidad.

Investigaciones muestran que la participación en grupos de apoyo materno está vinculada a un mayor bienestar emocional y a una mayor satisfacción en el rol de madre (Negron et al., 2013). Estos grupos no solo ofrecen consuelo y compañía, sino que también proporcionan un espacio seguro para compartir preocupaciones y recibir sugerencias útiles.

Pedir ayuda no es un signo de debilidad, sino una muestra de fortaleza. En la maternidad, como en la vida, hay momentos en los que sentimos que todo está bajo control y otros en los que simplemente necesitamos una mano amiga. Reconocer que no tienes que hacerlo todo sola es una de las lecciones más importantes que puedes aprender. Buscar apoyo, ya sea emocional, práctico o simplemente para sentirte escuchada, puede marcar una gran diferencia en tu bienestar. Afortunadamente, hoy en día no solo contamos con la cercanía de familiares y amigos, sino también con el poder de las comunidades online y los grupos de apoyo. En la próxima sección, exploraremos cómo estos espacios pueden ofrecerte el soporte que necesitas, incluso en los días más difíciles.

Grupos de Apoyo y Comunidad Online

La maternidad puede ser una experiencia profundamente gratificante, pero también desafiante. En un mundo cada vez más conectado, las madres ya no necesitan depender exclusivamente de su entorno inmediato para encontrar apoyo. Con la proliferación de redes sociales, foros en línea y aplicaciones dedicadas a la maternidad, es más fácil que nunca conectarse con otras madres que comparten experiencias y desafíos similares. Estos grupos, tanto presenciales como online, ofrecen un espacio seguro para compartir dudas, preocupaciones y alegrías, y muchas veces sirven como un recurso invaluable de información, consuelo y apoyo emocional.

Beneficios de los grupos de apoyo

Unirse a un grupo de apoyo puede marcar una gran diferencia en el bienestar emocional de una madre, especialmente durante los primeros meses y años de crianza. Estos grupos proporcionan un espacio donde las madres pueden conectar, compartir sus experiencias y aprender de otras personas que están atravesando situaciones similares. Además, permiten construir una red de apoyo, lo que reduce la sensación de aislamiento y facilita la crianza compartida.

1. Sentido de pertenencia

Uno de los beneficios más importantes de los grupos de apoyo es el sentido de pertenencia que generan. La maternidad puede ser una experiencia solitaria, especialmente si la madre no tiene familiares o amigos cercanos que estén pasando por las mismas etapas. Unirte a un grupo, ya sea presencial o en línea, te permite conectar con otras madres que están experimentando los mismos desafíos, lo que reduce los sentimientos de soledad y aislamiento.

Sentirse comprendida y apoyada en un entorno donde las personas comparten experiencias similares proporciona un alivio emocional importante. Según investigaciones, el apoyo social es un factor clave en la prevención del estrés materno y contribuye a una mayor sensación de bienestar (Dunham, 2011). Estos grupos permiten a las madres sentirse acompañadas y apoyadas, lo que impacta positivamente en su salud mental.

2. Compartir experiencias

Los grupos de apoyo ofrecen la oportunidad de compartir experiencias personales y escuchar las historias de otras madres. A menudo, solo saber que otras personas están pasando por las mismas dificultades puede ser un gran consuelo. Este intercambio de vivencias no solo normaliza las dificultades que pueden surgir en la maternidad, sino que también proporciona perspectivas y soluciones que quizás no habías considerado.

El intercambio de experiencias fomenta la empatía y la comprensión entre las madres, creando un ambiente donde las preocupaciones se escuchan y validan. Un estudio realizado por Lazarus y Folkman (1984) muestra que el apoyo social percibido y el intercambio de experiencias son esenciales para mejorar la resiliencia emocional y la capacidad de afrontar el estrés, lo que es especialmente relevante para las madres primerizas.

3. Aprendizaje conjunto

Uno de los beneficios clave de los grupos de apoyo es el acceso a una comunidad que comparte información y consejos prácticos sobre una amplia gama de temas relacionados con la maternidad. Desde la lactancia y el sueño del bebé hasta la alimentación complementaria y el manejo de las emociones, estos grupos son una fuente invaluable de conocimiento colectivo.

El aprendizaje compartido permite a las madres adquirir nuevas habilidades y estrategias para enfrentar los desafíos de la crianza. Este tipo de intercambio también promueve el empoderamiento, ya que las madres se sienten más seguras y capaces de tomar decisiones informadas para el bienestar de su familia. Según un estudio de Rosenberg et al. (2010), el aprendizaje colaborativo en grupos de apoyo mejora la confianza de las madres en su capacidad para cuidar de sus hijos y tomar decisiones acertadas en el día a día.

4. Acceso a información profesional

Muchos grupos de apoyo, especialmente los que tienen un enfoque estructurado, incluyen la presencia de profesionales de la salud, como consultores de lactancia, psicólogos o pediatras. Estos profesionales no solo moderan las discusiones, sino que también ofrecen consejos basados en evidencia científica y en su experiencia profesional. El acceso a este tipo de información puede ser crucial, ya que ayuda a las madres a resolver dudas o preocupaciones de manera precisa y confiable.

La orientación profesional en un entorno de apoyo facilita el acceso a recursos de calidad que pueden ser difíciles de encontrar de manera independiente. Además, contar con la opinión de expertos ayuda a tranquilizar a las madres y a proporcionarles estrategias respaldadas por la ciencia, lo que refuerza su confianza en la toma de decisiones (Hoddinott et al., 2006).

Conectarse en línea: opciones y recursos

Con el auge de la tecnología y las redes sociales, las madres ahora tienen la opción de conectarse con otras mujeres de todo el mundo a través de plataformas en línea. Estos espacios ofrecen la misma sensación de comunidad y apoyo que los grupos presenciales, con la ventaja añadida de la flexibilidad en cuanto a tiempo y ubicación. Desde foros hasta aplicaciones especializadas, las madres tienen a su disposición una amplia gama de recursos para encontrar el apoyo que necesitan.

1. Redes sociales y foros

Las redes sociales, como Facebook, y los foros en línea, como BabyCenter y Mumsnet, son algunas de las plataformas más populares para las madres que buscan apoyo. En estos espacios, las madres pueden participar en grupos dedicados a temas específicos, como la lactancia, la crianza respetuosa o el sueño infantil. Estos grupos suelen ser dinámicos, con un flujo constante de preguntas, respuestas y consejos de madres de todo el mundo.

- **Grupos de Facebook**: Existen innumerables grupos dedicados a la maternidad, que permiten a las madres hacer preguntas, compartir experiencias y obtener consejos prácticos en tiempo real. Estos grupos también pueden enfocarse en intereses específicos, como la crianza basada en apego o la lactancia prolongada.

- **Foros de BabyCenter y Mumsnet**: Estas plataformas ofrecen una gran cantidad de discusiones sobre todos los aspectos de la maternidad, desde el embarazo hasta la educación infantil. Son espacios donde las madres pueden buscar respuestas a preguntas específicas y encontrar apoyo de otras personas que han pasado por las mismas situaciones.

2. Aplicaciones de maternidad

Las aplicaciones móviles han revolucionado la forma en que las madres pueden conectarse entre sí. Existen aplicaciones diseñadas específicamente para facilitar la comunicación y el apoyo entre madres, así como para proporcionar información sobre el desarrollo infantil.

- **Peanut**: Esta aplicación está diseñada para conectar a madres de la misma área geográfica y facilitar conversaciones sobre temas relevantes en la maternidad. Peanut permite a las madres encontrar "match" con otras que comparten intereses o desafíos similares, lo que facilita el establecimiento de conexiones significativas.

- **The Wonder Weeks**: Esta aplicación, además de proporcionar información detallada sobre los hitos del desarrollo del bebé, cuenta con una comunidad activa donde los padres pueden compartir sus experiencias y recibir apoyo en cada fase del desarrollo infantil.

3. Grupos presenciales

A pesar de las ventajas de los grupos en línea, muchas madres aún prefieren el contacto personal que ofrecen los grupos presenciales. Estos grupos, organizados por hospitales, centros de salud o comunidades locales, ofrecen la oportunidad de establecer relaciones más profundas y recibir orientación cara a cara.

- **Centros de salud y hospitales**: Muchos centros de salud y hospitales locales organizan grupos de apoyo para madres. Estos grupos suelen estar dirigidos por profesionales de la salud, como pediatras o consultores de lactancia, que proporcionan orientación práctica y emocional a las madres.

- **La Liga de la Leche Internacional**: Este es un recurso global que organiza reuniones de apoyo para madres lactantes en todo el mundo. Ofrecen un espacio para que las madres compartan sus experiencias y preocupaciones sobre la lactancia, al tiempo que reciben orientación de consultores de lactancia certificados. La Liga de la Leche no solo promueve la lactancia materna, sino que también fomenta la creación de una red de apoyo emocional entre las madres.

Cómo crear tu propio grupo de apoyo

Si no encuentras un grupo de apoyo que se ajuste a tus necesidades, otra opción es crear uno propio. Organizar un grupo local de madres o iniciar una comunidad en línea puede ser una excelente manera de construir la red de apoyo que estás buscando. Muchas madres están en la misma situación que tú y también buscan un espacio para compartir y aprender. Crear un grupo te permite personalizar las discusiones y actividades para satisfacer las necesidades específicas de las madres de tu área o de tu comunidad virtual.

Conectarte con otras madres que están pasando por situaciones similares puede ser una fuente increíble de consuelo y ánimo. Ya sea que te unas a un grupo de apoyo local o encuentres una comunidad online donde puedas compartir tus experiencias, estos espacios te permiten descubrir que no estás sola. A través de estas conexiones, aprendes que los desafíos que enfrentas son más comunes de lo que piensas y que siempre hay alguien dispuesto a ofrecer una palabra amable o un consejo útil. A medida que cerramos este capítulo, quiero que te lleves la certeza de que el apoyo está al alcance de tu mano. Solo tienes que abrirte a recibirlo y a conectarte con los demás.

Conclusión del Capítulo

Crear una red de apoyo sólida es uno de los pilares más importantes para asegurar tu bienestar emocional y físico durante la maternidad. La idea de que una madre debe hacerlo todo sola es un mito que a menudo genera presión innecesaria y sentimientos de agotamiento. La realidad es que la maternidad, aunque profundamente gratificante, también está llena de desafíos que pueden ser abrumadores si se intentan enfrentar sin ayuda. Pedir apoyo no solo es aceptable, sino que es un acto de autocuidado y fortaleza. Saber cuándo y cómo pedir ayuda es una señal de madurez y sabiduría, ya que cuidar de ti misma es crucial para poder cuidar de tu bebé de la mejor manera posible. En este viaje, rodearte de personas que te apoyen te permitirá enfrentar las dificultades con mayor tranquilidad y disfrutar plenamente de los momentos felices.

La maternidad, especialmente en los primeros años, puede ser emocionalmente intensa y físicamente agotadora. A menudo, las expectativas de la sociedad o de nosotras mismas nos hacen pensar que debemos poder con todo: cuidar al bebé, mantener el hogar en orden, trabajar y seguir con nuestras vidas como si nada hubiera cambiado. Sin embargo, aceptar que no es posible hacerlo todo sola y que está bien buscar ayuda es un paso importante para evitar el agotamiento y cuidar tu bienestar mental. Al construir una red de apoyo, ya sea con familiares, amigos o profesionales, te aseguras de que no tengas que cargar con todo el peso por tu cuenta. Recibir ayuda para tareas cotidianas o simplemente tener a alguien con quien hablar puede hacer una gran diferencia en tu experiencia como madre.

Además de buscar apoyo en las personas cercanas, conectarte con otras madres puede ser especialmente beneficioso. Las experiencias compartidas con otras madres que están pasando por situaciones similares a las tuyas te permiten sentirte comprendida, validada y acompañada. Participar en grupos de apoyo locales, clases para padres o comunidades en línea dedicadas a la maternidad puede brindarte un espacio seguro para compartir tus dudas, preocupaciones y éxitos. La conexión con otras madres te recuerda que no estás sola en este camino y que muchas de las emociones y desafíos que enfrentas son comunes. Estas conexiones pueden convertirse en una fuente invaluable de ánimo, consuelo y amistad a lo largo de los años.

Es importante también recordar que tu red de apoyo no solo te beneficia a ti, sino que también tiene un impacto positivo en el desarrollo de tu bebé. Crecer rodeado de personas que lo aman, lo cuidan y lo apoyan contribuye significativamente a su bienestar emocional y social. Los abuelos, tías, tíos, amigos cercanos y otros miembros de tu comunidad pueden ofrecerle a tu hijo una variedad de interacciones y vínculos afectivos que enriquecen su desarrollo. Además, al ver cómo tú te apoyas en los demás, tu hijo aprenderá el valor de la cooperación, la empatía y la construcción de relaciones saludables.

Pedir ayuda y aceptar el apoyo de los demás no es un signo de debilidad, sino una muestra de sabiduría y amor propio. La maternidad, aunque es una experiencia transformadora y hermosa, puede ser agotadora tanto física como mentalmente. Al pedir ayuda, te das la oportunidad de recargar energías, cuidar tu salud mental y dedicar tiempo a tus propias necesidades, lo cual es esencial para mantener el equilibrio en tu vida. El autocuidado no es un lujo, sino una necesidad, y es importante que recuerdes que cuando te cuidas a ti misma, también estás cuidando mejor a tu bebé.

Tu red de apoyo puede ser tan amplia o tan íntima como desees. Para algunas madres, esa red puede estar formada por familiares cercanos que ofrecen apoyo diario; para otras, puede consistir en amigos, vecinos o incluso profesionales de la salud. También hay quienes encuentran consuelo en comunidades virtuales de maternidad, donde pueden compartir consejos y experiencias con madres de todo el mundo. Lo importante es que sientas que tienes un lugar donde acudir cuando lo necesites, sin temor a ser juzgada o criticada. Esta red debe ser un espacio de empatía, comprensión y apoyo incondicional, donde puedas sentirte libre de compartir tanto los momentos difíciles como las alegrías.

Al construir esta red, también es esencial recordar que el apoyo emocional es tan importante como el apoyo práctico. Tener a alguien con quien hablar sobre tus sentimientos, tus preocupaciones y tus logros en la maternidad puede ser profundamente sanador. Ya sea un amigo cercano, un terapeuta o un grupo de apoyo, contar con alguien que te escuche y te ofrezca perspectiva en los momentos difíciles te ayudará a sobrellevar los altibajos de la maternidad de una manera más equilibrada.

En resumen, construir una red de apoyo sólida no es solo un acto de autocuidado, sino una parte esencial de tu bienestar como madre. No tienes que enfrentar los desafíos de la maternidad sola, y pedir ayuda es un signo de fortaleza, no de debilidad. Conectarte con otras madres, recibir el apoyo de tu familia y amigos, y encontrar comunidades donde puedas compartir tus experiencias te brindará el respaldo emocional y práctico que necesitas para navegar los momentos más difíciles. Al rodearte de personas que te apoyen, no solo te estarás cuidando a ti misma, sino también a tu bebé, quien crecerá rodeado de amor, cuidado y apoyo constante.

Al finalizar este capítulo, me gustaría dejarte con un consejo que puede transformar tu perspectiva: no te sientas culpable por pedir ayuda. Ser madre es una tarea monumental, y no estás diseñada para hacer todo por ti misma. Mi consejo es sencillo: permítete recibir apoyo sin juzgarte por ello. Todos necesitamos de otros, y tú no eres la excepción. Rodearte de personas que te comprendan, te escuchen y te apoyen no solo te beneficiará a ti, sino también a tu bebé. Así que la próxima vez que sientas que necesitas una pausa o una palabra de aliento, no dudes en buscar esa ayuda que está ahí para ti.

Consejo del autor: Rodéate de personas que te apoyen y te comprendan. La maternidad es un viaje hermoso, pero también desafiante. No te sientas culpable por pedir ayuda cuando lo necesites, y recuerda que compartir tus experiencias, preocupaciones y alegrías con los demás te fortalecerá a ti y a tu bebé.

Con este consejo en mente, quiero invitarte a un ejercicio reflexivo. Tómate unos minutos para pensar en los momentos en los que has sentido que necesitabas ayuda, pero no la pediste. ¿Qué te detuvo? ¿Qué emociones te invadieron? Este ejercicio es una oportunidad para reflexionar sobre la importancia de dejar de lado la idea de que pedir apoyo es un signo de fracaso. Más bien, es un paso valiente hacia el autocuidado. Reconocer tus límites y aceptar el apoyo te permitirá ser una madre más fuerte y tranquila. Vamos a sumergirnos en esta reflexión que te ayudará a conectar con tus verdaderas necesidades.

<table>
<tr><td>

Ejercicio reflexivo

</td></tr>
<tr><td>

Reflexiona sobre las personas que ya forman parte de tu red de apoyo y cómo te han ayudado. Haz una lista de:

</td></tr>
<tr><td>

- ¿Quiénes son las personas en tu vida a las que puedes acudir en busca de apoyo?

</td></tr>
<tr><td>

- ¿De qué maneras te gustaría mejorar tu red de apoyo?

</td></tr>
<tr><td>

- ¿Qué tipo de ayuda crees que te beneficiaría más en este momento de la maternidad?

</td></tr>
<tr><td>

Escribir estas reflexiones te ayudará a identificar áreas donde puedes fortalecer tu red de apoyo y te permitirá tomar pasos concretos para hacerlo.

</td></tr>
</table>

Después de haberte tomado un momento para reflexionar, es hora de volver a lo práctico. Pedir ayuda puede tomar muchas formas, y en la siguiente sección te compartiré algunos tips y trucos que te permitirán delegar y organizar mejor tu día a día. Desde formas sencillas de involucrar a otros en las rutinas diarias hasta cómo hacer uso eficiente de las comunidades online, estos consejos están diseñados para que puedas aligerar la carga y enfocarte más en disfrutar del tiempo con tu bebé. No estás sola en este viaje, y estas herramientas te ayudarán a recordarlo.

Tips y trucos

1. **Pide ayuda específica**: Si necesitas apoyo, trata de ser específica. En lugar de decir "necesito ayuda", di algo como "¿podrías venir a ayudarme con el bebé un par de horas esta tarde?" Esto facilita que los demás comprendan cómo pueden ayudarte.

2. **Acepta la ayuda**: Muchas veces, las madres se sienten culpables por aceptar ayuda, pero es importante recordar que aceptar apoyo no te hace menos capaz. Te permitirá descansar y recargar energías.

3. **Conéctate localmente**: Si bien las comunidades en línea son útiles, trata de conectarte con madres que vivan cerca de ti. Tener apoyo cercano en momentos de emergencia o simplemente para compañía diaria puede marcar una gran diferencia.

4. **Sé parte de la red de apoyo de otros**: La maternidad es un camino de reciprocidad. Así como recibes apoyo, también es gratificante y fortalecedor ofrecer ayuda a otras madres cuando lo necesiten.

Ya tienes en tus manos algunos consejos prácticos para hacer la maternidad más llevadera, pero a veces es útil saber que hay más opciones de apoyo disponibles. En la próxima sección, te presentaré recursos adicionales que pueden brindarte ese acompañamiento extra cuando lo necesites. Desde redes de apoyo locales hasta plataformas digitales que te conectan con profesionales y otras madres, estos recursos están pensados para que siempre tengas un lugar al cual recurrir. Recuerda que rodearte de ayuda no solo te beneficia a ti, sino también a tu bebé. ¡Vamos a explorar juntos estos valiosos recursos!

Recursos adicionales

- **Libros recomendados**:
  - *El cerebro de la madre* de Katherine Ellison: Ofrece una mirada fascinante sobre cómo la maternidad transforma el cerebro y las necesidades de una red de apoyo.
  - *Crianza feliz* de Rosa Jové: Proporciona una visión integral sobre la crianza basada en el amor y la empatía, destacando la importancia de una comunidad de apoyo.
- **Aplicaciones útiles**:
  - **Peanut**: Conecta a madres de diferentes partes del mundo para compartir experiencias y apoyarse mutuamente.
  - **Meetup**: Plataforma para encontrar y unirse a grupos locales de madres y actividades relacionadas con la maternidad.
- **Grupos de apoyo y webs**:

- *La Liga de la Leche Internacional*: Ofrece apoyo en lactancia y proporciona una comunidad de madres.

- *Postpartum Support International* (PSI): Brinda recursos para madres que enfrentan depresión posparto y otros desafíos de salud mental.

"A veces se necesita una comunidad entera para criar a un niño." – **Proverbio africano**

Preguntas Más Frecuentes:

1. **¿Cuándo debo empezar a cuidarme durante el embarazo?**

   - Respuesta: Comienza tan pronto como sepas que estás embarazada. Establece una dieta equilibrada, realiza ejercicios moderados y sigue las recomendaciones médicas.

2. **¿Cuánto peso es normal ganar durante el embarazo?**

   - Respuesta: El aumento de peso varía, pero en general, se recomienda un aumento saludable de 11-16 kg. Consulta con tu médico para determinar la cantidad adecuada para tu situación.

3. **¿Cómo elijo al pediatra adecuado para mi bebé?**

   - Respuesta: Investiga y entrevista a varios pediatras. Busca recomendaciones, verifica la ubicación de la clínica y asegúrate de sentirte cómoda con su enfoque y filosofía.

4. **¿Cuáles son las señales de trabajo de parto?**

   - Respuesta: Las señales incluyen contracciones regulares, rotura de aguas, y cambios en el moco cervical. Si tienes dudas, comunícate con tu médico.

5. **¿Cómo manejar el sueño del recién nacido?**

- Respuesta: Establece una rutina de sueño, responde a las necesidades del bebé y considera la posibilidad de compartir la habitación. Paciencia y consistencia son clave.

6. **¿Cuándo debo comenzar la alimentación sólida y qué alimentos debo introducir primero?**

   - Respuesta: Generalmente, se inicia entre los 4 y 6 meses. Comienza con alimentos blandos como purés de frutas y verduras. Consulta con el pediatra para una guía personalizada.

7. **¿Cómo fomentar el desarrollo del lenguaje en mi hijo?**

   - Respuesta: Habla y lee con tu bebé desde el principio. Anima la comunicación, responde a sus balbuceos y favorece un entorno rico en palabras.

8. **¿Cuándo es el momento adecuado para iniciar la educación preescolar?**

   - Respuesta: Alrededor de los 3 años es común, pero depende de las necesidades y desarrollo del niño. Observa señales de preparación social y emocional.

9. **¿Cómo manejar los berrinches y el comportamiento desafiante?**

   - Respuesta: Establece límites claros, utiliza la disciplina positiva, y ofrece alternativas.

Comprender sus emociones y comunicarte efectivamente es clave.

10. ¿Cuándo debo hablar con mi hijo sobre la pubertad y la sexualidad?

- Respuesta: Inicia conversaciones abiertas sobre el cuerpo desde temprano. Ajusta el nivel de detalle a medida que crece y asegúrate de responder a sus preguntas de manera honesta y apropiada para su edad.

¡Mas Preguntas!

1. **Nutrición para tu bebé:** Recuerda ofrecerle leche materna o fórmula según sus necesidades. Si ya ha comenzado con alimentos sólidos, asegúrate de proporcionarle opciones saludables y variadas para fomentar un crecimiento y desarrollo óptimos.

2. **Horarios y rutinas:** Establecer rutinas puede ser clave. Un horario regular para dormir, comer y jugar proporcionará seguridad y previsibilidad para tu bebé. ¡No olvides programar momentos para ti también!

3. **Estimulación temprana:** Realiza actividades que estimulen los sentidos de tu bebé. Juegos suaves, música relajante y hablarle en tono suave ayudarán a su desarrollo cognitivo y emocional.

4. **Seguridad siempre:** Asegúrate de que su entorno sea seguro. Revisa regularmente los juguetes y la cuna para evitar peligros. Mantén los productos químicos y objetos afilados fuera de su alcance.

5. **Consulta médica regular:** Programa citas regulares con el pediatra para chequeos y vacunas. No dudes en hacer preguntas sobre el desarrollo y la salud de tu bebé.

6. **Momentos de juego:** ¡Diviértete con tu pequeño! El juego es fundamental para el desarrollo social y emocional. Juguetes educativos y tiempo de calidad juntos fortalecerán vuestro vínculo.

7. **Auto-cuidado:** Ser una super mamá también implica cuidar de ti misma. Descansa cuando puedas, come bien y pide ayuda si la necesitas. ¡Eres increíble y mereces momentos de tranquilidad!

Recuerda que cada bebé es único, así que confía en tus instintos y disfruta cada momento con tu pequeño. ¡Eres la mejor super mamá que tu bebé podría tener! 💙

- ❖ **¿Qué es lo que hace un niño a esta edad?** En la primera etapa del desarrollo, los recién nacidos, generalmente hasta el primer mes de vida, experimentan un período de sueño prolongado, alimentación frecuente, llanto para comunicarse y breves momentos de alerta. Su visión es borrosa y se centra principalmente en objetos cercanos. Aunque aún no pueden sostener la cabeza, comienzan a responder a estímulos visuales y auditivos.

Recién Nacido a 3 Meses:

- Sueño prolongado, generalmente entre 14 y 17 horas al día.

- Alimentación frecuente con leche materna o fórmula.

- Llanto para comunicarse, ya sea por hambre, sueño, incomodidad o necesidad de cambio de pañal.

- Breves períodos de alerta donde comienzan a responder a estímulos visuales y auditivos.

- Incapacidad para sostener la cabeza por sí mismos.

- Desarrollo visual limitado, prefiriendo patrones de alto contraste.

4 a 6 Meses:

- Desarrollo de habilidades motoras gruesas, como girarse y rodar.

- Descubrimiento de las manos y los pies.

- Inicio de la introducción de alimentos sólidos.

- Mayor interacción con el entorno, como agarrar objetos.

- Posibilidad de sentarse con apoyo.

7 a 12 Meses:

- Desarrollo de habilidades motoras finas, como agarrar pequeños objetos con los dedos.

- Exploración activa del entorno, gateo y posiblemente los primeros pasos.

- Mayor capacidad para comunicarse, como balbucear y entender algunas palabras.

- Desarrollo de la coordinación ojo-mano.

- Interacción social más intensa con sonrisas y risas.

En cada etapa, es importante brindar un ambiente seguro y estimulante para apoyar el desarrollo físico, cognitivo y emocional del niño. Cada niño es único y puede alcanzar estos hitos a su propio ritmo. Siempre es recomendable consultar con el pediatra para asegurarse de que el desarrollo del niño sea apropiado.

- ❖ **¿Es normal que tenga tanto hipo? ¿Y qué estornude?** El hipo en los recién nacidos es común y normal. Sucede debido a la inmadurez de su sistema nervioso y su tendencia a tragar aire mientras se alimentan. Estornudar también es común y puede ser una respuesta a la irritación nasal, polvo o incluso el contacto con el aire. Ambos son comportamientos normales en los bebés.

Sí, es normal que los recién nacidos y los bebés tengan hipo con frecuencia. El hipo en los bebés es común y generalmente inofensivo. Puede ocurrir debido a la inmadurez del sistema nervioso central del bebé y a la tendencia a tragar aire mientras se alimentan. No suele ser motivo de preocupación, y la mayoría de los bebés superan el hipo por sí mismos.

El estornudo también es común en los bebés y puede tener varias causas. Puede ser una respuesta a la irritación nasal, polvo, cambios en la temperatura o incluso el contacto con el aire. Los bebés tienen sistemas respiratorios y nasales sensibles que están en desarrollo, lo que puede hacer que estornuden con más frecuencia que los adultos.

Ambos, el hipo y los estornudos, son parte del proceso normal de adaptación y desarrollo del sistema respiratorio del bebé. Sin embargo, si notas que el hipo es excesivamente frecuente o persiste por períodos prolongados, o si los estornudos van acompañados de otros síntomas como fiebre, irritación ocular o congestión nasal, podría ser prudente consultar con el pediatra para descartar cualquier problema subyacente. En general, la mayoría de los episodios de hipo y estornudo en los bebés son fenómenos normales y temporales.

> ➢ El hipo en los bebés generalmente desaparece por sí solo y no requiere tratamiento específico. Aquí hay algunas sugerencias que podrían ayudarte a aliviar el hipo en un bebé:

1. **Espera pacientemente:** En la mayoría de los casos, el hipo desaparece por sí solo en unos minutos. Trata de mantener la calma y espera a que pase.

2. **Ofrece pequeños sorbos de agua:** Si el bebé ya está tomando líquidos, puedes darle pequeños sorbos de agua. Esto puede ayudar a calmar el hipo.

3. **Evita alimentar apresuradamente:** Si el hipo ocurre después de alimentar al bebé, asegúrate de que esté tomando los biberones o el pecho de manera tranquila y sin prisas para minimizar la ingestión de aire.

4. **Burp al bebé:** Después de alimentar, asegúrate de que el bebé eructe para liberar cualquier exceso de aire en el estómago, lo que puede ayudar a prevenir el hipo.

5. **Cambios en la postura:** Modifica la posición del bebé. Puedes levantarle suavemente la cabeza o cambiar su posición para ver si eso ayuda a detener el hipo.

6. **Evita estímulos bruscos:** Evita actividades que puedan sobresaltar al bebé mientras tiene hipo. Mantén un entorno tranquilo y relajado.

Es importante destacar que, en la mayoría de los casos, el hipo en los bebés es inofensivo y desaparece por sí solo. Sin embargo, si el hipo persiste durante períodos prolongados o si estás preocupado por la frecuencia, es aconsejable consultar con el pediatra para descartar cualquier problema subyacente.

❖ **¿Es normal que se asuste tanto?** Sí, la sobre sensibilidad a estímulos externos es normal en los recién nacidos. Los sonidos fuertes, cambios bruscos de luz o movimiento pueden asustarlos. Su sistema nervioso está en desarrollo y es sensible, por lo que es importante brindar un entorno tranquilo y suave para ayudarles a adaptarse gradualmente.

Sí, es normal que los recién nacidos y los bebés pequeños sean propensos a asustarse fácilmente. Durante los primeros meses de vida, los bebés están experimentando y adaptándose a un mundo completamente nuevo. Su sistema nervioso está en desarrollo y es muy sensible, lo que los hace más propensos a sobresaltarse ante estímulos externos.

Factores como ruidos fuertes, cambios bruscos de luz, movimientos repentinos o incluso ciertos olores pueden ser suficientes para asustar a un bebé. Además, su capacidad para procesar y entender su entorno está en desarrollo, lo que puede contribuir a su reacción ante estímulos que pueden parecernos triviales.

Como cuidador, puedes ayudar a reducir la frecuencia de los sustos siendo consciente de su entorno y evitando situaciones que puedan ser abrumadoras. Mantener un ambiente tranquilo y suave, hablar en tonos calmados y manejar al bebé con cuidado contribuirán a su sensación de seguridad.

A medida que el bebé crece y se acostumbra a su entorno, es probable que estos sobresaltos disminuyan gradualmente. Sin embargo, es importante seguir proporcionando un ambiente amoroso y de apoyo para ayudar al bebé a desarrollar la confianza y la seguridad emocional.

❖ **¿Los recién nacidos ven?** Sí, los recién nacidos pueden ver, pero su visión es limitada. Ven mejor a distancias cortas y prefieren patrones de alto contraste. Con el tiempo, su visión mejora y se desarrolla.

Sí, los recién nacidos son capaces de ver, pero su visión está en desarrollo y es limitada en los primeros meses de vida. Al nacer, la visión de los bebés es borrosa, y suelen preferir patrones de alto contraste, como blanco y negro. Los bebés recién nacidos pueden enfocar objetos a una distancia de aproximadamente 20 a 30 centímetros de sus ojos, lo que coincide con la distancia entre el bebé y la cara de la persona que lo sostiene.

A medida que los meses pasan, la visión de los bebés mejora gradualmente. A los 2-3 meses, pueden comenzar a seguir objetos en movimiento con sus ojos y a mostrar interés por caras humanas. Durante el primer año de vida, los bebés experimentan un rápido desarrollo visual, y alrededor de los 6 meses, la mayoría de ellos tienen una visión más aguda y son capaces de ver colores con mayor claridad.

Es importante proporcionar estímulos visuales apropiados para apoyar el desarrollo visual del bebé y estimular su curiosidad. Juegos con colores contrastantes, juguetes llamativos y la interacción visual con los cuidadores contribuyen al desarrollo saludable de la visión en los recién nacidos.

❖ **¿Cuándo se cae el cordón umbilical?** El cordón umbilical generalmente se cae por sí solo en las primeras dos semanas de vida. Es importante mantener el área limpia y seca para prevenir infecciones. Si hay enrojecimiento, inflamación o secreciones inusuales alrededor del ombligo, es recomendable consultar al pediatra.

El cordón umbilical generalmente se cae por sí solo en las primeras dos semanas de vida del bebé, pero este período puede variar. Puede ocurrir entre los 7 y 21 días después del nacimiento. Durante este tiempo, el cordón umbilical se seca y eventualmente forma una costra antes de caerse.

Es esencial cuidar adecuadamente del cordón umbilical para prevenir infecciones. Aquí hay algunos consejos:

1. **Mantén el área limpia y seca:** Limpia suavemente el área alrededor del cordón umbilical con agua y jabón suave durante el baño del bebé. Asegúrate de secar cuidadosamente el área después del baño.

2. **Dobla el pañal:** Al poner el pañal, pliégalo para que no roce el cordón umbilical y permita que el área esté expuesta al aire.

3. **Evita sumergir al bebé en agua:** Durante los primeros días, es recomendable evitar sumergir completamente al bebé en agua, como en una tina. Opta por limpiar el área con esponja hasta que el cordón umbilical se haya caído.

4. **Consulta con el pediatra:** Si notas enrojecimiento, hinchazón, sangrado o cualquier otro signo de infección alrededor del cordón umbilical, es crucial que consultes con el pediatra de inmediato.

Recuerda que cada bebé es único y el tiempo exacto para que el cordón umbilical se caiga puede variar. Si tienes alguna preocupación o preguntas sobre el cuidado del cordón umbilical de tu bebé, no dudes en consultar con el profesional de la salud que sigue el desarrollo de tu hijo.

❖ **¿Cuándo y cómo debo bañar al niño?** Puedes comenzar a bañar al bebé cuando el cordón umbilical se haya caído y la herida haya sanado. Utiliza agua tibia y jabones suaves diseñados para bebés. Asegúrate de tener todo lo necesario a la mano antes de comenzar y sostén con firmeza a tu bebé mientras lo bañas.

El momento y la forma de bañar a un niño pueden variar según las preferencias de los padres y las necesidades específicas del bebé. Aquí te brindo algunas pautas generales:

1. Cuándo bañar al niño:

- **Frecuencia:** En los primeros días de vida, cuando el cordón umbilical del bebé aún está presente, es recomendable esperar a que se caiga antes de sumergirlo completamente en agua. Después de eso, puedes comenzar a bañar al bebé varias veces a la semana, ajustando la frecuencia según sea necesario. Muchos padres encuentran que bañar al bebé dos o tres veces por semana es suficiente durante los primeros meses.

- **Mejor momento del día:** Algunos padres prefieren bañar al bebé por la noche como parte de la rutina para ayudar a relajar al bebé antes de dormir. Sin embargo, puedes elegir el momento que mejor se adapte a tu rutina y a las preferencias de tu bebé.

2. Cómo bañar al niño:

- **Reúne los suministros:** Antes de comenzar el baño, asegúrate de tener todo lo necesario, como una bañera para bebés, toallas suaves, jabón y champú suaves, y ropa limpia.
- **Temperatura del agua:** Asegúrate de que la temperatura del agua esté tibia, no demasiado caliente ni demasiado fría. Puedes probar la temperatura con el dorso de tu mano para garantizar que sea cómoda para el bebé.
- **Manejo cuidadoso:** Sujeta al bebé con cuidado y sostén su cabeza y cuello con una mano mientras lo bañas. Al principio, puedes optar por lavar su cara y cabello con una esponja y agua, reservando la inmersión completa en la bañera para más adelante.
- **Duración del baño:** Los baños para bebés no necesitan ser largos. Algunos minutos son suficientes. Mantén el baño breve y evita que el bebé se enfríe.
- **Secado y vestimenta:** Después de sacar al bebé del agua, sécalo suavemente con una toalla y asegúrate de prestar especial atención a los pliegues de la piel. Luego, vístelo con ropa limpia y seca.

Recuerda que cada bebé es único, y puedes ajustar la rutina del baño según las necesidades y preferencias de tu hijo. Mantén un ambiente tranquilo y relajado durante el baño para que el bebé se sienta seguro y cómodo.

❖ **¿Cómo debo limpiar sus genitales?** Limpia suavemente la zona genital del bebé con una esponja o un paño húmedo durante el baño. Es esencial secar bien y evitar irritaciones. Si es niño, ten cuidado con la limpieza del prepucio.

Limpiar los genitales de un bebé requiere cuidado y suavidad. Aquí te proporciono algunos pasos básicos para limpiar adecuadamente los genitales de tu bebé:

1. **Lávate las manos:** Antes de comenzar, asegúrate de lavarte bien las manos para evitar la transferencia de gérmenes al bebé.
2. **Reúne los suministros:** Ten a mano todo lo que necesitas, como toallas suaves, algodón y agua tibia.
3. **Prepara un recipiente con agua tibia:** Puedes usar un recipiente pequeño con agua tibia para mojar el algodón o una esponja suave.
4. **Coloca al bebé en una superficie cómoda:** Pon al bebé en una superficie estable y cómoda, como un cambiador o una toalla suave.
5. **Limpieza para las niñas:**

- Si tienes una niña, limpia con cuidado de adelante hacia atrás para evitar la propagación de bacterias desde el área rectal hacia la uretra.
- Utiliza un algodón mojado con agua tibia para limpiar suavemente el área genital externa. Puedes utilizar un movimiento de barrido desde el ombligo hacia la parte exterior.

6. **Limpieza para los niños:**
   - Para los niños, limpia alrededor del pene y los testículos con cuidado. No es necesario tirar hacia atrás el prepucio en los bebés, ya que aún puede estar adherido. Solo limpia la parte externa.

7. **Seca suavemente:** Después de limpiar, sécalo con una toalla suave. Presta especial atención a los pliegues de la piel.
8. **Hidratación (si es necesario):** Si es recomendado por el pediatra, puedes aplicar una pequeña cantidad de crema hidratante específica para bebés para mantener la piel suave.

Es importante realizar esta limpieza con delicadeza y prestar atención a cualquier signo de irritación, enrojecimiento o incomodidad en el bebé. Si tienes preguntas o preocupaciones sobre el cuidado de los genitales de tu bebé, no dudes en consultar con el pediatra.

❖ **¿Cuándo puedo cortarle las uñas?** Puedes empezar a cortar las uñas del bebé cuando notes que están lo suficientemente largas como para causar molestias o rasguñarse. Usa tijeras o cortaúñas para bebés, y asegúrate de hacerlo con cuidado para evitar cortar la piel. Puede ser útil esperar a que el bebé esté tranquilo o dormido para facilitar el proceso.

Cortar las uñas de un bebé puede ser una tarea delicada, pero es importante hacerlo para prevenir arañazos accidentales. Aquí hay algunas pautas generales sobre cuándo y cómo cortar las uñas de un bebé:

1. **Cuándo cortar:**
   - **Cuando estén largas:** Por lo general, las uñas de un recién nacido pueden ser bastante suaves, pero pueden volverse más afiladas a medida que el bebé crece. Comienza a cortarlas cuando notes que están lo suficientemente largas como para causar molestias o riesgo de arañazos.
   - **Después del baño:** Cortar las uñas después del baño puede ser más fácil, ya que las uñas están más blandas. También puedes intentar hacerlo mientras el bebé duerme, para evitar movimientos bruscos.
   - **Cuando estén visibles:** Observa las uñas regularmente y corta cuando veas que se han

alargado lo suficiente como para necesitar atención.

2. **Cómo cortar:**
   - **Utiliza tijeras o cortaúñas para bebés:** Utiliza tijeras o cortaúñas diseñados específicamente para bebés. Estos suelen tener bordes redondeados y son más seguros para la delicada piel del bebé.
   - **Ilumina bien el área:** Asegúrate de tener buena iluminación para ver claramente las uñas. Es posible que necesites ayuda de otra persona para sostener al bebé de manera segura mientras cortas las uñas.
   - **Corta recto y con cuidado:** Corta las uñas rectas para evitar bordes afilados. Si tienes dudas o no te sientes cómodo, puedes optar por limar las uñas con una lima de uñas para bebés.
   - **Ten cuidado con las yemas de los dedos:** Asegúrate de no cortar demasiado cerca de las yemas de los dedos para evitar lesiones. Cortar solo la punta es generalmente suficiente.

Recuerda que cortar las uñas del bebé puede ser un proceso gradual, y puede llevarte un tiempo sentirte completamente seguro haciéndolo. No dudes en pedir ayuda a otro adulto si es necesario, y siempre mantén la seguridad del bebé como prioridad.

❖ **¿Como atender a los bebes que le están saliendo los dientes?**

El proceso de dentición en los bebés puede ser un momento incómodo y doloroso. Aquí hay algunas sugerencias sobre cómo atender a los bebés que están saliendo los dientes:

1. **Mordedores Refrigerados:**

   • Proporciona mordedores específicos para la dentición que puedan ser enfriados en el refrigerador. El frío ayuda a aliviar la inflamación y proporciona alivio a las encías doloridas.

2. **Pañuelos o Juguetes de Tela Fríos:**

   • Envuelve hielo triturado o cubitos de hielo en una gasa o pañuelo de tela y permite que el bebé lo chupe. Asegúrate de supervisar de cerca y evitar el contacto directo con el hielo para prevenir la congelación.

3. **Masaje de Encías:**

   • Lava bien tus manos y, con un dedo limpio, masajea suavemente las encías del bebé. Esto puede proporcionar alivio y distracción.

4. **Alimentos Fríos:**

   • Ofrece alimentos fríos y suaves, como yogur o puré de frutas refrigerado. Asegúrate de que los alimentos sean adecuados para la edad del bebé y no presenten riesgos de asfixia.

5. **Anillos de Dentición:**

   - Utiliza anillos de dentición diseñados para enfriarse en el refrigerador. Estos pueden proporcionar una superficie segura y fría para que el bebé mastique.

6. **Gel o Cremas para Dentición:**

   - Consulta con el pediatra y utiliza geles o cremas específicas para la dentición que puedan aplicarse en las encías del bebé para aliviar el malestar.

7. **Cuidado Extra Durante la Noche:**

   - Si el bebé se despierta durante la noche debido al dolor dental, brinda consuelo adicional. Puede ser útil darle un mordedor refrigerado o realizar un masaje suave antes de volver a dormir.

8. **Distraer con Juegos y Actividades:**

   - Proporciona juguetes y actividades que puedan distraer al bebé durante este período incómodo. La atención adicional y el juego pueden ayudar a reducir la incomodidad.

9. **Consulta con el Pediatra:**

   - Si el dolor parece ser intenso o persistente, o si hay otros síntomas preocupantes, como fiebre, consulta con el pediatra para descartar cualquier problema más serio.

Recuerda que cada bebé es único, y lo que funciona para uno puede no ser efectivo para otro. Observa las señales de tu bebé y ajusta las estrategias según sea necesario. Además, siempre es recomendable consultar con el pediatra antes de utilizar cualquier medicamento o tratamiento para la dentición.

¡Gracias por acompañarnos en la lectura de "La Más Preguntadas por Mami"! Esperamos que este mini manual haya proporcionado respuestas útiles y consejos prácticos para guiarlos en el emocionante viaje de la crianza de bebés. Ser padres es una experiencia única, llena de alegrías y desafíos, y estamos aquí para apoyarlos en cada paso del camino. Siempre recuerden que cada bebé es único, al igual que cada mamá, y no hay un manual único que sirva para todos. ¡Les deseamos a todos ustedes, mamás y papás, lo mejor en esta hermosa travesía de la maternidad y la paternidad! ¡Hasta pronto!

De la Panza a la Vida

Aquí tienes 50 consejos importantes en la crianza de Bebés:
Embarazo y Recién Nacido:

1. **Cuidado Prenatal:** Inicia el cuidado prenatal temprano y asiste a todas las citas médicas.

2. **Educación Prenatal:** Informate sobre el parto, la lactancia y los cuidados del recién nacido. *

3. **Preparación para el Parto:** Considera clases de preparación para el parto para estar mejor preparada.

4. **Habitación del Bebé:** Prepara la habitación del bebé con anticipación.

5. **Bolsa para el Hospital:** Ten una bolsa de hospital lista con elementos esenciales para el parto.

6. **Establecer Rutinas:** Establece rutinas desde los primeros días para ayudar al bebé a adaptarse.

7. **Lactancia Materna:** Considera la lactancia materna. Busca apoyo si es necesario.

8. **Cambio de Pañales:** Aprende a cambiar pañales de manera eficiente y segura.

9. **Dormir cuando el Bebé Duerme:** Descansa siempre que tu bebé duerma para recuperar energías.

10. **Control de Visitantes:** Limita las visitas al hospital y en casa durante las primeras semanas.

Desarrollo del Bebé:

11. **Estimulación Temprana:** Practica actividades que estimulen los sentidos del bebé.

12. **Tiempo Boca Abajo:** Supervisa el tiempo boca abajo para fortalecer el cuello.

13. **Hablar y Cantar:** Habla y canta al bebé para fomentar el desarrollo del lenguaje.*

14. **Juegos Sensoriales:** Introduce juguetes y actividades sensoriales según la edad.

15. **Vacunas:** Mantén el calendario de vacunas actualizado según las recomendaciones médicas.

16. **Desarrollo Motor:** Observa y celebra los logros en el desarrollo motor.

17. **Socialización:** Promueve la interacción social con otros bebés y adultos.

18. **Monitoreo de la Salud:** Esté atenta a signos de enfermedad y realiza chequeos regulares.

19. **Tiempo al Aire Libre:** Proporciona tiempo al aire libre cuando sea posible.

20. **Introducción de Alimentos:** Introduce alimentos sólidos según las indicaciones del pediatra.*

Cuidado Diario:

21. **Cuidado de la Piel:** Utiliza productos suaves y adecuados para la piel del bebé.

22. **Baño Seguro:** Aprende a bañar al bebé de manera segura.

23. **Cortar Uñas:** Corta las uñas del bebé con cuidado para evitar arañazos.

24. **Vestimenta Apropiada:** Ajusta la ropa del bebé según la temperatura ambiente.

25. **Monitoreo del Sueño:** Establece una rutina de sueño y monitorea patrones de sueño.

26. **Posicionamiento para Dormir:** Coloca al bebé boca arriba para dormir para prevenir el síndrome de muerte súbita del lactante (SMSL). *

27. **Prevención de Estrangulamiento:** Evita peluches y objetos sueltos en la cuna para prevenir riesgos de estrangulamiento. *

28. **Cuidado del Cordón Umbilical:** Limpia y cuida el cordón umbilical según las recomendaciones médicas.

29. **Atención Dental:** Inicia la atención dental temprana, incluso antes de que aparezcan los dientes.

30. **Prevención de Accidentes:** Asegura el entorno para prevenir accidentes, como caídas y golpes.

Vida Familiar:

31. **Auto-Cuidado:** No descuides tu bienestar. Programa momentos para ti misma.

32. **Comunicación con la Pareja:** Mantén una comunicación abierta con tu pareja sobre las responsabilidades y desafíos.

33. **Ayuda Familiar:** Acepta ayuda de familiares y amigos cuando la necesites.

34. **Tiempo en Pareja:** Encuentra tiempo de calidad con tu pareja para fortalecer la relación.

35. **Planificación Financiera:** Planifica el presupuesto familiar y ahorra para gastos inesperados.

36. **Reconoce tus Límites:** No tengas miedo de pedir ayuda cuando la necesites.

37. **Participación del Padre:** Involucra al padre en la crianza desde el principio.

38. **Desarrollo Profesional:** Ajusta expectativas profesionales durante los primeros meses.

39. **Educación Continua:** Mantente informada sobre nuevas investigaciones y recomendaciones en la crianza.

40. **Tiempo de Calidad:** Prioriza el tiempo de calidad con tu bebé, aunque sea en pequeñas dosis. *

Aspectos Emocionales y Mentales:

41. **Cuida tu Salud Mental:** Presta atención a tu salud mental y busca apoyo si es necesario.

42. **Manejo del Estrés:** Desarrolla estrategias para manejar el estrés y la fatiga.

43. **No Hay Padres Perfectos:** Acepta que no hay padres perfectos, y está bien cometer errores. *

44. **Celebración de Logros:** Celebra tus logros como madre, incluso los pequeños.

45. **Conexión con Otros Padres:** Conéctate con otros padres para compartir experiencias y consejos.

46. **Sueño de Calidad:** Prioriza el sueño de calidad para mantener tu bienestar emocional.

47. **Tiempo para Ti Misma:** Establece momentos regulares para actividades que disfrutas. *

48. **Escucha a tu Instinto:** Confía en tu instinto maternal y sigue tus decisiones.

49. **Aprender de los Desafíos:** Ve los desafíos como oportunidades para aprender y crecer.

50. **Disfruta del Momento:** Aprovecha cada momento, ya que el tiempo pasa rápidamente.

Recuerda que cada bebé es único, y lo más importante es seguir tu intuición y adaptar estos consejos según las necesidades y personalidad de tu hijo. ¡Disfruta cada etapa de la crianza y celebra el increíble viaje de ser madre!

"El Poder de Ser Mamá: Un Viaje de Amor, Fortaleza y Crecimiento"

Querida mamá primeriza,

Has recorrido un camino lleno de emociones, retos y descubrimientos. Ahora, al llegar al final de este viaje de preparación, quiero recordarte algo muy importante: eres increíble.

La maternidad no es un destino fijo, es un viaje continuo que te transformará y te mostrará nuevas facetas de ti misma cada día. No existe una madre perfecta, pero lo que sí existe es una madre que da lo mejor de sí misma, que aprende de cada experiencia y que, sobre todo, ama profundamente a su hijo. Y esa madre, ¡eres tú!

Los días pueden ser agotadores, llenos de incertidumbre, pero también estarán llenos de momentos que te harán sentir más fuerte de lo que jamás imaginaste. Recuerda que cada pequeño paso que das, cada duda que resuelves y cada sonrisa que ofreces es una victoria. Cada lágrima de cansancio se convertirá en una anécdota de tu fortaleza, y cada obstáculo superado será una prueba más de tu inmenso amor.

Confía en tus instintos, en tu capacidad y en tu amor. Tú tienes lo necesario para criar a un hijo feliz y saludable. Si en algún momento sientes que te falta algo, que no sabes o que no puedes, respira profundo y recuerda que no estás sola. Siempre puedes apoyarte en los que te rodean y, lo más importante, siempre puedes confiar en ti misma. Tú puedes con esto.

Imagina la vida que estás construyendo, la relación maravillosa que tendrás con tu bebé y todas las sonrisas que están por venir. Sigue adelante con la certeza de que lo estás haciendo increíblemente bien.

¡Felicidades por este hermoso viaje que recién comienza! ¡Tú puedes lograrlo!

Bibliografía

- American College of Obstetricians and Gynecologists. (2020). *Your Pregnancy and Childbirth: Month to Month* (6th ed.). American College of Obstetricians and Gynecologists.

- Cohen, S., Janicki-Deverts, D., & Miller, G. E. (2018). Psychological stress and disease. *JAMA*, 298(14), 1685-1687.

- Field, T. (2012). Exercise and pregnancy: a review of the literature. *Journal of Perinatal Education*, 21(1), 1-7.

- Hayes, S. C., Strosahl, K. D., & Wilson, K. G. (2011). *Acceptance and Commitment Therapy: The Process and Practice of Mindful Change* (2nd ed.). Guilford Press.

- McDonald, S. J., Middleton, P., Dowswell, T., & Morris, P. S. (2013). Effect of timing of umbilical cord clamping of term infants on maternal and neonatal outcomes. *Cochrane Database of Systematic Reviews*, 7, CD004074.

- Monk, C., Lugo-Candelas, C., & Trumpff, C. (2016). Prenatal developmental origins of future psychopathology: Mechanisms and pathways. *Annual Review of Clinical Psychology*, 12, 171-197.

- National Institute for Health and Care Excellence (NICE). (2021). *Intrapartum care for healthy women and babies*. NICE Guidelines. https://www.nice.org.uk/guidance/cg190

- Neff, K. D. (2003). Self-compassion: An alternative conceptualization of a healthy attitude toward oneself. *Self and Identity*, 2(2), 85-101.

- Nolen-Hoeksema, S. (2012). Emotion regulation and psychopathology: The role of gender. *Annual Review of Clinical Psychology*, 8, 161-187.

- Pennebaker, J. W. (1997). *Opening Up: The Healing Power of Expressing Emotions*. Guilford Press.

- Zhang, J., Troendle, J. F., Yancey, M. K., Klebanoff, M. A., & Fraser, W. D. (2010). Reassessing the labor curve in nulliparous women. *American Journal of Obstetrics and Gynecology*, 202(3), 232.e1-232.e6.

www.ingramcontent.com/pod-product-compliance
Lightning Source LLC
Chambersburg PA
CBHW051248250726
48656CB00004B/1193